CW00394628

# LE MAT

## *The Fool*

## Ian Russell

© 2018 IAN RUSSELL ALL RIGHTS RESERVED

For my very dear
friend Sue.

With love Ian
xxxx

Although opening chapters of Le Mat are based on true events, it is a work of fiction and must be regarded as such.

Names, characters, businesses, places, events, locales, and incidents are either the products of the author's imagination or used in a fictitious manner.  Any resemblance to actual persons, living or dead, or actual events is purely coincidental.

My thanks to my wife Dee for proof reading my story, and to my brother Michael for the cover artwork.

THE FOOL .

It is not possible to evolve without questioning if there is more to be discovered.

A new path will have unforeseen risks and dangers, mistakes will inevitably be made.

When the opportunity presents itself, you must be willing to sacrifice convention.

I would
I could
I should
If only those around me...
I do
I can
I must
Because of those around me...
I did
I was allowed to
I had to
Despite knowing in my heart...

As a child, I learned to lie to others
As an adult, I learned to lie to myself with greater conviction

With hope, Homo Sapiens' successes may one day be recognised by those who will follow, Homo Illustratum, The Enlightened.

Ian Russell
2009

Le Mat or The Fool is the first of two novels which together see a young merchant navy navigation cadet begin a journey far beyond his comprehension. Adventure on the high sea will give way to a journey into the paranormal and beyond.

What if heaven is not a place, but access to every life you have ever lived; a chance to reengage with every person, relive every experience, say and do the things we wanted to have said and done?

Would you leave heaven, to be born again in another time and place?

For the two people that are my legacy, my daughter Lucy (White Mist) and my son Alexander (Little Bear); for my brother, my sisters and their loves, my dearest friends around the world, close and distant relations, those who I have known, the people who made my life what it was; and those I will meet, the people that will make my life what it will be and most of all for my wife, best friend and partner Dee.

My thanks to everyone that takes the time to read my story.

# XXI   THE WORLD

P ride. Once considered the fundamental requirement for personal development. With such passing of time I no longer recall the emotion or even the sensation of the vice that was once so encouraged by our parents, teachers and leaders throughout history. Of all the so-called seven deadly sins, it is surely that from which all others arise, the anarchic destroyer of love and the seed of injustice.

There are no heroes in my tale, certainly not I. If I have learned anything at all, it is quite simply that such vanity above all else, interferes with our recognition of the needs of those and that which is around us. Envy, gluttony, lust, wrath, avarice and sloth are but the bantling brats that tug at the skirts of pride, whilst fear is its alter ego.

If we take pride in our achievements should we not set them against our failures? Mistakes, I have made many, but there is no learning without mistakes.

If one can balance one's mistakes with successes, one is undeniably fortunate.

My friends the ancient Egyptians believe that when the heart of your soul is handed over to Osiris. It is placed it on a great golden scale and balanced against the white feather of Ma'at, the feather of truth and of harmony, on the other side. The truth is that we are our own judge and jury throughout life until our dying day.

When we replace pride with love and respect our thoughts and deeds take on a different perspective. When we approach our life's end we learn to respect the lives of even the smallest of creatures.

The downfall of Homo Sapiens? Simply money.

Of course, there were those who lived an altruistic life, asking nothing for themselves, but there were too few.

\* \* \*

The dinosaurs ruled this Earth for one hundred and eighty-million years; so-called Knowing Earthling, in his arrogance, has once again managed to destroy the balance of nature in just two hundred and fifty-thousand years. He has ceased to evolve in the last fifty-thousand. Once again, he has lost the desire to grow.

Without intervention, such civilizations inevitably bring about their own extinction, as many have done before.

Can Homo Sapiens evolve? It would seem only with the guidance of a New-born, one with no preconception of what is right or what is wrong can balance be restored, and even then, the New-born must be shielded from the world of commerce and bigotry while they grow, lest they be influenced by the desire to fit in, to feel part of the flock. Only a New-born raised in an environment free of elitism can fulfil their destiny, all others will fall.

In a world where elitism exists, greed will exist at every level, everyone wants just a little more than they can have, no one is guiltless.

Homo Sapiens, the incident, for that is all it was, is only worthy of a place in history as a lesson to those who follow.

This is my world, the world I have inherited.

# THE WORCESTER

## 0  LE MAT

Sunday ~ 14th October 1973

I know that when my journey began, I had been so very proud of myself, standing there naively smug waiting to board the Worcester.

At school I had achieved enough, with the minimal of effort, learning was easy, I was never challenged.

\* \* \*

She lay fifty yards out in the Thames off Greenhithe, a part of maritime history and a part of the lives of so many officers in the Merchant Marine.

As I walked along the river bank to the jetty, I caught my first sight of the white lines that stretched along the length of her hull.

At first glance she reminded me of HMS Victory, Nelson's resplendent flag ship of Trafalgar fame. The Victory stood in dry dock at Portsmouth, fifty miles from my home in the New Forest.

My first impressions of the Worcester would soon change standing there on the jetty with just a few more moments to note her utilitarian forward and stern deck alterations. As she was, I could only surmise that she must surely have been modified by Chinese Junk builders rather than English shipwrights.

I did not know that a far more elegant ship of fame was once moored behind her. The Cutty Sark had served as the sister training ship since 1938 as a part of the Thames Nautical Training College and moored alongside the Worcester. On that grey October afternoon, she resided up river in permanent dry dock at Greenwich, opposite the Isle of Dogs.

Despite my judgment of the adulterated ship before me I was bursting with excitement and enthusiasm, although I cannot say what it was that excited me most, wearing the blue serge double breasted uniform and the white peaked cap of a Merchant Navy Officer, the thrill of leaving home to begin the adventure of a lifetime or the thought of one day aspiring to become ship's Master. I hungered for them all.

I stood on the riverside, one of six young individuals, each of us in a private and silent world of his own. There were female cadets, at least in the BP Fleet, but very few and none apparently joining with me. The Merchant Marine was very much a male dominated environment. For me, it was the beginning of the dream that I had fostered throughout my final year at school. The seed had been planted by a television series just two years before, having been seduced by the romance of the sea and a certain Captain James Onedin's struggle to succeed as a Captain and sailing ship owner.

The Worcester would be our home for the next two weeks on the short induction course that would begin our careers in the Merchant Marine.

"Are you boys from BP?" asked Paul.

I turned around to see the latest arrival. He was dressed in the same navy blue, double-breasted uniform and white peaked cap that we wore but that was where the likeness ended. Unlike us, his tie was loose around his neck, his hat casually yet purposefully tilted to one side and his double-breasted jacket was unbuttoned in the same casual manner.

"Yes, I am," announced the young-looking boy beside me.

"Paul!" I said in surprise.

I looked around at the other cadets and saw three of them nodding their heads.

In that moment I felt that I knew them all.

"Thought I was late!" he announced, then he turned to me and shook my hand briefly.

"Jimmy!" he acknowledged with a smile.

He was nineteen, three years older than I was. I knew it without knowing why. There was no reason why I should have known, I had never met any of them before.

The other lads looked older, in their early twenties. At sixteen, I was the youngest except for the boy beside me who looked younger still, although I also knew that he too was sixteen.

"How do you do Paul, my name's Roy, Roy McClair."

Roy's elocution revealed a sophisticated education, which was in marked contrast to Paul's 'Michael Caine' accent. Clearly, he had attended a better class of school than either Paul or me.

He shook Paul's hand then turned to me.

"James Cummings pleased to meet you," I said shaking Roy's hand.

Until Paul arrived, we had all been content to stand in silence.

"It looks like you were just in time, that's our boat if I'm not mistaken," said Roy, looking towards the small diesel clinker-built launch that chugged across to the jetty. "Are you two old friends?"

"Friends? I hope we will be, but we just met." I answered.

"You knew Paul's name," Roy pointed out mitigating his question.

It was true, and it was then that I realized that I had spoken to him by name.

"Watch him lads, we have ourselves a company spy here," Paul joked, trivializing the subject.

I felt a sudden loss, something hard to explain, almost physical, as though I had for a brief moment been given something which was then quickly snatched away, more profound than simply a feeling of déjà vu and leaving me to conclude that I had been the butt of some practical joke and perhaps just not understood.

The feeling, intense as it was, evaporated quickly, there was just so much else to think about.

# COMRADES

P aul put down his case and straightened his hat and tie.

"Better look sweet for the officers," he said nodding his head towards the river.

I looked down at the little boat to see what Paul was preparing himself for, the crew were all young lads like us.

"Ok you boys get your gear into the boat and we'll get you on-board ship," shouted the coxswain as they moored.

We took our suitcases down the jetty and one by one boarded the little boat. My own was a large blue wooden ribbed specimen almost big enough for me to fit inside, purchased along with my uniforms from Miller Rayner's, the outfitters in Southampton.

It was a short trip across the water to where the Worcester lay at anchor. The accommodation ladder led up from the small boarding jetty to a doorway amidships, entering onto the main deck. It was then that I realized the ship was anchored at both bows and stern, parallel with the river bank and the river current.

Once on board my feelings about her changed again, she was indeed a fine old ship. Looking at her from the inside, I felt some sense of her historic past. The varnished wooden interior looked as though it had been painted with thick, sweet honey. It smelled old and seasoned by years of sea air. Someone had spent a great deal of tender love and care on her.

We were directed to a duty officer who summoned an orderly to escort us below to find our bunks which for us were two decks down on the orlop deck directly below.

We passed some older lads in casual clothes going the other way, their bunks were on the lower deck immediately below the main deck. From their casual manner, it was obvious that this was not their first visit to the college, they didn't even acknowledge our presence. They were not intentionally rude, we simply weren't a part of their world and therefore did not exist.

All cadets now had bunks instead of the more traditional hammocks that had once provided sleeping for two hundred boys.

Like most ships, the stairs were almost vertical, which is why they were referred to as ladders. Our bunks were in rows of three down each side of the ship. Each bed faced its own grey locker, which stood six feet tall; and each row of lockers formed a dividing wall separating the next row of beds, while the row behind the beds formed another. There was no predetermined allocation, so I took the middle bunk, Roy took the bunk on my right against the starboard hull and Paul the one on my left. I sat down on my bed contemplating my new home. My journey had begun.

Roy was on the short side, with a child-like face and straight dark brown hair parted at the side. He reminded me of one of Billy Bunter's comic book friends. It seems easier now to picture him dressed in a Greyfriar's school blazer and grey trousers than in his Cadet's uniform, although I never saw him in that way at the time.

I probably looked just as youthful to Roy. I had a short crew cut, and dressed in my fine new uniform, I was probably smarter than I had ever been before. Until my interview in the summer, my hair had been unkempt, long, down to my shoulders. I had never really concerned myself about the clothes I wore or had the money to buy them anyway.

I was slightly bigger and broader than Roy, but shorter than Paul. Paul was older and physically much more mature than either Roy or me.

As we unpacked our uniforms, we began to relax and talk freely.

"Y'u won't need any a' those." said Paul, as I lifted my white tropical uniforms out of the case.

I knew he was right, October on the Thames is hardly the place for a tropical uniform, but they were mine and they had become a part of the entourage that would follow me everywhere, two whites, two khaki and one navy blue uniform.

"They didn't tell us whether to bring them or not." I protested defiantly.

"Good afternoon gentlemen. My name is Ferris. You will address all the officers on board as Sir. I am your Induction Course Officer."

He appeared from nowhere and spoke abruptly startling me.

"You won't be needing those lad," he said looking at my whites now hanging in the locker. "I want you all changed in to your working uniforms and in classroom two in fifteen minutes. You'll find it on this deck just astern. All the classrooms are numbered. You will have time to unpack the rest of your gear before supper tonight."

He made deliberate eye contact with each of us before moving on to the next row of beds. As soon as he moved on we all got out our navy-blue dungarees, thick light blue cotton shirts and black working boots as requested.

* * *

I had been in a romantic world of my own since leaving the village station in Sway. It seemed quite natural to me that people must always look at a man in uniform in the same way that I did, wondering where its owner might be going or where he had been. It then occurred to me that perhaps I was deluded and that it was only me with my wanderlust that wondered about such things in reality.

As I looked around the carriage at my fellow passengers, I was glad that only I knew my destination was actually Greenhithe. I so much wanted them to believe that I was about to be flying off to Hong Kong, Sydney, New York or any more exotic destination.

The illusion was over abruptly, it was time to discard the appearance of a junior officer and put on the attire of a deckhand. That was the first thing we would have to aspire to, not that many of us would ever have been considered 'a good hand' by the genuine breed.

# ALFIE

P aul broke the silence.

"I s'pose they'll keep us shut up here tonight."

"What do you mean?" asked Roy.

"I would very much like to see my new bird tonight," he replied with a smirk.

"Where are you from?" I asked.

"Landon!" he answered with a smile and a heavy East End accent.

"And you?" I asked looking at Roy.

"Guildford," he answered eloquently.

"Oh!"

I was not really sure exactly where Guildford was, but I thought it was somewhere close to London.

"I'm from Hampshire, near Southampton, down in the New Forest."

There was a brief silence.

"Where did you want to go then Paul?" I asked.

"Just out with this bird. She lives about half a mile away," he answered.

"Have you known her long?" I asked.

"Nah!" he laughed. "I only met her t'day, at lunch time, in the pub. She said she fell for the uniform, but I think it was really my sophisticated nature that won her over. We've been in bed all afternoon. Insatiable she was."

I looked at Roy and his face told me that he was as astonished as I was. Nobody picked up girls and went to bed with them in the same afternoon.

"You're kidding." I said naively.

"Of course he is!" Roy piped up.

11

Again, I was reminded of how much better his elocution was than Paul's or my own.

"Now why should I wanna wind you two boys up eh? Besides you saw 'er drop me off at the jetty."

Although some of my school friends had been promiscuous at a young age, my own experience with girls had been limited to say the least. I had only had one girlfriend. I was twelve years old, and she broke my heart. We had kissed passionately, lying in the long grass, but apart from that it was very innocent, it ended before it had started.

"She could have been your sister," I suggested, now implying that even having a girlfriend was too much to believe. "And anyway, I didn't see her!"

"Nor did I!" Roy echoed while exchanging a brief glance of disbelief with me.

We finished changing in an uncomfortable silence.

I felt out of my depth with Paul and I realized that he didn't just sound like Michael Caine, he reminded me in every way but looks of Alfie, the Cockney ladies' man that I had seen on the television only a few months before. The most significant difference was Paul's short black hair. 'No matter', I thought to myself, I felt comfortable with Roy.

# THE WORCESTER

T he three of us walked toward the classrooms astern, past some of the other lads that had we been waiting with up on the jetty.

The classrooms like the forecastle, were utilitarian modifications that were totally out of character with an old sailing ship. Unlike the Victory there no cannons of course and probably never had been, round portholes lined the various deck instead of gun ports.

There were already eight other cadets seated at desks inside the classroom. The desks were not unlike those at my school, wooden with a lift-up lid and ink well. Unlike the twin desks at school they were all single desks, so each person sat alone.

Roy headed straight for one of vacant front desks, I followed Paul to the third row. Paul went straight for the desk beside the porthole and I took the desk beside him feeling more comfortable with him than sat at the front where I could not see the others. The rest of the cadets followed us in to the room within the next couple of minutes and then Ferris made his entrance.

"Good afternoon gentlemen, welcome to the Incorporated Thames Nautical Training College HMS Worcester. You all know who I am. Please write your surname on the card in front of you with the felt tipped pen which will be passed around, then fold the card like this and place it on the front of your desk."

He had already written 'SIR' on his own card. He lifted it and folded it in half to form a tent-like plaque as he spoke.

"I'm sure I don't have to tell any of you that you are on board a ship. As I have said, the name of the ship is HMS Worcester. Please do not call her a boat, she is not! For your information 'boats are what ships carry'.

We may well be permanently moored here in the Thames; however, a ship she is and the most important thing on board ship is safety."

Roy lifted his hand to ask a question and Ferris looked down at his card to read his name.

"McClair," he said without qualification.

"Sir are submarines not also classified as boats?" he asked.

"The navy considers all vessels ships; however, submarines are historically referred to as boats due to the nature of the first submarines. A boat in naval terminology is a vessel that is launched or tended from a larger ship. The earliest submarines required support vessels to maintain and launch them, hence they were considered and remain boats."

His irritation at being interrupted was reflected in the accuracy of his answer. His voice had an air of absolute authority, it was not cold, but his tone made it crystal clear in the first few moments of contact that he was in charge.

He explained the safety procedures in detail, methodically pointing out the location of fire alarms and extinguishers, stressing the importance of raising the alarm in the event of a fire, first aid boxes, the ship's sick bay and other important information on a diagram of the ship's layout.

"You will find copies of this diagram at information points around the ship. They are at the top and bottom of every ladder. Study them! They may save your life!"

He paused deliberately to let us absorb the safety aspects. "You are all at the beginning of your career as Merchant Navy Officers and I stress beginning. During your two weeks here, you will be introduced to the correspondence course you will follow throughout your cadet training at sea. Tomorrow morning, we will begin with some assessment tests in mathematics and science."

Paper and pencils were handed around and we produced a timetable for the two-week course with no break for Saturday or Sunday.

"Rules?" He asked the question for us and then gave us all the answers. "You will be permitted to use the ferry to go ashore between 1830 and 2300. The last ferry back is at 2315, do not miss it! Those of you who are old enough to drink alcohol may do so in moderation, there are plenty of public houses within a short walk."

He went on to describe the other facilities on board ship and ashore.

"Finally, during your stay you will address all officers as Sir and you will address the nurse simply as Nurse. Supper is served in the mess from 1730 hours, breakfast from 0700 to 0830and lunch from 1300 to 1400. You will be served in or out of uniform, your working uniform will suffice provided it is clean."

It was a very rehearsed welcome.

"Do you have any questions?" he asked. I raised my hand and looked around to see that I was the only cadet who had. "Yes Cummings, what is it?"

"Sorry Sir," I mumbled. "Why is the ship called HMS if this is a Merchant Navy College?"

"That's an interesting question," he replied. "Does anyone know the answer?" he asked provokingly. Clearly my question was welcomed, whereas Roy had interrupted his flow.

Roy put his hand up at the front of the class.

"Yes McClair."

"Because it's a Royal Navy vessel Sir?" Roy suggested.

"No McClair, I'm afraid she is not!" he replied appearing to enjoy correcting him.

He hesitated briefly drawing breath and then began the next equally well rehearsed speech.

"This HMS Worcester is the third ship to bear the name Worcester. Vickers Sons and Maxim at Barrow-In-Furness built her in 1905, to the order of the Metropolitan Asylums Board who later merged into the London County Council.

"Formerly the Training Ship Exmouth, she was rigged as a three masted Barquentine. Sir John Biles, an eminent naval architect, drew her lines and was immensely proud of the finished ship. She is three hundred and fourteen feet in length, fifty-three feet beam, with a mean draught of eighteen feet six inches, her hull is riveted iron below the boot-topping to resist corrosion, and mild steel plate above.

"Under the ownership of the Metropolitan Asylums Board she was used as a Poor Law Training School to provide nautical training to boys in its care, enabling them to enter a life in either the Merchant Navy or Royal Navy.

"During the Second World War, she saw service first as an accommodation ship for the Volunteer Fire Brigade, then as a minesweeper depot ship under the White Ensign at Scapa Flow.

"After demobilization she arrived in the Thames on July 6th, 1945 and was towed up river to Messrs R.& H. Green and Silley Weir in the East India Dock Basin to begin her new life.

"When she first took up her moorings off Greenhithe, jury-rigged, with just half a bowsprit and the stump of a main mast, she looked the ugly duckling very much alongside the Cutty Sark."

In fairness, the Cutty Sark was the epitome of elegance, a tea clipper built for speed, while the Exmouth had been a purpose-built training ship.

"Like most depot ships, she was in a deplorable condition. Thanks to the hard work and enthusiasm of Worcester Cadets and staff, the first watch of Cadets was able to join the ship on 31st January 1946.

"On February 2nd representatives of the Worcester Committee formally commissioned her into service.

"Now in answer to your question Cummings, 'why H.M.S.?' It is a special privilege granted by the Admiralty to the Merchant Navy Officers Training Establishments."

He must have recited the ship's history many times before because he rattled off the names and dates as though they were members of his family and their dates of birth.

"Are there any more questions?" He asked finally.

No one else raised their hands or asked any questions.

"You may now return to your unpacking. I will see you all here at 0900 hours tomorrow morning, Good evening gentlemen, enjoy your stay."

# THE TAROT

$I$t was only four fifteen when we left the classroom, by five o'clock we had all finished unpacking and made our beds. Starched cotton sheets and thick red blankets had been laid out for us. I punched up the pillow and sat with my feet up and my back against the iron bed-head. Roy stood by the porthole, which was just above sea level, looking north across the Thames.

Paul had finished before either of us and was stood at his locker with his back to us. He turned around and walked back to his bed and sat down in the middle. He began to shuffle a pack of cards, then laid them out methodically on the flat blanket at the end of his bed, in a configuration I now know to be the Celtic Cross.

"Hi, my name's Mike, this is Bernie, Pete. We're from next door," said another cadet, appearing beside Paul's bedside and nodding his head towards the row of beds beyond our lockers.

Bernie nodded in acknowledgement.

"What line are you with?" asked Mike.

"We're all B.P." I answered.

"Me too!" said Bernie, "Mike and Podger are from Shell."

"Podger?" I asked.

"Pete. Podger's his nickname. They went to the same college and joined together," explained Bernie.

Pete's grinning face gave a clear indication that he was at ease with his moniker.

"What have you got there then?" asked Mike provokingly.

Roy stepped back from the porthole, sat down on the side of his bed and looked across at Paul.

"Tarot," said Paul emphatically.

He didn't look up, he knew Mike was talking to him. I suppose it was obvious really, but it was strange the way he said it. His emphasis on the word suggested the reverence he held for them, and it was obvious from the care and attention he gave the cards that they were highly treasured. It did seem strange to me at the time that he referred to them in that way, 'Tarot' not 'Tarot cards'.

"So, can you tell my fortune then?" asked Mike sarcastically.

"Would you like to cross my palm," answered Paul, refusing to bite.

"You want me to pay you?" he sneered.

"Do you actually want me to read the cards for you?"

Paul's manner was becoming terse.

"Yeah, alright then," he said grinning at his chums after pausing for a second of thought.

"You'll have to come back later."

"Why not now?" he asked impatiently.

"Because I need a shower!" Paul's answer was blunt and contemptuous.

He packed away his cards in a dark blue velvet envelope and put them back in his locker, feeling no need to explain further. Picking up his towel and washing kit he turned to Roy and me.

"You two going to clean up before supper?" he asked.

It was obvious from his tone that Paul was not as friendly towards Mike as he was with us, but I had no idea why, perhaps just because we were younger.

"I could do with a quick wash," said Roy.

"Me too, and I fancy a quick look around," I added, not that I was accustomed to showering before supper, and I had had a bath that morning.

We had showers at school to clean ourselves after sports, at home we had a bath, typically using the same water as another member of the family, or shivering in cold water. The only shower we had was a rubber hose that connected to the bath taps to wash our hair.

We grabbed our gear and followed Paul over to the stairs.

"See ya later," I said as we left.

Roy half raised his hand with an embarrassed wave to our visitors.

Paul had not really been rude to Podger or Bernie, nor was he surprised by Mike's interest in his cards. The cards appeared to be a commodity that he did not intend to give away freely.

We wandered to the 'dhobi room' as Ferris had called it, 'navy talk for laundry room, actually a word to describe an Indian washer-man or woman,' he'd said. It was to be found on the upper deck below the foremast. Above it on the ship's forecastle the ship's water tanks were housed in large white utilitarian rectangular cocoons, in front of which was the equally unsightly bridge and boiler funnel, rising from the boiler room on the tier deck at the bottom of the ship.

Inside the dhobi room there were enormous washing machines being used by cadets, bigger than anything I had ever seen before. There were three lads ironing and two more were hanging out their clothes to dry on long poles which pulled out of a large drying room in sections like huge towel rails and pushed back into a large drying cupboard. We walked through stopping only to scan the equipment and on into the adjacent cadets' washroom and toilets.

Roy and I stripped to the waist for a wash, Paul stripped naked and got into the shower.

"Gotta look good tonight," shouted Paul from the shower, there were no other cadets there.

"Are you going out with your girlfriend then?" I asked.

"Yeah, but I'll stop off for a quick pint wi'v you two lads if you're goin' out."

"Yeah ok, what d'ya think Roy?"

Roy spat the residue of his toothpaste into the sink.

"I've never been in a pub before, but I've got nothing else to do."

His innocence didn't seem to bother him. I would have felt an idiot admitting that I have never been into a pub in Paul's company. At least I had been to the pub many times when working with my older brother.

Paul stepped out of the shower brazenly drying himself neither concerned about exposing his flaccid though impressive manhood, nor any indication of judgement about Roy's inexperience.

"Great, we'll get changed and go out straight after supper," he answered.

He walked over to the basins having wrapped his towel around his waist, got out his shaving gear and started to shave. Roy and I looked at each other and both took out our own razors; neither of us really needed it, once a week would have sufficed but nobody said anything.

We queued up for supper at six twenty. The cadets' mess was on the lower deck, one level above our bunks, forward of the senior cadets' bunks; beyond that in the bows was the galley. The Ward Room was in the stern on the main deck below the Captain's quarters.

The cadets' mess provided a canteen style service with rows of long tables each seating twelve people. The food was much like school dinners with two choices, good and wholesome 'meat and two veg' type dishes with pie and custard to follow.

Mike, Bernie and Pete came over to join us at our table. Mike sat opposite Paul, which seemed to irritate him, then a few of the other cadets came over and filled up all but one of the remaining spaces at the table.

"This is Paul, Roy and James," said Mike pointing us out, "Ron, Phil, Alex."

They nodded as their names were spoken.

"Phil and Alex are from P&O and Ron is from B.P. Paul's going to tell my fortune with his Tarot cards later," he said turning back to his new friends.

"Not tonight, I'm going out, garden with mi lemon," said Paul nonchalantly.

"Garden? Lemon?" I asked, bemused by the significance.

"Date! Garden gate date, lemon curd bird," he explained.

"Lucky you," said Pete enviously having heard Paul's translation. "We're off down the pub later so we'll join you!"

Although Pete was more than a bit on the podgy side, he had a very warm smile and his weight suited his character.

Paul finished his supper quickly and sat impatiently willing Roy and me to finish our meal.

"I thought I ate quickly," I said looking at Paul. "I've got a big family at home and if you don't eat what's put in front of you someone else will."

"I want to get out of here," he griped.

I finished my food soon after Paul, and Roy stopped to look up at us.

"I won't be long."

He knew Paul was getting impatient. Eventually Roy pushed his half-eaten pudding bowl across his tray.

"Eat your food," said Paul not wanting to deprive him.

"It's alright, I don't want it," said Roy standing up from his chair.

"Let's go then boys," said Paul.

"Aren't you boys going to wait for us then?" asked Mike.

"No!" said Paul.

He didn't seek our opinion. It was already clear that Paul was a bit of a loner. He didn't seem to mind Roy and me, I didn't know why, maybe because we were the youngest of the cadets or perhaps simply because we shared his space. It was equally obvious that Mike was a bit of an organizer, but then at twenty-three he appeared to be the eldest.

"Maybe we'll see you down there," I said.

"Maybe, maybe not," said Mike dismissively.

# THE PIER

---

Wе were not the first cadets waiting to go ashore, some of the older cadets were there before us waiting for the first trip. Paul had insisted on changing into civvies. He wore a very fashionable pale grey suit. His jacket had wide lapels and underneath a waistcoat dropped to points at his waist. It was set off with a maroon shirt and matching tie. Roy and I had not changed clothes and were still dressed in working uniforms and with our short tidy haircuts there was no mistaking we were cadets despite the fact that our clothes bore no insignia.

The ferry crew ate at the same time as us and were not so eager to begin their evening shift but still in a humorous mood. They arrived at exactly six thirty, got straight into the small boat and started up the diesel engine while they chatted to each other. The queue was now beginning to grow but we got ashore on the first trip. We followed a group of senior cadets down the road to the first pub, The Pier. We had to wait ten minutes for the bar to open anyway, having forgotten that it was Sunday opening times. The sun had set shortly before and the air was quickly growing colder.

"We've got another batch of green middies here for you Fred!" shouted one of the older cadets as he walked in.

Fred was already pouring their beers as they walked up to the bar.

"Evening lads!" he shouted.

Paul walked straight over to the bar and took a crisp pound note out of his wallet and waved it above the beer taps. Roy and I stood behind him both getting our wallets out.

"What yu avin then?" asked Paul.

I had been drinking shandy for the last six months when I had been out with my older brother, somehow, I felt it was the time to move on to straight beer. I looked at the bar but saw nothing that I recognized.

"I'll have a pint of keg!"

I didn't really know what keg was, but my brother always asked for it and got a pint of Whitbread Tankard, so it seemed like a good idea. Roy was still groping around with his wallet.

"I'm buying," said Paul.

"Oh, okay thank you, I'll have half a pint of shandy please," he said as he put his wallet away. To my surprise Paul didn't tease him about the shandy.

"Good evening lads, my name's Fred. Take no notice of those lads, them's still fresh off their mother's titties themselves," he said. "Now what can I do for you?"

"Evenin' Fred, nice to meet you; Paul!" he added with his hand outstretched to introduce himself. "Pint of Stella, pint a keg and alf a shandy please squire."

Fred began to pour our drinks.

"Old sea dog eh?" asked Paul looking around the bar at all the maritime memorabilia.

"I am that," he said, "Joined in '37, did my twenty-five years with the Grey Funnel Line."

"The Royal Navy," Paul explained, plainly aware of our mystified expressions. Merchant ships paint their funnels in the distinctive colours of the owners.

The walls were scattered with ship's badges and pictures. I suppose it was obvious really but neither Roy nor I had put two and two together. We were too self-conscious about our age, but nobody batted an eyelid.

"That'll be twenty-two new pence young man."

We had been using the new currency for nearly three years but some of the older people still referred to it as new.

We stood at the bar chatting and gradually relaxed. Keg was a big change from shandy, it was easy to understand why it was called bitter, but I drank it as though it was my usual, trying desperately not to screw my face up.

We got to know a bit more about each other as we talked of our families and our homes. I bought another round of drinks and we moved to a table, by the time we finished the round Roy and I felt much more self-assured. When Roy ordered a round, he too opted for a whole pint.

"Fred, can I have a Pernod please," shouted Paul.

"Ice? Water?"

"Just a drop of water please squire!"

He paid for the chaser himself and Fred handed him a jug of water. The bright yellow liquid turned into a white milky cloud as he added a splash of water.

"What the hell is that stuff," I asked.

"It's French, aniseed."

He placed the glass to my nose.

"Shit!" I said screwing up my nose. "That's awful, smells like strong liquorice to me!"

"Liquorice, my young friend, is made from the seeds of the herb anise. Pimpinella anisum!" he explained again. "Don't you boys know anything? Odjus, beautiful!" he declared, drinking it down in one.

We carried on drinking and chatting for a while and then without warning Paul jumped up out of his chair.

"Sorry lads, I godda go now, it's almost eight," he said as he finished his beer. "I'll pop in on the way back if you're going to be here."

"No, I've had enough for one night, this will be more than ample for me," said Roy.

Paul left us at the bar and rushed off to meet his girlfriend; within minutes of him leaving, Mike, Pete and Bernie came into the pub.

"Where's Mr Personality?" asked Mike.

"If you mean Paul, he's gone to see his girlfriend," I said.

I took offence at the way Mike was getting at Paul behind his back, even if Paul wasn't exactly friendly towards him, I could not condone his retaliation. They passed us by and went up to the bar for a drink.

24

Roy and I finished our beer and went back to the Worcester. We had another look around the ship and ended up in the TV lounge, finally we went to bed at about half past eleven.

# THE GUNNERS

W hen we got there, Paul was already undressing. "Well how did you get on then?" I asked.

"We had a quick drink and then went straight back to her place where she dragged me into her bed. She has got such a lovely body, not one o' them skinny birds, curves, in all the right places," he said sliding his hands around an imaginary torso, pausing to smile and reflect on what he had said. "How about you two, did you stay long?"

"No, we came back here and watched the television," said Roy.

Paul sat down on his bed with his Tarot cards and started to deal them out again in the same pattern as before, a sort of cross shape.

"What are you up to?" I asked.

"Reading the cards."

"How often do you do that?"

"All the time, whenever I want to know how to deal with a situation. It kinda clears my mind. Yeah, that's the best way I can describe it, helps me focus my thoughts!"

"You mean you really believe in all that stuff?" asked Roy.

"Of course!" answered Paul, turning to look Roy in the face with his voice full of conviction.

Roy sounded naive to me, the cards bothered me, they were taboo, a part of the unknown, something dark that I didn't understand and wanted no part of.

I remembered as a third year at secondary school, a bunch of friends held a séance at a party during the first term. They came back to school the day after telling everyone the story that they had contacted some spirit. When we questioned them, they said it had predicted that Arsenal would win the FA Cup. Few of them had any real interest in football and none supported Arsenal.

The party had really been a chance to drink and smoke marihuana with the hope of getting the girls to let down their guard, so nobody took any notice. Arsenal finished twelfth in the league although they had won the European Fairs Cup that summer.

Arsenal had started the season badly losing to Stoke 5-0 in September. As the season progressed and Arsenal entered the Cup with the other first division teams people began to taunt the group waiting for the Gunners to fall, but it never happened. They went on to win the Cup 2-1 against Liverpool, having already beaten Tottenham Hotspur 1-0 to become League Champions just five days before and leaving us all wondering if there had been any truth in what they had said.

Despite my unease and the instinctive feeling that it was something inherently wrong and evil, I was definitely intrigued.

"Where did you learn to do it?" I asked Paul as he studied the cards.

"My mother taught me."

I realised that although Roy and I had talked about our families earlier that night, Paul had said very little about his background.

"Where did she learn?" I asked

"Well she wasn't my real mother," he paused smiling to himself. "I lived with Romani for a period of my life, she was the mother of many. She gave me the cards and taught me how to use them."

"So what sort of things do you use them for?" asked Roy.

"What will face me tomorrow, who I can trust and who I should avoid, the questions you ask yourselves all the time."

He really believed in it all, at least his voice and his manner suggested so. He never took his eyes off the cards as he spoke, he just continued with the ritual. If he really understood them and was not faking it, it must have been a regular habit because he sustained conversation without stopping to interpret the cards. He reminded me of my brother in law Richard playing patience whilst holding a conversation and perhaps even listening to the television all at the same time.

"So what do your cards tell you about Mike then?" I asked.

"That, my young friend, is my business!" he declared.

# THE QUERENT

Next morning we were up at seven o'clock, woken by a cadet on orderly duty. We showered and shaved, made our beds and dressed for breakfast. At twenty-five to eight when we were ready for breakfast, Mike came around to our beds and walked over to Paul.

"How about now?" It was Mike's turn to be nonchalant. There was no 'good morning lads' or 'how are you boys'. He was almost deliberately rude.

"If you wish!" answered Paul, unperturbed by Mike's discourtesy.

"Hey Bernie, Podger, do you wanna watch this?"

Pete and Bernie came around from behind the lockers and stood beside Paul's bed. Paul was totally unaffected, he walked to his locker and picked up the blue velvet envelope. After taking the cards out of their protective sheath, he placed it back on the locker shelf, turned around with the cards in his right hand and holding out the left towards Mike. Mike responded by reaching into his pocket and handed over a ten pence piece.

"It'll cost you at least one Pernod!"

Paul's hand stayed where it was until Mike put a second into his hand. "I only drink Pernod as a chaser!" Paul added, and Mike dropped a third coin into Paul's hand, then he closed it and pocketed the coins.

Thirty pence seemed a lot of money for someone treating the whole episode as a joke, my cadet's wages were only just over £8 per week, although Mike being older may have earned a little more. It suggested to me that not only did Mike really want to know about his future, but also that he was concerned about something that lay ahead.

"What would you like to know?" he asked.

"Will I become an officer?" asked Mike turning and grinning at Roy and me.

"Is that all? Could you be more specific?" Paul was surprisingly polite.

"Ok! Will I get my master's ticket then?" Mike demanded.

"Sit," Paul said invitingly. He offered Mike the tail end of his bed with an open palm and took a position at the top so that Mike could face him, then offered Mike the cards.

"What do I do with them?" Mike scoffed, looking first at the cards and then at his friends.

"Firstly, if you don't want to take this seriously you can have your money back and forget the whole thing," said Paul, drawing back the deck. "You came to me remember? It is important that we both focus on what you are asking."

"Ok, I just don't know if I believe in this stuff."

"Then why did you pay me thirty pence?"

"I need to know!"

My thoughts were confirmed.

Mike hesitated for a moment and the smug grin on his face was replaced by a contorted pout of submission due to the implication of what he had just said. His eyebrows lifted as he contemplated his own question and Paul handed him the cards.

"Spread the pack in front of you and shuffle the cards on the bed. Move them freely, don't worry about which way up they are, ask yourself the same question," said Paul.

Mike took a few minutes to shuffle the cards then picked them up and handed Paul the deck.

"Now cut the deck," said Paul.

Mike lifted a quarter of the cards from the deck and placed them in Paul's left hand, then Paul covered the smaller pile with the other cards.

Bernie, Pete, Roy and I all watched in awe and suspicion as Paul dealt out the cards in what had become a familiar shape.

The first card he placed between them contained a bright star with the word 'L'ETOILE' written at the bottom. The second he laid across the first, was the Nine of Wands. The next card was the Page of Pentacles, he laid it upside down above the first two cards. Stood at Paul's right shoulder; I realised then that the first card, The Star, had also been placed upside down and I wondered whether there was any significance in that, or that they were simply facing Mike. I had no idea which way the second card was faced because it was laid horizontally. Next Paul laid the Seven of Pentacles at the bottom of the spread, again it was upside down. The fifth card was the Knight of Pentacles and was placed upside down on the left; the sixth card was the Four of Wands and formed the cross being placed on the right, and like almost all the rest upside down.

Nobody spoke; we had seen Paul deal his own cards in silence, but we hadn't seen him perform his divination for anyone else. He placed the deck to one side and clasped his hands prayer like in front of his face, the points of his forefingers touched his lips as he studied intensely what was before him. He remained silent for two or three minutes adding to the tension before he pointed to the Star.

"This is the general situation; the Star symbolises your dream. Clearly you want very much to fulfil your dream of becoming a ship's master; the star is your goal, the direction you are following."

Mike looked unimpressed at Paul's opening statement.

"However, the card is inverted."

"What does that mean?" Mike asked.

"The card is upside down and therefore takes on a slightly different meaning. The Star does indeed represent your hopes, your dream, your goal; however, inverted it suggests that you believe that it is beyond your grasp."

"Huh?" blurted Paul in a display of disbelief.

"I suggest you are in some doubt that you can achieve your ambitions, 'What's the point in trying?' perhaps."

Mike trembled almost imperceptibly before Paul continued.

"You are looking on the darker side," he added. "The Nine of Wands would suggest the need to learn to trust others. Again, the card is inverted and indicates pride getting in your way and you are hesitant to make a long-term commitment. You refuse help. You think you can do it on your own and quite frankly, you are struggling!"

He waited a moment before continuing.

"The Page of Pentacles shows me what is on your mind, it shows a respect for knowledge, study, learning and new ideas, but inverted it says to me that you are overwhelmed, perhaps being unrealistic. You lack concern and you wonder whether the end result will be worth the effort. You want to succeed, but do you want it badly enough to work for it? In this position the Seven of Pentacles symbolises the past three years, it suggests harvesting what we have sown, the rewards for our efforts. Again, the card is inverted it suggests laziness, reaping the benefits of someone else's hard work. You lack long-term vision. The Knight of Pentacles symbolises the past year, it suggests a keenness to develop your career, inverted it could mean unemployment or being bored with work, unable to find your vocation. Perhaps and excessive interest in material things, good food, good wine or sex."

"Sex! That's all he talks about," blurted Pete.

Mike glared at him briefly in response.

"The Four of Wands here represents what lies ahead of you, the coming year. It suggests working with others to produce a common goal, I believe that being inverted suggests that may be a problem for you. There is no such thing as a completely self-made man!"

"Is that it?" asked Mike feeling cheated.

Paul picked up the deck that he had previously set aside and dealt four more cards placing them to the right of the cross, beginning at the bottom, and ending at the top; all inverted. They were the Emperor, the Two of Pentacles, the Three of Wands and the Tower. "The Emperor is the gate way for you," he continued. "He achieves through his own effort, he has the strength of character that will help him win the battle. Reversed? You will have to work for what you want, and because you will not accept the help of others the only way you will achieve it is with a great deal of hard work.

32

"The Two of Pentacles represents your personal life. Reversed, it shows me a move, possibly several moves to further your career; what you desire.

"The Three of Wands are your hopes and your fears, it represents success, leadership but only achieved by demonstration. Again reversed, you will need to be able to lead by example, it is not going to fall into your lap unless you prove yourself worthy.

"The Tower is the whole, the overview, it suggests a stormy future, it will not be easy for you to achieve what you desire but if you build your career on strong foundations you will weather the storms that life will throw at you.

"You will have to be strong and work hard to get your master's ticket, but if you are prepared to make the effort you can succeed and understand contentment."

"Of course I'll have to work hard, we all will!" Paul proclaimed with an unconvincing smile.

"But you will have to work harder than most!" said Paul accentuating the word you.

"Thanks a lot pal!"

Mike's tone made it quite obvious that Paul was annoying him.

"You wanted to know!"

"Yeah is that right? So, I do get to become a captain?"

"I believe you will in the fullness of time obtain your master's ticket and you will become a ship's Master, but you may have to change lines many times before you do. You will need to work very, very hard during the first part of your cadetship or you will suffer the consequences."

"Great, I wish I hadn't asked."

"But you did ask," interrupted Roy.

Pete sniggered.

Mike turned around and glared at Pete again, his expression showed his displeasure.

When Pete's grin had been replaced by a sombre face of repentant respect he turned back to Paul.

"What else can you tell me? Will I meet any girls here?"

Paul dealt three more cards and placed them beside the sixth card, the influence of the coming year. He studied them, but this time did not enlarge on the individual cards. The Five of Cups, the Lovers and the Eight of Swords all lay upside down.

"Yes, you will meet girls, but you will not like them. Surely you knew that anyway."

I noticed then that his speech had changed. Throughout the reading he had lost his Cockney accent, he spoke much more clinically, at the time I was more aware of that change and the contempt in his voice than what he had said.

"I'm off for breakfast, anyone going to join me?" asked Roy ending the rueful silence.

"Yeah, me!" I said perplexed by the whole business and only too keen to leave them to it.

I didn't feel comfortable about the display of hocus-pocus and after watching Mike embarrass himself in front of us, I was more determined than ever that it was not for me.

# CREDENCE

After a full English breakfast, we all went to the classroom for the course tests. Ferris was already there, he had moved all of our name cards; which indicated that we had all changed places, to stop any cheating I supposed. He waited for us all to come in then walked over, then shut the door before saying anything.

"Good morning gentlemen."

"Good morning Sir."

The dry chorus echoed the reluctance we all shared in answering, it reminded me of a hall full of rebellious fifth formers being forced to join in morning assembly with the rest of the school.

"I'm pleased to hear you all in such good spirits," he said sarcastically. "I trust you all slept well?"

I was not sure if he had asked a question, the sarcasm had gone but there was no response.

He walked around the room placing question papers face down on each desk.

"Do not turn over the examination papers until you are told to do so."

When he had finished he went to his desk and sat down.

"Gentlemen please turn over your papers now, but do not open them."

In doing so I realized that the papers were actually a foolscap size booklet.

"Please fill in your name and today's date, Monday the 15th of October 1973."

He waited while we did so.

"The question booklet you have in front of you is a multiple-choice examination in mathematics. You will score one mark for each correct answer; however, you will also lose one half mark for an incorrect answer. Therefore, if you do not know the correct answer, leave the question blank. Do you all understand?"

We all nodded.

"I strongly suggest you read the questions carefully. You have two hours to complete the test. Please open your papers and begin."

As he said it, he started a timer set for two hours. We sat in silence and began the test.

When I read the front-page information, it confirmed the marks for correct answers but said nothing about losing marks, so I assumed that he was placing doubt in our mind. The truth was Ferris was simply trying to stop us guessing. Anyone who scored low would get a chance to go through the questions again. Since he would assess the papers I realised it was his call. The pass mark was apparently eighty percent.

When we had finished we were given a fifteen-minute break, after that we came back and sat the science test. By lunch time, we were all ready for food and a chance to talk.

In the afternoon we began some basic seamanship, going over some nautical terms and then beginning some knotting and splicing of rope. Our seamanship instructor Mr Tucker, Archie, as he was known to anyone that had been on-board for more than a few days, was far less formal than Ferris; he was older, and his chubby, red weathered face lent itself well to his friendly smile.

Monday evening was much the same as Sunday night, we all went ashore in the same groups. Once again, after we had each bought a round, Paul left Roy and me at the Pier to finish our drinks before returning to the Worcester. Paul returned on the last ferry with a huge grin on his face. He was in no rush to give us the details of his jaunt, he knew we could not stop ourselves from asking.

Like Roy, I was still very naive about girls. My first love had hurt and embarrassed me. I was only twelve at the time, too slow and naive for her needs. She too was only twelve years old; however, her lust had developed early in unison with the well-developed breasts she already boasted.

Despite my brief pre-teenage encounters, I was still convinced that Paul's tales were nothing but fantasy.

## Tuesday ~ 16th October 1973

The next day Ferris handed back the test results. I was happy enough with my results having come top in science and second in maths. Such was my conceit that it both surprised and amused me, not because I had done so well, but because I felt my mathematics was better than my science.

Ferris went through everyone's marks and we reviewed our papers. My two mistakes in the maths paper were a result of not reading the questions properly. Mike had finished bottom in science and second from bottom in maths.

"Hall, you answered every question in both tests." He looked directly at Mike, "yet your mark in the science examination was only thirty-eight percent! Had you listened to me we could have reviewed the questions you were unsure of as I will with the other cadets. I suggest that you will need to put some serious effort into your Correspondence Course. You will need to work very, very hard to keep up while you are away. Do not let your pride get in the way of asking for help from your fellow cadets and officers while you are away."

It was uncanny. I looked at Roy and then at Paul. At first sight, Paul might have appeared oblivious to what had been said, he sat there, staring at the pencil, which he rolled between his forefingers and thumbs in an 'I told you so' manner. It was no surprise to him to have his divination confirmed so soon, but he was taking it all in. Roy had obviously noticed it too. He sat with his mouth open staring at Paul in total astonishment.

Ferris walked over to Roy and stared at him, "Seen a ghost lad?"

Roy closed his mouth and looked around at Ferris, any discussion would have to wait.

"No Sir! I'm sorry Sir."

Ferris dismissed Roy's apparent lapse in concentration without a second thought and walked over to a large metal cabinet. He opened up the doors revealing piles of white folders inside it.

"This morning we will begin by reviewing your Correspondence Course. So if you'll form a queue down the side of the classroom."

We queued up at the filing cabinet and he handed out the white folders. These manuals would form the basis of all our training while away from college and assigned to a ship. They contained theoretical and practical training for each stage of our cadetship.

At the end of the two week Induction Course, our training schedule would be followed by a nine months period of sea service; two four and a half month trips with six weeks leave in between; then back to the Worcester for our first period of study at a shore-side college for an Ordinary National Certificate or Diploma in Nautical Science, lasting between four and six months; a second period of sea service of about twelve months, three trips; then a final  second period of study at a shore-side college for the ONC or OND again lasting between four and six months.

* * *

When we finally got out for lunch it seemed everyone with the exception of Roy and I, wanted to have a Tarot reading and their futures predicted by Paul, despite the seemingly negative implications.

Word quickly spread about Mike's reading and Ferris had just confirmed he would have to 'work very, very hard'. It seemed too much of a coincidence. The other guys soon started teasing Mike saying, 'he must be queer if he doesn't like girls'. Mike did not find these repercussions amusing. Paul had certainly not endeared himself to him by causing such accusations. It would take Mike several years to come to terms with his sexuality and the abuse he suffered as a child.

For myself, it was the first time I had really heard of such things, I was old enough to have understood what was meant even if I did not comprehend the desire, my desire for girls was still as yet hardly formed.

# THE OLDER WOMAN

In the afternoon we all had to visit the nurse for a check-up on general health and a long list of inoculations; my own had been performed by my local GP, but for some there were still a couple of boosters to be taken. None of us had seen the nurse so it created a bit of excitement and speculation about what she looked like. We were all lined up in a queue when she arrived.

"Good afternoon boys? How are you all settling in?" she greeted, not waiting for an answer. "I'll see you one at a time in a few minutes."

She disappeared into the sick bay and closed the door behind her.

We all looked around at each other, no words were needed to convey our thoughts. She was not a young girl relatively speaking, in fact she was probably in her late thirties. She had the look of Lady Penelope and it was quite clear that she appeared to arouse the manhood in all of us. She was curvaceous and very attractive. Of course, being the only woman on board ship emphasised that fact. Her voice and her demeanour were it seemed, intentionally provocative.

"What do think of that then Mikey?" asked Pete.

"Piss off fatso!"

In difference to Mike's pre-divination 'Jack the lad' nature, he took the remark as another insult, clearly angry about the recent innuendoes he had been subjected to. Pete overlooked his retort realising that he had touched a very sensitive nerve in his friend.

By the time it came to my turn to see nurse, I was already aroused by the general lust that had developed in the group, her every touch seemed to be sensual and I was very much aware that it made my hairs stand on end.

Memories of my first infatuation with a mature woman came flooding back. Miss Hamblin my First Form teacher at secondary school had taken up her first post after training at our school and we, 1H, were her first class. She was in her early twenties, all the boys and some of the teachers thought she was beautiful. She was my maths teacher as well as my form teacher, which made her even more attractive to me due to my love of the subject.

She lacked the ability to control the class and alas we made her life very difficult. Sadly, she moved on at the end of the year.

Nurse was another beauty, she seemed to enjoy flirting with the cadets, something Miss Hamblin would never have done, even if we had been sixteen years old.

I thought of Nurse that night after lights out as I lay in my bed. My thoughts were instinctive, I imagined myself drawn to her womanhood. I desperately wanted to pleasure myself, but I was afraid that the others would hear. Trying to put her out of my mind and not to submit to my need I found myself wondering about Mike and what he others were saying about him. I could not comprehend the scenarios of which the others spoke.

# A FRIEND IN NEED

Wednesday ~ 17th October 1973

Wednesday evening Roy and I went ashore with Paul again, but that night he left us at eight twenty, a little later than usual. Roy and I carried on drinking that night, he was still drinking his pints of shandy, and I was now beginning to acquire a taste for keg bitter.

Before long, Mike came into the bar, alone and already intoxicated.

"Where have you been?" I asked.

"On a pub crawl."

"It's only eight thirty," said Roy checking his watch and recognising Mike's slurred speech.

He came over and sat on a stool beside Roy and me.

"What have you done with Pete and Bernie?" I asked.

"They've gone back to watch the bloody football."

"Yes, I think I've had enough," said Roy, "I think I will go back myself and watch the game."

England were playing Poland in the crucial World Cup qualifying game at Wembley, and the match highlights were on the television later that night. "Are you coming James? It could be a good match, we need to beat Poland tonight if we are going to qualify for the world cup. We beat Austria 7-0 last month."

"That's right, piss off and leave me why don't you? Anyway, the Poles beat us 2-0 in June, probably do the same again tonight, then we'll be out of the World Cup before it starts!"

"I think I'll give it a miss if you don't mind Roy."

I didn't really want to stay but I was already under the influence of the beer and I was somewhat sympathetic to Mike's solitude.

"Cheers Jimmy boy," said Mike. "What you havin'? I'm in the chair. Fred!" he shouted out across the bar.

"I'll see you later," I assured Roy.

"Yes alright!"

Even after a couple of beers Roy never lost his refined accent.

"Fred!" Mike slurred loudly, despite the fact that Fred stood opposite us at the bar.

"I would like a pint of lager and a large rum and black for myself and whatever my pal is drinking please."

"Keg please Fred," I added.

"What about a chaser?" asked Mike. I had never drunk spirit of any kind, but I didn't want to look stupid, so once again I copied my elder brother.

"I'll have a Scotch and American please Fred. A single."

Fred looked at me for a minute with a patronising raised eyebrow questioning my need. I hadn't a clue what I was asking for and he knew it. He'd seen more than enough young sailors regretting the consequences.

We sat down at a table before Mike could fall down.

"You know that scoring thirty-eight percent in the science exam, means you probably scored just short of sixty percent with his half point deductions," I said, knowing that still meant he was twenty percent short and with no idea how many were guesses.

Statistically he should have scored twenty five percent but then with Ferris' way of marking he would have scored minus twelve and a half percent.

"Do you think I give a monkey's?" he replied, not wishing to discuss it.

By nine o'clock I had stopped asking for bitter and switched to Scotch; by nine thirty I had finished my fourth and was well past my limit, not that a 'limit' was something I had ever reached.

I persuaded Mike to come back with me to watch the end of the football but when we arrived at the jetty there was no ferry running.

"Where's the ferry?" I shouted out to a group of cadets at the top of the accommodation ladder.

"No more ferry trips till the football finishes!" someone answered.

"Shit!" I cursed.

"Let's go back and have another drink," said Mike.

"Yeah let's," I said, by then too drunk to realise what I was doing.

We got ourselves back to the Pier and carried on with the shorts.

"Make 'em large ones Fred!" Mike shouted across the bar.

By half past ten, we had each bought two more rounds, all doubles.

"Thank you," said Mike as we left the pub.

"What for?" I asked.

"For staying with me. Are you gay Jimmy?"

"Sorry?" I had never heard the term.

"Do you think I'm a queer?" he asked.

"I don't know what you mean," I answered truthfully.

He seemed to accept my answer. We staggered back to the jetty together and got into the ferryboat. When we got back on board, Mike disappeared below but I met Roy on the main deck, he had just been for a wash.

The cold air had taken its toll on me during the short walk back along the riverbank.

"Roy!" I shouted, "I godda clean my teeth mate. Can I use your toothbrush?"

Roy rushed over to me.

"I think we should get down below before the duty officer sees you!"

"Godda clean my teeth Roy!" I insisted having lost all sense of reasoning.

"Tomorrow James!"

"I godda clean my teeth Roy!"

I belched, and the taste of whisky and American dry ginger ale filled my mouth and throat.

"Yes tomorrow, James," pleaded Roy, now desperate to get me downstairs and out of sight.

"Now Roy!"

I could contain it no longer. I opened my mouth and vomited all over him and the honey-glazed deck. By then the duty officer had heard the noise and was on the scene, fortunately for me it was Archie Tucker not Ferris.

"Jesus wept! Get someone te help ye te get him cleaned up and put te bed!" he said to Roy shaking his head in disbelief. "Why me Lord?" he said, still shaking his head. "Orderly!" he shouted.

Roy rushed off and brought Paul back to help get me to bed.

"Why is it always me?" Archie repeated, raising his eyes to the heavens above.

# HELL

Thursday ~ 18th October 1973

The next thing I knew Archie was shaking my shoulder.

"What is it?" I asked, still half asleep.

"It's 6 a.m. son, get ye working gear on and meet me at ma office in five minutes. Here, drink this tea, it'll get some fluids into ye and warm you up. Its cald out there," he said.

I felt awful, I could taste the vomit in my throat, it was tainted with stale whisky. My head was aching, and my stomach was knotted, but somehow I managed to drink my tea as I dressed.

I recall the tea tasted of scotch, but I have no idea if he was giving me the hair of the dog, or simply the tea mixing with the contents of my stomach.

I met him at his office.

"Now how are ye feelin' laddie?"

"Awful," I answered.

"Well get ye' sel' down to the ferry and ye can clean up the jetty, the orderlies will give ye a bucket and a broom."

He wasn't angry or officious in fact he seemed quite sympathetic, but I had to learn my lesson. The cold air hit me at the top of the accommodation ladder, I struggled down to the ferry where the lads were waiting and got in.

"Jesus you stink!" one said.

They dropped me off and gave me the bucket, broom and a plastic sack.

"Put all the crap in the sack then fill the bucket with sea water and give the deck a scrub down with the broom."

It was a low spring tide, the lowest I'd seen, the jetty was completely exposed and looked disgusting, it was littered with everything from sanitary towels and condoms to a broken umbrella. There must have been sewage going straight into the river somewhere judging from the stench. It was a daily job that the orderlies would have had to do if I hadn't been selected, at least picking up the rubbish anyway.

I felt like I wanted to die, I was having the first and the worst hangover of my life and I was freezing to death on a filthy jetty on a cold grey damp day in the middle of October. I could taste the Scotch every time I swallowed which made me retch again and again, but there was nothing left to vomit.

At quarter to seven the orderlies came back to fetch me. The rubbish had been picked up, but I hadn't finished scrubbing the jetty.

"Come on then smelly!" shouted the coxswain.

I emptied the bucket and got in the boat. When I got back on board the Worcester, Ferris had replaced Tucker as duty officer.

"Cummings isn't it?"

"Yes Sir."

I held my head in shame, knowing that he would not show any compassion.

"What have you got to say for yourself then lad?"

He didn't sound quite as severe as I had anticipated.

"I'm very sorry Sir, I didn't know that the ferry had been cancelled last night for the football. I'm afraid I went back to the pub and ended up drunk Sir. I know I've disgraced myself."

My head was hung low, I really was too ashamed to look him in the face.

"You certainly did disgrace yourself and let's not forget your company and the college. I believe you owe Mr Tucker, your friends and the orderlies an apology. I might well have dealt with the episode a little more seriously; however, I am informed that you were with Hall. He's a bad influence lad and you would do well to give him a wide berth. You have potential at least on paper so don't throw it away. First time?" he asked.

47

"I have never drunk spirits before Sir. Or beer," I added.

"As I thought, we all make mistakes, just be sure to learn from it. Well I think you've been punished enough for one day, do not let it happen again on board this ship or any other."

"No Sir," I replied meeting his eyes for the first time.

I was astonished at the uncharacteristic compassion he showed in not coming down harder on me, he had obviously taken a dislike to Mike.

My successful application with B.P. had required a minimum of four GCE O Levels, including maths and a science. Surely Mike had to do the same with Shell.

"Now go and get yourself cleaned up, I'm afraid you have a rather unpleasant smell about you."

The taste of stale whisky and vomit was obviously just as pungent to others as the taste in my mouth was to me.

"Yes Sir. Thank you, Sir. I really am sorry Sir!"

I scurried off down to my bunk to collect my washing kit and some clean clothes. When I arrived, Paul and Roy were still in bed, it was still only five minutes to seven. I grabbed my gear and turned to run upstairs.

"How ya feelin'?" asked Paul.

"Bloody awful! I just had the worst experience of my life out there. I'll tell ya, don't go swimming in the Thames, it's a bloody sewer. I need to scrub my teeth and shower."

"Yeah," he laughed. "Rest assured, I had no intention of jumping into the river. You need a shower all right! I'll see you up there," he said grinning, then he rolled over again unwilling to sacrifice five more minutes in bed.

I made my way upstairs, conscious of the fact that I was the spectacle of the day. I showered and shaved, then cleaned my teeth over and over again but I still felt awful. I could still taste the Scotch, nothing would take the taste away, my legs felt like jelly and my stomach hurt from the constant heaving I had endured.

# CURSED

Paul and Roy entered the shower room together.

"Are you alright James?" asked Roy.

"I just want to lay down and die," I said.

"How's the head?" asked Paul.

"Blindin'! Have either of you got any aspirin?"

"Yeah, in my locker, help yourself me old china," said Paul grinning.

"Cheers mate."

"You'll find them on the middle shelf where I keep my washing kit."

"Ta."

I walked cautiously back down below to our bunks and over to Paul's locker; every pace seemed to shake my jaw, which in turn reverberated through my head. I opened the locker and saw the bottle of aspirin where Paul said it would be. I picked up the bottle, took two out, and threw them down my throat. I gagged as I struggled to swallow them, but they started to dissolve in my mouth. Even the bitter taste of aspirin was a grateful relief for a minute or two from the acrid taste of stale whisky.

As I replaced the bottle, I noticed Paul's Tarot cards on the shelf above. Over the previous five days, I had become more and more intrigued, despite my deep-seated fear of the occult. Watching Paul use them to entertain and counsel our colleagues had finally blurred my better judgement.

I picked up the blue envelope and looked at it briefly, then walked over to Paul's bed, sat down, opened it up and took out the cards. I began to place them out on the bed, not in the shape of the cross as Paul did but without design, one beside the other just to see what they all were.

"Oh no! Not you Jimmy, what the hell are you doing?" Paul's voice was grief stricken, almost pleading.

"Sorry mate, I just saw them when I got out the aspirin and I wanted to look at them, I should have realised how precious they are to you. I wasn't trying to steal them mate. Shit! If I was I wouldn't spread them all over your bed"

"It's not that I don't trust you Jim! You should never, ever, ever touch the cards unless I give them to you. The cards possess dark forces!"

Was he implying that the gift was not his alone, that the cards held within them some of the power he used?

"Yeah! If you say so." I answered dismissively.

Despite my previous discomfort, I reacted with the same contempt for the cards that any sensible adult holds for a magic wand. Surely, he must have been trying to have fun with me, but I had never seen him so distressed, and that bothered me.

"Believe me, you are in great danger!" he said melodramatically, and I noticed his accent had gone again.

"From what? The bogeyman? They are just cards for Christ's sake."

Even as I said it I doubted my words.

"Don't piss about," he pleaded. "Listen and listen well my friend, I've had this happen before. Six other friends have touched these cards and within days each and every one of them has suffered a catastrophe."

He was serious, I could tell somehow. It was the first time he had called me a friend and I realised he had never talked about our friends, none of us had.

"Well it's done now, I'm sorry."

"Hey, it's you I'm worried about. It's not my fault, the cards are cursed," he explained.

"Whose fault is it then? Cursed? Why?" I asked.

"It's a Romani tradition. My dai, my mother Isis, cursed the cards before giving them to me. Anyone else that tries to use the cards or takes the cards will face danger or ruin."

"Nice mother!" I said sarcastically.

"You have no idea," he smiled. "Erudita, she was a Shaman, La Madre de Cognoscit. The cards are cursed to stop them falling into the wrong hands."

'The mother of something,' I thought to myself. The rest meant nothing to me. I was silent while he recited some kind of foreign verse in the way a priest might utter a prayer at a moment of crisis and despair. It could have been Latin, I know now that it was Romani.

"The wrong hands? I asked.

"The fallen," he answered.

I didn't pursue my question despite not understanding the answer.

"Well what can I do, cross your palm or something?"

"If only! No that will do no good mon ami!"

His refusal really worried me further because Paul had been consistently business like with everyone else.

"Just be on your guard at all times."

"Well what happened to your mates then?" I asked.

I didn't really want to know but once again my curiosity got the better of me.

"One was killed, knocked off his motor-bike, one broke his leg skiing, one got caught nicking stuff from work and got sacked; one committed suicide because he failed his A-levels, he was a really good friend, and so happy before he touched the..." he paused again briefly before continuing.

I ended the sentence in my head.

"One got caught doing a burglary with some loser and ended up inside. He was always as straight as they come. The other one went crazy, separated from his Missus and ended up divorced and last I heard, he was on the streets."

"Nice bunch of friends you keep."

"Hey, I don't give a shit what you think of my friends, I'm just warning you before you become another statistic. Be careful, be bloody careful, and don't do anything stupid, understand?"

"Ok, ok, I hear you."

There was genuine anxiety in his voice, though it was noticeable to me at least that having listed the casualties his subsequent concerns were delivered in his Cockney accent, it had been dropped and even become Spanish at one point.

He picked up the cards and shuffled them then started to deal them out in the usual shape, this time with an urgency that I had not seen before. He remained silent while he examined the cards, in fact he didn't say any more about it during the rest of the course.

"Now let's get some breakfast inside you," he said after returning the cards to his locker.

"I couldn't eat anything," I answered.

"You need some grease inside you, it'll settle your stomach," he added.

I realised Roy had not returned from his shower, no one had. We had been alone for the entire exchange, frozen in a moment of time.

The initial fear passed during the morning and I gradually put the experience out of my mind.

# DESTINY

B y Thursday all the new cadets had got acquainted with each other, by Friday news of Paul's talents had reached the senior cadets and they now visited our bedside for some insight into their future.

Mike became much less open with everyone and isolated himself from any social gathering. It bothered me how greatly Paul's Tarot reading had affected his behaviour, and consequently my own experience with the cards kept haunting me.

The weekend came and went, there was no let up for us although it was largely physical work, swimming, survival and launching lifeboats. Rowing a full-sized gig against the Thames in full ebb was no fun, we barely cleared the davit rigging in thirty minutes of hard pulling.

Paul was always busy either with his cards or with his girlfriend. We never saw her, but he was always willing to talk about his exploits when asked.

Roy and I spent a lot of time together. Neither of us had any desire to have our fortune told and Paul never offered. He never sought out business with anyone, they always came to him. I think the whole thing scared Roy as much as it did me.

# V   THE HIEROPHANT

F inally, it was the last day of the course.  It seemed that during
those two short weeks we had all done so much, everything from
launching lifeboats to rope work, basic navigation, basic buoyage, IRPCS
regs, the International Regulations for Preventing Collisions at Sea which
had been adopted as a convention of the International Maritime
Organization the previous year, and survival training in the swimming
pool.

We finished the course before lunch and we were expecting a visit
from Captain Le Fevre, he was Head of Fleet Recruitment for Deck Cadets
at B.P.  All his cadets were gathered in the classroom when Ferris brought
him in, all of us from B.P knew who he was, he had conducted our
interviews and selection.

I sat anxiously hoping he had not found out about my drunken
episode, it would not go down well.  It was far from uncommon in the
service, however the Merchant Marine took a dim view of drunks on the
bridge naturally enough.  I still felt very ashamed at what had happened,
but nobody ever mentioned it again, nor the fact that I was only sixteen
and under age.

"Good afternoon lads, I hope the course went well.  I haven't heard
anything from the college, so I assume none of you have any
insurmountable problems."

I felt happier consoling myself that he had heard nothing from the
college, but I suspected there would still be a written report.

"I expect that you're all keen to know where you're headed but I'm
afraid I can't tell you just yet.  You will all receive your ship assignments
by the end of next week.  You will be glad to hear you get a rest now for a
couple of weeks or so before you have to leave home.  Most of you will

join a ship along with one of your colleagues here, although a few of you may have to travel alone."

I wondered who I would end up with, I hoped it would be Roy or Paul, I would have to wait and see like everyone else.

"I have brought along Miss Cooper from the office, she will speak to you all about what you need to take with you. There are also company reports you will need to complete and return to us during your time at sea, she will explain these too. Finally, I expect you're all anxious to find out how to get your hands on your salary. You will all have brought your bank account details with you I trust, you will need them when you talk to Miss Cooper. She will go over everything you need to know."

He paused, turned towards the window and stared out over the Thames adding drama to his dialog.

"I know you boys have been shut up here for two weeks, but I will not tolerate bad behaviour from anyone who works for me."

His statement came from nowhere and hit me like a stone in the middle of the forehead. I wanted to throw-up and I had to struggle to stop myself from retching. He was going to sack me here in front of everyone as an example to the others. Tears began to build in my eyes as I waited for his pause to end.

"When you are in the presence of any of the women that work in my department, you will behave like the officers you strive to become and the gentlemen I know you all to be. I know that I will not find it necessary to remind any of you about this in the future, my girls are not the street girls you'll hear all about at sea."

I let out a gasp of air as my chest relaxed.

Suddenly a premonition overwhelmed me. 'Sam, she is my destiny and I hers. Miss Cooper is Sam.' The thought crashed through my mind, coming from nowhere just like Paul's name had when we met on the pier two weeks before, almost as though I was listening to myself. Miss Cooper is Sam, and Le Fevre was protecting her like a farther protects his daughter.

I knew what she looked like from my visits to Britannic House, but more than that, I knew the touch her hands, the smell of her hair, and the subtlety of every curve of her body. He opened the door and called her in.

During the two weeks on board, I had been aroused by Nurse like most of the other lads, she looked so sensuous and she was so demonstrative with us all. Being away from home for the first time, I had become bewitched by her self-assurance and maturity. Then and for the first time, I realised Samantha was literally the girl of my dreams. I knew her in that moment before seeing her again and then she walked in.

She stood before me at the front of the room, petite with blue-grey eyes and long wavy blonde hair, tied in a pale blue silk ribbon at the top. Her nostrils seem to flare with elegance and a vibrancy that suggested a wild spirit fighting to break free, and her mouth unable to do anything except smile in a way that melted my heart.

"Good afternoon boys, nice to see you all again. Now, do any of you have your bank details with you now?"

I put up my hand and looked around to see Roy, Paul, John and Rob all with their hands up.

"If the rest of you will go and get them now I will make a start. Would you like to come up first James?"

She knew my name. The little card on my desk simply said Cummings. She looked straight at me and I got up at the same time as the others rose to fetch their paperwork. I looked at Paul and he winked at me knowingly. I sat down in front of her and we looked into each other's eyes.

My mind went into overdrive as a multitude of thoughts, powerful sensations of déjà vu, raced through my mind. The rest of the world seemed to stand still. All I wanted to do was take her in my arms and kiss her soft lips and taste the essence of her sweet neck. I knew how sweetly she kissed and how she loved me kissing her neck that way. I did not know or even consider how I knew it or if I had actually done it. It was surreal.

It seemed like an eternity, in reality it was only seconds. Then she smiled and regained her composure.

She explained the procedures and recorded all my details. I had the papers with me, but I had memorised all the details, my bank account number, passport number, discharge book number, seaman's ID number, employee number and my National Insurance number. I didn't know why I had bothered, habit and numbers I guess, suddenly it seemed a wise move because I couldn't take my eyes off her.

She was friendly and smiled the whole time despite my constant stare. I said nothing that would give away my feelings, but any fool would have realised how smitten I was, because my eyes only left hers to look down at her inviting shiny pink lips and hers broke off only to fill in her forms.

After just five minutes we had finished, I took her hand and gently shook it. She had a strangely firm grip, I knew it would be. One would have normally expected a light feminine gesture from such a pretty girl. 'She was just nineteen! How the hell do I know that?' I thought, realising that I knew but that it didn't make sense for me to know. I eased my grip on her hand, but she continued to hold mine for a brief moment as she smiled at me. I felt we both knew what was happening, yet with perhaps the exception of Paul, nobody else did.

"McClair is it?" she asked

Roy was beckoned with a beckoning finger and a smile. He took my place while I walked back past Paul. He looked up at me from his chair, his legs were stretched out at the side of his desk and crossed at the feet, his arms were folded across his chest. He pursed his lips and blew me a kiss then winked at me again grinning broadly.

Sam looked down at her list as Roy sat down in front of her.

"Now then, Roy isn't it," she confirmed.

\* \* \*

We left the Worcester that afternoon and I never got a chance to talk to her again.

57

Most of us needed to catch the train into central London and go our different ways.

Roy and I were both headed back to Waterloo station, from there we would catch different trains home. Paul walked with us back to the Greenhithe Station before going back to collect his luggage, he planned to meet his elusive girlfriend after seeing us off. When our train arrived, we shook hands.

"I hope to be sailing with at least one of you boys," I said.

"We'll have to see," answered Paul. "Kushti bok pral! You take care now! You too young Roy."

"You too," I answered. "And keep in touch!"

"Bon voyage Paul," said Roy.

There were new beginnings, journeys physical, mental and spiritual. I felt his energy, force, optimism and his contented gayety.

He would become my friend, my guide and mentor. He would never teach because we need to make mistakes to learn and he would neither encourage nor discourage my ideas or actions.

Roy and I boarded the train together and said good bye at Waterloo.

# THE DREAM

## THE FOREST

I watched the forest pass by as the train made its way from Brockenhurst to Sway; it had always been my private wilderness and childhood playground. I knew every tunnel intimately, though better from the bridges above than from the railway below.

The railway divided the heath; on the south stretching away to the Solent and the Isle of Wight, and on the north, the woods and Long Slade Bottom.

I recalled exploring every trail in that part of the forest at some time or another. I loved it and was so happy to see it again.

As children, we knew that Sway was locally famous for two things; the Tower, and the Treacle Mines. We all knew about the Tower, it was there for all to see. Peterson's Folly, or Sway Tower as it was better known, stood in the south of Sway and at two hundred and eighteen feet, it was the tallest folly in the world. It could be seen from any high spot on the forest, even from the Isle of Wight, something that became apparent while spending most of my summer holidays there in my early teens.

The tall slender tower was an experiment in the use of concrete as a building material before the addition of steel reinforcement. With almost four hundred steps and thirteen floors, it stands seventy feet taller than Nelson's Column, marking out my home like a titanic matchstick stuck into a map. It was built in 1879, coincidentally the same period that the mysterious legend of the Treacle Mines was born.

Most of the children of Sway knew about the legend of the treacle mines, and boasted of their existence to friends from surrounding villages; conjuring up imaginations of enormous caverns in the forest, lit by flaming torches, where lumps of treacle could be picked from the rocks. The little-known truth about these myths was far less romantic.

At around the same time that old Peterson was mixing his concrete, a new railway line was being carved through the forest. The station at Brockenhurst was the junction for Lymington and the ferry to Yarmouth on the Isle of Wight, while the main line went off to Dorchester via Ringwood. The upwardly mobile Victorian middle classes wanted quicker access to the beautiful seaside resort of Bournemouth, so a new line was needed that would cut across the New Forest through Sway to Christchurch.

More than one old navigator suffered a tragic end in the construction of that line, paralysed and drowned in a sea of thick orange treacle-like slurry erupting from the banks of the cutting. Pockets of it lay waiting to strike in a deadly silence unmatched even by the coiled adders, basking in the sunshine on the heath to the north beneath which the deposits originated. The heavy clay soil in the higher land soaked up water like a sponge, and golden treacle was the end result.

These events had long been forgotten, but more importantly to us children, so had the secret location of the mysterious caverns. Perhaps the entrance lay hidden beneath old Peterson's skyscraper, sealed for eternity.

The Ringwood Line was pulled up in the fifties but the clearway it left remained, cutting its way through Long Slade and out through Burley. We all knew it as 'The Old Railway Line'; it provided a wonderful source of hide-outs under the old bridges, or on the banks of the cuttings. It also formed a magical boundary, our own Hadrian's Wall protecting us from Lyndhurst and the imaginary barbarous north beyond. We would frequently venture way beyond its protection, and even camp on the forest in the bad lands of the north, having escaped from home with a tin of beans or even a string of sausages to sustain us on a warm summer night. Such expeditions were considered immensely dangerous, requiring extreme valour, but they made great stories to tell and retell.

It would always be my forest and my home. I dreamed of living in the woods, it belonged to me, despite the counter claims of my brother, some other passionate friends, a few hundred commoners and of course the Sherriff of Nottingham, otherwise known as the Forestry Commission. The history books were all wrong, we knew that Robin Hood's theatre of fame was there in the New Forest.

My train passed through the last tunnel and I watched the platform rise and run along the side of the train. I was home, it was time to get off.

# WANDERLUST

**M**y parents met me at the station. It was a pretty little example of Victorian architecture that frequently won awards for its beautiful floral displays. It still displayed the old green signs of Southern Railways, who had taken over the line from London and South Western Railways way back. There was no one else there except Joe, the Station Master.

It was good to see them and to be back home, not that I had been homesick, I just had so much I wanted to share with my family.

I realised that it was them that I wanted to see, my school friends had all gone their own way, most of my friends had started work, and most of the rest had gone on to Sixth Form College in Brockenhurst to study A levels. It felt strange not to be seeing them all anymore. I had met new friends and would make more in the weeks and months ahead. I also realised I would be leaving my family behind.

I spent a relatively quiet two weeks, waiting impatiently for the news of where I would be going.

My younger sisters were still at school, and my older brother and sisters were married and had left home, so I just had Mum and Dad for company.

My father was partially disabled, suffering badly with rheumatoid arthritis. He no longer worked, but he managed to drive and was more than happy to take me into Southampton to do my shopping. I think he shared in my excitement, he was definitely proud of me for getting the job.

I had saved a little money working through the long summer, having left school in early June as soon as I had finished my GCE's; with my B.P. wages coming through I was eager to spend it. I had developed a sense of urgency that was new to my life. Soon I would be leaving to go to sea and before I did I wanted new clothes, different clothes, and a cassette recorder to play my own music.

My outlook on life had changed since leaving home, the older cadets had influenced me in many ways and I wanted to fit in, be like them, there was a part of me that wanted to look good for Sam too, although our brief encounter now felt like it had been nothing more than a dream.

I found myself a nice portable radio cassette player in Southampton, which I acquired learning quickly from the sales man about the system of hire purchase credit. That left me with money to spare with which I was able to buy my first two album tapes to go with it, 10CC and Stealers Wheel, both albums coincidentally named after the band. I spent the remainder of my money on a new bomber jacket, two shirts and a pair of Foster Grant sunglasses, which I felt were particularly fashionable. It wasn't exactly a new wardrobe, but it was all I could afford.

Friday ~ 2nd November 1973

Each morning I waited at the breakfast table, eager for the post to arrive; finally, on Friday morning, I heard the letter box open and the sound of post falling onto the floor. I rushed out to the hallway to find a white envelope addressed to me with the green and yellow BP logo on it, lying on the floor in front of me. I picked it up along with the rest of the post and took it back to the dining room where I sat down with Mum, Dad and my brother.

John, my brother, ran his own car repair business from a small workshop in Brockenhurst, when and how he worked was to a point down to him, so he would often pop in for breakfast and a chat.

I opened the envelope with excitement and anticipation. I felt like someone who had won the football pools and was about to find out how big the dividend was.

Inside the envelope was a letter, a travel warrant for the train to London, and a blue crew list of all the ships in the fleet. I read the letter first, I was off to Kharg Island with Bernard Harris.

Bernie had been very quiet at college, but I could have done worse, he was friendly enough and like me, he played chess. I was no budding Grand Master, but I could play a fair game, at school I had been the team captain. I preferred to satisfy my need for mental stimulation, rather than running around chasing a football in the school field or talking to girls during the lunch breaks; besides, I wasn't part of either group. If it had not been for my laid-back attitude to study, I would have most definitely have been thought of as a geek. I did not care.

Mum got out the old Times Atlas and handed it to Dad. It had originally belonged to her father when he was alive and must have been at least thirty years old.

We looked up Kharg Island to find out where I was going, it was a second dividend, not a jackpot. I was off to Iran or Persia as the atlas said, at least a small island, fifteen miles off the Iranian coast in the northern Gulf; the atlas cited it as Kharag I. A little green spot off the largely orange and brown contoured map of Iran.

The more uplifting news was that my ship, the S.S. British Grenadier, was bound for Boston and the United States so it would be a good trip, down around the Cape of Good Hope.

We all sat around the table and began talking about Dad's wartime experiences in Egypt. He had been through Cape Town on his way to wage war against Rommel's Afrika Korp in North Africa.

At the outbreak of war, both he and my mother worked in reserved occupations, building Motor Torpedo Boats at the British Power Boat Company in nearby Hythe, on Southampton Water. Dad recalled that he had lied his way into the Royal Hampshire Regiment, by misleading the enlisting officer.

"When they asked me, 'What was your last job?' I told them about my previous job rather than my current job," he explained.

In his opinion he hadn't lied, he'd just differentiated between the words last and current.

Such people were exempt from being conscripted. In my father's case he was officially prohibited from enlisting on his own initiative and required to remain at his post, but he got away with it.

He spent almost two years based at Ramsgate, at the time when the British Armada made its way across the channel to rescue the British Expeditionary Force, in May 1940, and throughout the Battle of Britain, while the RAF in the skies above answered the threat of a German attack on the South East coast that summer.

As a child I had no comprehension of the desperate situation Britain faced at that time or the significance of his posting. Unbeknown to me my father had stood at the front line of Britain's ground-based defence.

At the end of 1941, he transferred to the Seaforth Highlanders Second Battalion, wishing to fight alongside his Scottish countrymen.

Thirty-one years before, almost to that day, he had narrowly escaped death during the first night at the second Battle of El Alamein. He very rarely spoke of the battle itself even to my mother, except to say that he and his comrades shared a strong dislike for General Montgomery, the man that replaced the Auk, their beloved General Claude Auchinleck, Montgomery's predecessor.

Over the years, we had learned that his close friend had saved his life that night, throwing himself over my father and shielding him from an incoming mortar shell. His friend took the full impact of the blast in his back, except for one fragment of shrapnel that pierced my father's windpipe narrowly missing his carotid artery.

He would never discuss his feelings about his saviour, not even his name, but we were all aware of the anguish he felt about his friend's sacrifice. Had his friend not protected him, none of us would have been born. Me, my brother and sisters all owed our existence to this unknown hero.

Almost a hundred men of the Second Battalion lost their lives during that fateful night.

Dad was found by a medic during the battle who performed an emergency tracheotomy in the field enabling him to breathe before being hospitalised in Alexandria.

Rightly or wrongly my father would say Montgomery was very much a strategic General, prepared to suffer heavy losses in order to win the war, perhaps that is why so many his comrades paid for the victory with their lives. In Monty's defence, he conceded that it was perhaps one of the most significant turning points of the war.

In May 1944 he was transferred again, this time to the Royal Engineers where he finished his war as the Skipper of a supply-boat working out of Port Said.

We spent some time talking about his brief stop in Cape Town and his experiences in Egypt. He always took great pleasure talking about that time after Alamein, when he served in Port Said. Having given and lost so much, he probably deserved to finish the war that way. He was extremely proud to have been the Skipper on a supply-boat and delighted in telling us that his Mate had been Skipper of a fishing boat before the war, but that 'he outranked him, so it was his boat'. He talked and talked of the trips to and from warships and the officers that he carried from ship to shore or even Alexandria, a city he loved. He got out some old photographs of the boat and some of him standing in front of the Sphinx and the pyramids of Giza.

The wanderlust surged inside me, I just couldn't wait to leave. I glanced through the crew list, my name was not there, but then none of my friends were there either, it was the previous month's list. It did tell me that the Grenadier was a fifty-five-thousand-ton ship. Her master's name was Alan Browning and there were six cadets on board, four Deck and two Engineering.

My brother John had forgotten about work and sat through dad's accounts with me. He was extremely envious but at the same time very pleased for me. He knew as much as my father, just how much I wanted this dream. I had spent some of the summer holidays working with him at his workshop in Brockenhurst. He was seven years my senior and until that year we had never really spent much time together, despite sharing a bedroom for most of our lives. During that summer we had become very close, somehow the barriers age had put between us became insignificant, we had worked, laughed and got just a little drunk together on several occasions.

My mother was tearful now, she was worried about me jetting off around the world, no one else in the family had been abroad except Dad, and then only during the war.

Realising that I only had one week now before I left and knowing at last where I was bound for, my impatience subsided; I developed a need to recharge my soul and refresh my memory about my home and background.

I spent most of the time alone, walking through the forest where I had spent my childhood playing. It was my way of saying goodbye to that childhood, and moving on beyond more distant barriers than the old railway line, that had once been our Hadrian's Wall.

# THE OLD MAN

I walked without thought of direction, across the heath and down across the plain, on through the gap that had once been one of many bridges carrying the old steam trains to Ringwood. I never did understand why those bridges had been demolished when the railway tracks had been removed, years later they would be replaced with new wooden ones for walkers and cyclists.

I carried on along the path that crosses the bog-land until I entered the woods. The temperature dropped significantly, along with the brilliant light from the sun's rays, partially blocked by the dense branches overhead.

Ahead of me to the right stood a long wooden fence, supported in part by its iron railed predecessor. Climbing the iron fence made the task of looking over the taller wooden one very easy. Beyond the fence was a large old house that stood silently in acres of grounds. All my compatriots knew about the location of the house and the old outbuilding, which stood just the other side of the fence.

In keeping with tradition, I once again climbed up and peered over at the estate. Standing majestically behind the ruined main house was an enormous rhododendron. In early summer, this magnificent shrub would be covered in bright red flowers, in marked contrast to the smaller, more prolific, pink-mauve petals of the wild variety that grew around the forest. Still wearing its white robes, it stood silently, like a huge iceberg large enough to have sunk the Titanic.

I was about to climb down when I noticed the smoke coming from the chimney on the little outbuilding beside me.

For years we had assumed both buildings to be derelict. As children, we had never ventured beyond the safety of the fence, for fear of the witches that lived there; if not witches, then perhaps the last remaining outpost of German or Japanese soldiers, that my young friends and I were all agreed, was where they had concealed themselves since the end of the war.

Despite the knowledge that either of these scenarios was unlikely, it was not without some trepidation that I placed my leg over the fence and slipped down the other side.

I crept over to one of the many broken windows, intending to look through to the darkness inside.

I could hear the crackling of burning wood, and as I peered into the darkness, I could see the flickering flames of the fire in the hearth.

"Come in."

I could now make out the figure of a man beyond the fire, sat in an old wooden carver chair.

"Come in come in!" said the man without pausing.

I opened the door beside me and stood in the doorway. The room was dark inside despite the flickering fire, and I hesitated, waiting for my eyes to adjust.

"Come in and close the door boy, it's cold."

I didn't recognise the voice of the tramp like figure that sat at the other side of the room, but I did as he requested.

"You don't recognise your old friend do you," he said not requiring an answer. "Sit," he continued, pointing to an old trunk on the other side of the room. "Pull it over, so that we can talk by the fire."

I dragged the empty trunk across the floor and sat down, while he threw more sticks on the fire from the pile beside him.

"Do I know you?" I asked.

"Not yet," he chuckled.

His hair was completely white and his body without muscle mass, thin with age. His accent was not recognisable, his words softly and slowly spoken. He looked very old, but I said nothing.

"Old! What is old? Time and age are illusions."

It appeared he knew what I was thinking.

"Who are you? Where have you come from?"

"You may consider me your guardian angel," he laughed.

"And you're here to protect me?" I asked, not realising I needed protecting.

"From fear."

"But I am not frightened."

"Really? Then let us agree on guide you," he answered.

"Guide me?"

I had not considered Paul's prediction of peril until he asked the question.

"You're a rebel aren't you? Different, unorthodox, demanding, and spoilt. You have never had to make an effort, and you make your own rules."

"What the..."

I did not finish speaking the question, 'What the hell is happening here?'.

I already knew I couldn't lie to myself and I just knew he would know anyway.

"Go on," I answered.

"You're going to sea. You want to travel but you don't know where, you want to be taken somewhere, anywhere."

"Yes, I do."

"Have you ever felt that you could do something, or work something out without knowing why?"

I considered the question quickly.

"Sometimes I feel like I can do whatever I put my mind to, but, there are things I can't do."

He waited for me to continue.

"I can't run, I had an op..."

He stopped me with his stare.

"People can run if they want to run."

I found that odd at the time, but I considered his point. The fact was that I didn't actually want to run, and derived no pleasure from trying. I knew I had never had to push myself to succeed or to understand things.

The things I wanted to do came naturally and I felt no need to stand out by being better than required.

"You are coming to the end of a journey and will have to choose between two consequences," he paused. "Trust in yourself my young friend. The rebel in you will know what to do when the time comes."

"It will?" I had no idea what he meant.

"Go now. You will find me here again when you need me. Bon voyage. Close the door on your way out, its cold out there."

"Right, yes, I'll... close the door."

I left as instructed, climbed back over the fence and turned for home.

Perhaps he was just some crazy old tramp, but something very profound told me I that I had known him at some point, I just couldn't place where or when. He also seemed to know me in ways I was aware of but never considered. I had no idea what he meant about the end of a journey, clearly that was wrong, I was about to begin the biggest journey of my life so far.

# SMITTEN

Monday ~ 12<sup>th</sup> November 1973

I met Bernie at Britannic House on the second floor. We were both dressed in our navy-blue number one uniforms carrying our white peaked caps under our arm. I felt ready for my new life.

Sam met us at the lift looking lovelier than ever. She wore a vivid green scarf, the colour of new spring leaves, tied in a bow, where before there had been a blue ribbon. She took us into her office and sat at her desk. I couldn't take my eyes off her and she knew it. As she looked me in the eyes, her pupils dilated visibly almost filling the blue-grey iris, noticeably dipping her gaze as she spoke whilst and barely acknowledging Bernie.

She gave us our plane tickets and explained how to check in. We were to be met in Dubai by B.P.'s shipping agents in the gulf, Gray Mackenzie. After she had finished the formal tasks, she stood up.

"Remember to write to your family, and don't forget your wives and girlfriends! You'll get your incoming mail every two or three weeks."

I had fallen for her and was completely besotted. It seemed she was encouraging me to write to her by the way she had worded things. I wanted to ask for her address right there and then so that I could, but fear of rejection and inexperience prevented me from doing so, especially in front of Bernie.

She picked up the phone and waited for an answer.

"They're ready to leave now," she said, and then put the phone down.

Captain Le Fevre appeared a few moments later.

"Well gentlemen, I trust you are both in good health. Is there anything you would like to discuss before leaving?"

"No Sir," I shook my head.

"No Sir," Bernie echoed.

"Well in that case may I take this opportunity to wish you both every success with your first trip. No doubt Miss Cooper has told you to contact her if you have any problems reaching your ship. Our agents in the Gulf are Gray Mackenzie, as you now know," he said turning his head to Sam for confirmation. She acknowledged with a single nod. "They will look after you when you arrive in Dubai. Well I wish you both bon voyage and good luck. Miss Cooper will take you to your car."

He shook our hands and disappeared through the interconnecting door.

Despite my preoccupation with Sam, I could not help to notice what a very distinguished man he was. If he did know about my indiscretions on board the Worcester, and he probably did, he had the grace not to mention it in public. I guessed my drinking habits and indeed others aboard ship would be recorded for review.

Sam handed us both her office contact details and apologised for not having already done so.

"I'm so sorry. I can't think why I forgot to give you these earlier, you must think I am so silly."

'No, no!' I tried to say, but not a sound came from my lips.

She acknowledged my thoughts subconsciously with her dilated eyes.

Business completed, she escorted us down to the ground floor, and took us out through the rear of the building to a chauffeur driven car, waiting to carry us off to Heathrow Airport. She shook my hand and smiled.

"Good luck James," she said.

"Goodbye Samantha."

"Sam," she countered with a smile, "and it's au revoir. You're coming back to me. Have a great trip," she added then turning to Bernie she made a polite though somewhat half-hearted gesture to shake his hand. "You too Bernard."

It pleased me that she didn't make the prolonged eye contact with Bernie in the way that she had with me, and that her handshake was noticeably less committed; but jealousy would probably be the wrong word to describe my feelings of uncertainty. On the Worcester I seemed to know what she was feeling, I knew her thoughts as intimately as I did my own. On that day in the office at Britannic House I recognised my own feelings for her, but there was only hope that she felt the same way about me.

"Goodbye Sam," he answered using the intimate name she had offered me.

She stood there, waving goodbye, and I watched her disappear as the car rounded the corner. I told Bernie how I felt about her and how much I had wanted to ask for her private address so that I could write to her.

"Bit old for yo', isn't she? You should have asked anyway! What did yo' have to lose?" he answered philosophically.

Whilst I felt that a relationship with Miss Hamblin or Nurse were beyond reasonable belief, it never occurred to me that Sam was too old. But he was right about the latter and it seemed to be too late to do anything about it.

"Well you'wull just have to send her a letter at the office and make it private," he added.

I began to notice his west country accent; to me at least, it seemed noticeably broader than my Hampshire accent.

"Yeah, I will!"

Logical thought had abandoned me, stupidly it hadn't yet occurred to me that it was that simple.

I sat back in the chair thinking about her and how she had looked at me, she was so very lovely in every way. 'You're coming back to me,' she said.

"So it's Doo-bi we-ere off to, not Iran!" said Bernie moving on. There was a distinct difference in the way Sam had pronounced it, which amused me.

"I've never heard of the United Arab Emirates," I answered.

Sam had told us that it was on the southern side of the Persian Gulf. Our flight was due to depart at half past two in the afternoon, and it was still only ten minutes to eleven.

\* \* \*

It was shortly after twelve thirty by the time I had checked in my enormous blue ribbed suitcase, crammed full and almost too heavy to lift. Fortunately for the people around me, my new cassette recorder was safely packed inside my case. I had not stopped to consider that I might want to use it before I checked in, so I was soon bored to tears, waiting in the departure lounge without music to ease the boredom. I sat down reluctantly and fidgeted restlessly.

It was dead time for me and being unable to speak to Sam frustrated me enormously. I knew we had a long journey ahead of us but for some reason a two-hour wait before we took off seemed like an eternity. I can still smile at the impatience of new love.

Bernie being well prepared for the journey, sat reading a book. I had never been very fond of reading, it was too slow, so I had not considered bringing one. I realised that it would be a good time to buy one, but I no longer had the money. I had spent most of what I had on clothes and what I had left I had changed into Dirhams at the office before leaving.

"Do you know where any of the lads are going?" I asked Bernie.

"Nope. I said I'd write to Mike and Pete when I got on board ship."

"Yeah, I told Paul and Roy I'd keep in touch."

He nodded and glanced around the departure lounge again.

"Did you let Paul tell your fortune then?" he asked.

"No, I wasn't very keen to know what lies ahead of me. I'd rather wait till it happens."

Paul's warning flashed back through my mind. I thought that I had put the incident behind me, evidently, I had not. The thought was brief, but it still sent a chill right through me and for a moment I felt like my chest had been opened by an invisible rapier.

"I know what you mean. I saw what he did to Mike, so I thought I'd pass on that one."

I noticed that in using the word 'he', Bernie attributed the blame to Paul. 'What it did,' may have been more appropriate. I saw it more as Mike's fault, he was the first person to ask Paul to use the cards; whereas

75

I had not sought the forewarning of impending doom that I received. It wasn't worth arguing about and Bernie knew nothing of my experience, so I said nothing.

"Have you been abroad before?" I asked.

"Yeah, I've been on holiday to Majorca and Spain, with my family a few years ago. You?"

"No, never." I shook my head. "I've never even flown before."

Some of my school friends had been fortunate enough to take a short flight on the new Boeing 747 Jumbo Jet a couple of years before, but the cost of the event was far beyond that which my parents could afford.

We chatted the time away, but my thoughts kept moving back to Samantha. 'Had her smile been no more than politeness? Had I read more into the handshake than there really was? Did she have a boyfriend? Was I simply too young for her? Perhaps it was no more than a spot on my nose that captured her gaze?' Only doubt filled my mind.

In a desperate need to be positive, I decided for the second time, I would indeed write to her as Bernie had suggested. What did I have to lose?

I remembered how attractive her legs looked in the short black skirt and black tights, though I had not been conscious of looking at them. Her waist was slim, and she filled the skirt in a beautiful curvy way that was extremely arousing, but it was her beautiful eyes that radiated her very soul.

I looked down at my white cap and then at the bright brass buttons on my uniform and felt full of confidence.

I stood up and walked across to a bookshop, putting my cap on as I crossed the floor, pretending to myself I was looking for a book. I made my way around to the end of the shelves, where I could see my reflection in the glass window. 'Why shouldn't she like me?' I thought trying to convince myself that I was a good catch.

It was very out of character for me, I had never been really bothered about the way I looked.

# THE FLIGHT

O ur flight was with Middle East Airlines, we would be landing in Beirut before flying on to Dubai, where ever that was. I wasn't sure where Beirut was either, I had no idea I'd be going there until we had checked in.

We were both impatient to discover what type of plane we would be flying on; I knew it wouldn't be a Concorde, they hadn't yet entered commercial service, but it could be a Jumbo jet.

The flight was called at ten minutes to two, and we moved quickly to the gate. It didn't seem that difficult to get on a plane, although I was following Bernie.

As the boarding coach pulled up alongside the plane, it was clear that it wasn't a Jumbo, it was only about half the size; the difference being blatantly apparent with a Jumbo beside it, on the other side of the coach. I noticed the green cedar tree emblazoned on the red tail.

The interior looked very comfortable as we stepped inside, first impressions would change within an hour. We both removed our jackets, and a stewardess took them away and hung them up for us. I loosened my tie and sat down beside the porthole. The Captain switched on the intercom and welcomed us to the flight, we were on board a Boeing 720B; we would be travelling at twenty-eight thousand feet, and our ETA at Dubai was 1.55 a.m. local time.

When he had finished the hostesses went through the safety procedures, with over exaggerated smiles, and eyes that stared blankly into space. I smiled as I thought back to Ferris's conviction performing a similar task. He may have been methodical, but every word he delivered was with such conviction, you knew that it might save your life one-day.

The engines throttled up to full power, and as the brakes were released I felt myself pushed back into the seat. The take-off was smooth; I watched the sombre grey November clouds fall away below us as we moved into the bright sunshine. The engines eased back as the plane levelled out, then the seat belt and no smoking lights went off together with a ping.

Having never flown before, it hadn't occurred to me that once we were above the clouds we would emerge into brilliant sunshine. I watched the blanket of very different snow-white clouds below me until we were across the Channel and moving across Germany. An hour or so later I decided to take some photographs through the porthole as we flew over the Alps, ignorant of the enormous difference between the powers of the human eye in comparison to a cheap camera lens.

We were served our evening meal just before five o'clock. Darkness had started to limit the view from the window before we started to eat, by the time we had finished, it was completely black outside with only the glow of urban lights scattered across the countryside below.

We both made ourselves as comfortable as possible and tried to sleep but it wasn't easy.

The landing in Beirut was my first but the brief bounce as the wheels touched the runway was not too great a shock, the roar when the braking flaps were raised was much more startling. We remained seated while some of the passengers disembarked and their replacements joined us for the onward flight to Dubai. The whole thing took about an hour.

I stirred as the stewardess brought us our jackets, then over the intercom the Captain informed us that we had commenced our descent into Dubai, and that it was now one forty-two in the morning local time. Bernie was already awake. We both adjusted our watches. The temperature in Dubai was seventy-eight degrees, warm for a November night I thought. The cabin lights were extinguished, and I sat back anxiously awaiting the landing. It was very smooth, this time there was just the faintest contact, cushioned by the suspension as the wheels touched the ground.

I watched the lights from the airport buildings race by the window as we rushed down the runway. The wind roared again as the braking flaps were raised and I turned around to Bernie.

"We made it!" I said, releasing my clenched fist from the arm rests.

"Yeah, nice touch down, but I didn't get much sleep, I'm knackered." His slow drawl emphasised the fact.

"Me too," I said. "Still we'll get some sleep at the hotel soon."

"We've gotta get through immigration and collect our bags first."

"Yeah so?"

"If it's anything like Spain that'll take at least an hour!"

The aeroplane finally came to rest, and as the pilot ran down the engines passengers started to undo their seat belts, despite the fact that the signs above still flashed to the contrary. Eventually the sign was extinguished, Bernie undid his seatbelt, standing up as straight as it was possible between the seats to stretch as he did so.

The door was opened in front of us and the warm air rushed in through the doorway filling the plane with a pungent aroma. It was a mixture of musty Arabian spice and salt from the sea, made heavy by the heat and humidity that forms over the desert sands so close to the sea.

I undid my belt and stood up as Bernie, having found space in the gangway, reached up to retrieve our flight bags.

We had to wait while the ground crew made the final checks that the stairway was secure before we could disembark. It only took a few minutes, but everyone was restless after the long journey and eager to get off. People were already jostling for a space in the gangway in a desperate attempt to be amongst the first to disembark.

As I stepped out onto the stairway, the full impact of the heavy, humid air hit me, and I began to perspire in the heat.

We queued up with passengers from other flights to pass through the immigration desk. Finally, I was confronted by a customs officer who after checking that the boy in the photograph was me, stamped the first immigration visa into my passport. Bernie was right about the cases, it was another half-hour before we retrieved them and passed through customs into the arrival area.

Even holding my jacket made me feel uncomfortable in the humidity, I wished I had worn something more comfortable for travelling. I chuckled to myself as I realised that my beloved 'whites' would be more suitable.

# THE WARRIOR

We were met by an extremely wiry and very dark-skinned man waiting in the arrival area, his very dark colour made him look more African than Arabian to me. I had no idea who did what in Dubai and I had expected a Brit or perhaps an Arab.

He stood waiting beyond the barrier holding up a board with 'B.P.' written in the familiar large green letters.

"Hi, I'm Bernard Harris and this is James Cummings, are you from Gray MacKenzie?"

"Yes Sir; Mr Bernard, Mr James. My name is Haji bin Jabir, I am from Gray MacKenzie. Do you have all your luggage?"

He had the physique of a long-distance runner.

"Yes," said Bernie as I nodded.

Haji turned around and shouted in what sounded like Arabic to a small Indian looking man who rushed over at his call. He continued with more instructions and the little man grabbed my large case, then proceeded to take Bernie's. The poor man looked too small to carry one let alone two, but he scurried off and we followed.

Once outside, we walked across the road to a heavy looking American Dodge van; Haji opened up the large side door for our access. After the little Indian had placed the cases in the back of the van, he came around to Haji who placed a coin into his hand. The little man muttered something, Haji responded in an abusive tone. Judging by his tone it sounded to me like he was swearing at him; whatever he had said, the little man walked away muttering in disgust.

"Gentlemen, we go to the Ras al Khaimah Hotel," said Haji, clapping and rubbing his hands together in front of his face.

"In Dubai," I asked.

"In Ras al Khaimah," he answered, considering the fact to be obvious, grinning at my stupidity. "Please!" He added ushering us into the van.

We set off into the darkness towards the city of Dubai passing what looked like an enormous palace, surrounded by large green lawns and illuminated under floodlights. I was relieved by the cool air that soon filled the van; it emphasised how warm and humid it had been outside.

Shortly after leaving the airport, we passed the dockside. I saw the sea on our left side as we moved out of the city along the Sharjah Road, towards Ras al Khaimah.

It was nearly five in the morning when we arrived at the hotel, back at home it would have been one o'clock. Haji escorted us to the reception desk while a porter brought in our cases. He explained that it would be two or three days before he came back for us.

B.P. had made our reservations and would settle the account through Grey MacKenzie; we only had to fill in a form and submit our passports before being shown to our room.

We shared a twin room with an en-suite bathroom. It was very large and spacious with sliding glass doors opening onto a small balcony. Neither Bernie nor I tipped the porter, we just thanked him and closed the door behind him.

"Big isn't it!" I said.

"Yeah at least there's plenty of room," Bernie replied.

"I'm sure our cabin on board the Grenadier won't be so luxurious!" he chuckled. It was a very spacious room.

I dropped my bags and went into the bathroom.

"Can you drink this water?" I called out, picking up the glass by the sink.

"I shouldn't! There's a bottle out here."

"Do you want some?" I asked.

"Cheers mate," he replied.

I picked up another glass from the sink and took it back to the bedside table. Bernie had walked over to the balcony and opened up the door.

"There's a swimming pool down there."

I followed him out onto the balcony. From there, I could see we were on the second floor and I realised that I had neither noticed the floor number in the lift nor the room number.

"It's warm," I said handing him the glass; it had been standing on the bedside table for some time, but I walked back to the bed drinking it anyway.

Bernie left the balcony door ajar even though the room seemed cool and walked over to the bed.

"I'm ready for this," he said, putting down the glass and laying down.

"I think I'll have a quick shower before turning in, I feel dirty as hell." I felt very uncomfortable, too uncomfortable to sleep despite being so tired.

"I'm too tired to care," he said still lying there.

By the time I got out of the shower he was asleep.

# AN ALIEN WORLD

Tuesday ~ 13th November 1973

I woke up before Bernie and looked at my watch, it was ten minutes to one. I poured out another glass of water, it was warm despite the room feeling cool, but I was thirsty, so I drank it then walked over to the balcony window and pulled back the curtain. The intense light broke through the room and fell onto Bernie's face, he screwed up his eyes as he stirred.

"Close the curtain for God's sake!" he cried in a painfully constricted voice.

I moved out onto the balcony closing the curtain behind me. I had never seen a sky so bright, there was not a cloud to be seen; the sun shone with a whiteness that seemed to drain the colour from everything around me.

I looked down at the swimming pool, it looked very cool and inviting. In the distance, I could see a small harbour, beyond that the sea stretched out to the horizon. On the right a range of what appeared to be sandstone or limestone mountains, rose steeply from the water sealing the vista, disappearing into the horizon like an endless fortress wall.

It was very hot, almost ninety degrees outside, but the heat had burned off the humidity of the night and the sea breeze made it feel much more comfortable. Inside was substantially cooler and I became aware of the sound of fans. I hadn't realised until then that both the hotel and the van were air-conditioned.

The desert that surrounded the hotel looked very different to the rolling orange dunes of barren sand that I had imagined. There was a sparse covering of green plants, small trees and scrub, scattered across the sand, which was a noticeably pale dirty greyish buff colour. There were no other buildings in sight except for a few down at the harbour. During the previous night's trip from Dubai, it had been too dark to see the landscape.

I left Bernie struggling to wake up and took another shower. I had begun to shave when Bernie came into the bathroom.

"Do you mind if I use the shower?" he asked.

"Help yourself mate."

"Cheers," he said, turning on the water and stepping in.

"Oh, that's wonderful!" he shouted.

"Yeah, and about time too! You were beginning to stink!" I said jokingly.

We both dressed and went downstairs to the restaurant where we ate a light meal from the salad bar. The food was not very appetising. It would take me a while to get used to Arabic food and the style of cooking. My exposure to foreign cuisine was limited to say the least.

"D'ya fancy a swim then?" I asked.

"I need another coke first," said Bernie, quickly swallowing what was left in his glass.

He belched involuntarily covering his mouth with his hand, then summoned the waiter and ordered another.

The meals were paid for, but I was not sure whether the drinks were down to us, and I only had three pounds worth of Dirhams to last me until we got on board ship. In the end we just signed for our meal and there was no request for money.

"Why don't we have one outside?" I suggested.

"Yeah, why not!"

We went upstairs and changed into our swimming trunks. I grabbed my towel, cassette recorder and my pocket chess set, and went down to the pool.

The hotel was very quiet, so I was not surprised to find that there was no one else there; we had the pool to ourselves. We had a long relaxing soak in the water, it was warm, but still a refreshing break from the heat.

When we eventually got out we ordered two more cokes, sat in the shade and surveyed the landscape.

"Hey there's a camel over there," said Bernie.

"There are four of them," I said pointing out three others beyond the scrub.

It seemed such an alien world to me.

# THE FILLY

Wednesday ~ 14th November 1973

**W**e spent the next morning soaking up the sun, swimming, playing chess and drinking ice cold cokes. I was glad that I had bought the cassette recorder, and now had three tapes to choose from. I had purchased David Bowie's 'Hunky Dory' before leaving for Dubai, 'Life on Mars' was my favourite track. Bernie didn't object to me playing the same tapes over and over again.

I wasn't sure whether we could buy beer, I was under age, and besides it was an Arab State. It didn't matter to me; keg bitter didn't sound refreshing, and my night on the Scotch still haunted me. Bernie never asked for anything but coke.

"Well then Jimmy, are you going to write to Sam before we leave here?"

"Yes, I suppose I should."

I asked a waiter to bring me some paper, ordered a coke for Bernie and a grapefruit juice for me; the coke seemed to be getting sweeter with every glass.

First, I wrote a letter to my parents to tell them everything and that I was enjoying myself, then I used up the rest of my first film taking pictures of the hotel, the pool and the camels.

Bernie had a Polaroid camera and he asked the waiter to take a few pictures of the two of us at the poolside.

"Here," he said, "you can send one of these to Sam and one to your parents."

"Great! Thanks Bernie!" I said.

I had only once written a letter to a girlfriend. Susan, the girl I had fallen for at twelve years of age, had ended our brief relationship, replacing me with an older more experienced boy. I wrote to her telling her that I loved her, opening my heart to her in an attempt to change her mind. My letter was so emotional that after reading it, Susan took it to school and showed all her friends, thinking only kindly of me. She told me that we could still be friends, but my young pride was deeply wounded; I was seriously embarrassed, although surprisingly no one teased me about it.

There were other girls that caught my eye, but apart from a kiss with a girl under a hospital bed that was it. Maxine and I had both had a tonsillectomy operation and were the only two children in the ward. We were eight years old and had escaped out beds briefly before being spotted by the ward Sister.

Subconsciously, I had delayed writing to Sam in an attempt to maintain the illusion of romance, fearing another rejection far more painful than my experience at school, even though few would ever know or care. The thought, when I considered it, that Le Fevre might find out that I had mistaken Sam's friendly smile for something much deeper seemed more daunting, though I felt sure Sam would not tell him and he would probably never know that she had received my letter.

I picked the best of the three photographs and wrote my first letter to Sam.

\* \* \*

S.S. British Grenadier
Wednesday, November 14th 1973
Dear Sam,

I'm not sure how many letters you get from amorous cadets, but I felt I had to write.

*Here is a picture of Bernie and me by the pool at the Ras al Khaimah Hotel in the United Arab Emirates. In case you don't remember me, I'm the shorter one on the right. You sent us out here to join the British Grenadier on Monday.*

*I have the strangest feeling that I have known you before and I don't know why. I have to say you are a very pretty girl and I love your nose, it reminds me of the horses on the forest where I live. I know that doesn't sound very flattering, but you have a habit of flaring your nostrils the way a young foal does, full of spirit and vigour. Any way it is a pretty nose and a very proud one too.*

*If you don't have anything better to do, drop me a line some time, tell me about yourself, I'd love to hear. Perhaps I could take you out for a drink when I get back to college or when I finish this trip. If you don't reply I will assume you would rather I didn't write.*

*If you do write perhaps you would send me a photograph of yourself."*

*Yours truly*

*James*

*PS If you do write, please let me know where to write to you, I only know the office address. Oh, and please don't tell Le Fevre I have written, I think he might fire me if you do!*

＊ ＊ ＊

I showed Bernie the letter.

"What do you think?" I asked.

"Looks fine to me apart from calling her a horse I s'pose. And I don't think she had a proud nose, all I saw was her great big smile looking at you. Not that I'm an expert on women mind!"

"Do you have a girl friend?"

"Sort of," he answered, "I've known her since we went to school together and we've been out with each other a few times. Here!"

He handed me a strip of black and white photos in a photo booth.

"Her name's Stella. I've just sent her a letter."

"She looks very nice." I said politely.

She was a very plain looking girl and it seemed to me that to call her 'pretty' would have been unconvincingly gracious.

"What does she do?" I asked.

"She works in a bank, at home in Ipswich," said Bernie.

"Is that where you are from? I thought you were from Cornwall or Devon judging from your accent."

"Nope. I'm from Woolverstone. It's a little village just outside Ipswich."

"Do you think I should add a kiss?" I asked dismissing his reply.

"Well you've asked her for a photo anyway."

"Yeah your right. What harm can it do?"

"I always put an 'o' after the 'x' for a kiss and a cuddle," he added.

Its seemed a nice thought so I added an 'o' after the cross beside my name then we took our letters through to reception. I paid for the postage using a five dirham note and was handed a collection of coins in change.

# THE WEDDING

Shortly after noon, Haji came back to the hotel and asked us to be ready to leave at three o'clock. Neither Bernie nor I were sad to be leaving, we were both keen to get on board ship and begin our new lives. We dressed for lunch, then went back to our room to re-pack.

"What are you going to wear then?" I asked.

"What d'ya reckon?"

"It's too hot for anything but our white uniforms, but I haven't got the balls to wear it. I think we're destined for a bit of painting and deck scrubbing. They'll probably think we're jumped up little farts if we wear our uniforms. I think I'm gonna go for my suit, it may be a bit hot, but it won't look like we think we own the place."

"Sounds good to me!"

Having to pack my cap meant that there was no room for my cassette recorder. Bearing in mind the possibility that we could have a lot more waiting around before actually getting on board, and after having been deprived at Heathrow, I decided to carry it separately in the brown cardboard box that it came in.

Haji arrived on time to pick us up with the Dodge. We set off back along the road for Dubai but then turned off towards the sea.

"Where are we going?" I shouted to Haji.

The local harbour was too small for a tanker, I hadn't seen anything bigger than a small dhow alongside the quay.

"Haji is taking you to boat in harbour. You must go by boat to your ship," he said, looking at me in the mirror.

When we arrived at the harbour we drove along the quay, beyond the view from the hotel, as we turned the bend I saw the supply boat.

91

Grayswift was fifty to sixty feet long with a twenty-foot beam, about the size of a war time MTB. The bridge was on the forward half of the boat, with a small upper deck area behind it; a cargo deck aft of that, about twenty-feet long, large enough to stack supplies. Below the bridge and upper deck, there was a large cabin, with four large windows on each side just above the gunnels. She looked well-proportioned beside the local vessels and was being loaded with crates of fruit, vegetables, crates of meat and other supplies when we arrived.

"You give Haji your passports, and Haji will get the exit visas."

There was only one man visible on the bridge, he was wearing the white shirt and shorts of a merchant navy officer. Haji escorted us up the gangplank onto the boat and down below decks to a large seated lounge.

"Your bags will be loaded for you, please make yourselves comfortable, Haji will return when we are under way."

'Comfortable' seemed to be stretching the imagination. There were six rows of very rigid looking brown plastic covered, utilitarian bench seats down each side of the cabin; it looked like an oversized bus. We both stretched out as best we could. There were no cushions, so we sat one per chair, our backs against the hull, and our legs stretched out along the bench seat. I turned on my cassette recorder, only to discover that the batteries were running low; very soon the music was nothing more than a slow dirge.

"I wonder if there's a pool on board, most of the bigger ships have a small pool," I muttered, thinking about the Grenadier.

"I don't really care, I just want to get on board and settled in. This is just so damn boring!"

I was frustrated about my batteries, but also feeling just a little anxious about how life would be for the next four months.

I turned around and gazed through the porthole.

"Shit! Look at that!"

Bernie turned around in his seat and peered out of his porthole.

"What?" he said looking from side to side.

"Down there," I said pointing down. "Right in front of us."

"Oh God, I hate snakes, they scare the hell out of me!"

"Me too! Oh shit it's ugly!" I said with an involuntary shiver.

It was only about three feet long, but it was bright yellow and lay there almost motionless, basking in the stillness of the harbour water.

"Do you think it's poisonous?" he asked.

"I don't know, to be honest I don't really plan on getting too close to it any way. I can't bear the damn things."

I shivered as I said it. The ugliness I imagined was in essence simply my intense dislike of snakes.

The boat vibrated as the engines started, the sound echoed through the hull. I looked at my watch, it was quarter past four.

"At last!" said Bernie." Perhaps we'll get some proper grub tonight!"

"Yeah, I'm beginning to get a bit peckish myself. Can't say I'm too fond of that stuff they served up in the hotel."

The boat started to move off and I wanted to go up and take a look around.

"Do you think we could go up on deck?"

"Aloft!" Bernie corrected me with a smile, we both wanted to sound like seaman.

"I think we better wait till Haji comes back."

"Yeah I suppose you're right."

We waited but no one came.

Watching the sea pass by the port hole, we saw more sea snakes basking in the sunshine, some drifting like pieces of discarded yellow hose on the surface of the water, others spiralling quickly away as we passed.

It was just after five o'clock when Haji appeared with two trays, one balanced on top of the other, each with a covered plate of food on it.

"Haji has some food for you gentlemen."

It was chicken and salad with boiled potatoes, it looked great as he handed us a tray each.

He took our passports from his back trouser pocket, examined the first to identify the owner, then handed them to us. My pristine new dark blue passport now had a distinct curve that echoed Haji's backside and contained two visa stamps, one entry and one exit.

"Those yellow snakes, are they poisonous?" I asked placing my passport back in my inside jacket pocket along with my Seaman's ID card and my Discharge book.

"Deadly poisonous! But they will not attack if you leave them alone, they have very small mouth, big problem to be biting men, men too big for them," he said with a grin.

He mimicked a cobra, one hand bent at the wrist with his fingers biting his other arm.

"Haji know many divers here, they don't bother them. They wrap around the scuba gear but the divers, they don't care!" he grinned again clapping his hands.

The skinless chicken was boiled and looked very pale and insipid. I had never tasted boiled chicken before and the anaemic colour affected my appetite. It was actually very moist and succulent, but despite my hunger I only picked at it. It wasn't the comfort food I craved for.

"Haji bring coffee," he said disappearing up the ladder.

He was back quickly with a large steel coffee-pot and two mugs; the pot had a screw on lid to keep the coffee hot.

"Coffee!" he announced, placing the tray down on a small table.

"Is it okay to go aloft?"

"On deck? Sure, is alright on deck, but no wander around," he said leaving us to our food.

"Chicken's good!" said Bernie.

Due to my limited experience of food it tasted sterile to me and judging by the taste without any salt. Bernie finished his while I continued to pick at it.

We poured ourselves some coffee; I recognised the taste, it was strong and mixed with evaporated milk, but I didn't care, there was obviously lots of sugar already in it. When we had finished the coffee, we decided to go up on deck and have a look around.

The sun was well down in the sky now and the temperature was more bearable, especially with the breeze produced by the boats speed. I looked back along the wake, the coastline was almost out of sight. The long range of mountains ran away to the east of us, to the Strait of Hormuz.

They had taken on a reddish-brown colour in the dusk. With the shore line below the horizon, they appeared to rise almost vertically out of the water to their peaks. They were the Musandam mountains, not cliffs. They were spectacular, and I wished that I had not packed my camera. I looked around in the direction we were heading but saw nothing.

"No sign of any ships!" I said.

"No!"

We wandered over to the ship's side and leant on the railings.

"I wonder what they're doing at home?" he said.

"It's Princess Anne's wedding day today!" I said realising the date. "It's a bank holiday."

"What time is the wedding?" he asked.

"Dunno! Two or three o'clock I reckon, that's the usual sort of time isn't it!"

"Is it on the tele' then?"

"Yeah, must be." I answered. "I s'pose they'll all be watching it soon. It must be about one o'clock at home. It seems strange to know what's going on at home and not be there."

We seemed to be moving towards a very large yellow buoy, I pointed it out to Bernie. It was quarter to six when we tied up alongside. The buoy was about ten feet in diameter at its base and stood a good ten to twelve feet out of the water. There were steps up the side leading to a hatch on the top surface, above that a cradle supported an enormous amber light, which was already flashing brightly. It was obviously a mooring point. Haji came out on to the deck and walked over to us.

"We must wait here for your ship. It comes maybe in two hours. You rest now, Haji will call you when ship comes. More coffee; yes?"

I still wasn't sure what country he was from, but his very dark skin suggested he was of African origin. We took his advice and went back below, had another cup of coffee and settled back down on the seats.

95

# XV  THE TOWER

Hagi returned at quarter to eight.

"Ship come now gentlemen, you follow Haji up on deck; yes?"

The engines started up again, and we were moving before we reached the top of the stairs. The sun had gone down over an hour earlier, the outline of the British Grenadier stood out clearly in the darkness; her bright deck lights temporarily lit for the crew change. She was still a few miles northeast of us, off our starboard side, having turned southeast around the Strait of Hormuz.

As she drew closer, her immense size overwhelmed me.

On the deck above us, her huge spotlights lit up a mass of green pipework running down the length of the ship, just visible over the gunnels; at the stern the bridge and crew's quarters shone brilliant white, the huge red and black funnel stood with its green shield emblazoned with yellow BP, clearly visible in the floodlights.

I lived on the south coast, just twelve miles from the huge ESSO oil-refinery at Fawley; looking up from the Grayswift that night, it seemed I had not seen such an enormous ship since my early childhood, when we used to visit Southampton to see the Queen Mary or the Queen Elizabeth at Mayflower docks. I was in awe imagining just how big one of B.P.'s largest two hundred and fifty thousand-ton Very Large Crude Carriers would be.

As the boat manoeuvred alongside the huge hull, we moved to the deck behind the bridge with Haji, two steps higher than the aft deck and clear of the cargo area.

A long staircase, the accommodation ladder, hung down from the tanker deck amidships; the supply-boat edged forward towards it. The bottom end was suspended thirty feet down the side of the ship.

In port, the bottom end of the accommodation ladder would have rested on the quayside, forming a staircase to the deck; at sea it hung down alongside the ship's hull, supported by a derrick on the deck and a thick steel cable that hung down to the top of a cradle, forming an archway at the bottom.

I looked up at the officers and crew looking down over the gunnels, silhouetted by the bright deck lights.

To the right of the bottom step was the pilot ladder, traditionally used by harbour pilots to board a ship and navigate her though the channels of his homeport; a simple rope ladder with wooden treads running straight down the hull, from the deck, down to just above the water. Every six feet the treads extended three feet out to the sides, to prevent the ladder from twisting or rolling.

The Grenadier's red bottomed hull showed up in the darkness, she was in ballast heading north to take on her cargo of crude oil. Her huge black hull towered out of the water. When returning, fully laden she would have been almost submerged with only a few feet of freeboard, almost level with the Grayswift.

Until that time I had not been aware of the swell, the sea was flat and calm, but as we drew close to the accommodation ladder it was apparent that our deck was gently rising and falling two or three feet against the Grenadier.

"You must climb up the pilot ladder and step across onto the accommodation ladder," Haji instructed.

It would not be a massive climb if timed correctly, two or three steps at most.

"What about our luggage?" I asked.

"It will go up in the net."

Haji pointed back down the boat and I saw our cases in a net waiting for the derrick above to lower its block and tackle.

"What about my tape recorder?" I asked Haji, realising I still clutched it under my arm, safely packed in its cardboard box.

"Haji put it in the net; yes?" he pointed down the boat.

"No," I said, considering the weight of the suitcases. "It'll get crushed."

Haji lifted his upturned hands out sideways, shrugging his shoulders as he nodded.

"You give it to Haji, Haji give it to you when you are on the accommodation ladder; yes?"

"Yes okay."

We were in position to go aboard. I looked up at the crew above once more; I could clearly see two officers who stood out in their white tropical uniforms, and five or six crewmen visible on the Grenadier's deck.

"Wait for the boat to rise then take the ladder with your hand; yes?"

"Yeah, sure thing," said Bernie being first in line.

The Grayswift rose against the Grenadier, which was unaffected by the swell, peaking about once every five seconds.

I watched Bernie step across onto the pilot ladder as it peaked, as he did, the Grayswift eased away from the hull.

The pilot ladder moved gently from side to side as Bernie made the short climb. Three steps and he was level with the accommodation ladder platform. As he moved across and started the long climb up the staircase to the Grenadier's deck, the Grayswift closed against the tanker hull again. Rubber car tyres all along the Grayswift's gunnels cushioned her against the Grenadier's black hull.

I had already handed my cassette recorder to Haji and moved into position. Having noted the step I was aiming for, I was ready to grab the pilot ladder as it peaked again.

Below me the boat deck fell away as I began the short climb. I made the same three steps, moved across onto the relative safety of the accommodation ladder platform, then turned around to retrieve my cassette recorder. Haji passed it up to me and as I took it, I nodded in thanks and turned around. Looking up the staircase I saw Bernie move onto the deck and shake hands with the officers.

I had only reached the third step when the steps beneath my feet evaporated.

* * *

I was at the epicentre of the chaos surrounding me, unable to actually witness the spectacle of what was happening. The next thing I knew I was underwater. The box containing my precious cassette recorder was snatched from my grip as I plunged into the depths below.

Time seemed to stand still. Paul's warning of catastrophe flashed through my mind, then bizarrely the old man beyond Longslade, who told me 'I was coming to the end of a journey and will have to choose between two consequences'. Was I to be a victim here? Drowning, or crushed? Were they my options? He seemed to be repeating his words to me.

I felt no panic suspended in the water and in time. If I should die there, I would never see my family again, and yet I had been given fourteen more years of life after surviving a major operation when I was two years old. Was there a heaven? Will I feel anything. Sam then consumed my thoughts. I could recall countless memories of a life with her that we had not yet shared, through my eyes and also through hers. I knew I had to survive somehow.

I could see the surface above me, the Grayswift had moved away to port about eight feet from the Grenadier.

I had not sensed hitting anything during my fall, it was all so fast. There was no rigging caught around me, I was free to get back to the surface, the bright lights above illuminating my path. I struggled in my suit and suede ankle boots, but my head quickly broke the surface between the two ships.

The 'fall cable' had failed, and short steel strands of wire shrapnel had blasted off in all directions.

The 'fall cable' is lowered by the derrick on deck and supports the 'bail' and its 'bridle chains' at the bottom end of the accommodation ladder. When it failed, the bottom end of the accommodation ladder had swung down in an arc, into the sea, dangling like a useless shattered limb. The forces building up at the point of failure are so great that the steel cable explodes.

I looked up at Haji's panic-stricken face. The view from where he stood must have been horrifying as tons of steel, with me at the core, collapsed in front of him.

I was quickly swept along the two hulls by the current between the two vessels, they seemed to rise above me like the sides of the Grand Canyon. Before I had time to think, I was clear of the supply-boat. I watched the two hulls come crashing together again squashing the car tyres along the gunnels of the Grayswift as I turned in the water. My heart missed a beat as I considered just how easily I might have been crushed between them.

Both ships were moving at six knots and the current that carried me between them was probably three times as fast. It did not occur to me that all this happened in seconds.

As soon as I was through the gap my relative movement along the tanker hull slowed, I had time to look up again at the Grenadier's gunnels. I could see faces peering down over the side into the water, desperately searching for me. I was in relative darkness whilst they were on the brightly illuminated deck.

I realised that the immediate danger facing me at that moment was the tanker's propellers, I had to get clear of the ship before I reached them.

It was a struggle to swim in my suit and boots, but I managed to move twenty yards away from the ship before the stern passed me. I glanced back at the foaming wake, thrashing my arms over and over as fast as I could; I rolled over onto my back and looked up at the flat face of the stern and the white painted accommodation above it. As it passed me, I saw a white flare go up high into the sky and begin its slow descent, suspended by a miniature parachute.

The Grayswift had not yet turned around to pick me up.

I caught my breath for half a second, then screamed with all my heart and soul.

"Help! Help me! Help me please!"

I screamed again and again realising the gravity of my situation. For all they knew I could have been knocked out or injured in the collapse of the accommodation ladder or caught on its submerged wreckage and drowned.

I screamed and screamed, but I could see no one at the stern of the tanker. I could not understand why the Grayswift had not turned around to pick me up.

I continued to scream for help again and again.

"I'm here!" I shouted, but the two ships continued moving away together without any apparent change in course.

My face was throbbing with pain, but I did not know why. My mind fell into wild confusion trying to understand everything that had happened. My destiny now lay in the hands of the Grayswift Skipper. Had Haji seen me? They must know I had surfaced and cleared the Grayswift.

I did not know the cable had failed or what had happened to the accommodation ladder, it all happened too quickly, nor was I aware that there had been an Indian crewman on the pilot ladder behind me.

Two Indian crew were supposed to join the Grenadier with Bernie and me; they had chosen to join their countrymen in the crew quarters on the trip out. One had already stepped onto the pilot ladder behind me, while I was looking down to Haji to retrieve my cassette recorder; he had been left, desperately trying to make the thirty feet climb up the pilot ladder, unable to risk a similar fate as me, attempting to re-board the Grayswift, his climb hampered by the fact that he had been injured with a number of wire shards in his face and arms. That was the reason for the supply-boat maintaining its course. They would have to wait until he reached the safety of the tankers deck; coming back down the pilot ladder was too dangerous.

Ten minutes had passed, there was now a mile between myself and the ship. My mind raced with wild panic and I remembered Paul's warnings of doom and those damned Tarot cards again. I was terrified, not just of being alone in the water and the blackness, now the thought that it was due to dark forces haunted me.

"Save me God, please help me," I prayed in the water.

As a boy I had been Head Chorister and Altar Boy at the local church, not that I had relatively strong religious beliefs, but because I loved to sing and to sing with others; I also got paid a small sum of money every three months, another incentive.

Alone in the sea and dark night, I prayed to my God with a hope and belief that I had never done before.

I began to calm myself and assess my situation.

The crazy old tramp! 'Trust in yourself my friend. You will know what to do when the time comes'.

I realised that my right hand was bleeding, I could feel the salt water stinging my left arm and the fingers on my right hand. I moved my right hand to my face to examine it; my fingers brushed a long metal splinter that had pierced my cheek, and I winced at the pain. My hand or wrist appeared to be bleeding badly and I began to think about sharks. I knew there were sharks in those waters and I also knew they were attracted by the smell of blood. The fear of a shark attack was replaced by the memories of the bright yellow sea snakes; I went into a terrified shock.

Panic overwhelmed me, and I began to scream almost without pause for breath, thrashing wildly in the water; my left arm began to ache.

My jacket sleeve was torn, I had obviously caught it on something when I fell.

# CONFUSION

## VICTOR

"They can't hear you!" The voice spoke clearly behind me and I swallowed a mouthful of seawater as I panicked trying to swing around.

"Jesus! Where the hell did you come from?"

A young man moved up behind me and I instinctively reached out to grab him in panic, but he seemed to be out of reach.

"Who the hell are you?" I asked in disbelief.

"I am a friend!"

"I don't wish to sound ungrateful, but you're not the first person to tell me that."

I swallowed another mouthful of water kicking and throwing my arms around.

He was not swimming, he was just there, the image of a motionless body or at least the head and shoulders above the water. His position seemed fixed as the water rose and fell around his torso like the waves around the leg of a pier.

I reached out for him again and my hands went straight through him.

"Oh God, am I dead?" I could not understand what was happening.

"You are not dead," he replied with a calm voice and a bizarre smile.

"Are you an angel?" I asked, thinking that he didn't look like an angel, without any idea of what an angel might look like.

"Your arm, it's hurting you!" he said, ignoring my question.

"What?"

My reply was more a state of complete confusion rather than a request for him to repeat his question.

"You are feeling pain in your left arm," he said.

"Yes I am."

I pulled my left arm out of the water and spluttered as my mouth dipped into the water. There was a three-inch tear through my jacket sleeve on the outside of my arm, the water around it was tainted with blood.

"You should heal that."

"Yeah sure! And you just happen to have a needle and thread on you I suppose." I said, still kicking frantically to keep my mouth above water.

My terror had been suppressed, I was totally preoccupied by the sudden change in the circumstances I found myself in, absurd and ridiculous as it was.

"I will help you," he said.

I sensed a strange feeling of warmth in my head and down my arm, my thoughts focused entirely on the pain in my left arm. Slowly the pain eased, and I felt a sense of elation as the pain diminished.

"You must remove your shoes," he said.

"What?"

"Take off your shoes, so that you can swim more easily."

I realised again that my clothes were making it hard to tread water; I held my breath while I reached down to unzip my left boot, took another breath and then removed the right.

Memories of the survival training that I had done in the swimming pool at secondary school came rushing back to me. I could make a buoyancy aid using my trousers.

"Now your jacket."

I did as he suggested, then lifting my arm out of the water, pulled back my shirt sleeve, breaking the cuff button as I did so. I examined the cut, but it was clean. The water around me was red but the bleeding seemed to have stopped and the pain had gone.

"Are you an angel?" I repeated my earlier question.

"No, I am not an angel," he grinned.

"Are you human, you look human but you're not swimming?"

"I am a mortal," he answered.

"Are you English? You sound English!"

"No, I am Eratean. I am not from this world," he continued anticipating my next question."

"Jesus you're an alien! Oh God, I'm dead! I'm seeing things! I'm going mad from swallowing seawater. Help! Help! Help!" I screamed.

"They cannot hear you. See how far away they are."

I looked around at the ship, the Grenadier was about two miles away now, still on its original course; the Grayswift had turned back and begun zigzagging its way towards me.

"You see, they will find you. Do not panic."

Absurdly his calming voice reassured me.

"Where have you come from?"

His voice was so reassuring; once again I was distracted from the danger I was in, trying to understand what was happening to me.

"I am from another world in this galaxy, over there." He pointed southward up into the sky into the Milky Way, which shone brightly above the blackness of the sea.

"How do you do that?" I asked.

"Do what?"

"How do you take your arms out of the water without swimming, why aren't you drowning?"

"Is that so important?"

"Yes, I'm getting tired."

"Does this help you?" he said, raising his body straight up out of the water until even his feet were in the air.

He hovered there motionless, like a painted statue, then slipped back into the water. He wore a long robe like an ancient Greek. The robe hung from his shoulders to his ankles and in common with his bizarre stance, the garment appeared to be completely dry.

"Oh shit. Help!" I screamed again frightened by what I had just witnessed. "I'm over here."

The supply-boat was still a mile away zigzagging back and forth, but making slow progress towards me. I knew the sound of my voice would never be heard above the sound of the engines at that distance.

"Take off your trousers," he said.

"What?"

"Take off your trousers," he repeated just as calmly as before.

"Why?"

"You know why. Take off your trousers, you know how to make a buoyancy aid with them."

"Yes I do, I learnt it at school."

I took off my trousers and knotted the end of each leg. I placed them behind my head, holding them at the waist with the knotted legs loose behind, then threw them back over my head in an arc, into the sea in front of me, trapping air inside the legs. I had to do it twice before I got enough air into them, but it worked.

The water was much warmer than I had ever experienced; I was able to rest my legs for a while by laying across the crotch of the upturned trousers, holding the waist tightly bunched below me.

"How did you get here?"

"I found myself close at hand, I saw the flare, and I came to help."

I had forgotten all about the flare.

"Well get me out of here!"

As I finished speaking, I felt the same sensation I had experienced standing at the jetty when I first met Paul. Suddenly I knew the person in front of me.

"Victor! You are Victor!" I said softly.

"Yes, it is I," he grinned. "You are not in danger now."

Once again, the sensation that had smothered me was gone as quickly as it had arrived. I was confused by the moment, but at ease with my companion.

"My hand is bleeding," I protested without conviction.

"It is not serious," he said.

"But the sharks!"

"There are no sharks here."

"There is blood in the water."

"That is drifting away from you now, and you are not bleeding anymore."

"Well there are sea snakes!"

"Where are these serpents you speak of?" he mocked.

"I don't know, all around here!"

"There are no sea snakes around us," he said reassuringly.

"Well what are you going to do?" I asked, feeling despondent.

"I will wait with you until they find you, that will be sufficient."

I realised that despite the seriousness of my predicament, I was out of immediate danger, as he had said; I had a made shift buoyancy aid and I was resting.

I looked at the sea around me and the calm surface glimmered in the moonlight, the wake of the huge tanker remaining as significant as runway lights leading the way to the ship in the distance.

I had recovered my breath and realised that my bleeding hand was not as bad as I had feared. I felt around my face, several long metal splinters had pierced my cheeks. I could not see them, but I had four short lengths of the shrapnel-like wire shards in my cheeks. It was fortunate that none had hit my eyes because they would have pierced them just as easily. Had they done so I would surely have become a victim of the Grenadier's huge propellers.

"So how do you move like that, float in the sky, you know what I mean?" I asked having regained some sense of reason.

"How do you breathe?" he asked avoiding the question.

"I move my chest in and out." I answered sarcastically.

"Yes, but how?"

"With my muscles."

"Yes, but how?"

"I give up! I'm not in the mood to play twenty questions."

"Well where would you like me to start? How much do you know about holograms?"

"This is insane. I'm in the middle of the Persian Gulf, a mile away from the nearest ship, talking to a sarcastic alien in the dark."

"The boat is only two hundred yards away," he answered, correcting me.

I looked up, it was indeed much closer now.

"Where is your space ship? How did you get here?"

"It is above you," he said calmly.

"Where? Show me!"

"I cannot point directly to it, because I am not actually with you, I am on-board; but if you look straight up you will see my ship."

I let my head fall back into the water and looked straight upwards. I saw a silvery blue triangle in the sky. I looked down again and towards the supply-boat, still zigzagging across the tanker's wake and getting closer with every turn. The spotlight scanned the water just ahead of me.

"Help! I'm over here!" I screamed, urgency returning to my voice.

I waved my right arm in the air and blood-stained water ran down my hand and arm.

"Over here!"

The boat drew closer and closer, its powerful spotlight shone down from the bridge scanning the water just in front of me. Eventually the beam of light passed over me and I waved my arms again and shouted.

"Here. I'm over here. Help!"

The beam of light went over me again and came back quickly. The boat turned towards me and I breathed a sigh of relief.

"They've seen me."

I turned around, but he was gone.

# DELIVERANCE

Hagi's face looked down at me in the water and threw over a bright orange life ring with a floating line attached to it. I grasped the line in front of me, discarding my trousers in favour of the safety it offered, then pulled the ring to me and slipped it over my head and arms. By the time I looked back up again someone had thrown a short rope ladder over the side.

I climbed up to safety, half lifted by the line and the men above.

"There's an alien out there in the water."

"What?" said Haji.

"An alien!" I shouted, he's still out there. He helped me!"

"He's in shock."

The voice came from the officer calling from the bridge.

"Get him inside and let's take a look at him."

Haji guided me into the bridge, removed my wet shirt, and turned me around looking for signs of injury; then he laid me down on a long couch on the port side and covered me up with a blanket. He looked at my right hand which was oozing blood, and seeing that my injuries were superficial, wrapped it in a bandage to stem the bleeding.

"If he's breathing okay give him a snort of this."

The officer handed Haji a bottle of whisky about a quarter full.

"The boy's in shock. Ali get some hot coffee," he shouted at a crewman. "Singhy, take the wheel and get us back to the ship."

He stepped to the side to use the radio, informing the Grenadier Skipper that I had been located and picked up safely.

"We should take the wires from his face," Haji said to the officer.

"Ok, do what you must!" he answered.

"You have some wires in your face," said Haji. "Haji take them out before they do more damage. Can you see Haji ok?"

He covered each eye with his hand briefly as he spoke.

"Yes, I think so," I answered now concerned that there was perhaps another splinter in my eye.

He opened up a large first aid box and pulled out a number of sealed plastic packages. He opened two and produced a foil tray from each. He filled the first with antiseptic, then opening another bag he produced a pair of forceps, which he dropped into the antiseptic. He undid more sealed packets and produced some lint swabs and placed in the other tray.

"Haji will try not hurt you too much," he said, with the sterilised forceps in his hand. "Drink some juice," he suggested, passing me the scotch.

I sat up propping myself on my elbow, took the bottle and had a large swig. It went down without any taste, washing the salt from my mouth. Haji nodded in approval; I took another smaller swig, swilling it round my mouth and throat, burning the inside of my cheeks before I swallowed. I handed back the bottle and laid down.

"Lay still now," he said.

I did as he suggested, and I saw the first splinter as he pulled it away from my face. It was a short single strand of nail-like twisted cable, about two inches long and about a tenth of an inch in diameter. I was horrified at the sight of it, thinking how lucky I had been not to have been blinded.

I was conscious of the fresh taste of blood inside my mouth, it had gone right through my cheek. He pulled out three more splinters, all approximately the same size, two from my right cheek and one from my left; strangely enough it didn't hurt at all. After he had finished removing the splinters, he bathed each wound with more antiseptic. Having tasted the fresh blood, I expected to taste the antiseptic, but the small wounds had already closed themselves.

"Rinse your mouth," he said passing me the whisky again. I took the bottle and filled my mouth; I felt a sharp sting from the small wounds as it swirled around my mouth. I spat the blood-tainted whisky back into one of the trays.

"How do you feel," asked the officer.

"I'm ok."

He looked down at me and I paused.

"I didn't imagine it, there was an alien out there, he helped me! I saw him; and his space ship!"

As I spoke, I saw the Grenadier's lights shining above. We manoeuvred alongside again.

"Can I get on board now?"

"I'm afraid not," said the officer. "I think you may have had a bump on the head, you could have concussion. I'm not sure what happened to you out there, but there's no point in taking chances; besides you'll never make it up the pilot ladder with that hand, it's a long hard climb at the best of times. Can't risk you go up in the net either I'm afraid."

I looked down at my right hand to see that I had lost the finger nail from my middle finger and the flesh from my fore finger knuckle.

"No one else is missing but we have one more crewman to get on board and we have to finish transferring the supplies. As soon as that's done we'll get you back to the hospital. I'll talk to the Skipper and let him know what's going on, maybe we can get you on board when they come back down. How's that sound?"

I hadn't really thought about climbing the pilot ladder, I still wasn't really sure what had happened.

"Does your head hurt anywhere?" asked Haji.

"No! Not that I know of." I said. "But then I didn't feel the splinters either."

Haji felt around my head, pulling my hair from side to side.

"No pain?" he asked.

"No pain!" I answered.

He checked my fingers for movement then asked me to wiggle my toes after pulling off my wet socks.

"Okay, you take off your wet shirt and underpants and lie down. You rest now while I hang these out to dry." he said, passing me a blanket to cover myself.

I did as he had suggested and considered what I had experienced. Perhaps I did have a bump on the head, perhaps it was my imagination, certainly nothing happened that was not of my own doing. My alien friend had not physically intervened, I knew how to use my trousers to make a buoyancy aid.

I realised that they would be more likely to think I was delusional if I kept on talking about Victor. No one believed me anyway, but he had a name, and somehow I knew him; I knew him like I knew Paul and then Sam.

The supplies were loaded, and the last crewman opted for a ride in the cargo-net, rather than risk the long climb up the pilot ladder. The Grayswift crew laughed and jeered at the contorted figure as he rose.

Finally, we took the outward mail from the tanker and began to move away. I noticed the change in light as we moved away from the brilliant deck lights. I sat up. Looking across the bridge, I saw the tanker moving away from us through the starboard window, the accommodation ladder hanging like a smashed limb, dangling straight down into the water.

The trip back was quicker, the Skipper feeling justified to open up the throttles on the relatively flat sea. While we travelled back, Haji cleaned my injured hand with antiseptic and bandaged it neatly.

When we reached Ras al Khaimah, Haji brought back my dry shirt, socks, and underpants, which were all I had left to wear; they had dried quickly in the warm air and twenty-knot breeze created by the Grayswift. When I had dressed, he escorted me off the boat and back the Dodge.

The night air was cooler, but more humid without the breeze.

"We go to the hospital in Sharjah."

"You're the boss."

I settled back in my seat and stared out of the window into the blackness, wrapped in the blanket.

"My passport! I've lost my passport. And my Seaman's ID book, my Discharge book, my wallet, everything."

All my identification documents had been inside my jacket pocket, and my wallet in my trousers.

"Don't worry Sir, Haji will sort out everything for you."

"But I have no money!"

"You will not need money," he said as we drove off.

I turned back to the window, looked out into the blackness and fell into a deep sleep.

# ANGUISH

Hagi sat in silence driving into the hot and humid darkness, unaware that I had woken; while I sat motionless with my head against the window. I had only slept for thirty minutes; when I woke, my mind had immediately slipped into a mire of confusion.

The danger was over now, but my thoughts raced against what felt like an onslaught of insanity. I tried to recall what had happened, trying hard to make some sort of sense out of something that just didn't make any.

I realised that what I had experienced was enough to send anyone into deep shock; I'd heard it said that the mind can do strange things when people are in desperate situations. Too many questions filled my head. Before I could stop to reason with one, another would take its place.

Why wasn't I on the ship? At least I would be with other Brits, Bernie would be there. There was no way for me to get on board. I couldn't have made the climb up the pilot ladder even with a safety rope tied around me, not only because of my hand, I didn't have the strength. I felt weakened by the events that had befallen me.

Paul's words of impending doom reverberated through my mind shaking my grasp on reality, frightening me more than the accident, more than the fear of dying out there, and more than coming face to face with an alien; at least the latter might have just been a shock induced hallucination. His premonition defied all reason, and it had taken place just three weeks before when things were rational. How could he have predicted such an accident? The thought overwhelmed me until the Tarot cards were all I could think about and that focused thought somehow slowly brought a kind of peace to my mind.

Slowly my pensive trance released its grip, calmness and rational thought returned sufficiently to make me realise that no one would believe my story.

I could not convince myself that I had imagined the alien, however I tried to twist things in my mind. Events that night had definitely happened just the way I remembered them.

I knew repeating it would only hinder my chances of getting back on the ship, and that was what I wanted most. But did I? If Victor was real, I wanted to see him again, I wanted to see Sam, and my family, and it couldn't wait four and a half months.

I looked down at my left arm, there was a scar where earlier that evening had been a deep cut. How could that be explained away?

I had always believed that there was intelligent life on other planets, but it didn't really make sense to see a perfectly normal looking human hovering in the darkness above the sea, speaking in perfect English with no noticeable accent. That had always been a weak point of my beloved Star Trek, too many life forms spoke English. Clearly a common language would be beneficial to everyone, but it seemed ridiculous to think an alien would speak English, when our closest neighbours the French refused to do so.

There was incontrovertible evidence, the scar on my arm, my thoughts kept coming back to it. I turned it over to have another look. It was not so much a scar as a clean mark down the arm, no blood, no pink cicatrix, just a long unnatural looking pale stripe of new skin. Haji hadn't noticed it and I hadn't mentioned it.

# SCRUTINY

---

**W**e arrived at the old hospital and pulled up outside the main door at twenty past midnight, at least that's what my watch read; it was steamed up under the glass face but apparently still working.

The hospital was a very sad looking, dilapidated building, cheaply made and apparently in the middle of nowhere. Haji opened the side door of the Dodge and I stepped out on to the sandy track, with his blanket wrapped over all my worldly possessions, my torn shirt, socks and underpants.

I decided that for the time being it would definitely be better if I said nothing to the doctor about my time in the water, it would only complicate and confuse things.

We walked in through the door and along the dimly lit corridor. The unmistakeable smell of disinfectant overpowered the musky aroma from the desert sands that seemed to permeate everywhere else.

Haji escorted me over to what must have been a waiting area, then walked through an open door to a dark but paler skinned Nubian looking man, sitting behind a desk in a small room. He began to babble away in what sounded like Arabic, then turned back to the doorway beckoning as he came.

"We will see the doctor now. He does not speak in good English like Haji. Haji will wait until we know what happens to you."

I got up and followed him further down the corridor to a small room with a desk and two chairs. The lighting seemed very poor everywhere. Where there were lights, they were dim naked bulbs suspended from the white plaster ceilings.

Another man walked into the room in a drab white caftan, his face was weather-beaten and heavily lined by the sun. His features appeared

Arabian, but the white knitted kufi he wore made me think he was not a native Arab. I did not realise then that Gulf Arab men also wear a similar cap beneath the ghutra; however, the man's subservient demeanour suggested he was probably not a local Arab, but possibly a Syrian, Iraqi or Iranian. A slightly smarter Indian looking man in white cotton trousers and neatly pressed smock top, followed him shortly afterwards. The man in the trousers sat in the chair at the desk and jabbered to the other in Arabic. The first man I assumed must be a male nurse, and the second the doctor.

It suddenly dawned on me that I hadn't seen Arab men or any women working anywhere since I had first arrived in Dubai.

Most of the Arab men I had seen at the airport wore traditional dress, a pristine white kandura and red and white headdress; most of the women were dressed in a black abaya and burqa.

The nurse popped a thermometer into my mouth, then produced a pair of scissors and started to cut away the clean white bandages from my right hand. The middle finger nail had been ripped out, leaving a bright crimson imitation where it had once been. The knuckles on the middle and fore finger had been shaved back almost to the bone, but I no longer felt pain in either. He moved away to dispose of the bandages and the doctor shuffled across the room on the wheels of his office chair.

The doctor spoke to Haji for few minutes and then Haji told me he wanted to know exactly what had happened and what had been done after I was picked up.

The doctor grasped both my hands, pulled them over his lap and examined both sides, only taking a few seconds before dropping them and producing a small torch to look inside my mouth. He glanced at my cheeks flicking my face around with his fingertips, then used his torch to examine my eyes and pupil dilation. When he had done that he checked the thermometer and handed it to the nurse.

He muttered something, and Haji told me he wanted to know if there was any pain in my head, at the same time he stood up and began to scrutinise it, probing it with his hands. When he was satisfied that my skull was intact, he asked to look at my chest. I stood up, put down the blanket and removed my shirt. He took a stethoscope from his right pocket and slowly patting his left hand on his chest, suggesting he wanted me to take deep breaths. After he had listened to my chest, front and back, he noticed the white stripe on my left arm. More Arabic chatter followed.

"He wants to know what caused the mark on your left arm," said Haji.

"It's an old cut," I explained without thinking, but the lack of scarring along the unpigmented skin looked more like the skin grafts I'd seen on RAF pilots with burned faces.

I knew it would be impossible to explain now with the language barrier even if I wanted to. Haji told the doctor what I had said, the doctor re-examined the wound saying something to the nurse and shaking his head. He didn't believe it and I knew that he wouldn't, it did look very strange and unnatural. He slid his chair back to his desk and made some notes then he spoke to Haji for a short time.

The nurse reappeared with a kidney shaped white enamel basin filled with what looked like an iodine solution; he smeared it around the exposed flesh on my right hand. I grimaced with pain as the liquid touched the open wounds. He took another piece of cloth and moved towards my face, but the doctor turned and stopped him, then he produced some clean bandage and a roll of cotton wool.

As the nurse lifted my hand again I saw that it was now a rich yellowish-brown colour. He positioned my hand out in front of me with all the fingers closed together, covered them with a square piece of the cotton wool tapping it down lightly, then he picked up the bandage and wrapped my hand and fingers together again. It seemed to me that I had been better off on the boat with Haji.

The doctor got up to leave the room but stopped and grasped my left arm again as he passed. He probed the stripe with his thumbs but there was no bruising or break in the skin. He walked off muttering to himself and shaking his head.

The nurse handed me a thin greyish white cotton hospital gown which tied at the back and folded my shirt over his arm.

"What now Haji?"

"You must stay here tonight, and I will pick you up tomorrow. The doctor say' you okay but in case you may have breathe problem if you swallow too much water. They will watch you tonight. Tomorrow Haji will take you to hotel."

"What about my things, my clothes?"

Haji suddenly realised my case was on-board the tanker along with Bernie's case and the fresh supplies. In all the confusion, nobody had thought to keep it.

"Haji will have to contact the office first thing tomorrow. They will arrange for your suitcase to be returned to you."

"You do have my suitcase?"

"Do not worry Sir. Haji will look after everything," he said, trying to reassure me. "I will see you tomorrow morning Sir."

"What do I do now? Where do I go?"

"Haji will come with you to your bed Sir."

# GUILT

The nurse led us down the dim corridor into an equally dim and drab ward, full of old cream painted, iron framed beds. All but one contained man or boy. Some of the men were sitting up smoking cigarettes, others laid still, some awake and some sleeping, but no one spoke. As we moved towards the one vacant bed, all the open eyes followed our progress through the ward, some even sat up to watch.

I was the only European in the room. I looked at the man in the bed on the left; his legs and waist were loosely covered by a white sheet thrown across them, and a blood-stained bandage was wrapped around his huge round abdomen. I looked down at his feet protruding from the sheet and saw that his left ankle was literally chained to the end of the bed. Looking up towards his head, I noticed that his left hand was secured in the same way; it was beyond my reasoning to work out how it had been achieved.

His wrist and ankle were wrapped in bent metal rings rather than shackles or handcuffs. Each ring resembled a tapered sausage shape, made by rolling dough between your hands with both ends tapering to a point, then forged into a circle like the crudest form of bracelet from the early Iron Age.

I could only conclude that they had been pre-formed and then squeezed into their final shape, around his wrists and ankles. It occurred to me that a man as big as he, might well be able to force the gap open again with effort. I dismissed the idea quickly.

The nurse pulled back the top sheet of my bed and pointed me towards it.

"What's wrong with him?" I asked.

Haji spoke to the nurse, then told me that the man had been shot by the police the day before, having murdered his brother.

I looked at the man again, he didn't look like a man that had just committed murder, nor even capable of such a crime. For some reason, I felt that I should be able to sense his crime or at least his remorse, but there was nothing.

"What's going to happen to him?"

Haji turned his back to the man, moved his hand up to his throat, and slid his extended forefinger across it. As he did so, he tried to imitate the sound of a slicing blade with a very quiet 'shuck' sound. I shivered as I sat down on the bed.

"I see you tomorrow morning Sir. Rest now."

"Ok, see you tomorrow Haji. Oh Haji, my name is James."

"Yes Mr James."

He strutted off down the corridor oblivious of my attempt to be less formal.

I picked my legs up into the bed and pulled the sheet over me. As I looked around the room, I was unsettled by the strange faces staring at me, so I turned onto my side to get some sleep, facing the prisoner in the bed on my right. He lifted a bottle of water from his bedside and offered it to me.

"As-Salaam-Alaikum," he said smiling gently.

"No thank you," I answered, waving my arm and assuming his words meant water. "Thank you. I'm just tired."

It struck me that he must have been aware of the fate that awaited him, but there was no suggestion of anguish in him, nor anger or remorse.

"You rest my friend," he said slowly.

It surprised me that he spoke English, for some reason it just seemed absurd. After all that had happened, I felt very alone in that strange place, apparently, with my only friend being a murderer, chained up to the bed beside me. I closed my eyes trying to forget everything and empty my head, but once again I remembered Paul's warning of imminent catastrophe.

My mind drifted back to my school days, in the autumn of 1970, when some of my friends held a séance. They said that they had made contact with a spirit, who had told them that Arsenal would win the FA cup that season, in the summer of 1971; the rest of the class laughed, no one believed them. It was the first and only other experience of strange predictions that I could recall, and my last thought before falling asleep.

# CONTAMINATION

I awoke the next morning to see two Arab Policemen in pale green uniforms at the bed beside me.

One of the men had a large hacksaw and was attempting to cut through the crude ring around my new friend's wrist. When he had finished, he produced a more conventional pair of steel handcuffs, and used them to replace the ancient looking bondage. He repeated the task on the ankle chains, having first removed the second pair of handcuffs from my friend's previously unchained wrist. After tugging each to test that they were secure, they left without a word, leaving the empty chains dangling from the bedstead.

I still could not understand how or why they had used the primitive bent bar in the first place, or where the chains had come from. Logic suggested that they must have been forged in a more open state, then when in place somehow squeezed closed with a hammer or some huge clamp. Why anyone should have such archaic bondages still bewildered me. Clearly, he hadn't been brought there by the police or they would have used handcuffs.

When they had gone, the man smiled at me and tugged lightly at his new wrist restraint, testing his bonds in such a way that I could see he was still restrained. He lifted up the bottle with his right hand and offered it to me, but another male nurse came over before I had a chance to refuse. I was thirsty, but despite his friendly demeanour, I was reluctant to take his water, fearing that his dreadful crime might contaminate me in some way.

The nurse took my temperature and checked my pulse, and having recorded the information, he hung the clipboard back at the end of my bed. After he had gone, my newly acquired friend offered me an orange. I wondered who would have brought this man oranges but accepted gratefully; perhaps the skin would prevent my imagined contamination of evil-doing, from reaching the fruit inside.

I stepped far enough out of the bed to take the orange from him, and noticed the other men began to jabber away as I did so. Looking around the room, it seemed I was the centre of attention again. I peeled the orange with my fingers and broke it in half, offering a piece back to its owner. He took it from me gently, waving it in a display that others could see, then thanked me before tasting it.

"Alhamdulillah! Shukran sadikee. Thank you, my friend," he said.

I supposed that he would have had little difficulty peeling an orange himself, with just one hand chained to the bed frame. He was just grateful that I had offered him a piece.

The taste of the orange was sheer ecstasy on my tongue and it eased my thirst.

I realised that he had the appearance of being much more well-groomed than the other men in the ward, despite the absence of any robe. The intricately woven skullcap he wore was clean and brilliant white, his beard was well trimmed, and his face although similar in colour to the other inhabitants, was smooth, not weather beaten like theirs.

I lay down again and reflected on what had been without doubt the most eventful day of my life. I still could not rationalise what had happened out there.

'My left arm!' I thought. I twisted it around to examine the stripe of white skin, but it was gone, there was no trace of it; the skin had the same lightly tanned pigmentation as the rest of my arm, and there was no longer anything to substantiate my experience. 'Perhaps it really was all in my imagination, perhaps I would never find out.'

Before long the nurse appeared back with the doctor, the same Indian looking man that had examined me the night before. He looked at the writing on the board at the end of my bed, then came over, looked into my eyes again with his torch, and examined my chest. He stood up, added a note to the records and returned it to the end of the bed. He muttered something to the nurse and turned to move on, then stopped, turned back, and picked up my left arm, looking for the unnatural stripe. When he saw that it was gone he rolled over my right arm, assuming that he had forgotten which arm it was. Realising that it was not there either, he dropped it and shook his head in disbelief.

'So, the doctor remembered seeing the stripe on my arm the night before.'

I looked at my arm again, but there was no sign of any cut or scar, nor did I have any pain.

There was also no doubt in my mind; the doctor's reaction had confirmed that the strange mark had been there, because he too had seen it.

The doctor stop at the next bed and prodded my friend's bullet wound with his fingers; the pain he caused was clearly apparent on the poor man's face, but he made no sound. The doctor signed his records and moved on again.

* * *

I was feeling very dehydrated by the time Haji came for me. I couldn't ask the nurse for water without offending my friend, despite my thirst, I still did not wish to share his bottle. It would require lots of gestures for all to see, since I had no idea how to say water in Arabic; apart from my friend, no one seemed to speak English.

"You come with me Sir. Doctor say you good to go," said Haji.

I walked around the bed next to mine, and shook the poor man's free hand, feeling nothing but pity for him. He was just an ordinary man.

"Good-bye my friend," I said.

"Ma' salaam. Fi Amanullah, good-bye my friend," he smiled.

Haji picked up my shirt and I left the hospital wearing a white cotton smock that the nurse had given me.

I would never know the circumstances of his crime. I sensed only kindness and warmth towards me, with no suggestion of bitterness or anger about his own predicament. Perhaps his brother had committed an even more heinous crime.

# ALONE

T he sand outside was hot under my feet as I walked out to the van,
a smell of burned nuts filled the air.

"Haji take you back to Ras al Khaimah Hotel Sir," he said, handing
back my wretched clothing.

"My clothes Haji?" I asked, as I stepped into the van.

"Your clothes are on ship Sir," he answered, explaining the apparent
obvious.

"What am I supposed to wear?" I asked holding up my socks and
shirt.

He shrugged his shoulders in reply. "I have no shoes!"

"Yes Sir," he answered, he agreed.

There seemed little point in continuing the conversation, there was
nothing he could do.

"Water Haji? I asked hopefully.

"In the box in front of the seat Sir, at the back of the bus."

"Thank you," I answered, taking two bottles.

I drank greedily, finishing the first, holding the other back for the
journey.

* * *

We arrived back at the hotel and Haji escorted me to my room.

"You can eat here in your room if you want Sir. Anything you want to
eat or drink you ask for. You want something now sir?"

"I'd love a cold coke, two in fact."

"You see!" he said, picking up the phone and dialling eight so that I could see. "Two cokes! Room two one six," he said bluntly, using English rather than Arabic.

"Two one six, your room number. You want food here in your room?"

"Yes please, I'm feeling pretty hungry."

"Haji will take care of it Sir."

There was a knock at the door, Haji opened it up and passed me my cokes. He spoke in Arabic to the waiter, then he reassured me that the waiters knew my bill would be paid for me; there could be no tips, I just had to sign for anything I wanted. The Indian waiter rocked his head from side to side, smiling as Haji spoke.

"He will bring you food Sir. Haji come back with your clothes Sir, very soon."

When both had gone I removed my hospital gown and underpants and placed them in the sink with some hot water and soap. I showered as best I could, holding my bandaged hand outside the curtain, then managed to wrap myself in a towel.

I washed the clothes with my one good hand and hung them over a chair on the balcony, leaving my torn bloodstained shirt to soak in fresh hot soapy water.

There was a knock at the door, so I pulled the sheet off the bed and wrapped it around my shoulders. It was the same waiter holding a tray of food.

"Your food Sir," he said removing the covers.

"Biryani, vegetables, sag aloo, dhal and chapati," he explained, pointing to each dish.

He ushered me to eat. It smelled good and I was hungry, so I tasted the rice dish.

"Oh, that is wonderful," I responded.

Although I had never tasted anything like it, the subtle flavours were warm and soft, it was as comforting as shepherd's pie.

"What meat is this," I asked, enjoying the tenderness.

"It is goat Sir. Very good," he smiled, rocking his head again.

"Sahib, my friends think you are a very brave man, a hero."

Haji had told one of the waiters about the accident.

All of his colleagues had made the trip from the west coast of India or Pakistan, sailing across the Arabian Sea in an Arab Dhow. Having survived being alone in the same sea, in the darkness of night, I was held in great respect. He gave me a slight bow and pressed his hands together in the gesture of Añjali Mudrā. I thanked him for his kindness.

I sat at a table and devoured the food I have been given; the dahl was strange but tasty, the whole thing was the best meal I had eaten since leaving home.

After eating, I laid down on the bed to rest. I had no books, no cassette recorder and there was no TV, I did not even have my pocket chess set, so I had nothing to do except go over everything in my mind again and again. I laid down on the bed and drifted off to sleep.

# TÊTE-À-TÊTE

## FIRST NAMES

Friday ~ 16th November 1973

I woke up feeling thirsty, and was about to order myself a coke, when I realised that my alien friend was sitting in the chair beside the balcony windows looking at me. He got up and pulled the chair closer to the bed.

"You're back! You're real!" I blurted.

"Yes of course I am real," he answered.

I realised I was naked having thrown the sheet off me during the night, due to the hot and humid air. He appeared oblivious to my lack of clothes.

"Would you mind passing me my things, my underpants and the hospital gown, on the balcony."

He handed them to me and I thanked him, pulling on my underpants to cover myself, and forgoing the hospital robe. I sat on the side of the bed and covered my legs with the sheet.

"What the hell are you wearing, you look like Ed Straker!" I asked, still half asleep.

He no longer floated the way he had in the water, his body moved normally. But for his clothes, he would have passed unnoticed in any street back home in England. He wore a pale cream suit and short white leather boots, the jacket had a Mandarin style collar, and there were no buttons. His trousers were more like women's leggings, tight fitting, with his white ankle boots covering the bottoms. I thought it quite comical and could only compare him with Gerry Anderson's fictional head of SHADOW, from the TV series UFO, but then fashion never had been of any interest to me. It occurred to me that perhaps I was dreaming or hallucinating and that his clothes were from my memories.

"How did you get in here?" I asked.

"I walked in! It wasn't difficult, there was a door you see," he said, as he sat down in the chair that he had positioned a little closer to me.

"Well what do you want from me?"

"Why should I want anything from you James?" he asked benignly.

His hair was red and thick, his eyes blue. He had a presence that put me at ease, not just a smile and a sarcastic sense of humour, but an aura of warmth that seemed to envelope me.

"I don't know, I'm sorry, let's start again. My name is James Cummings, Jim or Jimmy if you prefer," I said, offering him my hand, which he accepted and shook.

"Friendship, I am known here as Victor," he said calmly.

I had almost forgotten the moment of déjà vu that night in the water, when I recognised him briefly.

"Victor! What sort of a name is that for an alien?" I scoffed.

"It is the name I have chosen for myself here. You would not be able to pronounce my indigene name, so it is pointless telling you."

"Indigene?"

"Sorry, indigenous, native. I get confused about your colloquial dialects sometimes. I meant my name in my native language," he explained.

"Try me."

I felt a strange sensation in my head. I knew it was him communicating with me, but the sounds made no sense to me.

"You see!" he said.

He had spoken his name without opening his mouth. I heard his words inside my head.

"You are a telepathic!"

"And so it would seem are you," he answered, in the same way.

"How do yo...'."

I never finished the sentence.

"You do it all the time, you just don't turn up the volume," he interrupted, smiling at me.

"What?"

"You are born with it, but when people don't hear your thoughts, you just stop sharing them," he grinned, "you're just rusty."

He paused to let me digest what he had said.

"When you construct a sentence in your mind, you transmit a weak exchange, you just don't realise you are doing it. It is simply that you have forgotten how to use your mind. Your powerful thoughts are much clearer. I sensed your fear in the water on Wednesday, your panic and your fight for life, just as clearly as they would have been on the day you were born, expecting your mother to understand your thoughts but getting no response.

"I can hear your words through thought, but your mind is untrained; your thoughts overlap each other, making it almost impossible to understand them. It's like speaking with your mouth full," he grinned. "Order your coke, I will have one too!"

I hadn't mentioned the coke, but I was thirsty, sensing that my mouth was dry. I picked up the phone.

"Two cokes please, room two one six."

"Yes Sir. I will send them up right away Sir. Room two one six," he confirmed.

"Yes. Thank you." I said.

"It's on its way," I said to Victor. "You drink coke?"

"Yes, I like coke."

"Do you eat?"

"Yes, I eat, but I am what you would call a vegetarian, at least here on Earth."

"God I could murder a bacon sandwich right now. I don't understand how people like you can go through life not eating meat."

"You misunderstand me," he said. "My people do eat meat, but only on our home planet. Eating is one of the greatest pleasures in life, but to eat meat we must first hunt a wild animal.

"We do gather infertile eggs, milk and honey, we eat fungi and wild grain, but we do not eat anything that bleeds on an alien world. We would never compromise an endangered species or an alien life form.

"When we eat flesh on Erato, we do so in celebration of the beast, and all that it was. Many of your ancient civilisations have lived, and still live their lives in this way, nature maintains a balance and order. Er-ah-to," he added, using phonics.

"We share our world with other life forms just as you do. We eat the flesh of other species, just as we in turn die, and our flesh is consumed by the bacteria that live within us."

He spoke slowly and clearly, like a theatre actor delivering his dialog, using his voice rather than his thoughts.

"That sorta' makes sense I s'pose, although I thought it was maggots and worms and things, that tucked into dead bodies."

I reflected on his words for a moment, craving a fried breakfast.

"So, I can rest in the knowledge you're not here to eat me then?"

He smiled, and I knew somehow that there was truth in his words.

"Are you alone?"

"Yes, I am alone."

"Is this the first time you have been here? To Earth?" I added, qualifying the question.

"No, I have been here twice before."

"You look human, is that really you, or am I looking at some grotesque monster with a space suit on?"

"Do you see a monster?"

There was a knock at the door, I stood up wrapping the sheet around me and answered the door. It was the waiter with the cokes. The waiter placed the cokes on the bedside table and left the room.

"How have you been? What happened to you after the Grayswift found you? He asked.

I told him about the trip back and my night in the hospital; about 'my friend' in the bed beside me.

"Slave chains," said Victor. There would still be a plentiful supply of those.

"Slaves? Here?"

He chuckled.

"Oh my naive young friend, how much you have to learn. That will have to be another discussion. Your friend, he will feel only sadness for the thing he has done, whatever his brother will have done, it is a sad thing to lose all respect for anyone. His Muslim religion allows for him to take an eye for an eye, while teaching forgiveness, he will die under Shariah law. He should have let the police deal with his brother."

It was bizarre discussing the death of someone who had been kind to me confronted with Victor's absurd clothes.

"You don't feel a little conspicuous the way you are dressed," I asked. "You look very different from yesterday."

"Yes, you noticed. I had it made for me in Paris just last week. It's a sort of East meets West design."

"Paris? You were in Paris last week!"

"Ye-e-e-s-s," his reply drawn out, bewildered at my cross-examining him with such a pointless question.

"You had it made; so, you paid for it. You have money; so, you work."

"Your theory is non-sequitur Jim, your conclusion does not follow the premise," he grinned. "No, it is ambiguous, the two statements have no logical connection."

He realised that his own knowledge of the English language was more complete than mine, and that my Latin was practically non-existent.

"In the first instance, I might not have paid for it and in the second, it does not follow that I earn it. I create the money, I pay for my needs and nobody suffers."

"You forge money? That's criminal."

"Says who? My needs are but a drop in the ocean. Who do you think controls how much money is printed to control the economy, the governments? No my friend, it is your big banks who tell you what you can and cannot have. I simply make very minor adjustments in their accounting, a drop in the ocean, and, lotto, I have a bank account. Well several actually. Sorry bingo."

I hadn't corrected him verbally, he just knew what I was thinking.

"It is the way of your world, and pandemically abused. Money is just a piece of paper, a worthless token created by your banks, there was never anything to steal in the first place. Poverty will always exist in a world of commerce. Ironically, those who have least, have the least expectations."

I conceded I had no idea about finance and the global economy. He was right in a way, the tailor got his money, it provided work for others and apparently no one really suffered. His thoughts on the subject suggested that he considered money to be some kind of disease.

"So what happened to the dress?" I asked not knowing how best to describe it.

"I had the time to obtain something more suitable," he grinned.

"Ice?" I asked.

"No thank you."

I passed him the glass and picked up the other bottle for myself.

"Thank you," he said, pouring out half the contents.

He sipped it slowly and put the glass down.

"What you saw yesterday was a holographic projection of me. I was actually above you on-board my ship."

"Yes, a hologram."

I had never seen one, but I knew what they were.

"The clothes I wore were simply functional for purpose."

"Like a uniform?"

"Not in the sense that it represents anything, more over utilitarian or perhaps walking around your house in," he smiled, and I smiled with him.

"Your ship," I recalled. "Is that how you got here?"

"How do you think I got here, by train?"

His grin was now almost constant and very reassuring. His sense of humour was a huge respite for me after all that had happened.

"No stupid question I s'pose," I answered smiling back. "Where is it?"

"In the car park," he said with the same sarcasm.

"Yeah ok!"

I let it drop.

"So how do you project a hologram?"

"There is a system on my ship."

"Oh! I thought maybe you sort of projected yourself."

"Well I do actually, the system simply amplifies my thoughts. How are you feeling?" he asked, changing the subject.

"My arm is better but surely you know that. How did you do it, was that your systems too?"

"No that was simply my thoughts boosting your own."

"My thoughts?"

I had not been aware of healing myself.

"I just pointed you in the right direction, helped you focus," he said.

"There's no sign that I ever cut it now! How about these?" I asked, holding out my bandaged right hand. "And these," I added, pointing to my cheeks.

"Your face is healing normally; as far as your hand is concerned, the muscle and tendon structure is not damaged, although the dressing is very crude. You can practice on those yourself. Besides, the doctor has seen those, if I helped you heal them now, questions would be asked when you get home."

He could sense how bad my hand was without seeing the wounds.

"Home? Why should I be going home? I'll have to re-join the tanker on its way back down the Gulf."

I then realised the option was not be mine, logic would indicate that. Haji was going to bring me my clothes, the same clothes that were on board the Grenadier. The Grayswift would have to rendezvous with the Grenadier when it was on its way to Boston. By the time my suitcase was delivered to me, the Grenadier would be sailing south across the Arabian Sea, towards the cape of Good Hope; the Suez Canal had been closed since the Six-Day War, in 1967.

I was sad to realise I would be going home without ever getting on board, despite my wish to get back home to England, Sam and my family.

"I believe that your company will want to see you and reassign you to another ship. Questions will be asked about the accident of course. I suspect the Captain and First Officer have been recalled for their statements. The company will blame them, rather than us."

"Why should the blame you? How do they know about you? What are you doing here? I thought you said you were on your own here."

"I am a traveller like you, I travel alone, but there are many others from my world who are living here too, it is an interesting world. The SS British Grenadier has reported my presence on several occasions in recent years. Having been low enough for you to see my ship, the chances it was unseen by anyone on board the Grenadier crew, are very low. As I said, they have seen my ship several times before.

"The Captain and his mate will use any excuse not to accept responsibility for the accident. Accidents happen, but it is their responsibility to ensure the equipment is safe for purpose, cables replaced on a regular basis for example.

"The company will not release information about alien sightings, nor will they accept the blame for failing to replace equipment, even though they themselves control the budgets.

"They will have already dispatched a replacement Skipper and Mate, perhaps an accident investigator as well, to review the incident thoroughly. The Grenadier may take a day or two to get back here, and they will want to be on board before she leaves port."

I considered everything he had said, and I began to think about going home.

# DEMOGRAPHICS

**M**y thoughts turned back to Victor, there were so many questions I wanted to ask him.

"Slow down, your mind is so hungry it races for answers, which you will not wait for before asking more questions. You too are a traveller are you not? What are you doing here if you are not?" asked Victor, before I could ask the question.

"It's my job."

"Yes, but why have you chosen this profession?"

"To see the world, I guess. To travel. To go where no man has gone before." I answered, giving Spock's Vulcan hand gesture.

Victor responded with a smile and a nod, and I knew he understood its meaning.

"My world, Erato, can only sustain balance if we, the dominant species, limit our numbers there. We do not own our world, Erato owns us; the rest of us must live on other worlds for most of our lives. Only the young, the eldest, and those desiring to procreate may live there. Erato is our Eden."

"Are you from this time? Can you travel in time? How long did it take to get here?"

"I am from this time, though I was born nearly seventeen hundred and five of your years ago. I cannot travel in time, at least, not in the way you think; it took me nearly seven Terran years to get here. It is practical to go into suspension during deep space flight. I have spent many years travelling the stars and perhaps almost one hundred of those years in suspension, almost fourteen years to journey to and from my world and yours."

I noticed again that he spoke slowly and quietly. He looked about thirty years old to me, but it didn't seem worth pursuing.

"What is suspension?"

"The method of suspended animation. You understand?"

"Yeah, I've seen it on science fiction films and Star Trek; Khan! How come you speak in English?"

"I learned English before my first trip here. It is one of the most widely understood languages here, there are many others, I am fluent in many."

"Is that so? Not all of them!" I said sarcastically.

"I understand seven hundred and forty-three Terran languages and dialects, so I can converse orally, telepathy requires no language, your thoughts do not need to be translated."

I understood what he meant, it did seem to make sense. When he used telepathy, I felt his thoughts in my own voice rather than his, yet I knew it was him speaking to me. The thoughts had a structure of language beyond words, inherent in our minds. Telepathy felt like musical code.

"Well Victor? What do you think of the place?"

"I have been here for over twelve years now, I have seen and learned much about your world as it is now. I came here for personal reasons, but I also like to study your development and I am always looking for answers."

"Answers?" I asked.

"I have spent much of my life searching for something, or someone."

"Who?"

"I will know when I have found him, or her. Are you a religious man Jim?"

"That's a big question. If you had asked me that last week, I would have said not particularly. My father is an atheist, but my mother and her parents were devoted to the church. I used to go to church every Sunday with her, I was a choir boy and an altar-boy, I know many of the bible stories from the old testament; it was the music I loved. That changed on Wednesday. I prayed to someone, or something out there. But I guess I am looking for answers as well now."

"A search for your god," he smiled, "so that all your questions can be answered, and the answers can be accepted. My people view the matter from a slightly different perspective, although many of us believe a greater entity may exist; an energy, a creator even. We believe that parallel universes exist, but we do not know how to move from one to another or if these parallel universes are in fact the same universe at different times."

"I think that is why I wanted to travel," I said. "I have so many unanswered questions."

"I have visited several planets in this life, there are many worlds with beings like Homo Sapiens and like us. The Earth is currently visited by five other advanced races. We Erateans and they, share our technologies, we coexist on worlds such as this, but never on our own home planets. Our home-worlds are the hub of our existence, our life force grows from our home-world. Homo Sapiens are an evolving race largely unaware of our existence.

"We know that your kind has seen the destruction of several civilisations, the Old Testament you speak of, speaks of a God who tires of mankind's wickedness and wipes the slate clean. We believe a change must be close at hand if your kind are to avoid your own destruction."

"A change? I don't understand."

"All in good time," he answered.

"Have you travelled outside the galaxy?"

"No, Erato, our world, is on the other side of the galaxy, much closer to the core. There is never complete darkness there, so many suns surround the black hole at the centre of the galaxy. If it were not for interstellar dust, the core would appear like one mass of light, brighter than the light reflected by your moon. Erato exists in a binary system, there are two suns in our sky.

"My people have sent probes and attempted expeditions into the void, but those who have left us have never returned. We know nothing of what lies beyond."

"Black hole, void? I don't understand"

"At the centre of every galaxy is what your people refer to as a black hole. It is immensely dense, its mass is so enormous that it draws the galaxy towards it in an ever-decreasing spiral, like water draining from a sink. The black hole grows in density with every solar system that's it engulfs.

"The void is what we refer to as the space between our galaxy and the next, it grows slowly larger, while our galaxies are slowing collapsing. No probes or ships from any of the enlightened worlds, has ever made the journey to another galaxy and returned."

"Is it further to another Galaxy than your world on the other side of the Milky Way?"

He chuckled then replied, "The Milky Way is around one hundred thousand light-years in diameter, the Andromeda galaxy is approximately two and a half million light-years away."

"But that's, what? Only twenty-five times as far!" I interrupted, making the quick calculation.

"Indeed, but there are other reasons that enable us to make intergalactic travel much faster than extragalactic travel. Within the galaxy we can warp space, we believe this is not possible beyond the galaxy, we don't know why. We simply lose contact with anything that moves into the void which is why we call it so. It is possible that other galaxies are formed of antimatter, we simply don't know."

"So how big is the universe? How far is it to the centre?"

Victor laughed in amusement.

"We do not know. The only limit we know of, is the time that light from distant galaxies takes to travel to the Milky Way as you call it. As time goes by galaxies further away will become detectable; however, as I said the universe is expanding at the same time, possibly faster than the speed of light."

"Are there monsters on other planets? You know, lizard men?"

"There are unique animals of different shapes and colours on most planets, some have very similar life forms, essentially what you would recognise as humanoid races at various stages of evolution on all the populated planets. On almost all worlds, bipedal mammals are the dominant species. On other planets there are different animals that dominate their world, just as the dinosaurs once ruled the Earth."

"You've seen dinosaurs?"

"I suppose you could call them that. The word's origin is Greek, deinos, terrible and sauros, lizard."

"That must be incredible."

"The universe is surely more incredible, that is why we keep searching for a way to reach other galaxies."

"So it's not God your looking for?"

"No not really, the only words for God my people have is 'the unanswered'. We would like to understand more about creation, what the universe is, rather than how big it measures. My people have evolved without the wars and crime that plague your world. There is no commerce, no money and consequently no greed, no injustice, no sickness and no fear. No one's time is worth more than anyone else's. We own nothing, therefore there is nothing to inherit or to steal, everyone is free to live the way they choose. If you want to eat you must hunt, gather food or function as a group for mutual benefit."

"Sounds like a nice place. What do you do all day?"

"Our lives are long and there are many days to live. We don't rush through life the way so many Terran cultures do now. Life for us is one of many journeys and we embrace it. We share our knowledge and our experiences. Many devote much of their lives to art in some form or another, painting, sculpture, music, drama or storytelling. There is much that we have in common, but we take more time to share and savour life's simple pleasures."

"Do you have any children?"

He laughed briefly.

"I have had twenty-seven sons and fifty-five daughters."

"You have a partner then?"

He smiled before answering.

"I have had many partners during my life. My people have many children, never more than one with the same mate. Monogamous relationships are very rare amongst my people. Men and women have always lived in equality. We live our lives as independent people, but at the same time as a part of a collective."

"What does monogamous mean?" I asked naively.

It seemed absurd to be asking an alien for help with my own language.

"In the context of what I have told you, it means we do not limit ourselves to one partner, even for breeding. All of my children have different mothers. Unlike your females, women from my world do not only bear children during the early years of womanhood. It is extremely rare for a woman to bear more than one child with the same partner, most of us experience many partnerships in our life time. We believe that there is less evaluation of children with different parentage. It was understood many millennia ago, that comparing ourselves or our children leads to pride, we also believe that pride leads to judgement, and in turn to isolation."

"Oh!" I answered, without really understanding.

To me, it seemed a very strange way to live.

"So where are all your children?"

"I am not sure where they are. Some will be on our home-world, Erato, and some will be travelling like me. I have lost twelve boys and eighteen girls."

"Lost?"

"They have perished, died."

"How did they die?"

"On expeditions such as this. Sometimes my people are captured and killed by indigenous humans or taken by a predator species. We are not invulnerable."

"The children you have left, do you talk to them?"

"It takes as long to send messages to other worlds as it does to travel, but yes, I have had messages from them, and they from me. My children are all adult, my youngest child is thirty-three of your years old; my oldest is only thirty-five years younger than I am. I was on Erato coming here, intending to raise another child. I do not consider them as my children, they are equal, as I am equal with my parents, grandparents and the generations that came before them, individuals and yet a part of our harmony."

"What do you mean harmony?"

"The people from my world share each other in a way your people do not yet understand. There are those among you that do, and it is these people I seek."

"Hey, I'm thirsty, I need another coke. Would you like another?"

"No thank you, one is sufficient. It is full of refined sugar, which in excess is not good for the body."

I picked up the phone and asked for another coke, ignoring his advice.

"Are you happy being on your own for so long, don't you get lonely? Do you have friends, mates?"

"The people on my planet are very diverse, most live as I do with various partners throughout our lives living for long periods alone. Some spend their entire life alone and never take a partner, they devote their lives to spiritual or scientific learning. We bond with partners for no other reason other than reproduction."

"No, I didn't mean that, I meant friends, pals."

"I understood what you meant, but there is no concept of friendship in the way you imagine, all of my people are my friends. The Eratean way the life is very different from yours, the majority live a nomadic communal life style, moving from group to group, and of course travelling to other worlds. When my people form a mating bond, it can only be with a member of the opposite sex. Most of my people live most of their lives in what you would term bisexual relationships, sharing in the experience of others in a way you may one day understand. Some prefer mainly homosexual relationships, taking only partners of their own sex, others prefer to restrict themselves to partners of the opposite sex. There are some, not many, that live their entire lives with one partner either heterosexual or homosexual, while others that choose abstention or isolation; such people can spend long periods without food, essentially devoting their lives to meditation. We all know that we can be reincarnated into a new life; but we will talk more of this another time."

He knew that I wanted to know more about being reborn, but he was telling me I would have to wait.

"I've never had sex before!" I said, thinking about the relationships he spoke of.

"That's not unusual Jim. Unless you are raised sharing one room with parents or adults it is a painful learning experience; nomadic or aboriginal children grow up here having been present while others enjoy sex; it is after all one of the strongest desires. Sex on Earth in these times, is generally repressed, the masses are told that it is wicked and sinful, so there is great confusion for those like you.

"Eratean children grow in a world without repressed emotions and desires. When they reach puberty, they begin to experiment, exploring their body and physical pleasure. They do so with an open mind and the knowledge that there is no sense of what constitutes acceptable behaviours."

There was a knock at the door and I walked over to answer it.

"Your coke Sir," said the waiter. "Would you like me to fill the mini-bar sir?"

His accent was Indian, but his words were clear.

"Mini-bar?"

I had never stayed in a hotel before, so I had no idea what he meant.

"Yes Sir."

He walked around the bed, and as I turned, I realised that Victor had gone. The waiter opened what looked like any other cupboard, it was stocked with cold drinks, chocolates, glasses and more importantly ice. He turned to me to confirm that I had seen everything and rocked his head from side to side like his colleague; it was the Indian expression of 'Achha', its manner suggests the negative, but generally means the opposite; good, I understand, or even thank you.

"Thank you," I said, escorting him back to the door.

He bowed in the gesture of Añjali Mudrā, and then left.

I turned around and Victor was back in his seat.

"In the bathroom," he answered, before I could ask where he had been.

147

"Eratean? What does that mean?"

"It is the demonym of Erato, the adjective describing anything of my world, be it people, language or anything else from my world."

"Erato?" I questioned, taking a sip from my glass.

"Erato is the name our Terran guests have given our world, after one of the Greek Muses. Erato is the Muse of love and poetry, it means 'desired', or 'lovely, perhaps derived from Eros, one of their gods."

I knew who Eros was, but I knew nothing about the Greek Muses.

"What did you mean by acceptable behaviours?"

"Earth is largely a male dominated world that exploits women for sexual ownership; homosexuality is considered abhorrent, and there is no collective support raising children.

"Eratean mothers have no expectation of being supported after giving birth, their children become the responsibility of everyone in the collective, babes will suckle from any breast. Women hunt, fish, cook, build and create, just as men do. Men equally share in a child's needs.

"Fidelity is expected among many of your kind. It stems from fear and being unable to distinguish between the urge for sexual satisfaction and something deeper.

"On Erato, sexual freedom is at the core of our lives, like the hunt, sharing our food and raising our children.

"You are still young, perhaps too young to question and understand these things."

We talked about his people and then about my family and my childhood for what seemed like hours. Eventually he had to leave.

"Will I see you again Victor?"

"Oh yes, there is much more I would like to discuss with you," he said, getting up to leave. "I have a gift for you."

He lifted his jacket and produced a beautiful silver box.

"What is it?"

"Something to help keep you amused," he said, placing it on the table in front of me.

I removed the silver metallic lid. It was a small chess set, around five inches square in size.

"That's really very kind of you, it's beautiful. How did you know?"

He didn't answer.

"It's such a shame you have to leave."

"If you are alone, move this key into the other slot, I will show you," he demonstrated.

"Now, make your move."

The key itself appeared to be no more than a small rectangular stick; it appeared to be made of the same material as the box. It felt latched as I pulled on the key, but came out easily, pulling itself back as I reinserted it, like a magnet attracted to steel.

I picked up the king's pawn and moved it two spaces forward to its new square. The square under the black king's pawn and the square two spaces in front both lit up with a dull red glow.

"You see, you must move the black pawn."

I moved it to its new square and the glow disappeared.

"It is intelligent," he explained.

"That's fantastic, thank you Victor. How good is it?"

"It knows nothing except the rules of the game, it will learn from you and the games you play. You may win, at first," he grinned. "I will return tomorrow."

He opened the door and left without any concern for his appearance. I sat motionless for about five minutes, still covered with the sheet, thinking over what had happened.

I went to the bathroom and soaked my face with cold water, washing the dust from my eyes.

I would surely never be able to convince anybody about my meetings with Victor, but then, did I want to anyway? I knew that I wanted to learn more about Victor's home and the rest of the galaxy. 'What would it be like to live as one of them? No wars, no crime, no sickness, no fear, would it be heaven or hell?'

My hunger was getting the better of me and I recalled the chocolate bars in the fridge, but I had no desire for sweets, so I picked up the phone and ordered some bread and a portion of chips. When it arrived, it was not what I expected, the chips were much thinner than anything I had seen before, and the bread was unleavened, but it tasted good, I wondered why I hadn't asked for something more English before. They had added a selection of sliced meat and olives, which I ate because I was hungry, I had no idea what type of meat it was, or where it came from.

When I had finished I went back to my chess set and pit my wits against the mysterious box; I realised that I now had physical evidence of Victor, right in front of me.

As I began to play, I realised that the pieces were being drawn into the centre of the squares, rather than without direction, the way a magnetic board would.

The technology was surely far in advance of anything on the market. There was no one to tell, even if I wanted to.

# THE JIGSAW

## OUTPLAYED

I soon became bored with the confines of my room, and decided to take my splendid gift down to the swimming pool, to play at a table in the sunshine.

I retrieved my shabby white hospital gown from the balcony and made my way downstairs to the bar, picking up another coke before going out to the pool. Aside from the staff it was empty, and I had nothing else to wear anyway. Had I seen any other people I might well have scurried off back to my room.

Outside it was very hot and the pool looked very inviting; I wished that I had my swimming trunks.

Avoiding the heat, I decided to sit at a table under the shade of the hotel, directly below my own balcony. I began a new game.

Moments later, I heard a voice call from above, but I didn't understand the language, it sounded German. There was a man looking down at me from the second-floor balcony.

"Hello," I said.

"Schach, darf ich mich am spiel beteiligen?" he replied. "Können wie eine runde schach spielen?"

"Sorry?" I questioned.

"English?" he asked. "Chess ya?"

"Ya," I answered emulating his accent.

He gestured with his hands, moving them from his chest towards me. I nodded, and he disappeared from the balcony. Within minutes he appeared at the poolside and walked across to the table. I pointed to the chair opposite me inviting him to join me.

"Danke," he said taking his seat.

He called the waiter from the bar and ordered a drink for himself and another coke for me.

"Thank you," I said.

"Bitteschön. Bernd," he said, offering me his hand.

"James."

"Chess," he said pointing to the little chess set.

"Yes, do you play?"

He gave a sharp nod, so I removed the key and placed the little pieces back in the starting positions and placed the box between us.

"Das ist ein außergewöhnlich schönes und sehr gut verarbeitetes Schachspiel!" he announced lifting the board up to examine it.

"Sorry?"

"Bitte? Entschuldigen Sie mich.    Beaut-ee-ful.    Das ist ein außergewöhnlich schönes und sehr gut  verarbeitetes Schachspiel," he repeated, stunned by its beauty.

The gleam in his eyes said almost as much as his words.  It was an exceptionally beautiful piece.

"Würden sie es eventuell verkaufen?" he asked showing and tapping his wallet.

"No no, it was a present, a gift," I answered, and I tapped at my heart with my right hand.

"Entschuldigung. Sorry," he said.

* * *

It soon became apparent that the magnetic like positioning of the pieces had ceased; no longer were they guided into the centre of a square, the mode had changed with the repositioning of the key.

I thought that I was a reasonably good player, but after five straight defeats by the German, I realised I was not in his league. I had never met such opposition before.

It seemed so ridiculous to have a language barrier with a fellow European, after spending the morning talking to Victor. We had hardly spoken a word since he joined me, his English was not much better than my German, which was in reality, limited to quite inappropriate snippets from watching a sustained diet of war films on the television.

I thought about what Victor told me earlier, 'we all had the ability to be telepathic', and having experienced it, I now really believed I could do it myself. As we began our sixth game, I stopped thinking about the chess and focused my thoughts on my opponent.

Bernd opened the game and I made a few cursory moves.

Slowly as the game progressed I became conscious of his thoughts, I could feel his mind progressing moves. Although this only occurred from time to time, the sixth game took much longer than the previous five; I was now at times prepared for his attacks, but inevitably the outcome was the same.

I seemed to have puzzled my German friend, he appeared to have lost his sense of domination, despite having won again. I could not tell exactly what he was thinking, but I got the impression that I had struck a surprise blow to his ego. He looked at his watch, then pointed at it showing me the face; it was a quarter to six. He stood up and shook my hand.

"Dankeschön, auf wiedersehen," he said.

"Dankeschön. Auf wiedersehen," I mimicked, using virtually my entire German vocabulary; we shook hands again.

* * *

The sunset came quickly. I sat alone watching the colour of the sky and the mountains change their colours, until darkness had consumed the vista, eventually going back to my room. I spent the evening feeling very bored and restless but reluctant to wander around the hotel. I felt uncomfortable inside the building wearing the robe I had acquired, apart from having a grubby as well as unkempt appearance it was much shorter than the Arabian garments, only reaching my knees and tied at the back.

When I ordered my evening meal it was less appealing than lunch, so I ate lightly and went to bed early.

# MOTIVE

Saturday ~ 17th November 1973

Saturday morning I awoke to find Victor in my room again. He was sitting in the same chair, this time wearing jeans and a black T-shirt, emblazoned with a picture of white light passing through a prism, refracted into its constituent colours. His shirt read Pink Floyd above the prism, and Dark Side of the Moon below it. It meant nothing to me.

"What the hell are you wearing now?"

"What does it look like?"

"Jeans and a T-shirt?"

"Well you should know! Millions of people wear them every day."

"Of course I know what they're called. I just expected you to be wearing your space suit. Paris?" I asked.

"London actually," he replied. "And I'm not flying today, so why should I suit up darling?" he added in an overtly camp voice, typically sarcastic.

"Hell, I don't know, I just didn't expect you to be wearing jeans and a T-shirt."

"They're very comfortable. Don't you have any?"

"Not right at the moment I don't, no! All I have is that bloody dress," I said, desperately wishing I had my jeans.

"I find they're less conspicuous. Don't you agree?"

"Yes, I can see that they would be. You don't hide yourself then?"

"There wouldn't be much point in travelling the length of the galaxy if I stayed shut up in my ship all the time would there, I've been here for twelve years remember?"

"Yes ok! They are very nice, perhaps you could rustle up a pair for me!

155

"And how would you explain those, since you have no money and no shoes to go out with."

He was right of course, I would have to wait for my own clothes to be returned.

"I have tried the local Arab costume of choice, but people are disturbed by my red eyebrows. They don't understand exactly what it is that they notice, because my hair is covered. Red hair is common amongst the Israeli people, and it does occur in Arabic people, but very rarely. It is said that the prophet Mohammad had red hair, and that he would dye it with Henna when it began to grey with age."

I would have been grateful for anything respectable to wear.

"Where is your home, Erato?" I asked.

"As I told you yesterday, my home is on the other side of the galaxy. If you imagine the galaxy as a flat disk, with my home at twelve o'clock and approximately one tenth of the way out from the centre, your solar system is at four o'clock and approximately one third of the way out from the centre, in the arm of Sagittarius."

"Do you miss it, your home?"

"Yes, I miss my home. It is very like Earth in terms of environment and geography, except that it is never really dark, as I said. The surrounding stars are closer, they appear bigger and brighter. The Milky Way shines like a thick band of light at night; during the day the light from Mnemosyne is set against the glow of almost a hundred million stars that surround the core, at night the core shines like a single mass, brighter than your moon. Erato, itself, is slightly larger than the Earth and has two suns."

"Two suns?"

"Mnemosyne, nem-oz-iny, the Greek goddess of memory; and an orbiting sun called Zeus. Mnemosyne is what Terrans refer to as a yellow dwarf, like your Sun, but brighter; Zeus is much smaller than Mnemosyne, not much larger than Jupiter, what Terrans refer to as a Red Dwarf.

"There are four Eratean moons, two larger than your own moon, Luna, and two smaller. There is also a dead planet, Melpomene, melpom-iny, which moves very close to the orbit of our own; there is no water and no life there. It is a dry red and yellow planet almost as big as our world and close enough to our own to look like another moon when our alignment approaches. At times it appears about half as big as your moon does. When it comes into alignment with our suns it has an impact on our seas and our weather. Our year is five hundred and four days long and our days are nearly forty Terran hours long. We have deserts and rain forests, temperate and polar regions, forests and grass plains, lakes and mountains, just as you do."

"Do you, your people that is, live in the deserts and the polar regions? Can you make them green and temperate?"

"We do not fight against nature, we work with it. It cannot be long before your people realise that they must work with nature or they will not survive. My people knew that great care was required if we were not to destroy the balance on our own world and in doing so cause our own extinction, especially when our technologies were developing. We knew that we must reach out into space to find other inhabitable worlds, so that each of us could restrict our time on Erato."

We talked at length about his world, I listened while he told me about the things that he found most beautiful and missed the most about his home.

When he asked what I had been doing, I told him about the chess, how I had felt Bernd's thoughts almost as though they were my own.

Victor decided to teach me to further focus my thoughts, so that we could communicate by telepathy. It was difficult for him to receive my thoughts clearly, whilst it was easy for me to receive his. He could project clear thoughts into my head, but my mind raced, a muddled confusion of thoughts and questions all at the same time, making it difficult for him to unfold them.

"You must relax, slow your thoughts and focus on what you want to say. Stop thinking about how I look and what you had for dinner yesterday. I sense that your capacity to hear the thoughts of another is already well developed and much greater than normal."

"It's hard," I said, "I'm hungry, and I find it hard to accept that you look so human."

He was well built, muscular and on the larger side of average. His eyes were no longer blue as I had first thought but bright green and his hair reddish ginger. There was nothing obviously alien about his looks, I would have walked straight past him without a second glance anywhere but perhaps for the striking green eyes. I wondered why I thought they had been blue.

"It will come to you."

He had virtually stopped speaking orally now.

I was startled by a knock at the door. I got up to open it without a thought for Victor's presence. It was Haji with my suitcase and flight bag. Looking around me I realised Victor had vanished.

"Good morning Sir," he said with a huge grin. "Haji said he would look after you."

"Thank you Haji. I don't feel good wearing this caftan thing."

I opened up the case and pulled out a clean shirt, a pair of jeans, underpants and socks.

"How are you feeling Sir? You not see no man from space no more?"

"What? No, no! I must have imagined it. I'm okay now I've got these," I said, holding up my clothes.

"Haji is happy to see you so well Sir. This makes Haji very happy too. If you do not need me, Haji must go now. Is something else you need?"

"No thank you Haji. Do you know when I will get on board ship?" I asked, knowing the answer.

"Haji have no news of ship Sir."

"But what about my clothes? They must have come from the Grenadier!"

"Yes Sir," he answered, without grasping the implication.

There had been no need for him to be on the Grayswift when it rendezvoused with the Grenadier to retrieve my case.

"When will you be back?"

"As soon as Haji know what will happen to you Sir."

"How do I get in touch with you if I want anything?"

"You can ask for Haji at the hotel reception. They will call Haji."

"Ok Haji, I'll see you later."

"Goodbye Sir," he closed the door behind him.

I could not understand what had happened to Victor. Until I had got up to open the door, he had been sitting in the chair. There was no sound of him moving, and no time to move any way. I walked back to my bed, picked up my flight bag and pulled out my washing kit. I felt in need of a shave although the hair on my face could hardly be called stubble added to which my mouth felt disgusting. I was about to walk into the bathroom when Victor materialised in front of me.

"Oh shit, this is like something out of Star Trek! Can you beam in to places?

"No, I can't," he laughed. "We can project a holographic image of ourselves as you know. It has limited uses, but it sometimes serves a purpose."

"You're here now, it is you I'm talking to or a hologram? You seem real enough today, just as you were yesterday."

I reached out and touched him realising it was the first time I had. He really was there.

"How did you do that then?"

"I simply block the thoughts that I am here from your mind. I was here all the time, I did not want Haji to see me. He expected you to be alone and would probably ask awkward questions, which would cause unnecessary complications."

"And Haji, you blocked his thoughts too."

"It is not a problem to hide from a small group of Terrans, it just takes a little concentration."

"So why did you hide from me and not just Haji?"

"You would not have been aware that he could not see me, so from Haji's perspective, you would have appeared to be acting strangely. 'See no man from space no more'," he said mimicking the little African warrior.

"What about yesterday, when you said you were in the bathroom?"

"I was in the bathroom, rinsing my mouth. The coke is not good for you, the sugar is converted to acid by bacteria in your mouth and bad for your teeth. An old man like me must look after his teeth!" he laughed.

"Crazy!"

I shook my head in disbelief having discussed disappearing and tooth decay as though they were both everyday occurrences. There was no reason to doubt him, I certainly had no better theories.

"That reminds me. Will you excuse me for a couple of minutes, I need to clean my teeth and have a shower."

"I will leave you for a while, I too have some things to do."

"On your ship?"

"No, I am studying animal life in the desert."

"What for?"

"Because I like to study."

"What are you studying?"

"Sand gazelles."

"Gazelles? Here in the desert? Where are they in the mountains?"

"No. As the name implies their natural habitat is in the desert sands."

"What do you do with them, cut them up?"

For the first time, the thought that I might end up being probed and examined or even dissected, crossed my mind. I shivered briefly.

"Please do not concern yourself, I know you are frightened. Terran thoughts become focused when fear is involved. Where practical, I take what I find back to my ship for examination, but we never harm any life. Erateans have not harmed a single Terran life more advanced than a mollusc for thirty thousand of your years. We regard ourselves as a nonviolent race, we treat all life as a miracle and with the utmost respect. Anything I find will be returned to its natural habitat. On the contrary, it is your people that feel the need to dissect my people."

He paused briefly.

"I lost one of my sons here thirty years ago. His ship crashed in a place called Corona New Mexico in 1947. He was my youngest son."

"Crashed?"

"His ship collided with another ship.

"One of yours?"

"No, the other ship was piloted by another species, your people call them the Greys. The Greys are short bipedal humanoids, with grey skin, hence their classification; they are approximately four feet high, about the height of an eight-year-old Sapien, with distinctive sloping, almond shaped, black eyes."

"How old was your son?"

"He left Erato when he was fifteen years old, thirty-five of your years by the same measurement of time, but still just a child."

"Were you with him?"

"No, he was on a post educational visit with three other children. Two of his companions were killed, the other was critically injured in the crash and did not survive. My son chose to terminate his life, having suffered four years of interrogation, torture and confinement by the US military. I know this to be true because he was able to communicate with other Erateans on Earth up until that time. His body was dissected after his death."

"I'm so sorry Victor."

"Your people are afraid," he concluded.

"Thirty-five is hardly a child here, I'm only sixteen."

"The people of my world physically develop slower than Sapiens year for year. My son would have been as physically developed as a twelve-year-old Terran boy, but academically immensely superior. Our children learn more in their first twelve years than most of your people learn in their whole lives."

"Do you need schools then, if your transcriptors can teach them everything?"

His broad grin suggested my naivety.

"Our children are denied the use of transcriptors until they are ready to leave Erato. The transcriptors are an archive of all our memories, from lives going back hundreds of thousands of years, they have many uses as you will discover. Put simply they are living computers, they store data using deoxyribonucleic acid or DNA. Your people are beginning to understand its complexities and uses. Johannes Friedrich Miescher first identified what he called 'nuclein' in the nuclei of human white blood cells in 1869; in 1953 American biologist James Dewey Watson and English physicist Francis Harry Compton Crick discovered the double helix structure of DNA.

"We have no schools as such, children learn how to survive; how to fish, how to track and hunt, how to find water, how to create fire, what fruits and vegetation they can eat, what is poisonous, the dangers around them and most importantly how to live life; walk, run, swim, sing, dance, count, read, paint, sculpt, act, write, and imagine. Communal singing plays a big part in our lives as does dancing, and story-telling.

"We are all individuals, we do not want to create a race of automatons by force-feeding children things they do not need and do not want to know; we learn most when we really want to know, because then we understand the significance of the answer and its application. They learn to ask questions, and the questions are always answered, where possible by demonstration or experimentation; if the answer is not known, the question is put to others who will work to find the answer or solution, which they in turn share. As I said my people are nomadic and live a communal life style, people are constantly arriving and leaving; everyone is a teacher. Asking the question is actually of greater significance than knowing the answer."

"So, what would happen if your transcriptors broke down?"

"The transcriptors are just a tool, we still know how to live; transcriptors can be rebuilt just like anything else. In your world, when a civilisation dies, knowledge dies with it.

"By the time they reach twelve our children are ready to study the galaxy at first hand, then they may use the transcriptors to add the skills they will need."

"Your son?" I prompted, wanting him to tell me more.

"It was my son's first trip. He and his colleagues would have been in suspension during the journey to Earth, so their bodies would not have aged."

"What was his name?" I asked.

"You would not understand," he smiled, "he had no Terran name, he had no need and therefore not selected one. Post educational trips are observational only. No contact with Homo Sapiens was intended."

"Is that the personal reason? You said you had a personal reason for coming here?"

"Yes, in truth it is my primary motive for being here, not to recover his body as you are thinking; I fear that opportunity has long passed. Where possible we take our kind back to Erato, Erato is the source of our physical being, and we do our best to return our essence, taking nothing from our world. There is always the possibility of rebirth here."

"Rebirth? You mean he could come back from the dead?" I asked in disbelief.

"Not as you imagine. We know that our souls live on. Many of your civilisations believe reincarnation occurs. We have known this to be true for hundreds of thousands of years. I had hoped that my son may have been reincarnated here."

"Wow!" I said, "How would you know?"

"When you learn more about your mind you will understand," he explained.

As he said it I felt him touching my memories as they flashed through my mind, back to my birth and beyond into a warmth of some kind. He seemed puzzled.

"Have you found your son? Was he reborn?" I asked not knowing what puzzled him.

"I believe that he is reborn, perhaps a year or more before I arrived here, probably at some time in the 50's. We rarely spend much more than one Eratean year in transience. The period between physical existences," he explained, before I had a chance to ask. "Had I arrived earlier it would have been easier to find his soul.

"As a result of the crash and abduction in 1947, an Eratean delegation arrived here in 1954. An initial landing was made at Holloman Air Force base New Mexico, a second followed later that year at Edwards Air Force base in California to meet directly with President Dwight David Eisenhower.

"When news of my son arrived back on Erato I had been on a world your people once called Nebet-het in the Ra solar system."

"Your people met the president? So they know about you?" I answered with surprise.

"Of course, they know."

"I was born in 1957, your son would be about my age," I concluded."

I was overcome with wonder and amazement at the thought of reincarnation, but my elation was replaced by sadness and a sense of shame and guilt for the loss of his son. I wondered how I would feel if aliens had mutilated my son.

"We will talk more of this. It concerns you still, but you have nothing to fear."

I neither said nor consciously thought again about my safety with Victor, it was never really in doubt.

He got out of the chair and walked over to the door.

"I will come back tomorrow, continue to focus your thoughts while I am away."

I walked over to him with my right hand extended.

"I'm sorry," he said walking back towards me and taking my hand. "It's not customary everywhere you know."

I smiled at him then did my utmost to focus my thoughts in attempt to say goodbye to him.

'Goodbye.' I heard him inside my head.

# THE POWER OF THOUGHT

Despite the excitement, the simple act of cleaning my teeth felt wonderful and refreshing. I shaved the fine growth on my face, then had a long hot shower doing my best to keep my bandaged hand out of the water. When I had dried myself, I pulled my swimming trunks out of my suit case, grabbed a towel and went down for a swim.

The pool had looked so inviting, but it had been out of the question since I had returned. Reunited with my swimming trunks, I could not resist the temptation of lounging in the water and the brilliant sunshine.

I jumped in at the shallow end and swam to the edge of the pool, doing my best to keep my now damp bandage out of the water. Basking in the cool water I called a waiter from the bar and ordered a coke. I sipped the cool drink hanging on to the edge of the pool, wondering if my life would ever be the same again.

'How many other people have seen and talked with aliens?' I wondered. 'If the President of America knew, why had it been kept a secret? Did all the world's governments really know they existed? If what Victor had told me was true, then the American powers certainly knew about them and the Greys. Would they really have dissected Victor's son? Victor said, 'they are afraid', but I did not really understand why.'

I let myself slip backwards into the water and it flowed over my face. Perhaps it was all a delusion, perhaps I was actually losing my mind.

After a second coke and half an hour in the pool, my eyes were becoming tired; amongst other things, I had lost my beloved Foster Grant sunglasses in the accident, and my eyes needed a break from the brightness of the sun.

I was on my way through the hotel lounge when I met Bernd.

"Guten tag James. Chess?" he asked, smiling at me with the confidence of a champion.

"Ya! I have to dress. Clothes!" I gestured, moving my upturned palms down my torso.

He pointed at his watch and I looked at mine, misted up such as it was, it read 3:45. I hadn't eaten yet, but it was hot, and aside from the wonderful curry Haji obtained for me, I didn't find the food very appetising anyway.

"Four," I said holding up four fingers.

He gave a single military nod in acknowledgement.

I walked down stairs wearing a pair of jeans and a T-shirt, feeling liberated and human again. Bernd was waiting for me out in the shade beside the pool. I walked over to him and sat down, opened the chess set and placed it down between us ready for another pasting.

I opened the first game with my knights, moving both out into the centre of the board. Bernd replied quickly after each move, with his central pawns but soon slowed to his usual thoughtful game.

I sat waiting patiently for him to make his move but before he did, I thought I heard him say something.

"Pardon?" I asked instinctively, using my mind and not my voice.

He looked up at me, then from left to right and seeing no-one else around, raised his eyebrows at me, puzzled at my comment. I wasn't sure that he had heard me or understood me. He moved his bishop out into play and sat back with his arms folded. As usual, I rushed aggressively into moving my pawn up to challenge his bishop and sat back in my chair.

My eyes closed briefly in the bright white sunlight, expecting Bernd to take his usual time to think things through, I opened them again and sat up quickly when I heard him speak. He was going through the possible moves in his mind, so intense was his concentration, I could clearly sense his thoughts. He looked up again to see what had startled me, so I sat back and closed my eyes again. I listened to his thoughts and wondered if I could do a little cheating.

After studying his options, Bernd backed up his bishop one square. He continued to study the board and I waited for his thoughts to stop. Eventually he considered my own best line of attack, so I followed his advice and bought my queen forward in a bold attacking move.

The game continued at his slow pace with me taking more time to listen to Bernd's thoughts. Inevitably Bernd made his first oversight and cursed himself silently for being so foolish. Sensing his error, I reacted swiftly, eight moves later I won my first game.

Bernd could not speak English, but I seemed to understand his thoughts. Victor had said that telepathy required no language.

He shook my hand to congratulate me on my first win before resetting the pieces.

By six o'clock I had won five more games and it was obvious Bernd could not believe the transformation. With the score at six games each, I decided to make my excuses and retire for the evening. I didn't feel I could humiliate him by losing to a cheat, and I could no longer go back to relying on my own abilities, it would have looked like I was throwing the game.

After we had finished playing, his mind began to wander, and his thoughts became unclear. I tried hard to say thank you using only my thoughts, but he never acknowledged the attempt.

# EXPATRIATES

I made my way back to my room, not knowing what I was going to do when I got there. The chess had been fun, both in terms of reading Bernd's thoughts, and raising my game. Despite knowing what he was thinking, I still had to use my own experience for the kill. I had so far only exploited his oversights and taken more time over my own moves.

The thought of another meal in the hotel was not an inspiring one, at least I would be able to eat in the restaurant that night.

There didn't appear to be any English people in the hotel to talk to, in fact there weren't many people at all. Bernd was the only other person I'd seen for two days. I knew nothing about him, sadly his English was not much better than my German, even my criminal friend in the hospital had spoken better English.

I was about to pick up the phone to let reception know I would be eating downstairs that evening, when there was a knock at the door. I opened it up to find a middle-aged couple smiling politely at me.

"Good evening, it's James isn't it," said the man, with a familiar accent.

"Yes, James Cummings," I answered. "You're English!"

"Yes, we are, my name is Wilson, Graham Wilson and this is my wife Lissa."

"We heard about your accident and we thought you might like some company."

They were both very polite shaking my hand, one after the other.

"I live here with Lissa, so we know there aren't many English people around."

"My husband is the General Manager at the power station," said Lissa.

I hadn't seen a power station anywhere but then I hadn't seen a town either, for all I knew the power station might have been in Dubai or Sharjah.

"We were going out to a little get together and we thought perhaps you'd like to come along," said Graham.

"It's not far from here, there'll be English food and something to drink," said Lissa, instinctively knowing what would tempt me most.

She had said the magic words; the thought of English food made my mouth water.

"That's really nice of you. Do I have time to get changed?"

"If you want to, but it's just a few friends, there's really no need to dress up," said Graham.

"Well actually I've lost the only suit I had, and I suppose wearing a uniform is a little pompous," I answered.

"We heard all the details and I'd say you've earned the right to wear it son. Don't you worry though, you look fine, it's a casual little soirée anyway," said Graham.

"I think I'll just put on a clean shirt if you don't mind." My T-shirt was damp with sweat after sitting in the heat for so long.

"We'll wait downstairs in reception for you," said Lissa.

I climbed into the back seat of their large white Mercedes and we made our way to a large villa near the quay.

\* \* \*

"Nice to see you again James!"

It was the same officer that had skippered Grayswift on the night of my accident.

"And you. Do you live near here?"

"I share this place with the other two Skippers."

"I expect you would like to chat," said Lissa. "I'll get you a beer and some nibbles, I expect you could do with a drink."

"Yes, thank you very much."

I stopped myself from telling her how hungry I was.

"Eric," he introduced himself. "How are you feeling now?"

"Not too bad under the circumstances. A bit mixed up to be honest."

"You don't seem too bad for someone who experienced what you did. You are a lucky lad! Are you going to re-join the Grenadier?"

"I'm not sure what's happening, I thought you might know. I have my case back now anyway."

"Oh, well that means they have already turned around. They never tell us anything, we're just taxi drivers. She'll be on her way to her next port now, so it looks like you will be going home again."

"That would be nice."

Until then, I hadn't really accepted the fact that after all that had happened they would send me home again, even though I wanted it. Amongst English people who had chosen to live and work there, I suddenly felt very homesick.

Lissa brought me a cold beer and a plate full of sandwiches, sausage rolls and other party nibbles. It was heaven to taste something familiar again. The sandwiches were comfort food, the sausage rolls were not alas, quite what I was used to. When I bit into them, they appeared to be made with small frankfurter sausages rather than pork sausage meat, the taste was sufficiently different to be just a little disappointing.

"How's the food at the hotel?" asked Eric.

"I'm starving there to be honest, I can't eat the stuff they serve up. Haji did get a wonderful curry for me the first night I was back there though."

"It was probably what they cooked for the staff. Good to have a beer too eh?" he laughed.

I sipped at the golden lager beer, which tasted very different from anything I had tasted before, it was chilled, dry tasting and surprisingly refreshing.

# EXTRA TERRESTRIALS

Eric led me through to an office space wo that we could talk.

"So young man, what was all that stuff about aliens in the water, did you really see something out there or what?"

It would do nobody any good to talk about Victor here, no one would believe me and despite the chess set, I still didn't know how much I believed myself.

"I don't know what I saw, I was so damn scared."

"That's understandable, but I've seen some strange things out here recently, lights in the sky, you know. We all have."

"What do you mean?"

"Well just that really, lights flying across the sky, stopping, then shooting off at a tangent in another direction. Sometimes they fly around for two or three minutes and then they just shoot off into space."

I wondered if it could have been Victor.

"We get to see a lot of you guys through here, some of them we know quite well. We've all been out here for six years now," he paused for a moment. "There was a whole crew came through here, oh, about four years ago saying they had all seen a ufo trailing them. Hang on," he said, and popped out of the room briefly.

He returned with a cardboard folder, flicking through the pages inside.

"Yes, I thought it rang a bell. I talk to anyone that says they've seen U-fos, here are my notes. It was the same ship, the Grenadier funnily enough. Crew came through here in June, entire crew change except for the Skipper. He had already been pulled off near the Cape and replaced. According to my notes it began April 30th, 1969."

He showed me the open book to let me see his notes as he read through them.

"According to the crew the Grenadier was sailing through the Gulf of Mexico when a UFO appeared above the ship, they said it was spotted by a cadet taking a sextant reading to confirm latitude at local noon. He said it just seemed to appear, nobody else saw it arrive but it remained above the ship for the next three days. They reckoned it was about two thousand feet above the ship, 'certainly much closer than the aeroplanes normally fly,' it says here.

"They estimated between twenty to fifty feet long, dark blue during the day and silvery blue at night. Weather conditions were good at the time it was visible, a clear sky and calm seas.

"Chief Engineer reported that the ship's engines stopped without reason, only emergency lighting and steering available. Happened again on the next day just one minute after midnight. The crew managed to restart the engines, which took some time as all the pumps had to be shut down and restarted manually. It's all here."

"That's incredible," I said. "Is there any more? Did anyone see any aliens?"

"No," he said, "I've never met anyone that admits to a close encounter of the third kind before, which is why I'm interested in knowing what you think you saw."

He must have realised I had no idea what he was talking about.

"Seeing an alien. Sorry."

I was not sure if he sensed my ignorance.

"Defined by Dr. Josef Hynek, a U.S. astronomer, professor and ufologist.

"A close encounter of the first kind is a sighting of a u-fo. Flying saucers; odd lights; objects that cannot be attributed to known human technology. They called them foo-fighters during the Second World War.

"Second kind," he continued, "an observation of a u-fo and associated physical effects; heat; or radiation; damage to terrain; human paralysis; or frightened animals; electrical or radio interference. Oh, and lost time; a gap in memory.

"A close encounter of the third kind is an observation of what Hynek termed 'animate beings'. He isn't comfortable with that description or extra-terrestrials, but that's more or less what it refers to."

"Terrans!" I said, confusing the terms with the word that Victor used for Earthlings.

"Terrans? No just the opposite! "The word terra simply means earth or land, as in terra firma, solid ground, terrestrial, territory, or terrain for example.

He paused to recall what we were discussing before going off at a tangent.

"A CE4 is the classification for an abduction by a u-fo or its occupants. That type was not included in Hynek's original close encounters scale.

"There's more," he said looking back at his notes. "Next the food storage refrigerators shutdown without reason.

"On the third day just before midnight, the Second Engineer noticed that the lights were out in the ship's air conditioning room, and a door leading to the crew accommodation was opened. He passed through the door to investigate and spoke to two firemen.

"The next day on inspection the same door was found welded shut. They checked it out and the door had actually been welded before the ship left dock, because of a fault. The Second Engineer insisted it was the same door he used. A few minutes after the engineer was checking the door that night, the engines stopped again, leaving just emergency lighting and steering as before. This time the Chief Engineer was on watch, the engines were restarted again, and later discovered that the starter motor for the emergency diesel generator had been dismantled. All the parts of the generator were neatly placed by the machine as if someone had examined it.

"At exactly noon GMT on the third day the craft vanished in the same manner as it had appeared. That's all I have except the names and addresses."

Despite seeing Victor face to face, I was still shocked to hear the story. I decided I shouldn't say anything to Eric about Victor, but I was certainly keen to speak to Victor about it. Victor did say he had been here for twelve years.

"So I'd be interested in anything you can remember about Saturday night," he said. "Now that you've had time to recover from the shock that is."

"It's all a bit a blur I'm afraid. I'm not sure what I saw out there now, I was so scared, it could have all been an hallucination," I replied looking straight at him.

"Hey, no problem. Don't worry, these things are pretty spooky and not everyone wants to talk about them. I will just make a note that you initially thought you had seen an alien, for myself. Let's go through to the other room, we've got a film on, 'Bequest to a Nation', it's about Nelson and Lady Hamilton, Peter Finch and Glenda Jackson."

"Sounds good to me, mind you I'd be happy to watch the test-card for a while. I've hardly spoken to anyone since the accident and I haven't seen any television for over a week."

We watched the film but despite everyone else's desire to watch it, I hardly took in anything. All I could think about was seeing Sam and my family again, and when I stopped thinking about that, I thought about Victor. Perhaps I would never see him again and never get the chance to ask if the story I had just heard had anything to do with him. The thing I had seen in the sky sounded just like Eric's description and Victor, had been there more than long enough for it to have been him.

People began to leave the party as midnight approached.

"We're about ready to go now, but Eschelle is taking the boat out tonight for a crew change, would you like to go out with him?" asked Graham.

Eschelle was one of Eric's colleagues.

"Yes," I said without thinking, "I'd love to."

"I'll introduce you, come and meet him."

We went into the kitchen and found Eric, Eschelle and Steve sharing out the remains of a bottle of whisky.

"Eschelle this is James, he says he would love to go out tonight if that's alright with you."

"Sure. Hi James, are you ready to go?"

He stood against the worktop to prop himself up and raised his whisky glass which was half-full, probably at least four measures if not more.

"You bet," I said.

I said my goodbyes to Graham and Lissa thanking them for the evening.

# OFFICER OF THE WATCH

Eschelle and I drove down to the jetty in a pick-up truck and boarded the supply boat. There were half a dozen crewmen scurrying around, but Eschelle and I had the bridge to ourselves.

"Where are they from?" I asked.

"Four are Indian, one is Egyptian, and the other is from Iran."

"And Haji, where's he from?"

"Haji? He's from Zanzibar man," he chuckled.

"I've heard of that, I had a friend that lived there. Isn't that the big island on the east of Africa?"

"I think you mean Madagascar, but it's hardly an island compared to Zanzibar, it's bigger than Britain and Ireland put together. Zanzibar is a much smaller island but still about a hundred kilometres long, just off the coast of Dar es Salaam, Tanzania or Tanganyika as it used to be called."

"And you? Is that an Australian accent?" He was a very slender man, with a deep tan and blonde hair bleached by the sun.

"Me Oz," he laughed. "No man I'm from Suth Arfrica, Durban!" he answered emphasising his accent."

"Why did you laugh when I asked about Haji?"

"Haji is full of stories," he said with another chuckle. "He thinks he's descended from Ethiopian royalty. Man, he thinks he is descended from Solomon and Sheba. The crew all call him Hailie. You know? Haile Selassie, the Ethiopian Emperor! He started calling himself Al Haji after making the pilgrimage to Mecca. The Haj," he added. "His real name is Mohamad bin Jabir.

"Haj?"

176

"Yes, he's a Muslim. They're all supposed to make the trip at some point in the life. He's a good'un, misses his family."

"How come?" I asked.

"Not many jobs offer family status out here, you have to be pretty high up like the Wilsons to bring your wife and kids," he explained.

"The Wilsons have kids?"

"I think so, but they are grown up, back in England I think."

We were under way within a couple of minutes, and Echelle took the ship out into open water.

"Can you steer a ship?" he asked.

"Yes, I think so."

"Well in that case you're the Officer of the Watch. Take over," he said. "Keep her headed due northeast, 315 degrees on the compass, the throttles are set to 15 knots, and don't forget the radar. If anything happens or you spot any lights give me a shake. The crew will warn you if they spot something too close. Wake me up in an hour."

With that, he staggered over to the couch at the side of the bridge and laid down.

"Oh and wake me up in forty minutes or if you see any unidentified objects eh?" he said with a grin.

Clearly, he was not totally incapable, but he was probably not feeling his best.

It was a special experience for me being in control of such a large vessel, the crew had all disappeared below decks, despite what Eschelle had said, and Eschelle was asleep and there was nothing in sight except for the stars in the sky and the coastline on the radar screen. I knew very little about the radar, enough to know a blip on the screen meant something was there, I knew I could steer the ship.

I thought of my father in control of his supply boat during the war, and tried hard to speak to him, so far away back home in England, to let him know I was safe and well. I turned around to look at Eschelle. I wondered if Eric had been drinking the night we went out, then if there was any truth in the little warrior's ancestry.

# FULL ENGLISH

At 1.45 one of the crew came onto the bridge with two steaming mugs of coffee. He gave me mine without saying a word and then took the other over to Eschelle and shook his shoulder.

"Coffee boss," he whispered.

"Cheers Mostafa,"

Mostafa bowed his head slightly as he turned and disappeared as quickly as he had arrived. He was a pleasant man with a rounded face and an endearing smile, apparently well used to looking after his Skipper.

"How are we doing man?"

"Ok! I haven't seen any other ships around," I answered.

He took a look at the radar screen then moved up to the window.

"Spot on! See that yellow beacon?" he asked pointing about fifteen degrees to starboard. "Head for that!"

I turned the wheel very slightly and the ship moved slowly around to its new heading.

When we got close to the buoy, Eschelle called Mostafa onto the bridge and he took over from me. Eschelle picked up the radio microphone and started calling for the tanker. They were forty miles to the north coming down the gulf. Instead of tying up we changed course again, rendezvousing in the half-light just before sunrise.

There was only one person joining the ship, it was Bernd.

It was a large tanker but sat well down in the water unlike my fateful trip. Fully laden with crude oil Bernd only had a few steps up the pilot ladder to the deck. He never saw me on the bridge, but Eschelle told me he was the Chief Engineer. I wondered why he was boarding the ship leaving the Gulf and who he was replacing. I saw no one leave the tanker.

Eschelle let me take the ship back to Ras al Khaimah while he got some more sleep. The distant wall of mountains that ran all the way along the coast to the Musandam Peninsula, looked extraordinarily beautiful in the early morning light.

When we got home from my night's work, I was rewarded with a full English breakfast; eggs, bacon, sausages, beans and fried bread, with a piping hot mug of tea, all cooked surprisingly by a young Indian cook. It was the first English meal I'd had since leaving home, those guys knew how to look after themselves.

Haji arrived to take me back to the hotel before I had finished.

"Good morning Sir, you are looking well after your trip."

"Yes, I feel a lot better after that," I said placing my knife and fork on the empty plate.

I looked at his dark skin and deep brown eyes, wondering if the man in front of me could really have been descended from King Solomon.

"Well it is time to leave Sir, we must go to Dubai today."

"But I haven't slept yet."

"Haji is very sorry Sir, but we must first go to British Embassy to collect passport for you. Your plane leaves at ten past three this afternoon Sir. Haji will drop you at the hotel and pick you up at ten o'clock."

I looked at my watch, it was still only eight fifteen.

"Ok, at least I can get an hour's rest."

My case was virtually packed, I had only taken out the things I needed and most of those things would go back into my shoulder bag.

He dropped me outside the hotel at eight thirty. I showered and finished packing my case so that I would be ready, then dressed in my khaki uniform, having attached the cadet's epaulettes. As I looked into the mirror to do up my black tie I realised I was going home at last and I couldn't resist the urge to try on my white peaked cap to see how I looked. Happy with what I saw, I tossed my cap on the bed and laid down beside it.

I so desperately wanted to see Victor before I left, but there was no way of contacting him.

Tiredness overcame me, and I fell asleep exhausted.

# BLIGHTY

## ENGLISH GENTLEMAN

I was woken by a knock at the door. I opened my eyes to see Victor sitting in the chair waiting for me.

"Victor!"

I looked at my watch, it was ten o'clock; there was another knock at the door.

"That will be Haji, I have to leave."

"Leave? I wondered why you were dressed in uniform."

"I'm flying home today. Stay there," I said as I opened the door. Haji was waiting outside with a hotel porter. "I'll be down in five minutes. I just want to freshen up."

"Your bags sir?" asked the porter.

"Yes, just the suitcase," I said.

I opened the door wider for the porter standing behind Haji, keeping my flight bag for my last bits and pieces. Neither Haji or the porter saw Victor.

"Five minutes Sir," Haji reminded me.

"Yes ok," I said, and I closed the door. "Victor, I am leaving today, will I see you again?"

"I would like that very much if you wish it to be so," said Victor.

"Yes of course I do," I answered.

"Tell me where to find you."

"In England, you know where England is."

"Young man, I found my way across the galaxy, I was in Paris and London last week, I am confident that another trip to Europe will not be too great a challenge for me. Where in England is your home? Tell me and I will come to you."

I told him my home address, then went to the bathroom and washed my hands and face.

"I have to go now Victor. Goodbye my friend."

"We will meet again."

He shook my hand and smiled reassuringly.

"You can remove that bandage as soon as you get on board the aeroplane, but wait until you are sure Haji will not see your hand. I'm afraid they were unsuitable for the wounds. I have helped you seal them."

"Thank you Victor."

I took his hand in mine, placing my left hand on his upper shoulder, he smiled, put his hand other around my neck and pulled me towards him, embracing me like a long-lost friend.

\* \* \*

I met Haji in the hotel reception, there was nothing to pay, I just signed the bill and handed in my key. I walked slowly out to the Dodge with him.

"We have much to do Sir," he implored. "We must go to Embassy to collect your papers."

"I know Haji, you already told me."

My lack of enthusiasm to be on my way home, must have seemed strange to him after all that had happened, but my warrior friend only knew half the story. I was leaving behind something very significant, and I had not had the time to really come to terms with, consequently I did not have the same sense of the urgency that Haji showed.

I climbed straight into the Dodge, leaving Haji to supervise the loading of my case.

As we pulled away from the hotel I wondered if I would ever come back to this place, and if I would ever see Victor again. I reflected on the conversations Victor and I had shared, and I realised that most of them were absurd. There was little point in chastising myself. How often does anyone really have the foundations of their lives shaken so violently? I was nothing more than a boy when I started my journey, totally inexperienced in life. What should I have said or asked?

The sun shone dazzling white overhead as we drove back across the desert. As I stared across the hot shimmering sands. I wondered what questions someone older and wiser would have asked a man from the stars.

Having driven little more than a few miles, I succumbed to my tiredness and the intense light, and drifted off to sleep.

\* \* \*

I awoke as we arrived at the British Consulate in Dubai, just after eleven thirty. It was a quiet part of the city, there seemed to be nobody around. The Consulate looked much the same as the other buildings in the street, with its high garden walls and shuttered windows. An official wearing what must have been a very hot and uncomfortable dinner suit, met us at the door.

"We are from Grey Mackenzie Sir," said Haji introducing us.

"You must be the infamous young Mr Cummings, come in, come in both of you. Peter Jennings!" he said offering me his right hand. "We are going to need a couple of photographs first of all. If you would like to follow me, we can get started. Sorry but I'm in a bit of a rush and I'm on my own here at the moment. Of course, the Islamic weekend is Thursday afternoon and Friday, but we try to take the odd Sunday off when we can. Today there is a small function at the Palace!"

He was obviously expecting us and fully aware of my predicament. We followed him to a large comfortable room at the back of the house that appeared to be his personal office.

He took the photos himself with a Polaroid camera, then sat down at his desk without waiting for them to develop. He went through all the usual details, meticulously writing the information onto two identical large single sheet documents.

He wrote in an old-fashioned script style with a simple quill pen, which made a scratching sound on the paper, and had to be regularly dipped into a small ink well.

When he had finished, he produced two lengths of thickly woven blue ribbon. He folded one lengthways and snipped off a small piece with two cuts, forming a small V at the bend, creating two lengths which he then placed on the first copy.

Using a gold lighter from his jacket pocket, he melted a piece of red sealing wax so that it dripped onto the apex of the blue ribbons, picked up a small metal seal and pushed it into the pile of wax, fixing the two ribbons to the paper, then repeated the exercise with the second copy.

Next, he cut the two photographs down to passport size, sticking one to each paper, and finally he embossed each photograph using a large metal press on a table at the back of the office.

"There you are young Cummings, you're all legal and above board again. Leave one of these with passport control at Dubai airport, and hand in the second at immigration when you arrive back in the UK," he said, handing me the papers.

"Thank you very much Mr Jennings."

"Peter, please."

He offered his hand again.

"I've heard all about you from the Wilsons you know. You're quite a celebrity at the moment. Nothing much happens here as a rule, we live a good life but a fairly predictable one I'm afraid."

"Well it was nice to have met you Peter."

"You too young man. Have a good trip home to Blighty. If you'll excuse me, my wife and I are due at the Palace."

It seemed so peculiar to see what I could only assume was a typical British Civil Servant, dressed the way he was, in this remote part of the world. I had never met anyone in his position before at home, nor for that matter had I ever seen anyone dressed in a dinner suit, except on the television. To me he just seemed so out of place with everything else around me. Bizarrely, it was such an alien experience that it felt like I was actually playing a role in some black and white colonial movie, stranger than my accident, even stranger than talking to Victor, the meeting seemed almost rehearsed.

It occurred to me how little I knew about my own planet, and even my own country, its people and its customs. How much more mysterious then would Victor's home be? Beyond imagination! Would it be significantly different to Earth and if so how? After all, this place was nothing like my home, it was a lot hotter and of course barren, even the air felt and smelled totally different to me. Victor had said that there were many different landscapes and climates on his world too.

'What would it feel like?'

It was just after noon when we left the Embassy and I climbed back into the Dodge.

"Now you can go home Sir, see your family. That would be good, yes?"

"Yes, that would be good Haji."

"Do you have a family Haji?"

"I have a wife and three children in Zanzibar."

So what Eschelle had said was true, the little warrior was African.

"How long since you last saw them?"

"Nearly a year. Haji go home soon to see them."

I wondered what life was like in Haji's Zanzibar home, then my thoughts turned back to Victor. I had so many unanswered questions racing through my mind. There was so much more I wanted to know about Victor's world and his way of life. I would need to think out what questions I really wanted answers to in case I ever got the chance to see him again.

During the ride to the airport I sat nonchalantly in the back of the Dodge, much more at ease with myself and my surroundings. It no longer felt strange to be chauffeured around. Haji kept babbling away in the front seat talking and singing, his voice was tuneless, but it obviously made him happy and I chuckled inwardly at his contentment.

I looked down at the flamboyant papers with their long blue ribbons and they seemed to inflate my ego. My self-worth seemed to be growing rapidly and with it my confidence. Inwardly I felt like a conquering hero returning from some epic battle. I had been put to the test and I had survived. I had also been privileged to see things few people would ever see.

Along with this growth of inner strength, there seemed to be a new dawn in my wisdom.

During the last months of my schooling I had naively assumed that I had reached the lower summit on what I considered to be the mountain of learning. Of course, I knew that I still had more to learn, specifically the vocational development to become a Navigation Officer and perhaps one day a Master Mariner. I had thought that the summit was now just a short climb away; what a fool I had been.

It seemed clear to me that as I reached this insignificant crest, that instead of being able to see a reachable peak ahead of me, I could actually see a whole range of mountains growing eternally higher and higher, eventually disappearing into the distance.

I was just beginning to realise what an endless mass of knowledge there was. So many mountains that it would be impossible for any one person to see, let alone climb. I felt like I had been running up the staircase of wisdom all of my life, then looking up to realised that the staircase was in fact an escalator moving downwards beneath me. If I stood still on the escalator, I would in fact slowly lose ground.

Despite the realisation of my insignificance in this great universe, I no longer felt like a boy. I felt that I was growing up, becoming more experienced in life, maybe because I had come so close to facing death. I now had something to say about myself. Perhaps simply understanding just how little I knew about anything was the first step in that development.

A seed had been planted in my mind, though I did not realise the significance. A new sensory perception was growing inside me far more powerful than seeing, hearing or touching or even the sum of all three. Before I would realise the significance and power of telepathy, I would have to learn how to use it in the way someone who loses their sight, learns how powerful hearing and touch can really be.

That was the end of the beginning, my beginning, the last time I really felt pride. My journey through life had met its biggest crossroads, all I had to do was pick the route ahead. Which mountains would I now seek out and climb, and who would I climb them with?

In that short time, I had travelled half way around the world, all but killed in any of a number of possible ways, met and talked to an alien, spent the night in an Arabian hospital where I met and slept beside a murderer, and steered a sixty-foot supply boat out across the Persian Gulf.

Once more I felt so very proud to be wearing my uniform. It was the first time it had actually been appropriate to wear the khaki shirt and trousers intended for the sub-tropical climates. I felt like an officer despite the fact that the epaulettes only bore the single thin gold line down the centre, signifying a Deck Cadet.

# MILLION TO ONE

We arrived at the airport and I made no effort to move from my air-conditioned seat in the Dodge until Haji returned with a porter. He escorted me to the check-in desk and I handed the porter a one Dirham coin. Haji looked at me and smiled, but still found it necessary to shout what were surely Arabic insults at the porter. I had no idea if my tip was too big or too small. The porter nodded at me and made off away from Haji as quickly as possible.

I checked in at the MEA desk, Haji had my ticket and I still held the temporary passport papers from the consulate. When I had finished and was free of baggage I turned around to Haji.

"Goodbye Haji. I hope that we will meet again sometime."

I offered him my hand and he squeezed it tightly.

"Goodbye Sir. Haji hope to see Mr James again, next time Haji don't have to fish you out of sea!"

It was the first time he had referred to me by name unprompted.

I put a five Dirham note into his hand, which was most of what I had left.

"Haji see you to passport control," he said.

"Okay Haji, if you wish."

I smiled and walked off towards passport control at emigration with Haji following me.

I offered one of the identification papers to the Arab officer there, he called a colleague in Arabic and asked his opinion about the papers.

"Please," his colleague said politely.

He wanted both copies, so I handed him the second one.

"We take one of these, the other you keep," he decided, once again speaking very politely.

"That's correct," I answered, knowing what was supposed to happen.

He handed me back my copy and ushered me through into the departure area.

I shook hands with Haji and watched as he walked off, with his head turned back towards me, waving with a silly grin on his face.

Once inside I went straight over to the toilets and removed the tatty bandage from my hand. The knuckle had healed and there was little or no indication that it had ever been damaged. My fingernail was missing but the skin had healed where it would have been; the cuticle at the top of my finger had retained its shape in expectation of the nail re-growing. Without a close look you would never have noticed the nail was not intact. I washed my hands and threw the grubby blood and iodine-soaked bandage away.

I went back to the departure lounge and found myself a seat. I sat in oblivion, totally unaware of my surroundings, my mind too focused on Victor to take in anything around me.

My journey home would take about twelve hours including the train journey, that was all I had to relate travel time to. 'What was it like in suspended animation, do you dream?' I wondered.

I had no idea of the enormity of our galaxy in terms of light-years, despite a reasonably good appreciation of physics. I was unaware that Earth's nearest star Proxima Centauri was over four light-years away, over quarter of a million times further than our sun. If Victor's planet was across the other side of the galaxy he must have travelled at thousands of times faster than the speed of light.

It took almost exactly seven years for Victor to get here, that kind of distance seemed incredible. Victor had said that the galaxy was a hundred-thousand light-years across. Assuming the journey would be roughly two thirds of that, it equated to something close to ten-thousand light-years per year, ten-thousand times the speed of light. I could not recall if the NCC1701's trek had been within the galaxy or across the void, as Victor had called it. 'Perhaps Victor's ship could travel at warp factor ten,' I chuckled to myself.

Awareness of my surroundings eventually returned, I was back in the land of the living. I needed a pen and paper to make some notes. Looking around I noticed a newsagent's shop in the corner of the departure lounge, so I walked over and managed to find a small pocket note book and ball point pen, which I purchased using the last of the coins in my pocket.

'Now let's think this through,' I thought.

I sat down in the chair, opened the notebook and began to write. On the first page I wrote down my name address and phone number, on the second the number one, continuing with my list, answering the questions where I could, and to be confirmed later.

1. What is the name of your planet? Er-ato

2. What are your people called? Er-ate-ans

3. Are your people the only people on the planet or are there people from other planets? Others, some visitors from Earth

4. Are there any people from Earth on your planet? Yes

5. When will you go home?

6. How fast does your ship fly? Warp factor 10!

7. Do you have any weapons on board?

8. If you have no war and no crime is there any one or any race that you fear?

9. Are you the most advanced life form that you have discovered?

10. Why do you....

My concentration was broken by an outburst of English banter and raucous laughter. There must have been twenty or so English men of various ages, they all seemed to head straight for what appeared to be the only coffee bar in the lounge. Five of them came across to where I was sitting, the oldest of them sat down beside me. He was probably in his late twenties or early thirties, older than my brother John, the others were in their late teens or early twenties.

"On your way home?" he asked.

"Yes, how did you know?"

"Andy Morgan," he said with a wink of the eye. "It's not a difficult puzzle Watson," he said in jest. "You're in the departure lounge in

Dubai, you're in uniform," he added, leaning over to look at my cap badge. "BP eh?"

"That's right. You're seamen?"

Unlike me they were not in uniform.

"Shell! Whole crew change, twenty-six of us." he said sipping his coffee. "On your own then, that's unusual."

"I had an accident joining my ship. And by the way, I thought it was unusual for an entire crew change too," I answered.

"Not really. It happens from time to time. The ship needs some repairs so they're flying us all home. What sort of accident?"

I repeated my story to the five of them within hearing range, they were all interested in what had happened. I left out Victor, but I explained everything else in detail.

"Don't let it put you off the sea mate. I've never heard of anything like that before in my life, that was a million to one shot."

His words made me think again of Paul and those damned Tarot cards of his.

"Million to one eh?" I muttered. 'Maybe not,' I thought to myself.

Andy's friends nodded in agreement with him.

"James, James Cummings," I said as I offered him my hand, realising that I hadn't not actually introduced myself.

"They'll treat you like a king when you get back. Heads will roll," he said, shaking his head and tutting light-heartedly. "That sort of thing should never happen. You're damn well lucky to be alive. Can I get you a coffee? It's all there is I'm afraid."

"That's very kind of you, I could do with a drink."

"Joey, here's the cash go and get the boy a coffee will ya. Milk and sugar?"

"Please, two sugars," I nodded in response.

Joe stood up and did as he was asked.

We talked as a group about some of their experiences, especially Andy, he was a Second Officer. He already had his Chief's ticket and was studying for his Master's. His next trip would be his first serving as First

Officer, so he should have known all about safety at sea and crew changes.

He arranged to swap seats with one of the younger guys who had been allocated the seat next to mine, so that he could sit with me on the plane home. I was tempted to open up to him about Victor, he was the first person I had been able to talk to at any length.

We were due to stop off briefly at Beirut again on the way back; however, when we landed we all had to disembark and wait for another plane because of engine problems. They hadn't told us, but one engine was showing some sort of warning light as we approached, and they wouldn't take off until it was checked out.

We only had to wait for an hour, but we were left outside the departure lounge in the heat until the problem was resolved, and we could resume the journey.

Andy and I talked alone about all sorts of things, what made me join the Merchant Navy for one. The conversation drifted around to science fiction and Star Trek, Andy was a big fan like me.

"Do you think other life forms exist? From other worlds?" I asked him.

"They must," he said. "There are so many stars, so many planets, it wouldn't be very scientific to say categorically that they don't exist would it?"

"Have you ever had any experience of flying saucers?"

"We see some strange lights in the sky sometimes. I once saw a blueish light in the sky at sea. It shot across the sky at one hell of a speed and then stop dead, waited for a few seconds then shot off at an acute angle, stopped and did the same several times before zooming off out of sight. But that sort of thing always gets hushed up. We don't even like making reports, it's not good for promotion prospects and no one ever believes you."

"What do you think you'd do if you met an alien?" I asked.

"Shit myself probably," he laughed. "Run! God, I don't know! How about you?"

"I think I'd want to find out as much as I could about him, why he was here, where he came from, what it was like on his planet."

"Well you're a brave man!" he laughed. "You think there would be men and women then. You know on Earth that some species have only one sex, perhaps there could be several kinds of sexes, bees have workers and drones and only one queen."

It seemed an interesting observation, but I knew nothing about the sexes of bees. It would be a good question for Victor, we had not spoken about these things.

"I don't know I guess there could be millions of different species. I suppose it's arrogant to think that they are in anyway like us."

"Would you like to explore the galaxy?" he asked. "That must be every travellers dream!"

"Yes, I suppose I would." I hadn't thought of it until then. "I would love to see the stars."

"Have you heard about alien abduction? There are people that say they have been taken by aliens and subjected to all sorts of things."

"Really? And you believe that?" I asked.

"I told you nobody ever takes it seriously. Nobody believes any of it!"

He was right. Nobody believes the stories they hear, they never have; aliens, ghosts, even religion, people find it hard to accept someone else's word.

I took out my note book and looked at the unfinished question. 'Why do you' and finished writing it, 'Why do your people travel across space to Earth?' I added another, 'Are there more than two kinds of any life form, male and female?'

"What would you ask an alien if you met one?" I asked.

"What he wanted I suppose. Really? I think I would run as far away as I possibly could, I'm too young and handsome to die!" he laughed.

My circumstances in meeting Victor had been somewhat unique, I had been in a life-threatening position already and had nothing worse to fear from Victor. If he had wanted to abduct me or harm me in anyway, he could have done so at any time. Surely there was no need to fear for my safety. Victor seemed so caring for any form of life, and when he spoke verbally his telepathic thoughts seemed to substantiate beyond doubt that he was sincere. I added another question to my note book, 'Have your people ever harmed human life?' I added 'no', remembering Victor saying that they had never harmed any anything more advanced than a mollusc on Earth.

Eventually we boarded a replacement aeroplane and resumed our journey. Andy sat beside me again as we had to return to the same seats as before. We continued to talk for a while but we both fell asleep shortly after take-off.

# MEN IN UNIFORMS

Our flight landed at Heathrow at a quarter past seven. I was met at the arrivals gate at a quarter to eight by a man holding up a large white card, with 'James Cummings BP' written on it. I said goodbye to Andy and his friends, and made my way to the man waiting for me.

"Just a moment," I said sensing a presence close by.

I looked at the crowd of people waiting, trying to identify the person I sensed among them. Failing to identify anyone, I resigned myself to the matter at hand and caught the train home.

The driver led me outside to a car and told me he was going to take me to Waterloo station. He didn't talk very much, and I was feeling tired from the journey, so I never tried to make conversation.

He dropped me at the entrance to Waterloo, gave me a rail warrant for the train home, and waited while I fetched myself a trolley for my luggage.

At the ticket office I exchanged my warrant for a ticket, then made my way to the platform. It was a chilly evening back in England and I was dressed in just my shirt and tie. I wanted to unpack my raincoat from my suitcase, but the fast 91 train was due to leave for Basingstoke, Southampton and Bournemouth at 8.42. I could change at Southampton and pick up a slow train to Sway, which would be just a half hour trip.

The carriage was empty, so I took a seat near the door and pushed my suitcase under the table in front of me. It was warmer on the train, so I left my raincoat in the case. I took off my cap and placed it on the table in front of me.

Just before the train moved off, a girl opened the carriage door and sat down in the chair one row further along, facing me across the gangway. She was very attractive, about twenty years old, with dark hair and fair skin, brown eyes and bright cherry red lipstick; she wore a matching smart cherry red suit with a very short skirt. She laid a black leather briefcase on the table in front of her and put her red handbag on the seat beside her.

As the train moved off, I glanced across the corridor at her. I noticed her legs under the table. Her short skirt had ridden up, with her left leg crossed over her right. Her legs were on full display, and it was clear she was wearing black stockings. There was an inch of white flesh at the top of her right stocking, with a single black suspender strap visible, pulling at the dark ring circling her stocking top. I had never seen anything quite so seductive in my life, except in gentlemen's magazines. I looked up at her and knew instantly that she had seen me looking at her legs. She just smiled and made no attempt to change her posture or to adjust her skirt. I found myself looking down at her thigh again; I was embarrassed but I could not help myself.

She picked up her brief case from the table and placed it between her feet, then did the same with her handbag. Her legs were parted and pointed towards me. I caught a glimpse of her black silky knickers as she wriggled making herself comfortable.

There was something very powerful about that small area of flesh at her stocking tops. I felt myself stir between my legs. I tried to look away, but hard as I tried I was tormented by an animal lust inside me, and I could not stop myself from looking back at the mesmerising image between her stockings.

She picked up her handbag and pulled out a small bag, then touched up her red lipstick using a small mirror, glancing over the top at me as I watched her. When she had finished she stood up, leaving her brief case under the table.

"I'm just going to get myself a drink," she said. "If you are going to be here for a while, do you think you could keep an eye on my brief case?"

"Yes of course I could," I answered.

"Thanks, I won't be long."

She moved her briefcase on to the table to my left and walked off down the corridor. I watched her disappear through the door and looked around the carriage, confirming I was alone. When she returned, she had two cups of coffee.

"I bought one for you too," she said. "I hope you like sugar in your coffee."

"Thank you very much, yes I do."

It was strange, I had always been very shy with girls before, but she was so very confident, and her confidence began to put me at ease.

"You don't mind if I join you?" she asked, placing her handbag on my table, without waiting for my answer.

I pulled out my suitcase from under the table and pushed it across the gangway, placing it beneath the table on which her briefcase lay, making room for her to sit.

"You're in the navy, aren't you?"

"Yes, the Merchant Navy. I'm a Navigation Cadet with B.P. Tankers."

"Oh, I thought you were in the Royal Navy. That's a very smart uniform."

"Thank you, and sorry, to disappoint you, about the Royal Navy," I said.

"Oh, that's ok, I just like uniforms. They turn me on," she said brazenly.

"You don't look so bad yourself. That's a very attractive skirt you're wearing," I answered, emboldened by her direct attitude.

"I saw you looking," she said, "I could feel your eyes undressing me."

I dipped my head in embarrassment.

"It's ok, I like to be noticed!" she assured me.

"You have lovely legs," I said.

It seemed I was at her mercy, yet for some reason I was feeling much bolder.

"I know, they're my best attribute don't you think?" she said, moving them out into the gangway and raising the hem so that I could clearly see the darker lacy tops of her stockings.

"They're lovely, you have beautiful brown eyes too."

"Oh you're a flatterer aren't you!" she smiled.

"Sorry."

"Don't apologise, a girl likes to be flattered. Have you been somewhere exotic?"

"Not really, I've just got back from Dubai in the Persian Gulf," I answered casually.

On my journey to the Worcester just a few weeks before, I would have considered my trip to the United Arab Emirates very exotic. Having heard Victor's descriptions of his world, the scope of my imagination had somewhat changed.

"Sounds very exciting to me! I suppose you're on your way home to your girlfriend now."

I felt very guilty as I sipped my coffee, I was in love with Sam, but was that just a fantasy; Sam could not know that, and I had never so much as kissed her.

"No, I haven't got a girlfriend," I answered.

The glimpse at the flesh above her stockings had turned my head. Although I was being honest in principle, it felt like I was lying.

"I'm sorry I just assumed you would have."

"Why?"

"Well you know what they say about sailors, 'a girl in every port'!"

"Not me!" I dipped my head, breaking eye contact with her.

"You do like girls?" she dipped her head to look up into my eyes.

"Yes of course I do!"

"Well you hear all sorts of things. All those men on board ship with no women. I suppose you just use women and then forget them?" she said reproachfully.

"I wouldn't do that!"

"Tell me something, are you a virgin?" she asked.

I said nothing.

"You're blushing. You are a virgin!"

The next few seconds seemed like hours.

"Why don't we pop down to the bar for a drink?" she suggested.

I could sense the powerful lust in her mind as clearly as if it were my own. She wanted me in that moment and I knew it, my uniform excited her, and now that she knew I was a virgin, her thoughts were very clear, she wanted to be the one to take my virginity from me.

The sensation of hearing the thoughts of another person was no longer unfamiliar to me, having experienced it with Bernd playing chess. This was definitely more than a girl just giving me the right signals. I could actually read her mind. If I could sense her desires perhaps she could sense my own.

"Yes okay," I said smiling.

She picked up her briefcase and handbag, I put on my cap and grabbed my shoulder bag, leaving my case under the table, safe in the knowledge that only a fool would try to run away with it.

"Oh I do like that," she said, looking at my white cap.

Together we set off down the corridor.

"Why don't we slip in here for a moment," she said, opening the toilet door.

I moved in behind her, we dropped our belongings and I took of my cap.

"No, leave it on, it turns me on," she said.

I put it back on and she threw her arms around me, pressed her pelvis into my groin and my hands moved onto her hips, I felt the tops of her stockings and the soft skin of her legs. Electricity seemed to run from my fingertips, up my arms and across my chest. Her mouth found mine and she kissed me softly and seductively before opening her mouth and pushing her tongue against my own.

Natural instincts guided my hands, the sensation was new to me, enticing, mesmerizing, and intensifying the lust inside me exponentially. I wanted desperately to be inside her.

Before I could do anything, she slipped down in front of me, loosened my trousers and closed her mouth around me, caressing my swelling testicles with her hands.

All too quickly it was over for me, I exploded inside her mouth as she willed me to empty myself. She continued to tease me with her mouth and hands, and very soon I wanted her again just as desperately as before.

Then she was ready for me, I could sense the lust inside her demanding attention. I was ready for her and she knew that now I could satisfy her needs.

She wrapped her legs around me, and her eyes stared into mine with an intensity that matched her passion. She kissed me, and I tasted my essence on her tongue. Having already climaxed, I was able to prolong my lust long enough for her to reach her peak. Her soft moans of pleasure became shouts of ecstasy as she did. I sensed her thoughts willing me to fill her with another burst of my essence. Her eyes closed as she revelled in gratification.

"Yes, give it to me, give it all to me," she demanded.

I exploded inside her.

Like a devil stealing my very soul, my essence was her prize. There was no emotion in her, just a desire to have power over me, and I succumbed willingly.

"You can keep these as a memento," she said, handing me her black silk knickers.

"What's your name?" I asked. "I don't even know your name."

"That's right sailor boy, you don't! I always think it's more fun that way."

She had no intention of telling me, but did so without realising it. As she spoke her mind was focused, her thoughts where clear to me.

"Sharon!"

"How the hell...?" she shrieked.

"Just a guess."

"Listen, it very was very nice meeting you, we had some fun together, but I have to get off now."

"Basingstoke?"

"Yes," she said.

"My name is..."

"I don't want to know!" she interrupted, "It was fun, let's just leave it at that."

She was smiling, and I realised that she was a hunter, she had simply satisfied her hunger.

She kissed me firmly, pushing her tongue into my mouth, while her hands gently caressed the hair below my cap, and the last sensations of her climax slowly left her. When she had finished she said goodbye, opened the door and left me to clean myself.

When I got back to the seat, she had made her way to the door; she stood there looking back at me. The train stopped shortly afterwards, she turned to me smiling and she waved as she got off.

Losing my virginity that way was almost unbelievable. No recriminations, I knew her name, but she did not know mine, she didn't want to. She was extremely seductive, and I had experienced her lustful desire in a way most people on Earth have probably never done with their partner, I could read her mind. I had nothing to compare it with, I had felt her passion as she climaxed, and I climaxed with her. Her thoughts had danced through my mind and mingled with my own until I almost felt a part of her, as if we were almost one. I knew I had developed this extra sense during my time with Victor.

I chuckled to myself recalling how naive I must have sounded on the Worcester, listening to Paul's graphic descriptions of his exploits.

# SANCTUARY

Mentally and physically exhausted, I fell asleep in the chair, almost missing Southampton station, where I needed to pick up the slow train back to Sway. I was woken by the judder of the train stopping; I rushed to the nearest door and opened it before retrieving my luggage.

I ran up the steps as fast as I was able, laden with my huge blue suitcase, over the bridge to platform four.

There was a five-minute wait for the slow train, so I used the time to make a quick call home, calling the operator and reversing the charges. My brother John answered and accepted the charges.

"How ya doin' Higgs?"

"I'm in Southampton, I'm just about to get on the train to Sway."

"Mum and Dad have just left for the station. Someone from B.P. called and said you were on the train from London."

"They know the train doesn't get in till seventeen minutes past."

"I know, but they wanted to be sure they were there to meet you. I said I would wait by the phone. How was your trip back?"

"Have to go now John, I need to catch the train. I have so much to tell you, but it'll have to wait. I'll tell you later, you'll never believe it!"

"Okay Higgs, see ya soon," he agreed, using the personal nickname he had given me.

I had no idea why he called me Higgins or Higgs for short.

The slow train pulled in as I reached the bottom of the steps.

The last part of my journey home was familiar to me even in the dark. I knew all the stations and counted them of at each stop, Millbrook, Redbridge, Totton, Lyndhurst Road, Beaulieu Road and then Brockenhurst. I had made the trip so many times before. Soon the train was making its way from Brockenhurst to Sway, through the darkness of the forest and finally under the last bridge, just before the platform at Sway station.

As a child, I would run up to that bridge to catch the smoke from the magnificent steam engines that ran on that line. The sweet smell of coal and oil mixed with the rush of steam from the pistons was an experience I still recall.

As the train cleared the bridge, I put my head through the window and saw Mum, Dad and John all standing on the platform waiting for me.

I got off the train and dragged my suitcase onto the platform.

Mum grabbed me, throwing her arms around me.

Give your Old Fan a hug then Charlie," she said, beginning to cry.

The awful memories of the Grenadier moving away from me on that dark night went through my mind and I realised how lucky I was to be home.

"Are you okay son?" asked Dad.

"Yeah, I'm fine, just cold, my coat is still in the case."

John grabbed my hand, it was good to see him again. He looked at me in my uniform and then down at the green overalls he was still wearing.

"I think I'm in the wrong job. It's good to have ya back mate." he said with a huge grin. "I've been working at the garage today, I'll explain later."

He grabbed my suitcase and we walked out of the station gate towards the cars.

"They told us you had been injured, your hands and face. They said you couldn't get back on board the ship, and you'd been in hospital," said Mum, as her tears abated.

"Only small cuts. See, I lost my finger nail."

I showed her my right hand with the nail missing from my middle finger.

"That's healed up quickly, what about your face?"

"They were just splinters from the cable. I'm fine, really!"

\* \* \*

Within hours of the accident the local police officer had been sent to my home. B.P. Head Office had received a telegram from the Gray MacKenzie office as soon as the incident had been resolved, confirming that I was alive. The local constable P.C. Penny, was dispatched to inform my parents that a serious accident had occurred, but that I was alive and had suffered no serious injuries. A telegram from Gray MacKenzie followed the next day summarising the accident details.

*  *  *

Dad drove Mum and I home, while John put my suitcase in his car. Dad's little Fiat 500 was too small to carry the huge case.

All the family were there to greet me, my eldest sister Jean, her husband Richard and baby daughter Clare, John's wife Mary and daughter Jane, my sister Jane and her husband Charles and my younger sisters Jennie and Julie, the twins.

Mum had done her best to provide us with a buffet, everyone was ravenous. It was half past eleven at night by the time we got home, but they all wanted to be there, and no-one had eaten for hours. It was wonderful to taste some home cooked food again and see their loving faces.

I retold my story, and everyone sat in silence listening to the account. I could not tell them all that I had met an alien, or they too would have thought I had lost my mind. That would have to wait, and even then, I would probably only confide in John.

Dad was horrified at what had happened. Captain le Fevre had already arranged for him to go to Britannic House on Tuesday. They had all assumed I would not feel up to facing anyone that soon, so John would go in my place to accompany Dad, which was why he had been working that Sunday. They were right, I needed some time to get over the shock of everything before discussing things with Le Fevre, and a massive feeling of guilt suppressed my desire to see Sam again so soon.

Shock hit me when I got home, until then there had been so much else happening, but a feeling of sanctuary and love overwhelmed me, there at last I felt safe and secure.

## Monday ~ 19th November 1973

The next day nobody woke me, and I slept until mid-afternoon. The previous days had taken their toll and I was totally exhausted. The house was quiet with only Mum, Dad and my twin sisters who had decided to skip school and stay at home for the day.

My sister Jean had returned with daughter Clare late morning and stayed while Mum prepared my favourite meal. Sunday lunch had been postponed until my home-coming, we were having a small but special piece of roast lamb and onion sauce, a combination that had become my favourite since tasting onion sauce for the first time at Secondary School.

Normally Sunday lunch would have been chicken, it was cheaper, but today was my special homecoming treat. Jean's husband Richard had taken Dad to the local Working Men's Club for a game of snooker at lunch time the day before and Dad had won a huge joint of beef in the weekly dice game, but that had been placed in the freezer for the following Sunday.

By the time I woke, Jean and Clare had gone.

The five of us enjoyed our dinner together, Mum had even bought a bottle of burgundy for a special treat, but we all knew it was more special for her than the rest of us.

It was past five when we had finished eating. I spent the rest of the evening unpacking my gear and then settled down to a quiet evening watching the television with my family.

# SAUCE FOR THE GOOSE

Tuesday ~ 20th November 1973

Malcolm arrived early on Tuesday morning, he and my father had set off before I woke, travelling to Waterloo by train. My father's arthritis was too bad to drive that distance, my brother's Morris Minor was not up to the journey, and the price of petrol had shot up due to the oil crisis that followed the Arab Israeli war in October.

They arrived at the reception desk just before eleven.

"I'm here to see Captain Le Fevre, he announced.

"And your name sir?" asked the receptionist.

"Cummings."

"And what rank sir?" she asked.

"I'm retired," he answered.

His words made my mother laugh when she heard John repeat it later.

Sam met John and my father in the foyer and escorted them up to the Captain's office.

Captain Le Fevre compared the details he had about the accident with my father, and my father assured the Captain that I had suffered no serious physical injuries. Captain Le Fevre was a little surprised to hear that the injuries to my hand had healed so quickly but he did not pursue the matter.

My father was given a claim form for the clothing I had lost and a check for forty pounds as an advance for the same.

Le Fevre was eager to see me and wanted very much to get me back to sea as soon as possible. He asked my father to ask me, where I would like to go, what country I would like to see, and promised to do his best to get me there before Christmas. 'Anywhere in the world, as long as there was a B.P. vessel expected', nowhere was too far. He felt it was important 'for me to get back on the horse as quickly as possible, before I lost my confidence'. He also wanted to remind me that 'I could not afford to lose too much sea time if I was to re-join my friends at college again next year'.

They agreed that I would return with my father on Friday the 30th of November at 11.30.

At the end of the meeting, Captain Le Fevre escorted them to Sam's adjacent office and wished them a safe trip back, leaving Sam to sort out the travel details.

Having prepared everything during the meeting, Sam handed my father two travel warrants, one for their return journey, the other for he and I to revisit the following week. She also reimbursed him for his travel expenses.

"Mr Cummings, I would be very grateful if you could give this to James for me," she said, handing it to my brother.

"Sure," replied John, taking the letter. It was addressed simply 'James' and hand written.

"He's okay, isn't he?"

"Yes, he's just a bit shaken up, he'll be fine," he reassured her.

* * *

My brother was extremely impressed by the grandeur of Britannic House, he found the people very professional and the uniforms equally appealing. He was bored and frustrated with his work and looking for something more challenging.

Most of their journey home was spent discussing John's future. The heat was off me for the time being, I was safe at home and in an attempt to rekindle my wander lust, I could go to any country in the world, even Australia.

There was a lot of discussion when they got back. Mother couldn't wait to tell everyone about Dad's reply to the receptionist.

"He could have been an Admiral as far as they knew," she said. "Admiral Cummings," she laughed.

Despite the almost limitless choice of destinations on offer, I was still not ready to go anywhere, I wanted to talk in depth to John about Victor, and I wanted to see Victor again. If I were to leave, I would never get the chance. It would soon be December, and Christmas suddenly seemed very close. I wasn't at all sure I wanted to be on my own, away from my home and family at Christmas, having only just got home.

John gave me the letter from Sam.

"She's a very pretty girl Higgins," he grinned.

Only my father and the twins called me James, my mother always called me Charlie while I called her Old Fan, Jean called me Bugs or Bugsy, while Jane, well Jane had usually called me less savoury names the way sisters do.

"I know," I said, "I wrote to her from Dubai. It's strange, I feel I know her, but I don't know why. I'd like to read this if you don't mind."

I left them talking and went upstairs to my room. I opened the letter anxiously and found a photograph of Sam inside, my spirits lifted, and I began to read her letter.

---

*30B Highgate High St*
*Highgate*
*London*
*N6 5JG*
*19th November 1973*

*Dear James*
*This is actually the second letter I have written to you, I have already sent one to the S.S. British Grenadier.*
*I don't usually write to cadets, but I feel compelled to make you the exception.*
*I seem to know more about you than I can explain.*

---

It seemed like my heart stopped beating when I heard about your accident, although somehow I knew you were ok. I know now that you are safely back with your family.

I came to the airport to see you arrive, I just had to. I saw you, but you didnt see me.

There are times when I can't stop thinking about you, times when I think I've known you for ever. That day on the Worcester, when I called you up to take down your details was so strange, I could have written them all down from memory but I'd never seen them before.

I could have hugged you to death, but I don't know why. I know that I find you very attractive, but it's more than that, I hardly know you and yet at times I know so much about you.

I have no doubt that you will write back, in fact for some reason I already know you have written to me and asked for a photograph, but I can tell you, the letter hasn't arrived yet.

You probably think I'm deranged, but for some reason I feel I have to do this, it's like it's supposed to be.

I know your father is coming up to Britannic House tomorrow, I will give this letter to him before he leaves.

I hope you'll be up here soon, perhaps I could arrange a night up here for you, we could go out for a drink and a chat, there's just so much I want to talk to you about. I have a brother Kevin in the fleet, which is how I got into B.P., he's at Warsash at the moment down near you. He's doing his First Engineers ticket. We share a flat in Highgate above a baker's shop. It's a bit expensive but I love my independence and Kevin is away most of the time. The fresh bread downstairs is just divine for breakfast by the way. It's handy for work because it's just nine stops down on the Northern Line.

I'm looking forward to seeing you again soon and I know you'll want to stay, so bring some spare clothes.

Love Sam xxxx

PS I got a message from Bernie, he's fine and he hopes you're ok. I also got a message from Paul Caveat he was quite concerned about you and sent me a telex asking if you were ok. I sent a message back to let him know you had had an accident, but I don't understand how he knew unless someone on his ship heard something. He's on the M.V. British Poplar on route to Jamaica by the way.

Her handwriting was just as I expected, it was almost as beautiful as she was, very flamboyant, artistic and extremely neat.

For a few moments my heart was bursting with happiness, then I recalled what had happened just the day before, and I was with remorse about my experience on the train.

Sam had not received my letter, but then there was no way she could have, it would probably not reach her for at least another two or three days. I looked at the photograph, it was a picture of her in a garden wearing a short green skirt and white top. She had a summer tan, her legs and feet were bare, her blonde hair was tied up and her big green eyes sparkled. That proud nose of hers gave her the spirited look that I remembered so vividly. I placed the picture on my bed side table and made a promise to myself that I would never do anything to hurt her again, then smiling to myself made a second promise to myself that I would buy a picture frame.

* * *

Downstairs John was discussing the possibilities of going to sea with Mum and Dad.

"James, have you still got all the entry information you got from B.P.? John wants to follow you off to sea, as an engineer."

"Yes, it's upstairs in my drawer, I'll go and get it."

He had not discussed it with anyone outside the family, but having watched me leave home, John found himself being drawn towards a career in the Merchant Navy. After his visit to Britannic House, he felt quite strongly that B.P. was the place he should be looking. Like me, he wanted to travel, and it occurred to him that he might be able to use his engineering qualifications to gain entry as an engineer, he definitely wanted to get himself an Officers uniform.

I brought down the papers and we studied them together. At twenty-three, John was over the age of entry for an Engineering Cadet, but he already had City and Guilds certificates for a Diesel Technician, it would be worth making enquiries.

John left soon afterwards with my documents, he would need to discuss his plans with Mary. I wanted to talk to him alone, but it would have to wait, at least until the next morning.

# ANSWERS

T he next day I ate breakfast with Mum, Dad and the twins. After the girls had left for school, I decided to go for a walk. I wondered when I would see Victor again. I had no idea how he would make it known to me that he was here.

I was just turning the corner out of the estate, taking the shortcut to the forest when I heard his voice inside my head.

"Wait for me!"

I looked around, instinctively knowing where to look, he was there, a hundred yards behind me. I would have recognised him anywhere, he wore the same T-shirt and jeans as before, despite the cold weather. His ginger hair shone bright red in the autumn sunshine.

I wondered how I knew where to look. We sense sound with each ear so precisely that we can identify the direction three dimensionally, and our two eyes can judge distance. How did that work with telepathy? Perhaps he was also telling me where to look.

"Victor!" I shouted. "I thought I'd never see you again. How long have you been here?"

"I was here before sunrise this morning. I have been walking across this beautiful forest of yours!"

He was speaking orally again now as he approached me.

"It's not really mine ya know, the forest. It's good to be home though!"

"I know, it's always nice to go home. I have experienced the same happiness many times.

We walked down the hill together, through the cut to the forest.

"You have grown a little since we met," he grinned. "The experience on the train home."

"You know about that?"

The question was rhetorical and made me feel ashamed of my recent deeds.

His smile and thoughts told me that my feelings of guilt were naïve, and my indulgence had been a natural response, without malice or disrespect to anyone.

We crossed the road below the railway bridge spanning Manchester Road, and walked up the hill that ran along the railway embankment. The yellow gorse flowers braved the autumn frosts and the dying bracken was copper brown, crushed by the winds and rain. The forest was never a bleak place for me, the contrasting colours of the dying leaves on the deciduous trees set against groups of green pines were quite stunning. It was my home and I knew it so well.

At the top of the hill the railway line ran through the cutting that ran across the forest to Brockenhurst, the cutting where those old treacle mines had erupted many years before.

We crossed the footbridge across the railway and continued our walk north towards Longslade.

"You are focusing your telepathic abilities in your head, your brain, your ears and your eyes, you sense direction. Try to use your whole body to communicate, feel what I feel with every part of your body. You did it on the train if you recall."

I understood. I had shared all my senses with Sharon, I felt what she felt.

"What is it like on Erato?"

"For my people, spending time on Erato is like spending time in paradise. We live there in harmony with each other and with nature, it is my peoples' Garden of Eden.

"The planet is not dissimilar to Earth geographically as I have said, but larger.

"Only Terrans call it Erato, visitors from other words use their own names. Terrans renamed the planets in the time of Plato, almost three and a half thousand of your years ago.

"The name Erato is one of the nine Muses, goddesses in Greek mythology who control and symbolize the nine types of art known to the ancient Greeks. Erato is the Muse of lyric poetry, especially love and erotic poetry, she charms the sight.

"The other planets in our solar system are named after the other eight Muses, Calliope, Clio and Euterpe are the planets closer to our central sun Mnemosyne, Erato is the fourth planet and Melpomene is a relatively lifeless planet beyond Erato.

"Terran people refer to us as Erateans and our native language Eraean. We have only one native language, Erato is such a small part of the galaxy, and our people are migratory. Very few remain in one location long enough for regional dialects to develop."

"You do talk then, by mouth?"

"Of course, spoken language is a beautiful thing, but it is not possible over distance, telepathy is."

"I agree, talking is nice, and singing."

"We too sing when we come together," he acknowledged.

"Our collective knowledge is stored in what you might consider very sophisticated computer banks we call transcriptors."

I considered the chess set he had given me; I had known that a computer capable of playing chess existed, but it was a huge machine. The chess set he had given me was small enough to hold in my hand. Bernd had not known that my beautiful gift had actually been an intelligent machine, he had only recognised the craftsmanship.

"Your own development in computing technology is in its infancy, but it will develop exponentially I am sure. Transcriptors enable us to absorb large amounts of information at high speed, directly into the brain in the form of brain waves."

"Amazing!"

"It is the brain that is amazing my friend, you just don't know how to use it to its full capacity yet."

I reached into my trouser pocket and grasped my notebook.

"I have a notebook," I said holding it out for him to see. "I wrote down some questions that I wanted to ask you."

"Have I missed something? Let me see."

I handed him my notebook and he scanned it quickly as we walked.

"Ijani, one. What is the name of your planet? As I said, my home-world was named Erato by Terran migrants after the Greek Muse of lyric poetry.

"Feto, two. 'What are your people called?' My people are known as Eratean. You would not be able to pronounce or hear the melodic subtleties of the spoken language, there are subtle differences in our vocal and auditory capabilities.

"Mara, three. 'Are your people the only people on the planet or are there people from other planets?' There are other life forms on Erato, people from Earth, and from many other planets in the galaxy. Once invited, they may live more than one lifetime on our world if they wish, being reborn as Erateans. We are able to share physical pleasures, but it is not possible to interbreed naturally, and we have never considered it necessary to do so.

"It is not a common occurrence, but my people do invite alien life forms from worlds such as yours. Erato is more cosmopolitan than ancient Rome; however, time and space on our home-world is very precious. We only invite life forms from planets that have not developed galactic flight, those that value time and space on their world too."

"Rome?" I asked.

"Yes Rome. I was there when Constantine converted to Christianity in an attempt to bring order to the empire. The word cosmopolitan derives from the Greek word kosmopolitês, citizen of the world."

"You mean you were in Rome?"

"In Rome? Yes, it was my first trip in this life. I arrived here in the year Constantine became Emperor. Greece, Maya, China, Egypt and Samaria in previous lives. I have also spent time with lesser known communities, hunter-gatherers, nomadic pastoralists and tribal villages," he laughed.

"You have memories of your previous lives?"

"Extracts from our previous lives exist in the transcriptor databases. We are aware of our previous existence when we are born, and we can recall memories from them all; using the transcriptors we can experience much more vivid memories, much like you are able to recall distant memories by looking at photographs. When we die our physical form returns to Erato, and our soul is in a state of heaven. Heaven is not a place, it is access to every life you have ever lived, a chance to re-engage with every person you have ever known, relive every experience, say and do the things we wanted to have said and done. We exist in a timeless state until we feel the need to live another life in any time, past or future. Would you leave heaven, to be born again in another time and place?"

"I'm not sure about the time travel thing. How can you go back to the past? How can you go to the future if it's not happened, a single incident in the past could change either?"

"We believe that time begins and ends in a loop, so there is no beginning and no end, except that the cycle ends and restarts. Time is not a linear thing, it slows as it approaches any mass and no longer exists inside a black hole, where nothing escapes.

"Yes, there may be many possible futures, in a different universe. An infinite number of different universes that account for every alteration to the timeline. But for us there is only one future.

"Your people have a theory, the grandfather paradox, a paradox of time travel; if a person travels to the past and kills their own grandfather, before the conception of their father or mother, it would prevent the time-traveller's existence.

"Of course, one could wish to prevent their own birth and not care, but time cannot be destroyed. It can be speeded up, slowed down or even stopped, but it exists, more certainly than God.

"Time travel *can* exist because there is *no* paradox! If a person travels to the past, to a different timeline, and kills their own grandfather before the conception of their father or mother, everything that happened was always going to happen, in that time line. In the alternate timeline, the person leaves the time line and simply no longer exists there. Of course, if he could travel between alternate timelines, he could return to the first at the same point he left.

"When we want to live another mortal life, we wait for a new life to be conceived, possibly in a previous history or in a future millennium, most frequently a few years after our previous life ended."

It made sense, but there were still unanswered questions.

"Were you here when Jesus lived?" I asked going back to his previous comments.

"Jesus was only known to us for the brief period after he returned to his homeland. Many of my people who were close enough journeyed here to hear him speak, alas I was on Erato at the time and knew nothing of him until he had gone. There have been many of his kind, teachers and philosophers."

"Only creative sentient beings are invited to Erato, though we also try to find other developing worlds for endangered species. It is too dangerous to bring them to Erato. Every life form is a predator in some way, and such exercises can easily wipe out existing life forms. Perhaps a higher intelligence did the same once with our ancestors."

"You mean something planted our seed on a developing world?"

"Almost all the creative life forms we have encountered are essentially human in appearance and share a mammalian origin, some are oviparous, laying eggs that develop outside the body. Each has evolved from a different order. We are not all descended from primates.

"Logic tells us that an external influence probably brought about changes to the blocks of life across the galaxy. There were periods of rapid change and development in all our histories.

"It is not logical for so many species to be so similar in terms of size for example. The dinosaurs of your world grew to large sizes, as big as your blue whale.

"We are all made from the same building blocks, our blood may be different colours, but it pumps oxygen around our bodies and removes carbon dioxide just the same as yours. Our fauna turns carbon dioxide back to oxygen just as it does here. It is generally accepted that we have all evolved at least in part from common ancestors.

"Life will develop on any suitable planet given time but we all share a large proportion of what makes us who we are."

"Perhaps efficiency is drawing us together?" I suggested.

"Of course, that is without doubt highly significant."

"The core value of our philosophy is based upon improving knowledge, on our world and on other civilisations that we encounter; however, that is not a simple process.

"We have worked at times with some of your people, in the hope that they will use the information we give them for the benefit of all. Alas, your race has adopted a world of commerce that never existed on Erato, and it is that world of commerce that is holding back scientific discoveries that will one day change your way of life forever.

"We try not to become involved in the wars of other worlds, provided they are confined to their own world; however, we do from time to time intervene in an attempt to preserve peace.

"We have never encountered interplanetary war.

"Homo Sapiens are an advanced lifeform but we will discuss more of peoples and civilisations later.

"Even with the technology we possess, there are still millions of solar systems we have not visited.

"Apri, four. Are there any people from Earth on your planet? I think we have both covered that one.

"Maius, five. 'When will you go home?' Yes, I think I *will* go home soon, perhaps very soon. It depends on what happens over the coming weeks and months here.

"Iuni, six. 'How fast does your ship fly? Warp factor 10!' That is an interesting question.

"Your people have recently sent ships to Luna, your moon, two hundred and fifty thousand miles from Earth. I could reach it in less than two seconds and be outside your Solar System in less than thirty; light from Pluto takes almost four hours to travel the same distance. Theoretically, on a longer trip, such as coming here to Earth, we can travel at much faster speeds but that is because we are folding time and space.

"Iuli, seven. 'Do you have any weapons on board? We carry no weapons of war, but then what defines a weapon? The stone there on the ground could be a weapon; on the other hand, it could also be a tool. There is much on board my ship that could cause enormous destruction, and in the wrong hands could be considered an extremely powerful and dangerous weapon. For my people, they are tools.

"Ugu, eight. 'If you have no war and no crime is there any one or any race that you fear?' We have no crime, there is no need for anyone of my people, or our visitors to Erato to want for anything, we own nothing, so nothing can be stolen. With many life times, my people find it more difficult to limit their ambitions than to fulfil them. We fear no race, our people die as I have already explained, sometimes at the hands of your people or the other races we encounter.

"Is that the fault of those that kill, or should we simply not have been there. We accept responsibility for our actions and the consequences of our mistakes.

"Seta, nine. 'Are you the most advanced lifeform that you have discovered?' We are always searching for lifeforms more intelligent than ourselves, in particular, a race that we know once existed on our world.

"Oko, ten. 'Why do your people travel across space to Earth?' Why are we here? Terrans are an interesting race, you struggle with life because you conceal your thoughts, yet you still possess great love for each other, even to the point of sacrificing your life to save another. Even those you would condemn for heinous crimes possess the capacity for love. You are all trapped in a world of isolation; in desperation and frustration many of you seek pleasure in your darkest thoughts and emotions, knowing the barriers you put between yourselves will conceal it."

"There are some crimes that are unforgivable." I interrupted.

"Is that so?" he asked. "For us, isolation is itself the greatest crime, and the worst punishment at the same time. In order to hide one's thoughts one must block the thoughts of others. For us, living in isolation without hearing the thoughts of others is worse than living in a world without sight and sound in yours. My people would without doubt, choose to end their life rather than break one of our unspoken laws."

"Commit suicide you mean?" I asked.

"We Erateans have the ability to simply shutdown our physical life if we feel that we have achieved all that we wanted. Something similar frequently happens here on Earth; you would call it 'losing the will to live'. It often happens when a lifelong partner dies, and the other no longer enjoys life without them."

He allowed me a moment to absorb what he had said before continuing.

"And the unspoken laws?" I asked.

"They are unspoken, because we have no need to repeat them. We know them instinctively when we are born; we have no preachers or law makers. We will speak of these unspoken laws soon since you are not of our world."

"Like our Ten Commandments?"

He chuckled.

"The Ten Commandments pertain only to Jewish and Christian beliefs, other Terran religions have their own specific laws and beliefs. Shall I finish"

"Please do."

"Novo, eleven. 'Are there more than two kinds of any life form, male and female?' There are species both here on Earth and across the galaxy that could be classed as asexual or hermaphrodite.

"We have not encountered any advanced life forms of the asexual type but there are many hermaphrodite species.

"There are the sequential hermaphrodites, protandry where the organism starts as a male, and changes sex to a female later in life; and protogyny, where the organism starts as a female and changes sex to a male later in life. There are also simultaneous or synchronous hermaphrodite species that has both male and female sexual organs at the same time.

"There are occurrences of asymmetrical gonadal dysgenesis within a species, a condition where gonadal development is abnormal.

"Deo, twelve. 'Have your people ever harmed human life?' I have already told you that none of my people has ever consciously harmed a

Terran life form in forty thousand of your years. Like Homo Sapiens we are essentially hunter gatherers. When my people first arrived here they shared this world with Sapiens at a time when they too were highly telepathic. That changed forty thousand years ago when Sapiens began to hide their thoughts from us and then from each other. We still hunt for food on Erato and on other less developed worlds, where game is abundant and no one life form dominates the planet. Since that time, we have never hunted game here.

"Any more questions?"

"About the sexual classification of life forms? No not just yet," I grinned. "I'm still working on the sequential hermaphrodites."

"And if there had been another question? What number would that have been? He asked.

"Thirteen, dijani. Ijani, feto, mara, apri, maius, iuni, iuli, ugu, seta, oko, novo, deo; dijani, defeto, demar, dapri, demai, diuni, diuli, deugu, deseta, deoko, deono. You use base twelve."

"It is good," said Victor. "You are an enigma; you learn quickly."

I realised that he had two distinct personas; one minute he was a playfully sarcastic clown, teasing me, laughing at my responses, the next he would turn into a monastic teacher, bombarding me with an excess of information; but he knew I was eager to learn, I had coasted my way through school, the subjects I enjoyed I excelled at without effort, and the things that bored me I treated with contempt. He knew what I was thinking, and I understood his dryness.

"Sapiens have used base ten since first understanding numbers, you have ten digits on your hands and feet," he continued. "Mathematics is much easier in base twelve. Twelve is a highly composite number, divisible by; one, two, three, four, six, and twelve, it is also a simple division by eight, being two thirds, or nine being three quarters, and even ten being one sixth. Only five is not a simple multiple.

"The numbers you use are Hindu-Arabic developed around AD500; base ten, because you have ten fingers. The Greeks and Romans also used a base ten system but used letters to represent numbers, which is fine for counting tally, but useless for mathematics.

"The Babylonians adopted our system of mathematics, which at that time was sexagesimal, base sixty, it survives today in the usage of your measurement of time; sixty seconds in a minute, sixty minutes in an hour, and three hundred and sixty degrees in a circle. Sixty is a superior highly composite number, with factors of; one, two, three, four, six, and twelve, as is base twelve; but it is also divisible by five, ten, fifteen and thirty. We still use base sixty for complicated mathematics, but it is not used in our daily lives; base twelve is much more practical.

"Unlike the Romans and the Greeks, the Babylonians also had a true place-value system, with digits written in the left column representing larger values. This system clearly required a zero as a place holder; early use of the system simply left a space, later it was given a symbol. The use of a separator, or decimal point as it is called here, was realised by John Napier of Merchiston, born circa 1550, died April 4th, 1617. He was best known as the inventor of the logarithms you learned in school. He also invented a manually-operated calculating device for the calculation of products and quotients of numbers; the forerunner of the slide rule."

I was not yet fully aware of the fact, but I had been able to absorb all that he said. As he spoke he simultaneously transmitted everything he knew about the subject, implanting his knowledge directly into my memory. It was a time of transition, things that I had never heard of became clear to me and I could recall them all afterwards. I also sensed there was still more he was not telling me.

"What about bees, queens, drones and worker bees," I asked, remembering what Andy had said on the trip home.

"What about them? The Queen is responsible for laying the eggs that will grow into drones or workers. The drones are males, their role is to mate with the queen after which they will die. Half their abdomen will be ripped away as they attempt to fly away, because the barbs on the endophallus have locked it inside the queen. The workers are all female that lack full reproductive capacity."

"Are there any advanced life forms that breed that way," I asked.

"Not that we know of, he answered.

# INVITATION

We walked on in silence for a short while as I gathered my thoughts.

"How did you know where to find me?"

"Our transcriptors contain details of every domicile on Earth and associate it with its geographical co-ordinates. We have maps," he said with a broad grin. "To be truthful, when you left the hotel we shook hands.

"You may recall that I placed my left hand on the back of your neck. When I did, I placed a minute transmitter just beneath the skin. You would need some very sophisticated equipment to detect its output. It is not a radio transmitter, it is based on our transcriptor technology and it transmits on the same frequencies as the brain.

"Your people do not have the technology to intercept and decode this type of signal, but an electromagnetic signature could be detected."

I knew it was too much of a coincidence that he had turned up so conveniently.

"How did you get here? Where is your ship?"

"Up there, high enough to be out of harm's way," he said looking up into the sky. "I control the ship with thought."

I was becoming accustomed to the constant references to technologies that seemed impossible.

"So what now? What happens to the transmitter inside me?"

"It can stay there indefinitely, it will do you no harm. Who knows when I might want to find you again?"

I could see no reason to worry about it, he didn't have to tell me it was there. We walked over the railway bridge and off towards the woods.

"Do you mind if I ask you some questions now?" Victor broke the silence.

"Of course not!"

"Were you expecting the accident?"

"Are you crazy?"

"I know you didn't walk straight into it knowing what was going to happen but were you warned of danger?"

"How did you know?" I asked.

"You were then?"

"Yes, I was. My friend Paul, Paul Caveat, he warned me. He reads Tarot cards, predicts the future."

"And he read the cards for you?"

"No! No he didn't, I picked up his cards that was all. It scares me that hocus-pocus, it's like witchcraft. How can someone see into the future?"

"We all do from time to time."

"We do?"

"Yes, you dream, you don't usually remember the dreams but sometimes those very deep dreams can give you a glimpse of the future. You have experiences sometimes believing that you have seen something before, a situation, a scene, someone saying something. It is known to your people as déjà vu."

"Yes, I know, recently I've been experiencing that kind of thing more than ever before. My friend, Sam, she has experienced things about me, but we hardly know each other."

"I think I may have an explanation for that, but I cannot be sure and now would not be the time to tell you."

"Why?"

"Because I may be wrong, and I have no desire to corrupt your future with my thoughts or values."

"What do you mean?"

"I mean that, your life is your own and it is you that must decide which path you will follow. If I were to point you in the wrong direction it would be my responsibility, you could blame me for the mistake and with just cause, such things are forbidden by my people."

A group of New Forest ponies, normally very shy creatures, walked over to us and began to follow very closely. Victor stopped and turned around, and one of the horses pushed its nose into his hands. They stood motionless for a minute or two, then the horse moved away and the others followed.

"What was that all about?" I asked.

"She was in pain and I answered her, now she has no pain. It was not serious."

We crossed the road and walked down the slopes towards Longslade Bottom.

"What made you think I had been warned?" I asked.

"Have you forgotten? I can read your thoughts and besides, it was not entirely accidental that I was in the Persian Gulf when you had your accident."

"You mean, it wasn't an accident? Did you cause it?"

"No of course not, and as far as I am aware it *was* an accident. I have been following Paul Caveat for nearly twelve years now. We believe there are beings here that are not from our world or any world we know, they are the people I referred to earlier. We also believe that they possess powers even beyond our understanding. They no longer exist on Erato, but we know they once did. We have stories of our past, myths and legends even old records which refer to them, but no-one understands what happened to these people. I believe Paul is one of these people, we know them as Malakhi."

"Maluky? You think Paul is a Maluky?" I interrupted.

"Mal-ah-kai, ah like apple and kai like buy," he corrected me. "And yes, I believe Paul is a Malahk. Mal-ah-kai, Mal-ahk."

"Mal-ah-kai, Mal-ahk," I echoed.

As we reached the open grassland of Longslade he stopped and turned to face me.

"In terms of scientific evolution, my people were at the same stage of development as your people, over seven hundred thousand Terran years ago. It took Erateans less than two hundred of your years to move from our first space flight to reaching out into the galaxy. We have been visiting your planet for seven hundred and eighty thousand years.

"Your people have taken ten thousand years to achieve what took us less than one thousand and that is essentially because you live in a world of commerce.

"We are willing to share our knowledge with your people, but it can only be done slowly and with great care. Your people continue their attempts to reverse engineer our captured ships and technologies; however, they can only do so at the rate existing technology improves. They use developing methods to emulate the results step by step.

"Too much information and Sapiens would almost certainly have destroyed themselves. We never involved ourselves with your wars, judgement is our most revered law, that is, it is forbidden to judge anyone."

He sensed my puzzlement about what that implied but did not stop to explain himself further.

"We have been aware of the Malakhi for almost a million years, but they disappeared from our planet around the period we moved out into the galaxy and we do not know why.

"We believe that they are a much more advanced race although we have never studied one of these beings.

We walked on through the remains of the red brick railway bridge, its top demolished when the old railway line was decommissioned.

"So you think Paul is Malakhi?" I asked.

"He may be."

"So why did you follow me and not Paul? Paul is not on the Grenadier, I have been told he is on the Poplar in Jamaica."

"Because Paul told me six years ago that I would find my reborn son if I kept track of her. I suspected you may be in danger. I have been waiting for such an incident to occur."

"The Skipper from Grey Mackenzie, Eric, the guy on board Grayswift when I had the accident, he told me that the crew of the Grenadier had sighted a ship like yours back in sixty-nine. Was that you?" I asked.

"Yes, that was me. I remember tracking down the Grenadier, but not really knowing what I was looking for. At the time, there was another young cadet like you, he had fallen down a stairway between decks and was heavily concussed. What the crew did not know was that he had suffered a subdural haematoma."

'A swelling around the brain caused by bleeding from the cerebral veins,' he thought in parallel with his words

"He could have slipped into a coma and died, but fortunately I was there to help."

"You saved him?" I asked.

"I helped him stop the bleeding and relief the pressure, that is all," he answered. "I thought perhaps he was the person I was seeking so I spent a few days searching the ship for some clue. I soon realised I would have to wait and I have been following the Grenadier ever since."

"You were looking for someone? Me?"

"Perhaps."

"Do you think Paul is trying to harm me?" I asked.

"That makes no sense," he said. "The Malakhi are considered a pacifist race. I do not believe there was any intention to cause you harm."

"So where will you go from here? Back to Paul or back to the Grenadier?"

"Perhaps I will stay here for a while. I think my reasons for coming to Earth may be close to a conclusion and I feel the need to be with one of my kind again."

"A woman?"

"Yes, a woman. I would like to raise another child and I would like to share some time with a partner. I long to feel a woman's flesh beside me when I wake, and the pleasure of physical intimacy. I also hunger for the taste of freshly killed game, the thrill of the hunt and the blood warm livers eaten raw at the kill. I have been away for a long time my friend and I grow weary of the taste of nuts and berries. We have always been hunter gatherers just as you have, the difference is that we only eat wild game, and we have the greatest respect for the animals we hunt. Your people have in the main become accustomed to sanitised meat production, you no longer know what you are eating or how the animal lived its life."

"There must be billions of you, how do you manage not over populating your world?"

"We have, we number over two thousand billion. You know of course that your American cousins describe that as two trillion. The Eratean peoples are now spread all over the Galaxy as are the other visitors I spoke of. We hope we will soon possess the knowledge to move out of the Galaxy across the Universe."

"Could I come with you? To Erato?"

"That is a question I have hoped you would ask. I would be very happy to take you, if you wanted to come, but that is a very big decision and you will need time to reflect. I would need to be certain you understand the implications. By the time you could get back here at least fourteen years would have past, probably much more assuming you did not return immediately, and you would only appear days older. Your mother, father, brother and your sisters would all be older, perhaps even no longer alive."

"You're right it's a big decision and I need some time to think about it. Speaking of my father, is there anything that you can do to ease his pain?"

"I want you to consider that while I am gone. I want you to try to focus your thoughts each day. Find somewhere where you can sit and meditate. Clear your mind of what is around you and discover your inner thoughts."

"If I wanted to come with you, could I bring someone with me?"

"You have a friend you would like to come too?"

"Well it's early days but there is this girl, I can't explain it but we both seem to know things about the other and we believe we were meant to be together."

"Yes, the girl, of course! Tell me more about this girl. Is she telepathic?"

"I'm not sure, perhaps she is."

I began by telling him how beautiful she was and described the way she looked, smiled and spoke. I even described her meticulous hand writing to him.

He listened with great interest to everything I had to say, then told me he would have to leave and would be gone for a week or more. He said I needed time to consider where my future lay; he also wanted to find Paul and ask him to go to Erato with him, although he had little hope that Paul would go with him, even if he were able to find him.

I had enough to consider. I had to go to London to see Le Fevre and I desperately wanted to see Sam. If I were to leave with Victor, she would probably be my greatest consideration, I would find it hard to go without her. It appeared she felt the same way for me as I felt for her. I wasn't sure if I could leave her behind if she would not go with me.

We walked across the back of Longslade, close to the outbuilding where I had met the old tramp, but turned west through the wooded enclosures, talking about my childhood and the places I had played. Victor seemed very interested to hear about my childhood and particularly the way I spoke about the forest. As we walked he pointed out the fauna, flora and fungi that I had never noticed, explaining how each reproduced, what could be safely eaten and what could not, and those that possessed medicinal qualities. It seemed I did not really know my forest as well as I thought. Eventually I turned for home leaving Victor to himself near the edge of Wilverley Plain.

\* \* \*

Mum and Dad were content to let me find my feet again, they never pushed me to talk and I found it difficult to open up. I wasn't ready to talk to them about Victor, it would only worry them into thinking that I was suffering from some deep mental trauma as a result of the accident, perhaps I had. The only way I could be certain was for Victor to meet someone else. I desperately needed to speak to John and for him to see Victor for himself.

# FEAR

Thursday ~ 22nd November 1973

The next day John came in on his way to work, he had Mary and Jane with him, they were going to stay with Mum and Dad for the day.

"Well I have written a letter to B.P., Mary and I have discussed it and she will pop up to the post office for a stamp and post it today."

My father had always been proud of my decision to go to sea. John, Jean and Jane had all been eighteen when they married, none of them had stretched their wings and seen the world. It pleased him immensely to think that perhaps John would follow me into the Merchant Navy.

"So Higgs, do you fancy coming in with me today? I could do with a hand, I've got a Land Rover to re-spray for the S.R.G."

The Solent Rescue Group were an inshore rescue team that assisted in minor sea rescues in the Solent. John had been a member in his teens and still kept in contact with the guy that ran it.

"Sounds like a good idea son. Why don't you spend the day with your brother, you could be off again next week, and he might well be off when you get back."

"Yeah I'd like to. But I must be back by five, I have an appointment with Dr Stevens at 5.30."

"That should be okay," said John.

"Are you off now?"

"Soon as I've had a cup of tea."

John lived with Mary and Jane at his in-law's house in Ringwood. Mary's father, George, was a dairyman and lived in a good-sized tied farmhouse. They all got on well together, John had been dating Mary since they were sixteen, spending most of his weekends with them during the two years that they lived in Cirencester before they were married. He still liked coming home for a cup of tea on his way through to work, although he was normally provided with a farmhouse breakfast by Fran, Mary's mother. George would have already done the early morning milking when they sat down for breakfast.

I finished my breakfast while John drank his tea then we set off for Brockenhurst.

I didn't really know how to begin my story, so I let John do all the talking. We started work as soon as we got there, he had already sprayed the roof of the Land Rover in its navy-blue rescue livery and refitted the newly sprayed secondary roof panel, the rest of the body work was to be sprayed bright orange.

"Stick her up then Higgs and I'll mask up the underside."

I walked across to the Land Rover and pushed up on the ramp control lever. It was something I'd done many times before. I stared out of the open doors at the front of the garage and saw some of my school friends walking by on their way from the station to the college. It seemed like years had passed since I had spoken to them.

"James!" John's voice screamed out from his small office in the corner of the workshop.

I let go of the handle at the shock and the ramp stopped.

"What the fuck have you done? Get it down!"

I hadn't noticed the sound of metal against metal as the Land Rover's roof touched the steel garage roof strut.

John came running across the workshop and pulled the lever down before his words registered.

"Couldn't you hear it? What the hell am I going to do now? This is a brand-new Land Rover."

He glanced at the distorted roof panel then went silently to his tool box, picked out a two-pound hammer and walked out the back of the workshop. I remember hearing the bang of metal against metal. I went outside to see what he was doing. When I reached the back door, I could see he was smashing the hammer into an old engine block, again and again, with a slow purposeful rhythm.

'Don't say anything! Just don't say a damn thing!'

John wasn't saying it, although his words were almost inevitable, his thoughts were so focused that I could read his mind. Along with his anger there was a deeper emotion, his anger was simply the symptom of his desperation and fear, he was ultimately responsible for the damage.

He continued smashing into the engine block until he regained his composure, then turned to face me, anger released.

"Ok, let's take a look at the damage!"

We went back into the garage together and John studied the twisted roof panel.

"It's ok, I think I can fix it up. The actual roof's untouched, all I need to do is pull out the crease on the secondary roof panel and re-spray it, they'll never know."

"I'm sorry mate."

"What were you doing?"

"I'm sorry John, I wasn't concentrating."

The Land Rover was higher than any vehicle I had put up on the ramp before; a saloon car would go right to the top and still have two or three feet clearance. Luckily, the ramp had reached its limit, having only hit the secondary roof panel. If it had gone any further the actual vehicle roof would have been damaged and major repairs would have been needed, perhaps it would even have been a write off.

"We'll leave the roof until tomorrow," he said. "Let's get the body sprayed today."

He sprayed the lower body with the bright orange paint, and when that was done we went over to the pub for lunch.

"Pint please Tom. What are you drinking these days?" John asked.

"Same as you."

"Make that two please Tom."

"Glad to see you're alright James. John told us about your accident."

"It's good to be back." I answered.

233

"Don't mention the damage," whispered John. "They're lovely guys but they will think nothing of telling other customers and I really don't need any bad publicity, I need every penny I can get to set Mary up before I go to sea."

"I'm sorry."

"Forget it, no-one's ever gonna know. I panicked."

"I think I got that."

"Let's hope I can join you in the Merch'," he said picking up his beer. "Cheers bruv!"

He sipped at it smiling but shaking his head, still in disbelief at what had happened. I waited for Tom to move out of earshot before talking.

"John, I need to talk to you."

"Ok let's go and sit down then, we'll get some bread and cheese from the Island shop later."

I sat down at a table by the window. John put some money in the juke box then sat down with me.

"What's up then mate?"

I filled him in with the gaps of my adventures, everything that I had left out at home. I left nothing out, the girl on the train, Sam, and everything that I knew about Victor. John sat in silence until I had finished, by then we were on our second pint and I was much more relaxed.

"My little brother has grown up and seen more of life than I have. Shit mate what do you want me to say? Are you takin' the piss or what? I believe your story about the girl on the train and of course I have seen Sam, but aliens? Flying saucers? That's probably just a bit too much for me to accept. It's not a good place to talk here where we can be heard. Let's talk some more about it when we get back to the workshop."

We finished our beer and stopped off at the shop to buy the fresh bread, cheese and tomatoes and took them back to his office as we often did.

# PHYSICAL EVIDENCE

Back in his office I repeated my encounters with Victor. Any paranoia was long past, I was entirely confident that everything I had told him was true. If I was suffering from a delusion, it was so powerful that there were no doubts in my mind. Of course, I failed to realise at the time that this is the essence of a delusion.

"Victor will be back soon and then you can see him for yourself. In the meantime, I have a present for you," I said pulling Sharon's black lace knickers out of my pocket and throwing them to him.

He grinned waving the knickers under his nose and the faint sex of womanhood convinced him that at least some part of my story was true.

"Keep 'um or throw 'um away," I said. "I don't want them."

"And you think I do? What the hell do you think Mary would say if she found me with these? No thanks Bro," he laughed. "They're your trophy and covered in your cum, you keep 'um or chuck 'um away yourself," he said throwing them back.

"Well take a look at this," I said producing the chess set from the bag I had with me.

He examined the box before removing the lid.

"What's it made of?" he asked.

"What do you think it's made of?"

"Silver? No, it's too light. Silver plate? It's definitely metallic, what is it?"

He opened the lid and saw the intricately formed chess pieces inside.

"Well it looks like a very expensive miniature chess set to me. It's beautiful! I assume this is the chess set that Victor gave you? And this?" he asked pulling the small key from its slot.

"That's the key," I said, taking it from him and inserting it into the functional slot. "Move a piece."

He picked up the Queens Knight and moved it out in front of the queen's bishop; the square under the opposing king's pawn and the one two squares in front of it, both glowed red. Instinctively he moved the pawn forwards and the red glow stopped.

"Well I've heard about computers being able to play chess, but I've never seen one, certainly nothing this small."

He lifted the pawn again and put it down sensing the pull.

"The weight doesn't match the size of these pieces, they must be magnetic?"

He tipped the board slightly and nothing moved. He continued turning the board until it was upside down and the pieces remained firmly seated to the base.

"There must be some steel or nickel in this stuff but it's so light."

He walked out of the office over to his toolbox and picked up a magnet that he kept for retrieving dropped nuts and bolts.

"It has no effect on the chess pieces," he said testing the pieces on it.

He tried the magnet against the box with the same result.

"Do you have some acid in the old batteries outside?" I asked.

"You're not going to tip acid on it and ruin it are you?" he asked in alarm.

"I really don't think it will. Just get me a few drops. It may not be metal at all."

He found an old coffee jar which seemed clean enough for our needs, then went out to the back of the garage to where the old tyres and batteries were piled up. He returned with half an inch of old battery acid in the jar. Meanwhile I had found the end of a welding rod and a plastic spoon in the bin.

I removed all the pieces and placed them in the lid for safe keeping, then turned the board upside down and spooned a small amount of acid out of the jar. I dipped the welding rod into the acid hoping to transfer a single drop with the end, but it fizzed around it, neutralizing the acid as it made contact.

"Give me the spoon," said Martin.

He took the spoon to the sing in workshop and rinsed of the residue of acid.

"Here you do it, it's your box. Just use the handle."

Using the plastic spoon the other way around, I applied a small drop of the acid to the base.

To our amazement, the acid drop formed into a spherical bubble and rolled around on the base like a droplet of mercury on glass. I tilted the base and ran the drop back into the coffee jar, the base was completely dry and unaffected.

"Perhaps the acid is too diluted," suggested John.

"So why is it forming into balls of liquid like that? I've never seen that before," I answered.

He put his hand in his pocket and produced a handful of change, picking out a particularly oxidised two pence piece from the selection of coins. He laid the coin on an old magazine and applied a similar amount of the acid solution to the coin face. The reaction was completely different. The drops spread instantly across the surface burning away the thin discoloured layer of oxidized material, revealing the brightly minted surface.

We looked at each other in amazement and John re-examined the chessboard. There was not even the slightest mark on it. He went out into the workshop and brought back a small needle file, then he picked up the base again and tried to scratch the bottom corner with the sharp tip.

"Nothing!" he said examining it. "Do you mind if I try to file a small nick on the corner edge here?"

"Be my guest," I answered.

He placed the file across the corner edge on the bottom face of the board and slowly slid it forwards. After confirming that the board was unmarked, he retried the experiment with a heavier stroke.

"Not a bloody scratch!" he exclaimed. "Ok! I'll buy it for now. Don't let anyone else see this just yet."

He handed me back the board but never released it; taking it back, he took the key from its slot, held the board beneath his desk lamp, and stared into the small opening.

"Can't see a damn thing! It looks solid to me."

I repacked the chess set and returned it to my bag.

After that, he never questioned anything I had told him, there was no doubt in his mind that I had told him the truth.

"I want you to meet Victor. First I need you to tell me I'm not losing my mind."

"I don't think so Higgins, not any more. When and where?"

"As soon as he gets back."

"Ok, but what's all this about you wanting to go to his planet? Doesn't that scare you?"

"Sure, I'm scared, but it excites me too. I'm not sure about going though. I'm rather keen on Sam or had you forgot."

"Take her with you!"

"I had considered that, maybe she would come with me."

"If she won't go, I will!" he replied without realising the consequences of such a journey.

There was so much to think about. He joked with me about the sexual episode on the train home while we ate the fresh baked bread, cheese and tomatoes.

"Think nothing of it Bro, I know you want to take her to another planet, but you haven't even had a date with Sam and she will never know! It was a one off," he said. "Besides no one would say you've done anything wrong, not even Sam."

John was a grafter and he had a job to do, so we didn't discuss anything more until he had rubbed down the Land Rover, ready for its second coat, and then we set off for home in the car.

"Are you going to tell Mum and Dad?" John asked.

"Not yet, at least not till you've seen Victor."

"Jesus, I still can't believe it."

"I'm not sure I do, but time will tell."

# OBSERVATION

I walked up to the surgery on my own, leaving John to talk with Mum and Dad.

Doctor Stevens was well-known to everyone in my family, he made regular visits to my father when he was suffering badly with his arthritis. He was a very tall man with a permanent hunched posture, probably due to constantly having to bend his head when he passed through most doorways.

He checked my blood pressure, examined my eyes and throat, then listened to my chest. We chatted for a while about the accident, and because he was such a good Doctor, he soon had me telling him more about the injuries to my hand than I intended to. He had no detailed records of the incident to refer to, so he didn't know exactly what took place that night; however, even with the brief letter he had he became curious having examined my hands and arms.

"Apart from the finger nail there is no trace of any cuts at all, not even a scar. From what you have told me I would expect to see some residual scarring especially around the knuckle and fingers, I really don't understand it!"

He examined both my arms and the fingernail again, even more thoroughly than the first time, then shook his head.

"Anything else bothering you?" he asked.

"Actually, I have had some pain going to the toilet."

"Urinating?

"Yes."

"Let's take a quick look at you then. Drop your trousers and take a seat on the couch."

I did as he asked, and he began his examination.

239

"How long have you had this discharge," he asked.

I looked down to see what he meant. I had not noticed it, but there was a very small cream coloured spot of mucus at the end of my penis.

"Ok, you can pull your trousers up now," he said, having finished his inspection. "It looks like you have picked up some sort of infection. I am going to give you a prescription for some penicillin, take two a day after breakfast. I'll sign you off work for two weeks; that was a nasty experience you went through out there. I think both you and your parents deserve a short break before they drag you off to sea again. We can have another chat again next week if you could make another appointment on your way out. I'd just like to take a blood and urine sample if you could oblige, I'll have the results when I see you next week." he said.

He actually took several blood samples, filling four small glass vials, then he gave me a small bottle and asked me to pop into the toilet and provide a urine sample.

On my walk home, I realised how difficult it had been trying to keep any mention of Victor from the Doctor when questioned. I knew I could not expect my Doctor to place the same trust in my sanity without producing the chess set, but of course I didn't want him to know anyway. I would have to take special care not to give him any more clues when we met the following week, or he could complicate things.

# COLLUSION

## FIRST WORDS

Friday arrived and there had been no sign of Victor. I received a letter of invitation to receive my GCSE and CSE certificates at my school prize-giving at seven o'clock on December 7th. It would be good to see my friends again, so much had happened, and since I could be about to leave behind everything I knew, it would be nice to get a chance to say goodbye to them.

That morning I took the train to Southampton to go shopping. Dad would have taken me, but this time I wanted to do things myself without asking him his opinion. I bought myself a replacement suit, less conservative this time; a new pair of shoes and a new cassette recorder, all slightly more expensive than their predecessors, but no-one would know that. I wasn't sure I would ever need any of them if I was to leave with Victor, but until I had made a decision I had to keep up appearances, and BP were expecting receipts for replacing my losses.

On the train home, I found myself getting more and more anxious about Sam. I would have to meet with Le Fevre the following Friday, so I decided the best thing to do was call her before I did, so that we could at least talk. I decided to use the phone box down the road, not wanting Mum or Dad to overhear me. I would need to go home and get the number for Britannic House, showing off my new clothes would have to wait if I were to catch her before she went home.

I stopped off briefly at home and dropped off my shopping, grabbing one of Le Fevre's letters with the phone number on it from my bedroom. Dad noticed I had the paper in my hand and I was sure he had put two and two together, having been there when Sam gave John the private letter. He didn't mention her, nor did he suggest I use our own phone when I said I was going to the phone box.

A friend had shown me how to tap out the required number on the receiver when using the public phone, paying nothing for the call, not that I had told my family of that fact.

The phone call was uncomfortable for both of us, despite the fact that we had both declared our feelings for each other, and both knowing more about each other than we could explain.

Sam knew I had received her letter and by then she had received mine.

Standing in the phone box, I tried desperately to read her thoughts, but it was impossible. Without seeing her it just wasn't the same, I couldn't focus my mind.

I was nervous, and she couldn't talk from the office, so she gave me the number of the call box in her street and asked me to call her at seven o'clock that evening.

# SHREWD

"Sam, would you be an angel and get me a cup of coffee please? I haven't finished yet and I need something to perk me up. Grab one for yourself if you want."

The coffee from the executive lounge was a rich black Italian blend that was very different from the coffee in the canteen, or worse still in the automatic vending machines scattered around the building.

"Certainly Cap'n."

She was the only person in the building permitted to abbreviate his rank. He would call her Sam when they were alone, but always Samantha in company. Likewise, Sam would always call him Captain or Sir when they were not alone.

When she returned, he was busy in his own office, but the interconnecting door was open, so she walked straight in.

"Thank you so much," he said, sipping the strong espresso. "I needed that."

"Actually Sir, I have a suggestion I'd like to put to you about Friday's meeting with Cadet Cummings and his father."

"Go on," he answered. He often took her advice when dealing with cadets, valuing the fact that she understood the people of her generation better than he did, male or female.

"Well Sir, I know that you want to get Cummings back on board a ship before he loses his confidence; to me it seems that the longer he stays at home surrounded by his family, the less likely he is to want to leave.

"Since he's coming up to London anyway it might be a good idea to invite him to stay for a night or two. I would be very happy to show him around, he must be so relieved to be back safe in his own environment, it might be an opportunity to get him away from home."

"Perhaps you're right, you are such a clever girl. Call him. Ask him if he would like to spend the weekend up here. If he does, book him into a decent hotel for the weekend and get him a travel warrant for Sunday. Let's keep him away from home as long as possible. What time are we seeing him?"

"11.30," she answered.

"Well we will be finished by lunch time, you can take the afternoon off if you like."

"I could. Actually, I had thought about asking him if he would like to stay with me and my brother Kevin. He's coming up from Warsash on Friday evening. I told him what happened to Cummings and he said he would be happy to talk to him about life at sea, remind him what he wanted. Kevin said he would sleep on the couch and Cummings could have his room."

He cleared his throat somewhat taken aback by her concern.

"That's very maternal of you," he said, exaggerating the age difference between us, "but very shrewd, getting Kevin involved. Call him and see what he says. Let me know when you have."

"Certainly Sir."

She went out to the office closing the door behind her.

She turned her notebook towards her, standing in front of her desk rather than behind it, picked up the phone and entered 911111111 on the push buttoned base.

"Hello Mrs Cummings. This is Samantha Cooper, Captain Le Fevre's personal secretary at BP Tanker Company.

"Yes

"Yes thank you.

"Yes, I am sure you are.

"Yes, extremely brave. We were all worried about him.

"Yes please, if he's there?

"Ah, I see. That's not a problem. I'll call again early in the morning if that's ok.

"Yes. Yes of course. Friday the 30th, 11.30.

"Tomorrow then.

"Goodbye Mrs Cummings.

"You too, take care."

She put down the phone and tapped on his door.

"Come!"

"Sorry Sir, I tried calling Cummings as you asked, unfortunately he's out with his brother and won't be back until after five. I said I would call again tomorrow morning."

"It's Saturday tomorrow," he reminded her.

"Yes I know. I can call from the phone box at home. I think it would be best to give him as much time to think about it as possible.

"Thank you Sam, you're such a big help to me," he smiled.

# ELATION

"Hi, it's me. Is that you?"

"Of course it's me. Were you expecting someone else?" she laughed.

We were both much more relaxed, knowing that we both desperately wanted to see each other, and both strongly attracted to each other.

"You're sixteen, your birthday is May 2nd and you are Taurean; I checked your file, but only to confirm what I already knew."

"You are nineteen, a Virgo and your birthday is the 8th of September," I replied.

I remembered the moment in Ferris' classroom when I first knew how old she was.

"I found it hard to believe I could fall for a sixteen-year-old but somehow it doesn't matter," she said.

"Yu know for a day or two I thought I had fallen for the nurse on the Worcester, and she must have been almost forty, so I have no problem falling for a nineteen-year-old."

Her laugh reassured me. She told me that she had heard all about the infamous Nursie from gossiping Cadets, some had even boasted of more than friendship with the woman.

She told me about her plan and I teased her about being so devious.

If Le Fevre knew about it, I thought my parents would swallow it. It seemed like a great plan.

"Oh, one thing. Kevin won't be there." she added. "He does know about you and what happened, but I want you all to myself next weekend."

I did not need to feel her thoughts to conclude that it would probably not be an entirely platonic weekend.

We agreed Sam should call me at home in the morning as planned. I would expect the call around 8.30 and be ready to answer her call, my

246

mother would know that the call was probably for me. We would then go through her proposal.

I had no reason to suspect that my parents would doubt me, I was sure they would accept the plan without a second thought. I had been half way around the world so a weekend in London was nothing to get uptight about.

That night I went to my bed desperately trying to imagine holding and kissing her.

# DISTRACTION

I awoke the next morning with a powerful erection. I had no choice but to relieve myself unless I was to remain in bed, hoping it would subside. I looked at my watch, the mist inside it had cleared and it still seemed to be working; it was ten past eight, Sam would be calling in twenty minutes.

I willingly succumbed to my basic instincts, relishing the thought of her body next to mine.

Sam called at exactly 8.30.

"That will be for you James."

I answered the call as planned, trying to remain as polite and business-like as possible, in case anyone overheard.

"I couldn't stop thinking about you last night," said Sam.

"Yes, I think that would be a good idea," I answered.

"I know you can't talk but just say yes or no, to keep up appearances," she replied. "Did you think of me?"

"Indeed. It's been on my mind for some time."

"Okay I know it's difficult, just say I'd love to."

I did as she asked, and we said our subdued goodbyes.

The stage was set. I explained to Mum and Dad that Sam had offered to put me up for the weekend, with her and her brother Kevin. Captain Le Fevre had thought it would help get me back in the saddle; Sam would show me the sights, and Kevin would give me some insight into life at sea. We all agreed it would be a great opportunity for me to see London and talk with Kevin.

\* \* \*

With no routine, Saturday now seemed indistinguishable from any other day of the week, except that the twins were not at school.

Outside it was raining heavily and the idea of a trip to the Saturday market in Lymington had lost its appeal, even a nostalgic afternoon watching Bournemouth play football seemed pointless since Ted MacDougall had moved on, so when the twins asked Dad to play Monopoly with them I gladly agreed to join in.

It was one of Dad's major successes just a couple of years before. I remembered him acquiring the game with some left over Green Shield stamps, while redeeming the bulk for some forgettable but obviously required item. The same day when we arrived home, he had explained the rules to the twins and me.

We played game after game at the dining room table, eating the food Mother had prepared without any interruption to proceedings. Dad was as engrossed as the twins and I were. I recall his strategy for the game rested in the significance of obtaining all four stations and though it defied any logic I was aware of, his successes seemed to support his theory, though I still felt that luck had more to do with it.

Playing again that day, I sensed that he was totally absorbed in the game; he had put all his pain and discomfort to the back of his mind, caught up in the fantasy of buying properties with toy money.

We eventually moved to the sitting room to watch the television in the early evening. Whilst the others were engrossed in the evening's entertainment, it was merely an occasional distraction from my constant thoughts about Sam and Paul. Sam and I had foolishly agreed to wait until Friday when we could talk face to face. If she were to call me at home our weekend plans may be ruined; if I were to disappear every night to go to the phone box it would be just as bad if not worse, by virtue of my furtiveness.

# THANKS

On Sunday morning Mother went to church. She no longer attended every week out of consideration for my father. The week before she would not leave home until I had arrived safely back from Dubai. That morning she was determined to give thanks to her God for my safe return.

My father had grown up in Dundee, and his only connection to the church had been with the Church of Scotland, even then he had been agnostic. By the time I was born, war had long since destroyed what faith he had; he had become an atheist, and the constant pain he was in did nothing to alter his feelings. He had never really shared mother's need to participate in matters of religion, even before the war.

My mother's upbringing had undoubtedly been influenced by her father, who had been an active member of the choir at Beaulieu Abbey, as well as the village band leader and cornet player, after returning from his army posting in India. He had been heavily involved with all aspects of the Abbey for most of his life, so it was natural enough for mother to inherit his strong beliefs.

I, like my brother John, also spent a great deal of time with the church choir and as an altar boy, or server, as we called it. Even the summer camps I had attended since I had reached ten years old, were organised through the Vicar and the church choir.

I recalled it had been 'my God' that I had pleaded to just a few days before when my life was in peril, even after my beliefs had been turned upside down by the Tarot and my awareness of alien life. I had no reservations about accompanying her myself and giving thanks for my deliverance.

After the service we spoke to my old friend the Vicar and later to Harry Gale. Harry was my old choirmaster and the church organist. They were both valued friends who were naturally interested in the accident and relieved to see me return safely.

The Vicar, Peter Were had a wonderful sense of humour, which I always found very refreshing, he brought laughter to religion. He had spent years entertaining children with his ventriloquist's dummy, and he had a great passion for the music hall and theatre. Despite his love of the arts and music, his apparent lack of both pitch and timing left much to be desired in my naive opinion. I later realised that he was actually a very good vocalist with enough talent to sing out of key for entertainment value.

Harry was the opposite of Peter, black and white, a perfectionist and a stickler for pronunciation pitch and timing. He was probably the only person to continually push me to do better, nothing short of perfect was good enough for him. His teaching always required us young choristers to practice those skills before the adult members of the choir arrived for service rehearsals.

At the time, I never realised how much self-belief Harry's passion for music instilled in me. I realised later that through music I had experienced unrecognised moments of tranquillity and contentment, harmony with my fellow members, not simply musical but spiritual harmony. Moments when our concentration and focus were as one, producing wonderful sounds that might bring joy and even a tear to the listener.

I know now how the harmony of music brings harmony to existence.

Both men were huge influences on my life, each in their own way. Peter's view of life was that everything should be questioned, while Harry believed that things were set in stone and rules should be rigidly adhered to.

# INSECURITY

**M**um invited Jean and Richard for Sunday dinner, to share the beef that Dad had won the week before. Jean stayed at home with Mum while Richard and I accompanied Dad to the local Working Men's Club for a game of snooker.

Dad's attitude to Richard would never be the same as it was for his own sons. It seemed nobody was good enough for his daughters, especially someone as outspoken as Richard.

Richard was born and brought up in the little village of Keyhaven and had accumulated an enormous wealth of knowledge about country life. His preferred past-times were pigeon shooting and wild fowling. The fact that Richard was a very talented darts and snooker player added to my father's frustrations and to the inevitable conclusion of their game.

This frustration, compounded by Dad's failure to win on either the one-armed bandit, or on the dice, meant Dad was not at his happiest when we returned home for Sunday dinner. He picked at the lunch Mum had prepared, while the rest of us gorged ourselves on large servings of prime beef.

I had never considered it before, but I sensed that my father, in his weakened and contorted state, saw my brother-in-law as a threat to his relationship with my mother, which as far as I could tell had never entered Richard's mind.

# THE MESSENGER

When John arrived on Monday morning, everyone expected me to join him at the garage.

"Are you coming in today?" John asked.

"Not today John! I have too much on my mind and I don't want to cause any more accidents!"

Mum and Dad thought I was referring to my accident, but John recalled only too well the damaged Land Rover.

"No problem! I understand. You should get some fresh air now while the sun is shining," he suggested.

The wait to see Sam and the absence of Victor were unbearably frustrating for me. I remembered what Victor had said to me about meditating and decided to find a quiet spot in the woods. I knew where I was headed of course, the woods and the old tramp.

The sky was clear, and the sun shone brightly against the heavy frost, indicating that the temperature had still not yet risen much above freezing point.

The forest always looked magical on days like that. You could almost believe that the whole world had turned white overnight. The leaves of the oaks and chestnut trees had lost most of the chlorophyll that gives them the lush vibrant greens of spring and the warm subtle greens of summer. They shone in frosted white collages of red, yellow and brown, set off against their silvery white frosted trunks and branches. The heather and the remains of the long dead bracken also wore their brilliant white cobweb shifts. Only the gorse and swathes of pine trees that dissected the hard wood forests retained their dark green overcoats, though even they were dusted with white sequins. The sound of the heavily frosted grass crunching, and the ice-covered puddles cracking under foot added to the illusion that snow had arrived.

Smoke was rising from the outbuilding chimney, so I climbed the fence and walked over to the door.

"Come in Jim."

He sat in the same old wooden carver chair, poking the fire just as he was when I had last seen him.

"Come in come in! Come in and close the door boy, it's cold."

"You're always cold." I replied.

"You still don't recognise your old friend then," he said. "Sit," he continued, pointing to the old trunk. "Pull it over so we can talk by the fire."

Once again, I dragged the empty trunk across the floor and sat down, while he threw more sticks on the fire from the pile beside him.

"I know you." I said.

"Here!" he said, handing me a small box. "Kushti bok pral!"

"Paul? Is that you?"

I recognised his words and accent immediately.

"Of course, it's me! Who do you think it is?"

"You are so old."

This time I could tell him.

"Old, what is old? Time and age are illusions," he repeated.

"Victor. Have you met Victor?"

"Yes, we have met. 'He seeks the reborn soul of his son'."

"I know. He thinks you are a Malakh."

He did not respond to the claim.

"I told him that if he followed the Grenadier it would lead him to his reborn son. He thought that he had found him."

"Did you know what was going to happen to me?"

"Yes, I knew. I had hoped to prepare you."

"I was afraid of the cards."

"I did not know whether you would have the mental strength to survive such an ordeal, many do not."

"So, the cards hold no power. It was you and not them that could see into the future."

"The cards are a window, a conduit of time. Of course, if I were Malakhi, I could manipulate the cards at will, or perhaps subconsciously, I really couldn't say. Keep the cards and study them, you will understand."

I could not hear his thoughts the way I could with Victor, or for that matter anyone else.

I opened the box in the dim light of the fire and pulled out a deck of Tarot cards.

"Are they the cards, your cards?" I asked, reverently pronouncing the word as 'thee'.

"They are not the cards you handled on the Worcester. It is selfish I know but they are very precious to me."

"Why all the pretence about girls?" I asked, assuming his words confirmed that he was Malakhi.

"Who said it was pretence? Are you telling me you have not experienced physical desires and enjoyed carnal pleasures? Let's just say it's part of the job," he smiled.

I conceded his point despite feeling that as a superior being he should have more significant things to achieve.

"So how do you feel having survived the ordeal?"

I recalled considering the same question when leaving Dubai, but there had been so many things changing my perception of life, all in such a short space of time.

"Stronger," I answered. "Mentally stronger, perhaps wiser but at the same time so insignificant. Victor has offered to take me to Erato."

"I know."

"Should I go?"

"I cannot guide you in this matter, what must be must be. But let me quote an old friend, "If you bring forth what is within you, what you bring forth will save you. If you do not bring forth what is in you, what you do not bring forth will destroy you."

"What does it mean?"

"I cannot influence what you will do, you should follow what is in your heart, if you don't you will regret it and regrets can poison the soul."

"You warned me about the accident, why can you not tell me now?"

"I simply told you to be careful. Only you could overcome the ordeal."

"So why me? Why are you so interested in me? Am I Victor's son?"

"You are not his son, Victor knows that now; but you will lead him to find what he seeks."

"And you? What do you want?"

"You may consider me your friend and ally, a devil's advocate," he laughed.

"You said you were here to guide me?"

"I am guiding you."

"Have you been to Erato?"

"You ask so many questions. Take the cards and study them. Understand what each card represents. Use the cards to meditate. Now go and leave an old man to warm himself beside the fire."

"Meditate? Victor told me to meditate, that's why I came out here."

"Well then do what he suggested and try to work things out for yourself. Consider how each relates to you and to the world around you."

"Will I see you again?"

"Go!"

"Do you know the future? Can you tell me what I will do?"

"Can anyone tell you what has not yet happened? The cards will help you understand what is possible."

"So I have a choice?"

"Choice is perhaps the wrong word. You will make decisions; the futures I see for you are as numerous as the stars."

He hesitated, mumbling frustrated curses at my impatience.

"This I will tell you, the people of the Earth have become a cancerous infestation, once again they have destroyed the balance of nature and they multiply like a malignant tumour, spreading through the body, intent on ultimately destroying its host.

"Many have tried to restore balance to this world, blinded by logic, confusing order with balance and of course many have recognised the obstacle that Sapiens face, story tellers, song writers and philosophers."

Again, he hesitated, searching for the words he would use.

"It was not robes that your forefathers used to hide their naked bodies, the cloak they donned was pride. Pride became the barrier behind which they could conceal themselves from each other. Behold, the man is become as one of us, to know good and evil. Will he struggle to follow the path of love?

There have been prophets who have tried to open the hearts and minds of the people of Earth in the hope of restoring love and harmony to this world. Now only a few scattered tribes are even aware that the ancient ways ever existed. They, like so many of the Terran species, have been driven to the verge of extinction. Too few now recognise the significance of the sun, the moon and the planets which surround them, and the effect they have on the lifecycle of this world."

"Are you a God?" I asked.

"No," he smiled. "No, I am not a God, I am a cantankerous old man, one of many, I am Malakhi. To consider what god is you must first recognise the word is a verb not a noun, god is creation and creation is ongoing, everything has its purpose, and everything is in balance. We will talk of this again.

"Did he tell you about the others?"

"Others?"

"You think the Nordics are the only visitors here?"

"Who are the Nordics?"

"Victor and his Eratean friends."

"Why do you call them Nordics?"

"I don't. Your people call them Nordics because of their long blonde hair. They know they know they call themselves Eratean."

"Victor has ginger hair."

"The Victor you saw may have ginger hair," he said. "So he hasn't told you yet. Ask him about the Greys and their masters."

"He told me about his son's accident here, he said his ship collided with another alien ship piloted by Greys. Who are their masters?

"Ask Victor to show you. Now leave me."

I did as he requested and left him adding wood to the fire.

I looked back as I climbed the fence and noticed that smoke no longer rose from the building, then realised that there appeared to be no sign that it had ever had a chimney.

As I made my way out of the woods and back to the sunshine I wondered how old he was, how he had looked not much older than me the month before seemed to be of little consequence.

I considered what he had said feeling resentful and insulted that he should refer to the people of the Earth as an infestation.

I wondered who were the others he spoke of, the Greys and their Masters?

# 0   THE FOOL

Iopened the box of cards as I walked up the hill along the edge of the woods. As I skipped through the cards I recalled that they seemed to be made up of two decks.

The first consisted of twenty-two named and numbered cards, each depicted characters or objects. These cards showed characters or scenes, and all were numbers from 0, The Fool, to 21, The World. The second deck seemed at first glance to be a conventional, if somewhat ornate deck. Having skipped through, it was apparent that there were four suits, Cups, Wands, Coins and Swords.

The morning sun now warmed the air, as I glanced around I saw that the white frost had surrendered, revealing the deep greens and browns of the heath.

I sat down beneath a large old oak tree and leant back against the trunk. When I looked again at the cards in my hands, I realised that unlike a conventional deck of cards, the second deck contained a Page in each of the four suits, in addition to the usual court cards. Every card seemed to be unique, each depicting a different scene.

There were too many to study at once, so I picked out the first card and placed the remaining deck back in the box.

I looked at the card in front of me, but all I could think of was a swarming multitude of people devouring the Earth like a plague of locusts. I felt utterly helpless, unsure of what I was supposed to be doing, so I returned the card to the box and stared blankly at the bright sun, and then down onto the ground beside me.

Dead leaves covered the ground around me having fallen from the oak above.

I noticed an ant crawling across the ground beside me, and soon realised there was an army of the tiny creatures, apparently all working in collaboration with each other for their common good. Regiments of the tiny creatures marched in lines, some going to, and a similar quantity leaving the nest, which seemed to have its entrance beneath the exposed tree roots. I wondered as I gazed, if they were aware of my presence. To an untrained eye such as mine, I seemed to have no effect what so ever on their actions.

Could we perhaps exist amongst and be totally oblivious to some greater beings? The bible told us that we were made in God's image. Did that mean we looked like God, or thought like God? Paul said God was creation, perhaps we were a part of God? Perhaps the stars in the sky are like the atoms that make up our bodies? Maybe the universe was one huge living entity?

As I considered the absence of any data I had to develop my theories, the ants deposited their cargos and formed a perfect square in front of me, they moved like a military unit without breaking formation, then suddenly resumed their duties.

I took out the Tarot cards again and selected the first pack, laying them in a line in front of me. As I looked at each card and studied its relationship with the next, it appeared to me that together they summarised a journey through life.

I looked again at the first card numbered zero, The Fool. It was a simple picture of a young boy in colourful clothes. He carried his belongings in a small bundle tied to a stick.

The image reminded me of the tale of Dick Whittington who went off to London in search of his fortune, except that Dick's friend and ally was a cat, whilst this young chap had a small dog for company. Instead of the image of London in the distance, there were only mountains.

I recalled the time that Haji was driving me back to Dubai just a few days before, when I had recognised the mountain as a symbol of knowledge, and that I had mountains of knowledge to climb. I also recalled the long range of mountains glowing amber red in the morning sunlight, along the coast of Ras al Khaimah and the northern tip of

Oman, up to the Strait of Hormuz which might have been my gateway to a different life had I joined the Grenadier.

I looked at the card again and this time I was reminded of Charlie Chaplin leaving town at the end of a film, carrying only his walking stick and a small bundle in the other hand. He travelled light with all his worldly possessions in the bundle, but where was he going? Like me, he did not really know, he would know when he got there, until then, he must continue his journey, or he would never know.

His path had taken him to a cliff edge, yet he gazed up toward the sky, ignorant of the danger.

The parallels with my accident were blatant. Was the little dog at his heels snapping at him trying to warn him, just as Paul had tried to warn me? The dog too seemed to be gazing up at the sky in the same direction as his master.

Why was he named the fool, because he took risks? He seemed to be prepared to search for something better and with the few possessions he carried, he could go anywhere.

# I  THE MAGICIAN

The next card was numbered one, The Magician.

My first thoughts about the card summed up my initial fear of the Tarot. I did not believe in magicians; however, I feared the hocus-pocus surrounding the dark arts. I wondered just what the words hocus-pocus meant and where they came from.

The card portrayed a young man, older than the boy in the first card, perhaps a teacher. I recognised the sign of infinity over his head from mathematics, but did not understand its meaning in that context. Imagining myself writing the symbol I realised that it was not only a never-ending loop, it consisted of two loops, two balanced loops, eternity and balance. Perhaps between good and evil? It also seemed to describe time in the way Victor had explained it, that time was a loop with no beginning and no end. From yet another perspective I could see space being warped, a single circle appeared to be folded against itself.

In his right hand he held what appeared to be a wand, while his left hand pointed down to the earth. He wore a belt around his waist that appeared to be a snake with its tail disappearing into its mouth. The endless cycle of nature.

In front of him, there was a table and on it a sword, a baton, a goblet and a coin. These objects were the same as the houses of the other pack. They appeared to be on display, like the goods on a market stall.

The Swords seem to indicate a fight for something, a challenge or struggle; the batons I discovered, were actually called Wands, it suggested mystical energy; the goblets or Cups, suggested love and relationships; the Coins suggested material wealth, something Victor despised. I realised that there was a connection to ordinary playing cards, the Swords spades, Wands clubs, Cups hearts and Coins diamonds.

As I looked at the figure in his white robe, it reminded me of my first sighting of Victor, hovering motionless in the water beside me. In some way, the sign of infinity now suggested telepathy and communication, perhaps also the balance that both Victor and Paul had spoken of, and I knew that I would have to learn these things from one or both of them.

I looked back at the first card and understood what Paul had meant when he asked me how the ordeal had affected me; The Fool represented me and a new beginning. My life was about to change in every conceivable way, and that was all I knew. I felt young, free and full of energy, like the young boy depicted in the card.

I repacked the cards and settled down to watch the world around me. I wanted to remember what I would be leaving behind. The time seemed to disappear as I sat watching everything, from the ants at my side, to the birds in the sky.

The temperature began to fall as the sun moved towards the horizon. Feeling the cold, I made my way home.

# DOUBTS

For three days I had been studying the Tarot cards, reading as much as I could about the Tarot and the symbols used in the occult and different religions. I had also been searching for Paul's quote, "If you bring forth what is within you, what you bring forth will save you. If you do not bring forth what is in you, what you do not bring forth will destroy you." It sounded like a quote from the bible, but I couldn't find it anywhere.

I had sought help from my old friend and Vicar, Peter Were, on Tuesday afternoon, but he had no idea where it came from. He thought it sounded like a quote from Jesus and I agreed. He asked me were I had heard it and I told him an old man had quoted it to me, without saying where.

Peter said that he would speak to his old friends and colleagues about it. He had been a curate in the Bristol area and had a network of priests, deacons and bishops he could ask. He told me he would call me as soon as he had any news.

When I got home from Lymington, Dad reminded me about the trip to Britannic House the next day. Apparently, Sam had called wishing to confirm that we were still coming.

"I'd better call her back," I said, speaking to Dad in the dining room.

"No need, I told her we would be there and that you were looking forward to staying with her and her brother in London."

"What a lovely girl," said Mum, from the kitchen.

"She said you could call her back if you got back before five thirty," said Dad quietly.

"Thanks, I will."

Our telephone sat in a small window at the front of the house, half way up the staircase. I closed the door to the dining room behind me, sat down on the stairs and called the office. It was still only ten to five, so Sam should have been there, but there was no answer on her phone.

"No answer," I explained, back in the dining room.

"Never mind son. Why don't you try again later, just before half past eh?" he suggested.

"Yeah ok. I will."

The thought that Sam might have had second thoughts about having a relationship with a younger boy, filled me with anxiety. It felt like weeks since we had spoken.


"Peter Were called too," said mother, having joined us in the dining room.

"Really? I think I'd better call him back then."

I went back to the phone, closing the door as I went, which probably seems odd to my parents, being very out of character.

"I think I know where your quote comes from James," he began. One of my young colleagues has been doing some research into the Dead Sea Scrolls, and came across something called the Gnostic Gospels; thirteen ancient leather-bound codices, supposedly older than the New Testament gospels, also known as the Nag Hammadi Library, they are considered to be very controversial. Apparently, the quote comes from what is described as the Gospel of Thomas."

"You mean 'doubting Thomas', the disciple?"

"The very same."

"If that is true why is it not a part of the New Testament?"

"As my young colleague pointed out, the content of the New Testament was selected by a Council of Christian Bishops, when the Emperor Constantine adopted Christianity. These codices were only discovered in 1945. According to my colleague, the quote is something Jesus is supposed to have said after the resurrection."

"Thanks Vic'."

It was fortunate that he was one of the few priests who would question the established belief. He did not question me more on the old man that had quoted the text.

I called the office again after hanging up, and this time Sam answered. She had been in a meeting with Le Fevre and unable to answer her phone. Ironically, she was just as anxious as I was, fearing that I might have changed my mind. We could not speak for long because Mum had come out to check if I was ready for tea, but at least we could now both rest assured that we would see each other the next day.

# INCENTIVE

Friday 30th November 1973

Dad and I caught the 8.33 to Waterloo, from there we took the tube to Moorgate on the Northern Line changing at Euston Station.

I wore my number one navy blue uniform and white cap, taking a small case with enough clothes for the weekend. We checked in at Britannic House reception, and Sam came down to meet us. She looked prettier than ever; her eyes sparkled like bright blue sapphires, and her hair was tied up in the same way as the photograph she had sent me, emphasising her long slender neck. Her smile melted my heart, she was the sweetest thing I had ever seen.

"Good morning Mr Cummings, lovely to see you again; James, I hope you had a pleasant trip. Why don't you leave your case here at reception," she said, assuming that it was just my clothes for the weekend.

"Thank you Sam."

I passed her my case and she placed her hand on mine briefly before taking the handle. I noticed Dad smile knowingly, leaning with both hands on his walking stick as I turned around.

"If you'd like to follow me gentlemen, I'll take you to meet Captain Le Fevre."

We didn't get a chance to talk before going in to see the Captain. I felt Sam's thoughts as she resisted her desire to wrap her arms around me, instead we exchanged the usual pleasantries as she escorted us into the lift and up to his office.

She knocked at his door and told him we were waiting to see him, then ushered us in.

"Mr Cummings, James," he said, shaking our hands. "Thank you for coming, it's nice to see you both again. Please take a seat."

I sat down, removed my cap and placed it on my lap.

"How are you James? Let me take a look at your hand."

I bent forward to show him; the finger nail had just started to grow again on my middle finger, but apart from that there was nothing to be seen.

"My goodness they've healed up well."

He was not as shocked by this as I had expected, but then he did not really know the extent of my wounds.

"Yes it has Sir," I said.

"How are you feeling now?"

"I'm feeling much better now. My Doctor says I'm physically fit, but he has signed me off for two weeks to get over the shock," I answered, passing him the medical certificate.

"You have had a very serious accident, and I'm not going to push you back to sea before you're ready; however, I do urge you to get back to sea as soon as possible. I believe it's the best thing for you."

"It was a big shock for me Sir. I would have preferred to have got back on board straight away, but they wouldn't let me."

"I know, I've seen the reports. It's very commendable of you. Have you managed to replace your clothes?"

"Yes thank you Sir. I've got the claim form here for you, and the receipts for my shirt, suit and shoes, and for the cassette recorder."

I took the remaining papers from my pocket and handed them to him.

"Ah yes the cassette recorder. You've got yourself a new one then?"

"Yes, thank you Sir."

"A bit better than the last one I hope eh!" he said smiling at me, he was no fool.

As he spoke, I realised that I had also lost my David Bowie cassette, still inside my old recorder, lying somewhere at the bottom of the Persian Gulf. I had been too busy with other things to think about music. Having bought more expensive replacements for my other losses, I decided not to raise the issue.

"I'll get Samantha to sort this out for you before you leave, we'll see if we can get you a cheque for the difference." He leant forward and touched the intercom on his desk. "Samantha could you come in for a moment please?"

"Yes, certainly Sir," came the answer.

He signed the claim form without checking it as Sam knocked briefly at the door and came straight in.

"Could you take this down to accounts and get a cheque for the outstanding balance please Sam?" he asked.

"Certainly Sir," she answered politely, and left the room again.

"Now then James, did your father ask you to think about what you would like to do now? Is there anywhere you would like to go, Australia, the United States? I can send you anywhere we have a ship."

"I'm not sure Sir."

"Well do you feel ready to go back after a short break?"

"I feel okay Sir, I'm just a little unsure of what I want at the moment. I need some time to think."

"I understand, let's leave it at that for now, but I'd like to get you on board a ship for Christmas, sunshine or snow, where ever you like. I know we could spoil you for a while."

He paused for a moment.

"Perhaps I could have a chat with your father now, I'll have Samantha get you a cup of coffee. Would you like one Mr Cummings?"

"I'd rather have a cup of tea please," he answered.

"Certainly, if you'll excuse me for a moment I'll just sort that out. James would you like to follow me."

It pleased me that Dad never tried to interrupt my conversation, it reflected his confidence in me to deal with things in my own way.

The Captain showed me into Sam's office, but she was not there.

"Take a seat James. Would you ask Miss Cooper to bring your father a cup of tea and whatever you would like when she gets back?"

"Yes Sir."

"Thank you."

269

There was little doubt that he wanted me back onboard a ship as soon as possible, and I felt sure that he really did have my best interests at heart, but like almost everyone else, he knew so very little about what really happened.

I sat down and waited for Sam to come back. Alone and with the prospect of talking to Sam about the accident for the first time, I began to relive the incident in my mind, waiting for her to return.

She wasn't long, she had waited in the accounts department while my cheque was prepared.

"James, I've been dying to see you!" she said quietly as she rushed over.

I stood up to greet her and she stood in front of me hugging her own waist tightly and shaking her heels like an over-excited child.

"Me too!" I said. "It feels so weird, like I've known you for ages, it scares me sometimes."

"I know. It's the same for me. I just want to put my arms around you and hug you."

"Feel free!" I said hopefully.

"I can't, not here."

"No of course. I'm sorry I didn't think."

She looked around briefly and seeing that there was no one there, she did it anyway. I responded quickly, we held each other briefly and she kissed me softly.

"Why are you out here, where's your father?" she asked standing back.

"He's talking to Captain Le Fevre."

"He's really a very nice man you know, he just wants to get you back on a ship as soon as he can. I think he's got it in his mind to give you a Christmas you won't forget."

"I know. I'm still mixed up at the moment though. There's so much I want to talk to you about."

"I don't want you to go back yet!"

"Nor do I! I,"

"Sorry James," she interrupted before I could finish. "It'll have to wait for a few minutes, it'll be lunch time soon and we can have the rest of the weekend together. I've just got to sort out this cheque for you and lock up my desk. Would you like a cup of coffee?"

"Yes please, white, two sugars. Oh yes, the Captain asked if you could get my Dad a cup of tea as well."

"Sure, there's my instant beside the kettle there on the shelf, it's better than the vending machines. Have you ever had an espresso?"

"What's an espresso? I'll get you one from the executive lounge and get your dad a proper cup of tea."

She glanced around the office then turned and gave me a quick peck on the cheek.

I smiled. I had imagined things would be much more embarrassing and awkward.

Sam returned with our refreshments on a tray, three very small white cups of black coffee and a cup of tea. She smiled at me and took two cups of coffee off the tray, before tapping on the captain's door and walking straight in, cheque in hand for Captain Le Fevre to initial. She came back out after a few moments and gave me the cheque.

She handed me one of the coffees and took the last for herself.

I smelt the thick dark liquid in my cup. The smell of roasted coffee beans filled my nose in a way coffee never had done before.

"Do you have any milk?" I asked.

She smiled.

"Just sip it, slowly."

I sipped at the small cup, the intensity hit me like a very strong piece of dark chocolate with a taste of iron and spice.

"It's very strong."

"Just sip it slowly, savour it in your mouth. Trust me it will grow on you."

I sat and drank my coffee waiting for the Captain and my father to finish their discussion. There wasn't much for them to discuss. Dad knew that Le Fevre wanted me back at sea as soon as possible, but there would be no real pressure, I had to be ready to go back, no-one was going to force the issue.

They had a brief chat about John while he was there, and Le Fevre suggested that John should write to him directly, with a list of his qualifications and details of his apprenticeship if he was serious about a career with BP. Although he was Head of Fleet Recruitment for Deck Cadets, he worked in parallel with his colleague on the Engineering side, it would ultimately be his colleagues decision; however, he promised to give the matter his personal attention.

They came out together, both of them smiling.

"I see Miss Cooper has tempted you with my favourite coffee. I hope you like it."

"It's very strong Sir."

"Yes, yes it is," he smiled.

"So, James, Miss Cooper has kindly invited you to spend the weekend with her and her brother Kevin, and show you a few of the sights at our expense. We feel that it will do you good to get you out of the house for a while, cheer you up a bit."

"Yes Sir, I am very grateful to you and to Sa...' Miss Cooper. I've been looking forward to it all week."

She really was a very astute girl.

"Ok, it's lunch time now. I'm taking your father up to the company restaurant for lunch. Would you care to join us or are you keen to get off?"

"I'd rather like to see a bit of the city if you don't mind."

"Yes, I'm sure you would. Well have fun, remember you're in uniform and as such representing the company."

"Yes Sir, thank you Sir."

"Sam, have a lovely weekend, I'm sure you'll look after James."

"Thank you Sir, I will."

They escorted us down to reception, where I retrieved my suitcase, before saying goodbye.

"Well I look forward to seeing you again soon. Miss Cooper will be in touch to arrange another meeting in a week or two."

He shook my hand and turned away toward my father, then stopped and turned around again.

"Oh, by the way, please give Kevin my regards."

He reminded me of the TV detective Columbo, turning back as he left the scene to make a final comment to a suspect, leaving you with doubt about how much he knew.

"Here son, before you go," he said, as he put a ten-pound note into my hand. "We can't have you living on charity. Spoil the girl! It's Christmas. I'll see you on Sunday son, have fun."

Ten pounds was more than a week's wages for me and a great deal of money to him. He had not worked for some time and what was left of the family at home still relied on his invalidity benefit.

"I think she's got a bit of a soft spot for him." I heard my father say as they left, the Captain was no fool either.

I wondered if he also realised I was happy to stall things for a while.

# RESURRECTION

## NEW-BORN

Monday ~ 26<sup>th</sup> November 1973

I was unaware that Victor had been following me since we parted, and had seen me enter the outbuilding where I had talked with Paul. Paul had disappeared along with the smoking chimney when I left, but Victor was determined to meet with Paul again.

"I know you can hear me," he said, standing inside the empty building, speaking both orally and with his thoughts. "Will you speak with me now?"

Paul appeared before Victor, sitting in his chair in front of the crackling fire, where no fireplace had existed before.

"Friendship," said Victor, in his native custom, having formally introduced himself on their first meeting.

"Friendship," Paul responded.

"The girl, Samantha. Is she my daughter's living soul?"

"Yes, she is."

"I thought it was James, but he has no memories of a previous life. I assume he is a new-born, but I have never met one before. Does he know?"

"Not yet, there is much for him to learn; he was born into a world where reincarnation is no longer realised. Do you know what the Malakhi are?"

"I know that they once existed on my home-world. I suspect that I stand before one now."

"We Malakhi were all New-born, born of our home-world for the first time. James' life ended in the Persian Gulf, he drowned, but he chose to return rather than be reborn in a new life, creating an alternate future; one where he died and the other where he lives. Your meeting with him in the sea and everything that followed never happened in the alternate timeline.

"James no longer exists in that timeline; however, his soul exists in both, one as a living spirit and the other as a Malakh. Now he has the ability to move from one timeline to another, but he does not know this yet.

"My name is Saul of Tarsus, I was beheaded and died in Rome during the reign of Nero, the same day that Peter was crucified. Like James, I was New-born and chose not to be reborn in another life, but to return. The body you see before you is the physical manifestation of what was. My mentor was Jesus of Nazareth, he also chose to return as did his mentor and all of those that came before him. All the Earth's religions are based on the teachings of Malakhi, each for its time, and the needs of the people; prophecy and religion are one of many ways by which we can guide those we watch over.

"We are many, and we will live until the Earth, our home-world, is absorbed into Helios the Sun, then we will exist in Helios until it is consumed by the black hole.

"The Malahk from your world have had no cause to intervene in your timeline for thousands of years. They exist, unrecognised among you.

"We all exist within the galaxy, a galaxy divided through changes to the timeline, dividing like a cell, into two identical cells, the definition of life. When necessary those new cells will divide again and again.

"You seek the answer to 'the unanswered', but 'the unanswered' is unanswerable. I can only tell you what we the Malakhi believe. Much of it your ancestors learned from your Eratean born Malakhi thousands of years ago.

"Time begins and ends in a loop, there is no beginning and no end, except that the cycle ends and restarts. Time is not a linear thing, it slows as it approaches any mass and no longer exists inside a black hole, where nothing escapes.

"Time does not exist outside the galaxy, nothing exists in the void except the seeds of life.

"An infinite number of parallel universes exist that account for every alteration to the timeline in every galaxy. For you there is only one future and one past, your time line is fixed. You also exist in many other timelines, but you do not possess the ability to move from one to another.

"The Universe and all its children began with a seed, a single black hole. It grew in strength, without dimension, until it exploded scattering its seeds into the void. Each seed gave birth to a Galaxy that exists in the void. Changes to the time line created alternate time lines like the branches on a tree, a tree with one trunk, one original timeline.

"Life in each Galaxy evolved, stars formed, planets became worlds with moons. Some of those worlds produced intelligent life; eventually one race fulfilled their destiny, moving out into space to find new developing worlds, and continue to evolve. Among them were the first Malakhi.

"They became the seed on younger worlds they encountered on their journey across the galaxy; possessing the knowledge to produce a hybrid race, with which they could procreate; Adam and Eve; The Lovers portrayed in the Tarot.

"Their children's destiny, to evolve and find developing worlds for their own children. There are many New-borns during this time of growth, born of their home-world, having lived no previous life; in time one of these did what James has done, choosing to return as a Malakh where Adam or Eve became their mentor.

"The Malakh became great teachers and philosophers, prophets and messengers.

"In time, the galaxy and everything that exists was consumed by the black hole at its centre. The black hole became a new seed in the void, growing in mass and strength, without dimension, until it exploded scattering its seeds into the timeless void. Each seed gave birth to another universe and the void expanded to absorb them. Creation became growth, physical and four dimensional.

"I am a tree of time, James will become one of my branches, just as I am a branch on the tree that is Jesus. I do not share all the timelines that Jesus created, and James does not share mine.

"James will be the shepherd for the world he has inherited, when and how he decides to influence his timelines is for him to decide. Each time he does it will create another time line which is his to mould. When a New-born becomes a Malakh in James' timelines, it will create another new timeline, and the new Malahk will be its shepherd, James will become a mentor, just as I will be James' mentor.

"What I have not yet told you is that I exist as a Trinity, I am the New-born, Saul of Tarsus; I am the mortal who lived his last life as Luke the Evangelist, disciple of Paul; I am also the mortal who lived her last life as Mary wife of Clopas, mother of James the Less and Keeper of Knowledge. My mentor was the New-born Jesus of Nazareth; he was also the mortal who lived her last life as Mary Magdalene, wife of Jesus; he was also the mortal Judas Iscariot, disciple and betrayer of Jesus.

"I tell you this because you seek answers to the unanswered. James will live as long as the Earth. He will take many partners in his life; one of the more pleasurable ways we can shape the future is procreating with mortals. We exist as a Trinity because we all need something constant in our lives, we cannot end our lives and be reborn as you can, we cannot be killed, we died and returned into the eternal circle of time.

"James has told me that you have invited him to Erato; you have come to Earth to find the soul of your son, Sam; Sam has been reborn from the Earth; you and Sam have shared previous lives together, as kin and as lovers; Sam and James souls have touched though they do not know it yet. Erato would be the perfect place for James to grow, raise a family of his own on a world where harmony survives, probably with Sam, you could be his guide.

"It is for each of you to decide your future, but I can think of no better match. If you decide to join him, you will exist with him as one, you will live until the end of the Earth and exist until the end of the galaxy. You will be able to travel in time and space. You will have access to all the timelines that James has.

"The metamorphosis from New-born to Malakh ultimately requires the New-born to seek out two mortals, who will in full knowledge of their options, join and become as one. The alternative is for the Malakh to lose their sanity for eternity.

"When a species becomes a threat to life and harmony on their world, the Malakhi must try to restore balance and harmony, so that all may enjoy the paradise they seek.  We must also prevent malignant corruptions spreading through the galaxy. There are many ways that we can steer them back towards their destiny.

"You are familiar with Freud's theories on the human psyche I assume. James could be considered the Id, the instinct steering the Malakh Trinity. Should you join with James when your life ends you have the experience and knowledge of harmony to be the Ego, bringing reality to the union.

"Sam lives her life as a Sapien woman, in time she will bear James' children, she may live for two hundred years if she returns to Erato with you, but no longer, her Sapien body will not live the lifespan you are both used to. She will age, and she will die and be reborn an Eratean, leaving James to live for eternity without her. James will always be able to revisit her in the time they share together, just as you can, in the heaven between lives; or she could join with him, and you, and having lived so many lives as a woman, be the Superego, the morality. You would think as three on equal terms, not as counsel.

"It was Mary Magdalene that was supposed to follow in the teachings of Jesus, not Peter. Mary is the female personification of Jesus and Judas. The Earth is a male dominated world and Mary was supposed to change that. Together they taught in Europe and Asia, trying to overcome the world of commerce and land ownership, and encouraged the growth of the Roma and the nomadic way of life still common in the aboriginal people of the Americas, south and central Africa and Australia. The church was never meant to be a rich and powerful judge. Constantine and his bishops defiled the New Testament, my writings and the gospels, many were omitted that should have been included, the Gospels of Jesus, Mary Magdalene, Peter, Thomas, Philip and many more. Jesus never used the word 'Abba', he said 'Eema', not 'forgive them father', simply 'forgive them mother'. God is not man, God is the eternal universe which gives birth to all life and is life. If God has gender than it is without doubt female."

"You must not share any of this with James or Sam until their souls have touched, which will happen very soon. Do not think on it until that time because we must not influence James or Sam until they have found each other. I advise you to avoid both of them until I tell you."

# SMALL TALK

T he Globe was almost directly across the road from Britannic House. Sam led the way avoiding any contact until we found space at the end of the bar.

We took each other in our arms and held each other in silence for what seemed like hours, to the rest of the world only minutes. Neither of us said anything, we were both content just to hold each other. I kissed her lightly on the neck and the cheek and ran my fingers through her hair, pushing off the clip at the back, letting her hair fall around her shoulders. We were oblivious to everyone else in the bar.

I kissed her soft neck lightly, using my lips and the tip of my tongue, moving my lips from place to place and I sensed her arousal. To the other people in the bar it appeared that we were lovers, reunited after a period of separation; dressed as I was in my uniform, perhaps having just returned from a long trip.

The bar went silent. It was the women who stopped talking first and then even the men stopped chatting. Such tenderness would not have looked out of place on the big screen in some romantic love story. It felt so wonderful to hold her and I wanted to stay there forever.

Eventually we moved apart and looked at each other, free to savour the experience for the first time.

She was beautiful, I could sense her emotion, she showed that in her eyes and her thoughts, but we did not exchange words that way. We had not had the opportunity to burn the image of the other into our hearts and minds until that moment.

"You can't imagine how much I've wanted just to hold you," she said.

"Oh I think I can," I answered with a huge grin. "Can I get you a drink?"

"Yes please, I'd like a small glass of white wine, Sancerre would be nice."

279

"Sure, you sit down while I order it."

I bought a pint of bitter for myself and a glass of wine for Sam. I had got used to buying drinks and no longer expected to be questioned about my age; being dressed in uniform probably made me appear even younger, but I wasn't questioned by the landlord.

"You look gorgeous," I said placing the wine in on the table in front of her.

"Thank you, I think you're very kind to say so. There's something about you, something so familiar. It's funny, I took to you straight away, but when I saw you on the Worcester you changed my whole world. I never had any intention of getting involved with a cadet, just the opposite. I know how much Kevin is away, I don't know if I could live with that."

"Then why the letter?" I asked taking off my jacket.

"No, leave it on!" she cried. "You look so handsome in it. You can leave the buttons undone. The letter? I don't know. You're not the first cadet I've been attracted to but this time it's different, I don't feel like I have any choice. Sorry I'm not being very romantic I know. I am normally a very romantic girl. Perhaps it's love at first sight. That's what I mean about the Worcester, maybe that's the first time I really looked at you. I don't know, I've never believed that it could happen that way, but I think of you all the time now, especially when I'm in bed cuddling my teddy. I changed his name to James you know!"

Without warning she pinched my arm as hard as she was able, so hard I was glad I was still wearing my jacket.

"What was that for?" I asked.

"Don't *ever* associate my appearance with a horse, a foal, or any other farm yard animal," she snarled, emphasising the word ever. "You may call me Princess," she laughed.

"Well Princess, I fell for you onboard the Worcester too, there's no doubt about that. I remember it was so strange, the feeling that came over me I mean. I suddenly felt I knew you intimately. We've been through all this though and I still don't have any explanations. It's just great to see you."

She took a packet of cigarettes and a very elegant looking gold lighter from her handbag.

"Would you like one?" she asked offering the open packet.

"I don't smoke."

"Try one," she said, putting the packet down in front of me, then lit her own. She tilted her head back in a very sensuous way as she slowly blew a fine cloud of smoke into the air above us. Entranced, I picked up the packet in front of me. I was obsessed with her good looks and charismatic charm.

"Kent! I've never heard of them," I said as I pulled a cigarette out of the box.

"They're nicer than the usual rubbish. You can buy anything in the city," she answered.

I had never realised just how sensual a woman could look smoking a cigarette. I had never smoked at school, but I had seen plenty of kids that did. They never looked like Sam did. Sam said nothing as she inhaled and exhaled with a dignified elegance, the pause in her speech emphasising her erotic posture.

"This is nice," I said picking up the lighter."

"It was a birthday present from Kevin, he bought it back from Dubai actually."

"What's he like, Kevin?"

"He's tall, about six one, blonde like me, of course his hair is short, a bit on the skinny side and a pain, but I love him to bits."

She drew another breath on the cigarette, tilting her head again to blow the smoke into the air above us out of politeness.

"He's having a whale of a time and I get to hear all the gory details, which is probably why I was determined not to get involved with a sailor. The saying seems to be true, a girl in every port. That's not what I've got in mind for a partner. Still he's unattached and plans to stay that way, at least for a while."

She continued smoking her cigarette and I decided to try one myself. I coughed taking my first puff.

"You'll get used to it," she smiled reassuringly. "I saw your brother, he's very like you, too old for me though, but then you are younger than me. I've never been out with a younger guy before, they're so bloody immature."

"Thanks! So why are you here."

"Don't get grumpy! I told you I'm here because I want to be here; I like you, and you know as well as I do, there's something strange between us. It's something I've never experienced before. I don't know what it is yet, but I want more of it."

"So, what have you got planned for me then, are you going to show me the sights of London or take me home to your bed?" I asked.

"You don't mince your words do you! You could at least be a little more romantic about it."

My expression must have changed, thinking that I'd blown everything, perhaps she sensed my regret.

"Don't worry, I'm no prude, but I am going to take you out to see London, and before I do you're going to get out of that uniform."

"Why? I thought you liked it?"

"Yes, I do. I know I see them every day, but I happen to have a thing about uniforms, especially you, and if you don't change into something else pretty soon I'm going to be tempted to start ripping it off you. Besides you're so damn conspicuous. I don't want to be spotted by someone from the office, Stuart is a great boss but he's very paternal. We can leave your suitcase at reception for now, as long as we are back before six."

We finished our drinks chatting and laughing, I teased her, and she teased me, pinching me when she felt like it. It was a game, a sparring match, and it was fun. I changed my clothes in the pub toilet putting on a pair of jeans, a shirt and my new bomber jacket, then we set out on the tube to see the sights, dropping off my suitcase as Sam suggested.

We took the same route back on the Northern Line, changing at Euston Station on our way to Charing Cross, first stop being Trafalgar Square. An enormous Christmas tree stood solemnly beside Nelsons Column.

"No lights I'm afraid what with the miners and electricity workers banning overtime, and the price of oil," explained Sam.

I had been too wrapped up in my own rapidly changing life to be up to date with current affairs.

I told Sam about the film I had seen at the Grayswift villa as we looked up at Nelson.

We walked down Whitehall, past the Cenotaph and Downing Street, to Westminster Square, Big Ben, the Houses of Parliament, and Westminster Abbey. We lingered around poet's corner. She had a love of the English language and of poetry, so it was a special place for her. As we walked around she astonished me with her knowledge of poetry and her ability to recite so many works. Sadly, my knowledge in that area was somewhat limited.

"Masefield, he's your man, you must know Masefield being a sailor," she said.

"Never heard of him," I answered.

"You should be ashamed of yourself! 'I must go down to the seas again, to the lonely sea and the sky, and all I ask is a tall ship and a star to steer her by'."

"Oh yes I've heard that before," I smiled.

We walked on north west, passed St James' Court.

"Do you think you would get a discount James? On account of your name?" she asked jokingly.

"Call me Jim, or Jimmy," I suggested.

"No, I think I prefer James for now, it suits you. I'll think of something appropriate later," she laughed.

We continued our walk around Buckingham Palace, then west along Constitution Hill to Hyde park, up to the corner of the Serpentine and then north to Speakers Corner, where we stopped to listen to a crazy old woman ranting on about the sins of alcohol abuse, and how Christmas had become an excuse for excessive drinking. It didn't take long for us to get bored, so we headed down Oxford Street and up Baker Street to Madam Tussaud's. Sam bought our tickets, telling me that Le Fevre would sign off the cost. We spent over an hour there, taking turns to take photographs with the camera Sam had brought, while the other posed beside the wax models.

I was having such fun getting to know Sam, it made me feel good just to hold her hand as we walked around. Every now and then I would make her laugh and she would wrap her arms around me and hug me tightly.

When we left Madam Tussaud's it was getting dark outside, so we got on the tube at Baker Street station, and after changing trains got out at Leicester Square. We wandered around the pubs for a couple of hours, then we bought a hot-dog and sat in the square under the leafless plane trees to eat it, oblivious of the cold evening air.

"Do you like living in London?" I asked.

"Yes, I do. Don't you like it?"

"Yes, what I've seen of it, but I could have had fun with you anywhere."

"Me too. I'm sorry I made those remarks about younger boys, you're not a boy, you're a man, my man, and you not immature."

"I've never really been out with a girl before, not like this. I feel so relaxed with you and so very happy."

"You said you needed to talk to me at the office, is there something wrong, are you worried about going back to sea again?"

"I'm not sure I want to go back."

"Why? I know you had an awful experience, but that sort of thing doesn't happen every day you know, I have certainly never heard anything like it before any way. I would give anything to travel."

"Would you, would you really?"

"Yes, I would!"

"Maybe I will marry an officer one day and go to sea with him after all," she said with a huge grin.

"Is that some sort of proposal?"

"Don't be stupid, we've only just met, and *you*, are not an officer, yet!" she said, emphasising the word *you*, and poking her finger into my chest as she said it.

"So it's not me, it's the uniform and the life that goes with it you want?" I said sarcastically.

"Don't be so silly, you know that's not true. I told you I had no intention of getting involved with a cadet, but I like you very much. Let's not look for problems we don't have."

She took out a hand rolled cigarette from her purse and lit it, taking a deep breath of the smoke, then offered me the cigarette. I looked around bewildered and noticed another small group of people passing around their own cigarette discreetly. I took the cigarette and inhaled a small mouthful of the smoke.

"Take it back and hold onto it, she said. I did as I was told and began to cough violently, causing some of the lads in the group next to us to look across and laugh.

"Actually, they're a much nicer smoke than the Kent," she said taking back the cigarette and drawing another deep breath.

She passed back the cigarette and waited for me to continue. I breathed in another small mouthful of smoke and this time it did not hurt when I drew it back into my lungs. We continued to share the cigarette. I became very relaxed and forgot to pass it back to Sam.

"What is this stuff?" I asked.

"Pleasure?" she answered.

I looked at her feeling very relaxed and contented. My thoughts drifted, I was contemplating just how happy I felt, then like a ghost from the past, the memory of what had happened on the train suddenly returned to haunt me. I felt so guilty and my mind seemed to dwell on it.

"You're feeling guilty about something, I can see it," said Sam, interrupting my thought. "I don't know what you are feeling so guilty about, whatever you did before doesn't matter. I'm sure nothing happened in Dubai, Kevin says there's nothing there. Whatever it is it is in the past. I'm not a virgin and it doesn't bother me what you have done in the past."

She had clearly sensed my thoughts but there was no anger in her voice. I was communicating my thoughts to her clearly, and because they were so focused she had picked up my sense of guilt.

My mind drifted back to my first encounters with Victor, I now had some inkling of what he had meant when we had talked about telepathy. My confused mind normally raced with constant interruptions from the environment around me, causing my brain to focus for only a fraction of time on any one thing. My mind had been fixed for what seemed like minutes on only one thought process. I seemed to be much more focused on just one thought at a time.

Sam was clearly feeling as relaxed as I was, she had no problem in discussing her sexuality openly. We began to kiss softly, I brushed my lips against her top lip and then her bottom lip, she responded with her tongue playing gently across my lips. It was a gentle and sensual exploring of each other. She slowly found my neck, my ears and again my mouth with hers. Her lips were so light and so moist that every touch was erotic. I became very aroused but at the same time I was so very relaxed. I was enjoying every moment and every touch, in no rush to do anything more. I found myself kissing her neck softly in the same way that she had kissed mine, she moaned softly. My hands caressed the outsides of her breasts beneath the cover of her arms and I felt the hardness of her nipples beneath my thumbs. Finally, Sam shook her self away from me.

"Oh God!" she mumbled. "We can't stay here. I think it's time I took you home."

I kissed her again and she smiled.

"You've got such very wicked eyes, very sexy, piercing, they go right through me and I could kiss you for ever."

"You're the one with the sexy eyes!" I said, and I meant it, they were very passionate, bright blue eyes. "And it takes two to kiss!"

We walked hand in hand back to the tube station and made our way back to Highgate.

# II THE HIGH PRIESTESS

S am showed me up to the flat and ushered me in, it wasn't far from Highgate tube station. She sat me down on the sofa, which was a big soft thing; brown with a red and blue throw draped over it, and with big soft cushions scattered along it. She lit the small gas fire and a dozen white candles around the little room, then two joss sticks in the hearth. She turned off the lights, sat down beside me and produced another hand rolled cigarette from her purse. She appeared to be about to light it, but she shook visibly, smiled at me and dropped the cigarette.

Before I had time to ask her if she was alright, I felt a pulse of energy wash through me and I realised why she was smiling. She was experiencing the same sensation that I was now feeling. I could read her mind clearly and she could read mine, different to anything I had so far experienced, it was clearer and faster, much faster. We exchanged thoughts rapidly, in those first minutes we shared a brief glimpse of our future, we knew we had a common destiny, at least in the short term. We would be going away together with Victor. Sam now knew Victor and we both knew we were going to leave the Earth, our friends and our family behind us. There was no need for me to explain things now, somehow she already knew what I knew.

We moved to face each other and sat motionless, our consciousness drifted away from our bodies into darkness and then light, brightly coloured surreal images cascading around us, while we exchanged subconscious thoughts about our lives. We kissed again, my hand found its way on to her soft thigh and moved up under her skirt. I had no control over my body and I knew she felt the same, it was as if we were being manipulated, yet at the same time enjoying the experience.

We both stood in silence as I undid her belt. I slipped my hands inside her skirt slowly easing it over her hips, letting it fall to the ground. She reached up and slowly undid my shirt buttons, slipped her hands inside over my chest and pushed the shirt back over my shoulders.

Sam undid the buttons on her blouse, slowly moving from top to bottom; while I stood back savouring every movement. She wore a very pretty white cotton brassiere, which cupped her firm and beautifully shaped young breasts. I eased the straps down over her shoulders, then she slid her hands around her breasts and caressed her erect nipples. I moved towards her and slid my hands around her hips.

She was the most beautiful woman I had ever seen, I sensed the same emotions from her, intensifying my feelings over and over. Our telepathic communication was not in the form of words, there was a direct transfer of emotion and longing between us, love and desire danced between us, wanting each other, more and more, until our minds became as one.

She kissed me again as softly as a butterfly landing on my lips, then moved away from me and sat on the sofa, her eyes fixed on mine. She touched herself through her tights and knickers, and I felt her arousal. We instinctively knew exactly what the other wanted, we savoured every moment, taking time to explore each other through sight, smell, touch, taste and thought. I realised we were now on our knees and as I kissed her breast. She eased her tongue deep into my ear and the sensation was electric. So erotic was our simple foreplay, she bought me to climax before I removed my trousers. Sam knew what had happened, she undid my belt, eased off my jeans and underpants, and teased me with her mouth and tongue. She stood up and removed her black tights and white knickers together, then laid down on the floor in front of me. My eyes focused on her exposed womanhood, and as I moved towards her I was drawn, by her thoughts, then her scent, and finally the sweet taste of her essence, it was a pleasure I had not known.

We made love there for the first time, on the rug in front of the fire. The candle light flickered around us as we both climaxed together, as one.

The sensation went far beyond anything I ever imagined. Our minds exploded, but we were locked together so fiercely that it just went on and on, until we both collapsed exhausted, having shared both the physical and the emotional ecstasy.

We lay naked on the rug together, physically incapable, but our minds raced away together like two wild horses, running out of control together. We exchanged memories, fears and fantasies. Things that I had forgotten surfaced in my mind and passed into Sam's.

Eventually we regained our physical strength and began again as if without a break. By now the candles had burned out, the only light came from the yellow fluorescent light across the street.

The dim yellow light was replaced by the early morning sunshine. We had made love time and time again throughout the night, and finally we collapsed more completely than at any other time, both submitting to a strange sleep.

Together, we rose above our bodies. I looked down at the two of us lying on the rug, my body spooned hers as she lay with her back against my stomach, my arms were wrapped around her and her face turned back towards me at an almost uncomfortable angle, her eyes closed in a blissful smile, and my face in her long blonde hair. It was the most beautiful thing I had ever experienced.

I looked around me and saw a familiar door, I seemed to be in the room I was born in at the family home in Sway. With Sam's hand in mine, I opened the door handle and floated through to a place I had never seen before. Instead of the staircase and landing that I knew so well, I found myself in an enormous circular auditorium. The walls were a misty lifeless grey, and the roof above formed the shallowest of domes. Thousands of people emerged amongst the grey mist as my eyesight became accustomed to the dimness of the shadows. I noticed that above the walls a band of bright white light seemed to support the domed ceiling.

I looked at Sam, she was still with me, then I looked back at the people who appeared to be dressed in rags, moving aimlessly passed each other.

We made our way across the room and found another door, unfamiliar to me, a heavy oak panelled door with a black iron handle.

I pulled on the handle and floated through, tumbling across space at incredible speed, passing stars, and looking down at the Milky Way with its bands of stars spiralling away from a brightly glowing mass of at the core.

I looked around and Sam was gone.

"Where are you Sam?"

"I'm here. I feel you, but I can't see you."

"I can't see myself, my hands, my feet, nothing."

"Nor can I."

* * *

It felt like we had shared some secret knowledge, I could feel what she felt, she had awakened a feminine side of my personality that I did not know existed; I knew there was more to be revealed, but I would have to be patient, I would discover more about the enigma I had fallen for, all in good time.

# AWAKENING

T he energy that we had both experienced deserted us at the same moment, and our minds experienced a synchronised parting of some kind. We were pulled back from time and space to our waking bodies.

It was dark outside. Sam woke first and screamed with panic as she realised that the day had come and gone. "Oh hell! Stuart is going to go crazy at me!"

"What?"

"Stuart will..." she hesitated. "Christ! Am I dreaming? Do you know too?"

I rubbed my eyes and shook my head trying to wake myself and collect my thoughts.

"I think so." I answered.

"Me? Us? Victor?"

"You know about Victor?" I asked.

"Of course, I know about Victor, and me!"

"Then I'm ok, and I know what we are going to do. We're both going with him! I've seen the future! Our future," I smiled.

"So have I! Just a little bit. Screw work! Who cares?"

She dropped her head back onto the floor beside me and stared at the ceiling.

"You know what must happen now, we shared it last night. We should tell everyone we have decided to clear off on a world tour. We can't take them all into our confidence, we can't risk it!"

She was buzzing with excitement and enthusiasm, but she was right, it all came back to me. We had shared so much that night I had forgotten, I was still waking up whereas Sam was now wide awake and more excited than a child on Christmas morning.

Everything that I had experienced in the days since the accident she was now aware of, but unlike me, had not had time to consider any of it. She turned onto her side to face me.

"Only John and Mary know about Victor and that is the way it must stay. Even Kevin will only know the truth in a letter from me and that will be after we have left. I'm worried that he will try to stop me if we tell him anything before we leave. I will explain everything in the letter and swear him to secrecy. If Kevin wants to talk to someone about it, he could talk to John and Mary."

"And you," I said, "it's so strange. How do you feel about knowing what you are?"

It was the first time she had an opportunity to consider what I was asking her, and at that point I had no idea what difference it made to either of us.

"I don't know what I think, but we have a lot to do! Yes, I have to hand in my notice and say goodbye to everyone?"

"You'll have to meet everyone first," I grinned.

"I know. I will meet your family and you will meet mine. You know the Olds are going to be furious about me wasting my inheritance from Nanna!"

"Why, we won't need any money?" I said.

"Of course we won't, but they will want to know how we plan to fund our world tour," she answered, pointing out the sort of planning required to maintain the secret. Her mind was working so much faster than mine, she was plotting everything as we talked.

"Of course, but we can let them manage the funds so that they know where we are. That way they retain some control and more importantly some reassurance. We'll take two hundred pounds to last us till we get passed Morocco."

"Wait a minute, it's Saturday night. You haven't got to be at work till Monday," I said, making sense of the reality around me.

"God! I don't even know what day it is. Do you remember what happened to us? I've had orgasms before, but last night was way beyond anything I can relate to. I was a part of you yesterday! We became one!"

"I remember," I answered.

"I remember my mind as we joined, erupting with your thoughts. I remember looking down at the two of us and seeing you do the same thing. I felt like I was travelling through space, out beyond the solar system and even the galaxy, into the universe and beyond into something, something indescribable. I left, no we left our bodies, became something different, a part of something, something that hasn't happened, something that has no concept of time, I don't know how long we were there it could have been years or even centuries."

"I remember too. It happened, I know it happened. I can't even begin to explain it."

She coughed and held her throat.

"Oh God, I'm going to die if I don't get a drink. Do you want some orange juice? I need some vitamin C!"

"Orange juice, yes, yes I'd love some. But how about a kiss from my princess first?"

She rolled on top of me and kissed me, then jumped up from the floor and ran off to the kitchen. She bounced back with two glasses and a carton of orange juice. In the dim yellow light her naked body looked like a marble statuette.

We were completely dehydrated. When we had finished the orange juice we both still needed water to quench our rampant thirst.

"Was that heaven?" I asked.

"What is heaven?" she answered philosophically.

"I can't describe it! I just felt..."

"Part of something." she answered, finishing my thoughts.

"Yes. Joined not just with you but like a small piece in a giant jig-saw puzzle. I felt a purpose and a contentment."

"No need for anything."

"Yes, no fear, no shame, no guilt, no expectations and no boundaries."

We talked through the experience as one person would recall it or ponder a question before answering himself. Not only had we shared completely the whole experience, it also seemed from the same perspective.

Having quenched our thirst, we soon realised how hungry we were. Sam cooked us scrambled eggs made with cream and butter topped with pieces of smoked salmon which we ate with granary toast made with bread from the baker downstairs. I had never tasted anything like it before. We were like a newly married couple waking together for their first morning of blissful union, except that the day had gone, and it was dark outside. We drank a large mug of hot sweet tea gazing into each other's eyes, then passion and lust took over and we went to her bed to continue where we had left off.

The night was endless and in some strange way felt like our first night alone, this time we were in complete control of our bodies and our senses. We both satisfied each other again and again before falling into a deep sleep in the early hours of the morning.

# III  THE EMPRESS

Sunday ~ 2nd December 1973

We woke just after 8.30 on Sunday morning, with a heavy smell of sex on our bodies. We bathed together soaping each other's body as we talked about what we should do, stopping to savour a kiss at every opportunity.

"My case!" I said, realising that we had not collected it from Britannic House.

"Well I don't think you'll be wearing these," said Sam, holding up my underpants in one hand, and the rest of our clothes tucked under her left arm. "I'll pop them in my laundry basket with your shirt. I'll find you a pair of Kevin's and one of his T-shirts after we've had some breakfast."

"What about my case?"

"We'll pick that up on our way."

Sam made toast with thick marmalade and more hot sweet tea for breakfast, which we ate at the table, wrapped in her white fluffy towels. She liked her tea very sweet and we both needed the sugar. The tea was aromatic, something I had not noticed the day before.

'Darjeeling, a distinctive tea grown in the mountainous districts of northern India,' I recalled. "I think your need for sugar is overpowering the delicate flavour of the tea my darling."

It was not a word I had ever used before, but it felt natural, it was what I called her."

I had been raised on the much stronger blend of PG Tips, and never in my life tasted anything quite like it. I then not only knew what it was and where it came from, I also had memories of drinking it for years. I also remembered the scrambled eggs and smoked salmon we had eaten the night before. I realised that I had previous memories of eating smoked salmon, the smoky, slightly salty taste as it was, not unlike that of smoked bacon, especially stirred into the eggs just before serving, but with a very different delicate texture. Until that night I had never

294

actually seen it before, let alone eaten it. It appeared to have nothing in common with the tinned variety my mother would buy for an occasional treat.

I gazed at the beautiful woman across the table. Her damp hair was drying in soft wavy curls and her face was pure and radiant as nature had intended. This was the woman I wanted to spend my life with, the woman with whom I had shared memories of things to come. She was not just a beautiful woman, she was clever, creative, well read and extremely knowledgeable; she had my love and my respect, she was caring and maternal, she would be a good mother, she was alluring in so many ways; I could easily have gone back to bed with her, but she was now on a mission. There were things we must do.

# THE MISSION

## REUNION

We took the tube back down the Northern Line to Moorgate, stopping off to collect my suitcase, then back to Euston Station and down to Waterloo. Sam knew all the security guards, there were often occasions when cadets travelled at weekends at short notice, needing their plane tickets and a ride to the airport.

As we walked from the tube steps onto Waterloo station I felt a hand on my shoulder.

"You must be Sam."

It was Victor, and I saw that he had his other hand on Sam's shoulder.

"What are you doing here?" I asked.

He was still wearing the same T-shirt and jeans but this time he had on a heavy woollen jacket.

"I'm looking for you!"

"Well I knew you were coming back, but I didn't expect you to be here."

"Here seemed as good as anywhere. I had to catch the train in myself, it's very difficult to find somewhere secluded enough for me to land my ship in London," he explained.

"Where is your ship?" I asked. Victor pointed upwards.

"In orbit?" asked Sam.

"No not exactly. Technically 'in orbit' refers to an object which is falling towards the planet at a constant velocity, while moving forwards at a velocity which matches the curve of the planet surface, thereby negating any loss in altitude above said surface."

"Sorry?" said Sam.

"He means that his ship isn't moving. His ship is hovering above us," I explained.

"In a way," said Victor. "But if it were hovering above you it would be in a geo-stationary orbit to maintain that position. It's actually in a fixed orbit with your Sun rather that the Earth. In respect to Earth, my ship is in a static position relative to Terra's rotating axis, at present directly above Nepal. If it were in orbit it would be much more conspicuous, as it is it would be easily confused as an object in the depths of the solar system."

"Now you're just confusing me," I said.

"No he's not. We understand. I know you must because I do. I don't know how, so it must be you, your thoughts," Sam interrupted.

"Yes, I suppose I do, I just didn't want you to feel stupid."

"I don't feel stupid. I know everything you know," she reminded me, "nor was I stupid before I met you!"

"No matter," he said. "So, you've made up your minds?"

"How did you know?" I asked.

"I have been back since you arrived in London with your father. I have been with you since then."

"You mean you were spying on us?" asked Sam.

"Not exactly."

Victor knew exactly what was going through her mind.

"Well what then?" she questioned.

"I have been sharing your thoughts," said Victor.

"What?" Sam was shocked.

"Physical and emotional gratification are linked, you will understand in time but for now please read my thoughts. There is no insult to you. You yourselves experienced the episode in many ways. You will understand soon."

He held Sam's neck above her right shoulder with his left hand, holding mine with his right. We were silent, oblivious to the people around us while he shared memories of the times they had spent together, as friends, as kin, and as lovers, in different lifetimes. It was the first time she was aware of the lives she had lived before. There was a deep bond between them; but her heart was mine, we all knew it, there was no sense of loss between them, only joy that he could take her home to Erato. Gradually she would recall everything that she had been in the lives she led before.

'I have completed my mission here,' he said in silence. 'You are my reborn son.'

'I am Eratean?" she asked in the same manner.'

'No, you are Terran. You were born of Terran parents, you have a Terran body and your personality was shaped by Helios, her planets and Luna. Your soul is Eratean'' he explained.

'My personality?' she questioned.

'Gravity is one of the most significant forces in the Universe. Once you understand its power and influence you can begin to understand movement through the galaxy, the manipulation of gravity is the way in which the three-dimensional galaxy can be manipulated, reshaped.'

We both saw Victor in his true form for the first time. He wore the same white robes he had worn when I first saw him, struggling for my life in the waters of the Persian Gulf.

His eyes were the most significant, appearing larger than normal but more significantly completely black. Had I seen him that way in the warm waters of the Gulf I may well have panicked and drowned. Apart from the black shark-like eyes, he was essentially very human like. His hair was blonde, not red and there was no indication of facial or body hair that we could see; his cranium was slightly larger than normal, big enough to make him look a little strange in its own right although not so large that in itself you would question his origin and it could easily have been disguised with long hair or a hat; his ears and nose were both large in comparison with Homo Sapiens, but his mouth appeared normal; his chin seemed slightly more pronounced than ours, emphasised by a set of perfectly formed if somewhat yellowish teeth; his upper torso looked powerful as did his limbs and his hands and feet were larger than ours, and he stood much taller than me, probably almost seven feet tall.

'The blackness you see is simply a membrane we have developed to protect our eyes from the pollution in the atmosphere here. We have no tear ducts and cannot clean our eyes the way you do.'

He retracted the black membrane to reveal his bright green cat-like eyes. There was no iris, the whole eye was green except for the black vertical pupil which was even more striking than the black membrane, but somehow less alarming.

The membrane closed again covering his eyes.

'We also need them for the light.'

'You mean like sun glasses?' I thought.

'No, just the opposite. On our world the light is brighter and as I said it is never completely dark. The membrane actually intensifies specific wavelengths of the light rather than block it.'

'When do you want to leave?' asked Sam silently.

'There are things I must do before I return to Erato. There will be questions about what is happening here when I return; as I said, messages take as long as travel and my people will want to know how your people are evolving.'

'Well can we stay for Christmas?' asked Sam.

'Christmas? Yes, we can stay as long as you wish. Time is not a problem now that I have found you.'

'In that case let's make it New Year. My father is Scottish as you know and it's a big thing for him. It would be nice to see the New Year in with the family," I said.

'January 2nd then,' he suggested.

'Agreed. Okay with you Sam.'

'Sounds great to me, and I know what I'm going to spend my money on. We are going to buy everyone the best Christmas present they have ever had before we go. And on New Year's Eve we're going to party and get absolutely wrecked.'

'Call me if you want me, I will hear you,' thought Victor.

'Where are you going now?' I asked.

'I have still have things to take care of here until you are ready to leave,' he answered without further explanation.

'Can these people see you the way we see you now?' I asked. Looking around at the crowds of people on the station, they seemed to be moving very slowly.

'They see me as you saw me with your eyes. There is no need to conceal myself here. I am just another face in the crowd. It seems strange to you I know, but we are communicating much faster than if we were speaking orally. That is why the people appear to move so slowly to you; your brain is giving you a different message and you have not had time to understand it. We have only been standing here together for seconds.'

'How can you control so many minds at one time, when we can only think one thing at a time? I asked.

'Why do you think that your mind can process only of one thing at a time? You overlook the fact that your nervous system is being monitored constantly, as are most of your physical needs. Your mind is processing thousands of inputs at the same time. Ah! You both seem to have a minor physical condition that requires intervention.'

We both felt a wave of energy ripple across us.

'There we are. As I said, most of your physical needs are being monitored simultaneously and you only use a small portion of your brain. Homo Sapiens use only a fraction of their brain capabilities and appear to have little recognition or control over the subconscious. We use our entire brain with thousands of separate thought processes running concurrently in the subconscious. Like you we have one conscious thought process which can be interrupted. Of course our brains are slightly larger than yours.'

"Well how can we ever do what you do?" asked Sam.

'Patience, these skills will come to you in time. I will see you both very soon,' he said as he walked away into the crowd of people.

He was out of sight before I remembered Paul. He said that he wanted to find Paul, which was why he went away. Did he know I had met him? I wondered if Victor had uncovered any of the answers he sought. I had not told anyone about the Tarot cards that Paul had given me, there was no need to tell Sam, she knew everything that had ever happened to me, everything I knew and remembered.

I cannot explain in words the depth of intimacy and security I shared with Sam, neither of us had any memories to conceal. Both of us accepted everything that had gone before, and both of us knew that at least our immediate destiny was to be shared.

# A WOMAN'S SCORN

We bought our tickets and boarded the train home at 10:45, we would be home by lunch time.

"Well big boy, d'ya wanna follow me, I've got plans for you," she said, trying to impersonate Mae West.

I knew exactly what she meant, and it embarrassed me immensely that she knew how I lost my virginity in such depth, especially because it had been such a short time before, but then I also knew that she had slept with her previous boyfriend only ten days before. She had been in a casual relationship with a twenty-year-old Jamaican wood-be actor called Reginald when I saw her on the Worcester, she had enjoyed his company and not expected to begin a relationship with me or anyone else. It had ended amicably, there had never been any commitment, and he knew that she was struggling to come to terms with her feelings about me. They parted, leaving the door open.

I followed her down the carriage to the toilet. As soon as I closed the door, Sam undid my trousers, bent down and took me in her mouth. This time I was able to savour the sensation for much longer than my first experience. Sam was not going to be outdone, it was a preconceived performance for her and of course she had the advantage of being able to read my mind.

"Not a bad effort," I said as I opened the door.

My sarcasm was answered by a very firm punch in my right kidney.

"Do you think he was listening in again?" asked Sam.

"Of course he is."

Sam shook herself involuntarily, it was still difficult for her to come to terms with the feeling of being observed some way, having been raised as a Terran.

"You're going to put me off sex for life if you carry on like that."

"Oh, I thought perhaps that little performance was because you thought we were being watched," I teased.

I winced in pain as my right kidney took another punch from behind, even harder than before.

"You're disgusting! Good God he was my father once! Spare me please!"

"He was also your lover in another life, more than one life I recall, any way you know I was only teasing."

We returned to our seats and continued to spar with each other like young lion cubs.

# THE PIANO

Once we were past Brockenhurst, Sam took great delight in describing the landscape around us, pointing out all the features that she now knew as well as I did.

The train eventually stopped at the empty station and we stepped out into the crisp December sunshine.

No one knew we were coming home together or even expected me home for Sunday lunch, but I was sure Mum would be intending to save me some.

"Now you know what we have to do don't you?" asked Sam reassuring herself.

"Yes of course I know. If we focus on our love for each other they will all sense the energy between us. That will alleviate their fears about what we intend doing."

"That's it. You know they will pick it up. And where are we going, Africa, America, Europe?" she asked testing me.

"I thought we agreed Africa is best, it will be easier for them to accept that we have disappeared there. But we'll say we are backpacking through France and Spain before getting a boat to Morocco."

"You don't think that John or Mary will tell them where we have really gone."

"No, at least not for a while. They both know that they would be ridiculed, no one would believe them. Later, when time has passed, when everyone begins to think we are lost or dead, people will sense the different emotions in them. John, Mary and Kevin will know that we are almost certainly still alive and well. The truth will come out at a time when the others are ready to believe them."

"Do you think Victor met Paul?" she asked.

I think Victor would have passed us something of what happened if he did, but I felt nothing. I even forgot to ask, the past forty-eight hours have been pretty eventful," I grinned.

"There is just so much information in my mind I don't know how to deal with it. I'm not used to knowing so much about someone else," said Sam.

"I know what you mean. I don't understand how Victor copes with it all, it obviously has something to do with how we use our brain."

"Well I hope he can help me soon otherwise I am going to forget my own name, my head is just buzzing. It's going to be hard to concentrate in there."

"Well you're going to have to, that's my house there." I pointed to the house at the bottom of the hill."

"I know where you live fool. I know everything about you, even what a bloody mess your bedroom is in."

"Of course. I'll get used to it."

I opened the back door and walked in with Sam following me. Mother was in the dining room laying the table with Mary and the twins were in the sitting room playing the piano.

'Perhaps more accurately described as playing 'with' the piano,' I thought.

"Jim, I didn't expect you back till tonight," said Mum.

I gave her a kiss and a hug.

"Mum this is Samantha."

Mum looked at Sam and at me sensing the affection between us immediately.

"Hello Sam, give me a hug then," she said, the way she did with everyone. There was no sign of surprise in her, perhaps my father had told her after he returned from Britannic House.

"Hello Mum," Sam responded, as if she had known her all her life. In fact, she had known her 'all my life', so it was natural for her to call her Mum even on their first meeting. Mum didn't pick up on it, she just gave her a great big squeeze.

"Hello Mary, how are you?" I said giving her a peck on the cheek. "Where's John?"

"He's taken your Dad up the club for a pint."

"Oh yeah!" I answered.

Mum had released her grip on Sam and they were both smiling happily. I focused my thoughts on my love for Sam as I introduced her to Mary.

"Mary, this is Sam."

"Welcome to the madhouse Sam. I've heard all about you from John. I must say you two look very happy together."

"Thank you, we are," Sam smiled.

I had never taken a girl home with me before but both Mum and Mary seemed to sense our feelings and took to Sam instantly. I recalled that Sam's astrological sun sign was Virgo, the same as Mary's, and the same as my rising sign, how others see us. It suddenly seemed odd that I had always been interested in astrology but so frightened of the Tarot. Sam's rising sign was Taurus, my sun sign.

"Come through to the sitting room and I'll introduce you to the twins," I said.

I led her through to the piano where my two younger sisters, Jennie and Julie conspired to encourage John's three-year-old daughter to bash at the piano keys with her tiny fist.

"Sam, this is Jennie, and this is Julie."

The twins looked around and sniggered at each other, then ran out into the garden without saying a word.

"Sorry, they're a bit shy," I explained. "And this is Jane, John and Sue's daughter."

"Hello Jane, my name's Sam," she said, kneeling down to be at Elaine's eye level.

"Hello Sam. Hello Uncle Jim," she answered. I picked her up and gave her a cuddle.

"Are you going to play the piano?" she asked.

"Yes, why not," I said.

I sat down at the piano, it was my Mother's. Dad had taken her to a shop in Southampton and bought it for her before any of us were born. She played by ear and encouraged us all to learn. Over the years, six children had taken their toll on what was once a beautiful instrument, it was now scratched and stained, parts of the ivory had been removed from one or two keys however despite the constant abuse it received, it was reasonably well tuned and still produced a pleasant sound.

I began to play Beethoven's Fur Elise and the sound was so beautiful that I became completely engrossed.

"Oh Sam, that's beautiful," said my, mother walking into the room with Mary behind her. She stopped immediately and stood watching intently as she realised it was me playing. I played the entire piece effortlessly and with excellent expression then turned around to Sam and the others.

"How did you do that?" asked Mum. "You couldn't play that well last week!"

I had taken some lessons at school some time before and was capable of playing simple two-handed pieces, but she was right, I could not have played that before. It was Sam, she was the piano player, our exchange of thoughts had been so complete it even allowed me to use her talents to play a beautiful if somewhat elementary piece of classical music from memory.

"I don't know, I said. "It just came to me."

"It's a gift from God, it's a miracle. I knew you were special," she said. "You've always been special."

"What else can you play?" asked Mary.

"I don't know. Lots of things, Bagatelle!" I said and turned to continue playing.

"Oh, what has happened to you, it's a gift!" My mother had a particularly strong, perhaps even eccentric religious beliefs, and was prepared to accept miracles without a second thought. Mary was more sceptical and naturally Sam knew exactly why I was able to play. She had been playing since she was four years old and had private lessons from the age of six until just the year before.

Despite the knowledge of how I was able to perform this way using Sam's talent, it still seemed a miracle by every definition I could think of. I could do things now I could not do before, so it was logical to asume that everything I could do, Sam could do likewise.

"Again," shouted Jane.

"No more," I answered.

I got out of the chair and Mum hugged me believing that I had clearly been chosen for some special purpose. Then she turned around and gave Sam a hug, carried away with her excitement.

"We'll tell the Vicar and Harry Gale."    I realised that in my thoughtlessness I had set off down a road to disaster and quickly decided to manipulate the situation to suit our purpose. Mary would hear the truth from John soon enough, she already knew about Victor, though this was the first evidence that anything mysterious had happened to me.

"Mum listen," I said, drawing her back into the dining room with my arm around her shoulder. "Something happened to me out there in the Gulf, when I had the accident. I don't know what it was, but I kept hearing a voice and I've been hearing it ever since."

I consoled myself that so far I hadn't told even the whitest lie.

"The thing is, strange things have happened to me since then and I can do things I couldn't do before. Any way the voice has told me I must go on a long journey, leave the navy, and I must set off on this journey after Christmas."

"Leave the navy, give up work?" she questioned.

"Mum, I know it sounds crazy, but I just know it's what I'm supposed to do. Sam is going with me!"

"Where are you going, how long will you be gone?" she asked.

"I don't know the purpose of the journey, but we are going to start off in Jerusalem."

It had suddenly occurred to me that the Holy Land would have a bigger impact than Morocco.

"He's telling the truth Mrs Cummings," Sam chipped in. "I've heard the voice myself and I know I have to go with him. I'm going to hand in my notice tomorrow."

"But you've only just come back!"

"I know Mum, but I have to do this," I answered.

"Well we'll have to talk to your dad."

"No! Dad mustn't know about the voice or the piano, he doesn't believe the way you do."

"What are you going to tell him?" She asked, realising that Dad would never believe what I had said.

"I'll tell him that I need some time to make up my mind about the Navy, and that we are going to get away together to do just that. I'll tell him that we are going to see North Africa and Egypt where he had served in the war. He'll listen, and he'll understand, I know he will."

"You said you were going to..."

"Israel!" Sam interrupted instinctively before she had time to finish. "We're going to start off in Israel and cross the Sinai into Egypt the way Mary and Joseph did with the baby Jesus."

"But there has been fighting there, it's been on the news all the time, and where is all the money going to come from?"

"I have an inheritance," Sam answered. Mary didn't know how to stop herself laughing. She knew how easily I could use Mum's faith to mislead her and she had a pretty good idea where we were really going but she would never talk. We were very close, and I could rely on her as much as I could rely on John.

"We'd better go and drag John and Dad back from the club," I said. "You think on it and tell me what you would do Mum. You've heard me play the piano. So you know something has happened to me."

"Yes, perhaps I should speak to the Vicar though."

She trusted the Vicar implicitly in all matters of religion, and she also knew that the vicar, Peter Were, was a good friend of mine.

"No Mum, the voice said no-one must know about it, I was only to confide in you."

I knew she would never risk going against the Almighty's will, though it seemed cruel and sinful to use her faith against her.

# TELEKINETIC

---

Ｗe set off up the hill to the Working Men's Club. I was a junior member and allowed into the bar to play snooker and darts, but I would not be served alcohol there.

I signed Sam in as a guest and we walked through into the bar, John was watching Dad roll the dice. It was a regular part of Sunday lunch times at the club, roll three ones, three twos, or three threes, and you would walk away with a huge joint of meat, or a tray of fresh eggs; meat for the ones or twos, eggs for the threes. Dad had three ones, a result he shared with just one other local.

John acknowledged us both silently as my father, oblivious of our arrival, prepared to make his throw. We watched the ritual in silence as he wiped the three dice from the table into a small red leather beaker at the edge using his contorted hand. Clasping his left hand over the top of the beaker, he moved it to his mouth and blew magic into the space between his thumb and forefinger. As he threw the dice his whole body seemed to follow his arm, due to the stiffness in his joints. After three throws he finished up with two ones and a three.

The other contender moved up and took his first throw; a one, a three and a six. He picked up the three and the six and re-threw them. One of the die seemed to settle briefly on a one. I knew that I was consciously willing it to keep rolling as it flipped over once more and became a three, the other die coming to rest as a four. I had no idea if I had any influence on the dice or not and no one else seemed to notice, it happened too quickly to be sure. He took his final throw with the two dice and threw a five and a six. Dad had won. He selected the best looking joint of pork and left John to carry it away.

"Hello son. How long have you been here?" he asked turning around.

"We just arrived, we didn't want to interrupt your concentration," I answered.

"Have you been home?"

"Yes, we just came from there. You know Sam."

"Of course we do. Hello lass, how are you, have you had a nice weekend?"

"I'm very well thank you Mr Cummings; John." she nodded, acknowledging my brother. "It's lovely to see you again. I've had a wonderful weekend with James thank you."

To call him 'Dad' would have been over familiar, he was not as forward as my mother; none of my in-laws called him Dad, and despite his insight, our brief relationship hardly gave reason to do so. Since I knew that, Sam knew it too.

"It's very nice to see you too Sam. I knew Jim had a thing about you, but I didn't expect to see you here today. You both look very pleased with yourselves," he said.

She was clinging to my arm, and I loved it.

"We're just finishing a game of snooker at the moment, we were just called over for Dad to do the playoff roll. Why don't you get Sam a drink Higgs? Here!" said John handing me a fifty pence piece.

We walked over to the bar and they walked off to continue their game of snooker.

"Higgs?" she asked me as we turned.

"My brother has always called me Higgs, or Higgins."

"Yes I know, your sister Jean calls you Bugs or Bugsy and your Mum calls you Charlie. I knew, but I don't know why."

"That's probably because I don't know either. My friends call me..."

"I know what your friends call you and we don't need to know why thank you very much," she interrupted. "Boys! They're so disgusting!"

I noticed that there were a few friends I had grown up with in the club that day, and I took great pleasure in introducing Sam to them.

"James, I need the loo, don't tell me, I know where it is," she whispered with her mouth virtually kissing my ear.

"How do you know that? I don't know where the ladies is."

311

"I saw the sign as we came in," she answered with a smile.

"Elementary my dear Watson," I grinned and gave her a small kiss. "What would you like to drink?"

"White wine please."

"Dry?"

"Aha'."

She disappeared into the entrance hall and I was about to order the drinks when one of my friends stopped me. We had been choir boys together along with his older brother Stuart, our fathers were both Scots and our mothers were good friends. His name was James too, but everyone knew him as Bogey, I'm not sure why, but it distinguished between us and to me it seemed natural to call him by something other than my own name.

"How on Earth did you manage to pull that mate?" he asked with a jealous grin.

"We pulled each other. She's from London," I said grinning.

"Nice one. What d'ya know about er?"

"Everything! Everything there is to know."

He looked at me puzzlingly.

"How long have ya known 'er then?" he asked.

"All her life," I said.

"Is she a cousin or somethin'?"

"No, she's my girlfriend."

"Well you never mentioned er before. How old is she?"

"Nineteen."

"Nineteen! Bloody-ell, that's two years older than me, three years older than you! How the hell did ya manage that? She's stunnin mate!" he said, shaking his head with envy and disbelief.

He was born in August and despite being in my year at school was almost a year older than me.

"She's the most beautiful woman I've ever seen," I replied.

"What?" he said, laughing at the words I used. "Your 'ooked matey! Mind you, I can't say I blame ya. Hey, are you going to the school prize-giving next week?"

"Yeah!"

"Are you bringin' 'er wiv ya?"

"Yeah, I think I will."

"I heard all about your accident by the way. Your mum told my mum."

"Seems like a life time ago now."

"Hey, I'll see ya at the prize-giving. She's gonna turn a few 'eds."

"Yes, I think she probably will," I answered.

It was true, I was very lucky, and very happy, Sam was all I could ever wish for and the depth of the relationship was something no-one else could have any experience of, at least no-one I knew.

I turned back to the bar to order the drinks as Sam returned.

"It's James isn't," said Sam. "My James has told me all about you."

"Sorry mate, this is Sam," I said introducing her.

"People call me..."

"Bogey, yes I know, what horrid people, I shall call you Jamie to distinguish you from James, Bogie sounds like some kind of ghost or demon."

He laughed, and I grinned.

"Well it's the young Mr Cummings. I see your dad's done well again this week! Looks like luck runs in the family at the moment," said Burt the steward, looking at Sam.

"Yes, that's a nice piece of pork for next weekend."

"I wasn't talking about the pork. Your dad and your brother have taken at least twenty quid out of the machine today. They've had the tenner twice."

"No wonder John was so generous."

"Hey there, he always is! You know that."

"Yeah I was only kiddin. Can I have a pint of shandy and a glass of dry white wine please Burt?"

He peered over the top of his glasses at me.

"It's for my girlfriend Sam, she's nineteen."

Sam smiled and slid her arm around mine.

"You want a drink mate, since my big brover is buyin?"

"Why not, I'll have another shandy with ya," said Bogie.

"Can I have another shandy for my ginger friend please Burt?" I asked.

"Since your brother's buying I'll serve you, but you know you're not supposed to buy alcohol yourself," he replied.

It amused me that he would take issue about the wine for Sam, yet think nothing of giving me a half a pint of bitter as long as it was topped up with lemonade.

"Wanna try our luck on the fruit machine?" asked Bogie.

"Not really mate, you heard what Burt said. You're not gonna get much out of that after John and dad have emptied it," I said. "But I'll watch you throw your money way if you like."

Bogie had left school at fifteen and started work as an apprentice motor mechanic and he loved to play the fruit machine. Being nearly seventeen and half he could just about get away with being under age.

We followed him over to the machine, and he put two ten pence pieces into the slot, giving him for spins. On the third spin, he punched the hold button on the two outer reels and re-span the middle one; a cherry dropped in between the two bars on either side. He put another ten pence in and once again the two bars dropped into the same place on his first spin. Again, he held the two bars and re-spun the middle reel. The third bar dropped down on place below the win line and I willed it back one space. Had it dropped down, it might have gone unnoticed, but there was no doubt it had gone backwards.

He looked at me with shock and some guilt as the machine rattled out the sound of tokens loud enough for everyone in the vicinity to hear.

"Let me," said Sam, "just in case someone moans."

Bogie moved to one side while Sam scooped up a hundred ten pence tokens and took them to the bar to exchange for cash. We knew that if any of the older members who had lost money in the machine complained about his age, he might not get his money.

"I'm sorry young lady, James should have told you you're not really supposed to play the fruit machines if you're not a member," explained Burt apologetically. "Are you a CIU member?"

"Of course, I'm a member of my local club in Highgate," replied Sam, knowing full well she was not.

"Well that's alright then," said Burt, without asking for proof.

He stacked up the coins in piles of ten in front of her, and seeing they were all there exchanged them for two five-pound notes."

Together we walked around the bar to watch John and Dad finish their game. Sam handed Bogie his winnings as we sat in the corner out of sight from the bar and said nothing.

Neither Dad nor John were particularly good snooker players, it was a real struggle for Dad with his arthritis, but they loved to play now and again. Watching my dad struggle with the snooker cue reminded me that I had asked Victor if he might be able to do something for him. He had told me to consider that myself. Surely if I was thinking about it, Victor would know it, but I heard no voice answer my call, I would have to bring it up when we next met. I know that I would have given anything to stop his pain, and I tried to focus on his suffering as Victor had suggested while they finished the game. John won shortly afterwards, so we said goodbye to Bogie and went home for lunch.

# CHECKMATE

Malcolm handed Mum the pork as we walked in.

"Again? That's two weeks on the trot." Dad had actually won the beef that Mum was cooking, two weeks before, which was why John and Mary were there for lunch.

Sunday was normally a big thing for Mary's parents, her father was a farmer. To say they never went short of food was probably the understatement of the century. I remember eating Sunday roast there and it always seemed like half a cow had been placed on the table.

Dad then handed over a five-pound note to Mum and winked, everyone was in a good mood.

We all sat down for lunch, but we never mentioned our fictional forthcoming journey. I knew it would be better to discuss it with Dad when we could be alone. John and Mary would know what we really intended, and Mum would probably tell him everything that we had discussed in her excitement, despite being asked not to.

"Are you going back to London tonight Sam, or would you like me to make up a bed in the twin's room for you."

The twins' room was enormous and was once used by all four of my sisters. It was the room I was born in, sixteen years before.

"No thank you Mrs Cummings, I must go home tonight. I have to be at work in the morning."

"Yes of course dear. What time are you going back?"

"I'm catching the train at quarter past seven. Can I help you with the washing up?"

"No, you can help me with the washing up." I said, and John nearly choked on his second helping of beef.

"What's this then, you never wash up," John scoffed.

"Nor did you," said Mum, coming to my defence.

"You go and watch the film with Dad," I told Mum.

Sunday afternoons were meant for falling asleep in front of the television after a wonderful lunch.

"We've got apple pie and custard or treacle tart first," said Mum.

Mary helped Sam and me clear the dinner plates while Mum brought in the second course and the dishes. When everyone had finished Sam and I began the task of clearing up while everyone else went into the sitting room to watch the film.

"Can you make it back here by six thirty on Friday?" I asked.

"Yes, I suppose I could. Why?"

"It's my school prize-giving and I'd love you to come, I want to show you off."

"I'd love to come. If I hand in my notice tomorrow morning, I can finish on Friday morning and have the afternoon off. I'm owed nearly a week's holiday so that will come in useful because we can have some time with my family before Christmas."

"That's great. I'll talk to Dad tonight about us, just to prime him. I'll start talking about his war time activities in Alexandria, he loves to talk about that, well some of it."

We finished the clearing up and went in to join the others, they were all sat watching the Sunday afternoon film, 'Flight of the Phoenix', with James Stewart apparently stuck in the middle of the Gobi Desert.

I sat down in the only vacant arm chair and Sam sat on my knees. Watching the crippled aeroplane be rebuilt and rise from the ashes to fly again, struck a chord with what was happening to Sam and me.

When the film was over, John turned around and asked me for a game of chess. It was John who had taught me when I was nine years old, and it frustrated him that I could more than hold my own against him. I played regularly at school, while he only ever played me.

"Sam will give you a game, she's not bad."

She gave me a strange look, she had never played before in her life and the thought seemed preposterous to her.

"Great!" said John.

He set up the chess at the dining table and I watched them play with Mary and Jane. It was more like draughts than chess, just the way I would have played John. He always became very frustrated if I exchanged piece for piece that way. He could never see through my tactic, simply not allowing him to play his game.

"You're very good," said John after being beaten. "How long have you been playing?"

"About seven years, my brother taught me," she answered, and I smiled.

After the game had finished, Mum laid the table for tea. Sam told me that she could read John's mind when they were playing, I could too. She knew how I had been able to read other people's thoughts when their concentration or emotions were strong, and she could now do the same.

At seven o'clock Sam said goodbye to everyone and John took us both to the station.

"Goodbye Sam, I hope I'll see you again soon. I'll wait in the car and leave you two alone to say your goodbyes."

"Count on it! I'll be back next Friday. Goodbye and thanks for the game of chess, it was my first. James will explain."

She leant forward from the back seat and gave him a kiss on the cheek.

"I'll be about ten minutes mate," I said.

"I'll be here," he grinned.

We walked along the station platform into the little waiting room and sat down in front of the little gas fire. We were alone at last, Sam put her arms around me and gave me a big hug and we kissed for almost five minutes.

"If you think I'm going to let you take advantage of me here and make me miss my train you can forget it," she said breaking away.

"You were thinking it too," I answered.

"I know but we'll both have to be patient. I'm going to hand in my notice tomorrow. I want to go home to my world and live my life there with you, and when we die, we will both be born again as Erateans, so that we can be together again. I've had a wonderful time with you and I have...' no *we* have, experienced things very few others could have. I want more. I think I love you; I don't really know what love is, but I love being with you. I also believe that Victor was once my father, and perhaps my lover in other lifetimes. Somehow I know that Erato is my home and where I belong."

"I think that I fell in love with you that day on the Worcester. After everything that's happened this weekend I'm going to miss you like hell."

"It's only till Friday, we've both got so much to do and you're going to have to meet my parents next weekend. I want to spend some time with them at Christmas if that's alright with you. Can we?" she asked.

"Yes of course we can. Bloody hell I don't know how I am going to survive the week without you. I hope they like me as much as my lot like you."

"I know they will. Somehow I felt that your whole family could see a part of you in me."

"When could they have seen us?" I asked, twisting her words into a tasteless joke. "I'm, sorry, I will try to stop being coarse, I know you hate it. I do know what you mean, I already know your parents through you. Hows about spending Christmas Eve with mine, have a few drinks at the pub with Dad, John and Richard, Christmas Day and Boxing Day with the Olds and Kevin, then back here for New Year's Eve? I asked, using the alias she had for her parents.

"Great I'll call Mum tomorrow morning. But what about Mary, Jean, your mum, Jane and Charles? Can't they come to the pub too?"

"Mum won't go to the pub, Charles doesn't drink and doesn't like pubs, so he and Jane probably won't come, Jean and Mary might be persuaded if Mum will baby sit. We can only ask. We can do Midnight Mass with Mum when the pub shuts. We all love singing carols."

She already knew what I was saying but she wanted to ask.

"I know you do," she smiled.

What are you going to do about your Le Fevre?"

"I'll tell Dad I want time to think about it and if I have to, I'll leave. We are going to Israel to begin our world tour, just like you said to Mum, ok? Not France!"

"Yes, agreed."

We walked outside together to check on the train, there was no sign of it arriving yet, so we began to kiss again. I was just tugging at her skirt when we heard the station master open the office door. The train appeared right on cue and we hugged until it pulled up in front of us.

"I'll call you tomorrow night." I said.

"No, I'll call you," she said. You never know who's going to be in the phone box so it's easier for me to call you at home," she answered.

"My phone number...'"

"Sway 324. I know stupid." she interrupted.

"Yeah I keep forgetting."

She climbed into the train and closed the door, opened the window and grabbed my cheeks in an attempt to kiss me one last time.

The station master blew his whistle and lifted up the little green flag he carried.

"Keep clear now," he shouted to me. I stood back and waved her goodbye. I felt so sad to see her go but so very happy about our future. She was still waving and blowing kisses when the train disappeared beyond the tunnel.

I got back in the car and smiled at John.

"Are you going to explain then?"

"What?" I asked.

"The chess!"

"Tomorrow. I've got so much to tell you, you have to know it all before you'll even begin to understand. Ask Mary how much my piano playing has improved."

"What?"

"Just ask her and I'll explain tomorrow."

"Ok. You're a lucky son of a bitch you know."

"Yeah I am."

"Yes you are, you smutty worm!" thought Sam from the train. She was communicating with me. I could sense it was her voice clearly in my mind. It was the first time she spoken to me in that way. "You're a slimy slug for screwing that tart on the train when you wanted me. If I didn't know she seduced you, I'd make you sorry. And please dispose of her underwear immediately! Goodbye for now my handsome bear."

"I love you." I answered with my thoughts.

"I love you too mate," said my brother.

"Sorry?" I asked.

"I said I love you too." John had picked up my thoughts. Whatever I was doing now in using telepathy, I was doing it better. The problem was now I couldn't contain or direct my thoughts.

# NEW MEMORIES

I t felt strange to be alone again that evening. I had only spent one
weekend with Sam, but she was now a part of me and of my life. I
knew everything that she was, yet without her at my side, I felt so very
lost and vulnerable.

When John and Mary had gone, I decided to take a walk in the cold
crisp December air.

I wanted so much to be home for Christmas and yet somehow it
seemed to have lost its excitement. It had never been quite the same
since I lost my singing voice. Up until that time, my sisters and I would
be planning to go carol singing all over the village before mid-December;
we had to go early because as Christmas grew closer I would be out carol
singing with the church choir. The memories of each filled me with
emotion. Tears formed in my eyes and ran down my face, chilled by the
cold night and I realised I had no idea whether they were tears of joy or
sadness.

Carol singing with my older sister Jane and her friend Joanie, had
always been remarkable, not only for the sound we produced together,
but sadly because it was the only time of the year when Jane and I were
close, she could sing every bit as well as me and for that matter my
brother, who was also a choir boy. At any other time of the year we
fought constantly as siblings often do. Our harmonies would even get us
invited into houses to perform and be richly rewarded for doing so. The
money was always divided equally between the three of us and used to
buy presents for the family.

Singing carols with the choir was a different experience but equally
enjoyable. The choir would be invited into the homes of members of the
congregation who made sizable donations to the church funds. They and

their guests would have the privilege of being entertained in the comfort of their home. We would be rewarded with small sausage rolls, mince pies and other Christmas niceties. I had been Head Choir Boy during my last two years after Bogie's older brother Stuart had left, and as such was expected to sing the odd solo. Despite feeling honoured to do so it was the blend of melodious harmonies and verses of powerful unison that filled me with emotion.

I loved the traditional atmosphere, the smell of the tree, the same old decorations that would come out each year, the Chinese lanterns that would replace the lamp shades around the house, the Christmas cards, sprigs of holly with bright red berries and mistletoe with its clusters of white pearls. All the seasonal food, turkey, ham, mince pies and sausage rolls, fruit, nuts and lemonade. It was a package that seemed to be just the way Christmas should be. Presents were simple, but they were given with the love and kindness that made them special.

Now I was almost an adult, my school days were over, there was a new generation of Cummings', and for the first time there was a girl, no a woman, in my life and it appeared I not only had my own memories of Christmas, I had Sam's as well. The taste and smell of her mother's divine spiced potato and onion stuffing, the small candles that sat on the ends of the Christmas tree branches held on by little tin clips, waking in the half-light wondering how anyone had managed to get a tricycle upstairs to the bedroom, stretchy red crepe paper, paper chains, the paper balls and bell which folded flat and were brought out each year, her parents and grandmother wearing their party hats and listening to the Queen's speech.

They all seemed so vivid. Why then did such pleasant memories fill my eyes with still more tears? Perhaps the sadness that together we would soon be saying goodbye to everything we had ever known. I just did not understand what makes us cry.

I wondered about the deeper meaning of Christmas and how much what had happened had affected my Christian beliefs. So far there was nothing that contradicted with anything I had been taught. I had always believed that there was extra-terrestrial life and that had no bearing on

Christianity as I saw it. To me, the essence of Christianity was a life based on love, forgiveness, kindness and compassion. All of these things Victor strove towards, perhaps the Erateans were more in harmony with Christianity and the other religions of the Earth than the people of my world seemed to be. Was there a special time in the year when they too felt the joy in giving and sharing? And what of my fellow men? Did the other religions of Earth celebrate their faith with the same joy we did? I had no idea.

# IV  THE EMPEROR

Later that evening I sat down with my father and we talked about his experiences in North Africa as planned. He actually enjoyed his posting in Al Ismailiyah, despite the fact that the world was at war, and that he was far from home and the woman he loved.

He was enormously proud that he had been chosen to skipper his supply-boat, while his friend a regular seaman and former Skipper before the war, was selected as his Mate.

"I'd like to see Egypt," I said.

"Why don't you tell Captain Le Fevre, he'll send you there," he suggested.

"I'm not sure what I want yet Dad. I'm not ready to go back. I want some time to think it over before I make any decisions. You must know how I feel after the accident. It's not confidence, it's more like second thoughts about whether this is right for me. I want to get away for a while see something of the dry land on this planet before I go back to sea."

"For how long son? How could you afford it?"

"We can work our way round."

"We?" he asked.

"Sam and me. She's going to hand in her notice and she has some money to get us started.

"She's a bonny lass son, but you hardly know her, and I brought you up to know you have to pay your own way in life. How long would you expect to go for?"

"I don't know yet, but I'm no good to B.P. as I am."

"I suppose not, if that's how you feel. You know I only want what's right for you, don't you?"

I knew that in his heart he desperately wanted me to pursue my career in the Merchant Navy.

"Course I do Dad, that's why I know you'll understand me. You're not bothered about me going with Sam then?"

"Good God boy, Sam can't be worse than anything you would have seen in the Navy. She's a bonnie lass and I'm pleased you've found someone special."

"Thanks Dad."

My elder brother and sisters had all been married at the tender age of eighteen, which wasn't much older than I was. I realised that in Dad's perception, I had suddenly grown up and could make decisions for myself.

"I'm in no position to help you out financially I'm afraid. It's a shame your granddad wasn't still alive he might have given you something to be goin' on with."

"What shall I do about work?"

"Nothing. You've another week sick to think things through, there's no need to say anything now. Use what time you've got to think things through."

"But Sam's going to hand in her notice."

"That's up to Sam. What is she going to say to Le Fevre?"

"Nothing. She won't say anything to him about us, there's no need for him to know anything yet."

"Let's just see what happens. Maybe I can talk them into giving you a few months to think things through, you're still very young."

"Sure, whatever you think Dad."

It was pointless me trying to explain to him that I knew I wouldn't be going back to sea. I had already made up my mind or at least my mind had been made up. It was impossible to stop myself doing something that I had already realised was a part of my destiny. I felt an irresistible duty to do what I knew must be done.

I thought about what Paul had quoted to me, supposedly from the Gospel of Thomas, '"If you bring forth what is within you, what you bring forth will save you.  If you do not bring forth what is in you, what you do not bring forth will destroy you.'

I wondered just how old Paul was; was he a Malakh as Victor had said?  What part would he play in my new life?  He would be the key to the unanswered questions I had, not Victor.

### Monday ~ 3rd December 1973

"What's this Sam?" asked Captain Le Fevre as she handed him her letter along with the morning post.

"It's my resignation Captain," she answered.

"Resignation? Why? What on Earth has brought this on?" he asked, shocked and totally bewildered.

"I need a change and I have decided I want to do some travelling," she answered.

"Travelling?  This is all very sudden, have you come into some money?"

"Not to speak of.  I plan to work my way around for a while, doing whatever comes up."

"Have I upset you in some way?"

"No of course not! You've always been like a father to me."

"And what about young Cummings, what may I ask does he have to do with all this?  Has he upset you or let you down in some way?  You know it's not worth giving up your job just because you get upset by a cadet."

"I'm not upset, and James hasn't done anything.  I'm very fond of James, but he has a life of his own and I'm not sure I plan on becoming a Cadet's girlfriend."

"Then why?  Have I upset you or has someone else here upset you?"

"No, I told you, no-one has upset me, especially not you.  I've enjoyed working for you so very much, you've always been so very kind and very professional.  It's just that I have a friend you see, and she's decided she wants to see the world.  We met up yesterday after James left and she talked me into going with her. I'm young, and I want to see the world too."

"Well I don't want to lose you so if there's anything I can do let me know. Promise?"

"I promise."

"If you're determined to travel you could even consider becoming a Cadet yourself. I don't want to lose you, but I will do everything I can to help you."

"That's very kind of you, but that's not really what I had in mind."

"He's going to be upset you know."

"Who is?"

"Cummings. It's obvious he's very fond of you. You know you're like a daughter to me, I'm very, very fond of you myself. I saw the way you looked at each other on the Worcester and it made me wonder just how I will feel when I see my own little girl look at a boy like that for the first time."

"She's only twelve."

"She's growing up very quickly and she is becoming quite a precocious little madam!"

"He'll be alright," she said. "He's going to do his own travelling remember."

"He's got to you hasn't he, that's what this is all about isn't it," he insisted.

"No! I'm simply aware that he won't be around for a while either."

"I hope you're right, he has a good brain. His Induction Course results were very promising, he has a good future ahead of him provided he's not led astray. When do you intend to go?"

"Friday, it's in the letter. I'm owed nearly a week's leave," she answered.

"Yes of course, I'll take a look. I'd better prepare for this morning's meetings. We'll talk later."

He was a very considerate man and she had enjoyed her time at Britannic House. She had worked for him for a year since leaving college and he had helped her from the day she started. There was no need for her to tell him any more about us, he was shrewd enough to do some checking if he smelt a rat, he was a very perceptive man, better by far to keep as much from him as possible.

* * *

John picked me up that morning to join him at the garage. Mum and Dad thought it was good for us to spend time together and John always appreciated the company having worked alone for nearly two years.

"Mary told me how much your piano playing talents have improved. Can I assume this has some connection with Sam's chess playing?" he asked as he drove.

"Yes mate, one and the same!" I never spoke the words, I merely thought them.

"How is that possible?" he asked without noticing.

"We have joined in some way and shared our knowledge."

"I bet you did, you dirty little bugger, but what's that got to do with it?" he laughed.

"Look at me John. Look at me now."

We pulled up at the cross-roads and he turned to look at me.

"How do you think I do this?" I asked.

He flinched as he heard the words but watched my fixed mouth.

"How did you do that?"

"That was my question?"

"Shit this is weird. I can hear your voice but you're not talking."

"How do you think I learned to play the piano so well?"

"Just use your mouth will ya! It feels weird listening to you this way."

"I know, believe me. I've been there," I said switching back to conventional speech.

I could sense he instantly felt more comfortable.

I explained everything that had happened as well as I was able. John mocked me about the physical aspects of my story but there was no need for me to go into detail. He told me he was ready to see Victor for himself and felt sure he and Mary could keep our secret.

John was developing a wanderlust of his own, but with a wife and young daughter to consider, he was sure he wouldn't be planning to leave the planet.

As the morning progressed, I forgot to use speech and simply used telepathy to communicate with John. He became more comfortable about it when I explained I couldn't read his mind; however, he pointed out that I would have to be careful not to do the same thing with other people.

"Can you talk to Sam or Victor from here?" he asked.

"Sometimes. Sometimes I can communicate with Sam if she's trying to communicate with me. We have to focus our minds simultaneously to talk. When I talk to you this way you expect to hear me answer. I haven't trained myself to focus on more than one thing the way Victor can. He can hear us, but I have never heard anything from him except when he has been with me."

"Well I wonder what the New Year has in store for us. How long do you expect be gone?" he asked.

"It's going to be at least fourteen years in your time just getting there and back, weeks, months or years in ours depending on how long we stay. I guess we could be back while your still in your thirties."

At twenty-three John was seven years older than me, so if we stayed for a year or two he would be approaching forty by the time we got back.

"And what about you? How old will you be?"

"Well in reality I will still be seven years younger than you, the same as I am now, but physically I should only be a year or two older, at least that's how I understand things from Victor."

"Do you think Sam will want to come back? If she is Eratean then surely she will want to stay there."

"She has Terran parents remember, I'm sure she will want to come back if only to see them and let them know she is alive and well. I will want to return myself for the same reasons. I know I'm going to miss you, all of you."

"Well I'm going to send Le Fevre all my details tonight, so we could both be leaving here pretty soon. I need a change and I think that BP has something to offer me."

"I hope it does and I hope it's what you want. This is what I want, I think I always have."

We put in a hard day's work that day. Since John worked for himself the harder he worked, the more money he made, and he was keen to have as much cash behind him as possible. If he moved to B.P., the salary for a Junior Engineer would not be high.

# THE PHYSICIAN

**M**alcolm dropped me off at home that night but did not stop to come in. I was surprised the Doctor was there. It was not uncommon for him to call around to check up on Dad when he was going through a bad spell, but he wasn't. In fact, he was happier than I had seen him for some time.

"What's wrong," I asked.

"Your father seems to have made some dramatic improvements over the weekend. He seems to be in some sort of remission and we don't understand why."

The pain that was normally so cruel and so constant had eased off at some point over the weekend, but despite the fact that he felt significantly better than usual, he had not consciously been aware of any change until that morning. He found he could hold on to things much more easily and became aware that he felt no pain.

The arthritis had taken its toll on his body, his muscles were wasted, and his bones damaged, but something had definitely changed, and I suspected Victor had something to do with it.

"I'm going to take some blood samples from your father to see what we can find out. I would like to see you afterwards if that's convenient with you."

"Sure, here or at the surgery."

"Well actually at the surgery would be better. I'll give you a lift if you want. I've got my evening appointments to get back to anyway."

"That's ok, I'll take him up and wait for him," said Dad eager to drive the car.

I left them to it and went upstairs to wash and change. When I came down the doctor had already left.

As I followed Dad out of the house, it was obvious that he was far from cured. He still walked with short slow steps, his back was still hunched, and his fingers were badly contorted around the walking stick he still used. If Victor had cured him, how long would it take for him to fully recover, or was I expecting too much.

"What do you think he wants with you then?" Dad asked.

"I've no idea."

"Well it must be important if he needs to see you tonight."

* * *

"Take a seat young man." I did as he said.

"So, what's the problem Doctor?"

"Your blood tests."

"Yes?"

"It would seem that you had time to pick up a nasty little bug on your travels; however, aside from that you seem fine."

"This bug, what is it?"

"Well that's why I wanted to have a talk to you. Did anyone ever talk to you about sexually transmitted diseases?"

"At school we saw some films," I answered.

"Well if you are going to have sex with prostitutes for goodness sake use a condom. I'm not judging you, I know these things happen especially in the Merchant Navy, I'm just trying to impress upon you the need for cleanliness. I know that you get checked up for these things in the Navy; however, prevention is better than cure."

"I haven't been with a prostitute!" I protested.

"Oh, I'm very sorry, I just assumed! Well you've picked it up from somewhere."

"Picked what up exactly?"

"Neisseria gonorrhoeae! Gonorrhoea to you. Nasty little blighter as I said, but quite treatable provided we treat your partner. You do have a partner?"

I realised that it could not have been Sam who infected me, the blood tests were taken before we spent the night together, but that meant I could have infected her.

"Yes, I have a girlfriend, but it can't be her fault. I met someone before her."

"Do you know how to contact this person?"

"No, I don't know her name."

He made no apparent judgement about my promiscuity, but I could sense his thoughts of disapproval quite clearly.

"Can I take it you won't be seeing the young lady again?"

"No, no I won't be seeing her."

"Your girlfriend, have you had sex with her? Is she a local girl?"

"Yes, we have had sex together and no she's from London."

"When will you be seeing her again?"

"Friday, she's coming down."

"Right, I'll give you a letter to give to her, I'm afraid she's not my patient, so I cannot treat her. Ask her to go and see her Doctor as soon as possible and give him the letter. In the mean time I must ask you to refrain from sexual activity. I suppose I'd better examine you. Go behind the curtain and slip your pants down and I'll be with you in a minute."

I did as I was asked while the Doctor washed his hands and put on some surgical gloves. I found myself looking as keenly as the Doctor, wondering what exactly he was looking for.

"You don't appear to have any visible irritation at all, and no evidence of any discharge. "When did this encounter take place?"

"A couple of weeks ago on the..." I stopped midsentence realising that to let him know it had happened on the train was more than he needed to know. He ignored the incomplete comment and continued his examination.

"Well the incubation period anywhere between two to thirty days. It has showed up in your blood test plainly enough. Have you noticed any pain or discharge?"

"No, nothing, except when you examined me," I answered.

"Oh well, sometimes the symptoms can be very minor. Some people are asymptomatic. Alright you can dress now."

He pulled off his gloves, dropped them into a bin and then washed his hands again.

"Well I'd better give you a prescription for the treatment anyway. Two tablets a day, one in the morning and one in the evening for ten days after meals. I'll see you again for a check-up in two weeks' time."

He wrote out the prescription and then wrote a short letter stamping both. He sealed the letter in an envelope and handed it to me.

"This is for your girlfriend and this is for you. Ask your girlfriend to give this to her doctor," he said handing me the prescription.

"Thank you Doctor."

I shook his hand as I stood up. He was such an exceptionally tall man it seemed I must still look like a child to him, but for the first time I was aware of the difference in our relationship, he no longer spoke to me as a child, even if I acted like an idiot.

"If you must submit to your urges then please make sure you use a condom and wash thoroughly afterwards."

"I will Doctor," I said unable to stop myself grinning despite the seriousness of my ailment.

I went straight into the chemist and picked up my prescription.

Dad waited until we were on our way home in the car before asking me what the Doctor had wanted. I told him he just wanted to have a chat and to tell me that all my blood tests were clear.

"He's given me some vitamins to take to help build up my strength though," I said.

"I don't suppose you're going to need any more jabs before you go, but it might be worth telling him you're off to Egypt before you go, just in case you need any others."

"Yes I will, I forgot, but I think I'm pretty well covered."

When we got home, Mum said that Sam had called and asked me to call her back at eight. Knowing that I would need to tell her I had picked up a Gonorrhoea infection I decided to use the public phone again. She too would need the antibiotics that the doctor had prescribed for me.

I took the pills in secret after dinner, just in case anyone examined the bottle.

* * *

"Hi Sam?" I asked when the phone was answered.

"James, how are you? Victor is here with me."

"I'm fine, how are you two?"

"Fine, everything went smoothly at work. Le Fevre was most upset to hear that I was leaving but he's been really kind. He really is a nice guy you know. Victor met me after work and we have spent some time talking about his son, my previous life. It's so strange because I know nothing about it and yet in some ways it explains things I have felt all my life. Apparently, I was a bird before I was Victor's son."

"A bird? You mean a girl?"

"No stupid, a swallow! Well something very like a swallow."

"Oh good," I said bemused by her words. "I'm glad you've had a chance to talk anyway. I know he is happy to have found you. Listen, I went to the doctors tonight, he was round to see my dad and he asked me to come to the surgery. Seems I picked up an infection from Sharon on the train. It can't have been from you because we didn't, ya know, we didn't ... until after I'd had the blood test."

"You cheeky little...! How dare you!"

"Hey I'm sorry! I said it can't have been you, but I have a letter for you to give to your doctor." There was a brief silence.

"Don't worry," she said, "Victor says he has already taken care of it the other day at Waterloo station. He says you won't need the medicine."

"Oh, well that's a relief! Ask him if he has had anything to do with my dad. The doctor was there to see him today because he is in some sort of remission."

Sam passed Victor the phone and he explained that my father's genetic structure had been modified. He explained that it was my father's own immune system that was causing the illness and that it would take time to have any significant effect. Although his body would produce its own pain killers and his pain would go almost immediately, muscular strength and mobility would take time to restore.

I could hardly remember a time when my father had not been in pain. Even when I was a young boy he had problems with his back and those problems seemed to lead to his rheumatoid arthritis. I was so happy to think that he would be able to walk properly again and not suffer the constant torture he had endured for so long.

"Thank you Victor, I will be eternally grateful to you for what you've done," I said.

"Then you understand the gratitude that I have for you in restoring my son to me; however, it was you that gave your father the power to cure himself," he answered, and he handed back the telephone to Sam.

Sam told me she had called her parents and said we would be coming up to Chawton to see them on Sunday. She hadn't told them yet that she had given up her job. On Saturday we would do some shopping in London and have the night to ourselves.

"Love you loads Teddy Bear!" said Sam ending the call. "Oh, and Victor says he will see you and your brother tomorrow morning."

# COGNIZANCE

## COLD WAR

Tuesday ~ 4<sup>th</sup> December 1973

T he next day Victor was waiting for me down the road. He had spoken to me as I woke, I answered saying that I would meet him outside as soon as I had washed and dressed.

"Aren't you cold in that tunic?" I asked.

I saw him as he was in my mind, using my eyes he wore the same T-shirt, jeans and winter jacket.

"Actually, my himation is not made from natural fibre and it is an excellent insulator against cold or heat. Terrans selected the ancient Greek name for them, like so many other things. The word tunic comes from the Roman tunica. We Erateans usually greet each other when we meet."

"I'm sorry Victor, good morning."

"Good morning to you James. The Eratean custom is to greet each other with the word 'friendship' if we have met before. If it is the first meeting, we introduce ourselves formally by adding the words 'I am known as...' or 'I am known here as...'"

"I thought you said you had no concept of friendship?"

"We don't, not an exclusive way, that is the point of our welcome, everyone we meet is considered a friend."

"Gotcha. Friendship, I am known as James."

"Very good," he smiled, "friendship, I am known here as Victor. You are on your home-world, so you don't need to use the word 'here', I am not from here, so I do."

We walked off in the direction of the forest as usual and he explained that there was more we should discuss before Sam and I left with him.

"James, you must take great care not to discuss me or anything I am going to tell you with anyone, not even those that you would trust with your life," he began.

"I have only told my brother John about you," I replied.

"Our presence here is becoming more and more dangerous, not just for me but also for you and Sam."

There was no need for oral speech between us now, so no one would hear our discussion.

"In danger, from who?" I asked.

"From any of the many agencies that have been set up by the world's governments and from the secret societies that control them."

"What agencies? What secret societies?"

"Agencies that were set up over twenty years ago, before I arrived here," he answered. "The National Security Agency and the Central Intelligence Agency are a significant threat. These agencies were originally established to hide the truth of our existence from the public, they will go to any lengths to ensure that secrecy is maintained. They work with your Ministry of Intelligence departments here in Britain and many other agencies across the world, even part of the Komitet Gosudarstvennoy Bezopasnosti in the Soviet Union; the KGB."

"But I don't understand. Why do they keep it a secret?" I asked.

"They fear that if the public knew of our existence it would create mass hysteria resulting in the collapse of civilisation," he answered.

"Even the Russians realise that the political and financial structures that exist in the west have a significant effect on global stability.

"Knowledge of our existence could cause mass hysteria, perhaps even trigger nuclear war. We cannot be sure that the public would not fear our existence as greatly as the military powers here do," he explained. "That is why we have not simply confirmed our existence by landing in a city centre for all to see. You must understand that your people react badly to fear, and they are more than capable of destroying themselves."

"You mean nuclear weapons, I remember something about that or perhaps Sam does! Sometimes I can't tell if it's my thoughts or hers. It was the Cuban missile crisis, Kennedy right? JFK?" I continued vocally.

"No not Jack Kennedy," he laughed aloud. "And not the Cuban missile crisis either. Are these your thoughts or Sam's?" he asked.

"I don't know, does it matter? I remember reading about them as a teenager, but then I have never read the newspapers, so it must have been Sam."

"Let me tell you something about that episode. Jack Kennedy was elected as the next President of the United States on November 8th, 1960. On  November 9th, 1960, Premier Khrushchev sent a message to congratulate Kennedy on his presidential election, hoping that relations between the United States and USSR could move towards those developed in President Franklin Delano Roosevelt's time.

"Tensions were high after Soviet Air Defence Forces had shot down a United States U2 spy-plane on May 1st, 1960, while it was performing a photographic aerial reconnaissance mission deep into Soviet territory.

"Khrushchev suggested to Kennedy that the USSR wanted to begin negotiations with the U.S. on nuclear disarmament and a German peace treaty, expressing a desire to discuss anything which might an ease and improve the relationship between them.

"Kennedy responded thanking Khrushchev and their relationship looked set to improve after President Kennedy's inauguration on January 20th, 1961. I quote a significant part of his inaugural speech:

*Finally, to those nations who would make themselves our adversary, we offer not a pledge but a request: that both sides begin anew the quest for peace, before the dark powers of destruction unleashed by science engulf all humanity in planned or accidental self-destruction.*

*We dare not tempt them with weakness. For only when our arms are sufficient beyond doubt can we be certain beyond doubt that they will never be employed.*

*But neither can two great and powerful groups of nations take comfort from our present course--both sides overburdened by the cost of modern weapons, both rightly alarmed by the steady spread of the deadly atom, yet both racing to alter that uncertain balance of terror that stays the hand of mankind's final war.*

*So let us begin anew--remembering on both sides that civility is not a sign of weakness, and sincerity is always subject to proof. Let us never negotiate out of fear. But let us never fear to negotiate.*

*Let both sides explore what problems unite us instead of belaboring those problems which divide us.*

*Let both sides, for the first time, formulate serious and precise proposals for the inspection and control of arms--and bring the absolute power to destroy other nations under the absolute control of all nations.*

*Let both sides seek to invoke the wonders of science instead of its terrors. Together let us explore the stars, conquer the deserts, eradicate disease, tap the ocean depths and encourage the arts and commerce.*

*Let both sides unite to heed in all corners of the earth the command of Isaiah--to "undo the heavy burdens ... (and) let the oppressed go free."*

*And if a beachhead of cooperation may push back the jungle of suspicion, let both sides join in creating a new endeavor, not a new balance of power, but a new world of law, where the strong are just and the weak secure and the peace preserved.*

*All this will not be finished in the first one hundred days. Nor will it be finished in the first one thousand days, nor in the life of this Administration, nor even perhaps in our lifetime on this planet. But let us begin.*

"On February 22, 1961, President Kennedy sent Premier Khrushchev a letter, for the first time, suggesting a meeting, stating that he 'hoped it will be possible, before too long, for us to meet personally for an informal exchange of views.' Premier Khrushchev accepted Kennedy's summit proposal, and plans began for the two leaders to meet.

"After the failed Bay of Pigs invasion on April 17, 1961, tensions between America and Russia escalated, both President Kennedy and Premier Khrushchev were eager to meet face to face and work towards a peace treaty.

"The two men met for the first time at a summit meeting in Vienna on June 4th, 1961, and discussed the issues in the relationship between their countries.

"The Eratean people established direct contact with the Kennedy brothers and indeed with Nikita Khrushchev at great cost to all. I myself met with the two men face to face briefly on July 27th 1961, shortly after I arrived here."

I knew the name Khrushchev, but it existed in my memory like a memory once forgotten, until he reminded me of Kennedy's Soviet counterpart.

"We hoped to encourage a peace process by confronting them both, proving our existence to them beyond all doubt. Until that year neither Jack nor Nikita had experienced personal contact with my people. Both countries had secret departments who had been monitoring us and attempting to understand and reverse engineer captured alien starships; however, personal contact at that level had not existed for some time."

"How did you manage to bring them together again?"

"That was not difficult," he smiled. "Initially, one of my compatriots was sent to contact Nikita Khrushchev. He was able to impersonate head of the KGB Alexander Shelepin, who ironically became Deputy Prime Minister later that year."

"Ironically?"

"Khrushchev had denounced Stalin at a closed meeting at the Kremlin on February 25th, 1956, it later became clear that Shelepin wanted to restore the Stalinist system."

"Under his guise, he was able to kidnap Nikita and drive him to a waiting ship. The deception was regrettable, but we could think of no other way to bring these two people face to face to talk privately. What Nikita saw when we reached the ship was a secret KGB office guarded by a number of KGB agents. Once inside we were able to reveal ourselves and discuss the meeting."

"A few weeks ago, I might have thought that too incredible to believe," I said.

"He was remarkably unshaken by our appearance and agreeable to the meeting, so we proceeded with the second stage of our plan. We were able to walk into the White house unseen just as easily. As you know, we have the power to conceal reality from people's minds. We revealed ourselves to Jack Kennedy and his brother Bobby in the privacy of the Oval Office. We sensed that they were both aware of our existence, but it was apparent that both were clearly keen to resume personal discussions. All detailed information concerning us was highly classified and out of reach even to their eyes."

"Out of reach? Kennedy was the president!"

"I'm afraid the president of the United States of America has been little more than a puppet figurehead since 1952, when President Harry Truman established the National Security Agency. Since that time, those who make real policy decisions meet in secrecy.

"That's incredible!"

"Nikita knew more about us than Jack. He was a very worried man, it was easy for us to demonstrate to him that we understood that. Unlike his United States counterparts, he was permitted access to almost all secret information; however, he also knew that there was very little influence he could have on any of it."

"Almost all?"

"Nobody is immune from investigation in either country. The Soviets had put Gagarin into Space just three months before on April 12th, and the Americans were determined they would not fall behind in the Space Race. On May 25th, 1961, Jack Kennedy announced that 'Before the decade was out, the United States would land a man on the Moon and return him safely to Earth', speaking to a Joint Session of Congress. In June 1961, he approached the Soviet Union for the first time about making that a joint effort; Russia was far ahead of America in terms of space technology."

"I had no idea that the Americans wanted a joint effort."

"The Americans didn't, Jack Kennedy did. It was June 26th when he made his famous radio and television broadcast about his commitment to the people of West Berlin."

"Ich bin ein Berliner!"

"You remember?"

"No, but Sam does," I smiled.

"Seven weeks later, on August 13th, construction of the Berlin Wall began, rendering West Berlin an 'Island of Freedom' formally controlled by the Western Allies, in the Soviet controlled German Democratic Republic. As I said, both men had no option but to walk a political tightrope with those that did not trust the other side."

"In the weapons race, the United States was developing the Polaris missile with launch capability from a submerged vessel, a significant advantage over the Soviet Hotel Class submarines. The Russian project was rushed through on limited budgets and at the expense of safety. The following month, July 4th, one of the newest Hotel Class Soviet nuclear submarines, K19, suffered a severe accident. It was the first of its type equipped with surface launched ballistic nuclear missiles, meaning it would have to surface in order to launch. She was conducting exercises in the North Atlantic close to Southern Greenland when she developed a major leak in her reactor coolant system. Eight men died of radiation poisoning during the following three-week period. Just one of many disasters that would cost the Soviet Union dearly, not just financially but in the race for nuclear strike capability."

I was able to comprehend everything he was telling me in a way that my mind would not have done before; I assumed that was due to Sam's knowledge of events even though in July 1961 she would only have been six years old.

"Sapiens behave much like the other animals that live on this planet. Few of you ever really conquer and savour fear; it spreads through your people as quickly as it does when an antelope senses a hunter, and the whole herd reacts almost as one. Uncontrolled fear makes a man likely to strike out to defend himself before considering the consequences. We explained to the Kennedy brothers that we had Nikita onboard our ship, and that we had taken him there to discuss nuclear disarmament face to face. By revealing the inner thoughts of each to the other, it was clear to both, that each genuinely feared aggression from the other; it also became clear to them that in reality, neither had reason to fear the other, and that each wanted nothing more than peace for his people and for the world."

"So why the Cuban missile crisis? Why did they bring the world to the point of nuclear war?" I asked.

"You see everything so naively. Regrettably the worlds of politics and war are not as black and white as your chessboard my friend. It was by no means the first time the masses were deliberately deceived, it has happened many many times before, and since, and I am sure that it will not be the last. People want to trust their leaders and governments, and their leaders and governments need the backing of the people."

"Well I'm with you there!" I said realising my ignorance.

"Both men were leaders of their nation; however, neither man possessed the power to convince their people of the truth. People's beliefs are easily influenced, they generally want to feel that they are doing what is right, most no longer see through the lies and deceit. They had been conditioned to believe that the perceived enemy intended to destroy them and their way of life.

"The people of both countries wanted security. Most Americans were proud of their way of life, their independence and their freedom. Almost half of them voted against Jack Kennedy in the Presidential elections. Most Soviets had no choice but to adhere to the ways of the State.

"Nuclear weapons brought with them a sense of security that dispelled the fear of attack because each could retaliate. The entire world grew up knowing about and believing in a strategy of mutually assured destruction. In order to begin the task of disarmament, the people of the world would have to recognise that their sense of security was flawed.

Only by bringing the people to the brink of war, would they realise how vulnerable they really were."

"I don't understand. You mean they did it on purpose?"

"You do understand. Why do you play chess the way you do with your brother? Deception comes naturally to you, I know, I have felt it. Only when the people of the world wanted it for themselves could the process of disarmament begin. Having faced the reality of Armageddon, a new movement for peace began. We agreed to help develop world technology when disarmament was complete as an incentive to both sides."

"They tricked the world into disarming?"

"They tried."

# MURDER

Two years after I met him, Jack Kennedy was assassinated, murdered."

"I know! He was shot by Lee Harvey Oswald!"

"A sad conspiracy I'm afraid. I spoke with many of the people that witnessed the assassination. One of my people was able to speak directly with Mr Oswald before he too was murdered. We know that he did not shoot Jack Kennedy, nor did he know who did; however, he did smuggle a 6.5 mm calibre Carcano rifle into the Texas School Book Depository building, leaving it on the sixth floor as instructed.

"Immediately after the incident the building was searched by the Dallas police and sheriff's deputies, Oswald's rifle was found by Deputy Sheriff Seymour Weitzman and Officer Gene Boone where Oswald had hidden it among cartons on the sixth floor.

"We know there was a conspiracy, the cover up operation was blatantly obvious. Having infiltrated security following the assassination, our own investigation confirmed that the killing shot came from the car directly behind the presidential limousine.

"The first two shots were fired from the book depository by a Mafia hitman, Charles Nicoletti; the first was deflected, the bullet hit a traffic sign and ricocheted off injuring a bystander, James Thomas Tague, further down the road, the President instinctively dropped his head hearing the shot.

"A moment later the second shot hit Kennedy as he ducked his head, entering his back between the shoulders, close to the spine, and exiting through his neck; having hit no bone, it entered the back of John Bowden Connally Jr, Governor of Texas, entering his back below his right armpit, and began cascading as it shattered his fifth rib and exiting his chest, tumbling, it hit his wrist shattering his radius bone, spinning down and finally entering his left thigh.

"The third shot fired was in fact two simultaneous shots fired milliseconds apart; the first was the killing shot, fired by United States Secret Service Special Agent, George Warren Hickey Jr., using an AR-15 rifle carried in the car immediately following the presidential limousine as I have said; the second, was fired by James Earl Files, associate of Charles Nicoletti, using a .221 Remington Fire Ball pistol fitted with a telescopic sight.

"Files thought that he had killed Kennedy, but he had faltered when Kennedy's head moved, and his shot missed.

"The two men were hired by the CIA, who used Kennedy's cancellation of the second air strike following the failed Bay of Pigs operation as the motive, rather than allow the real reason to be known.

"Some say his vice-president, Lyndon Baines Johnson led the conspirators, but he was simply another puppet replacement for Kennedy, an exoteric face for the faceless.

"It matters not who pulled the trigger. The fact is that the men around him and the societies that really controlled the United States discovered that they had been duped by their own President. They felt that they had been betrayed.

"It was the faceless that decided Kennedy had over stepped himself and could no longer be trusted, and it was they who signed his death warrant. Very few knew what they had done.

"We believe that Kennedy's motivations were finally accepted as justification for permanent elimination when he sent National Security Memorandum 271 to James Webb, Administrator of NASA on November 12th, 1963. His murder took place just ten days afterwards. I can quote it for you. The subject was, 'Cooperation with the USSR on Outer Space Matters'. The text begins:

'I would like you to assume personally the initiative and central responsibility within the Government for the development of a program of substantive cooperation with the Soviet Union in the field of outer space, including the development of specific technical proposals.

I assume that you will work closely with the Department of State and other agencies as appropriate.

These proposals should be developed with a view to their possible discussion with the Soviet Union as a direct outcome of my September 20 proposal for broader cooperation between the United States and the USSR in outer space, including cooperation in lunar landing programs.

All proposals or suggestions originating within the Government relating to this general subject will be referred to you for your consideration and evaluation.

In addition to developing substantive proposals, I expect that you will assist the Secretary of State in exploring problems of procedure and timing connected with holding discussions with the Soviet Union and in proposing for my consideration the channels which would be most desirable from our point of view.

In this connection the channel of contact developed by Dr. Dryden between NASA and the Soviet Academy of Sciences has been quite effective, and I believe that we should continue to utilize it as appropriate as a means of continuing the dialogue between the scientists of both countries.

I would like an interim report on the progress of our planning by December 15.'

"We lost communication with both him and his brother the same day. We believe that the obvious conclusion is that he intended to share all knowledge of alien contact with the Russians, and therefore almost certainly considered far too great a risk to the secret societies and military chiefs. Five years later, his brother Bobby suffered the same fate when his intention to follow his brother into presidency became a realistic possibility, having defeated Senator Eugene McCarthy in the California primary election."

"That's right Nixon became president," I interrupted. His ability to quote such a lengthy document from memory no longer surprised me.

"It appears that Richard Nixon's presidency will not survive for much longer. We suspect that the resignation of Vice President Spiro Agnew and the appointment of his replacement Gerald Ford is not a mere coincidence."

I did not know these people and it appeared by my complete lack of knowledge that neither did Sam.

"These secret people, societies, whatever they are, they murdered them both! They killed them because they wanted to work with the Russians."

"Try not to judge them. As far back as the Majestic Twelve the consensus of opinion was against that and perhaps the risk justified the action. They may have been right."

"To kill them?"

"Murder and judgement are equally unacceptable for Erateans, both are common enough occurrences for Sapiens, for you murder is worse. The cost in lives may have been much greater had they not done so. No one will ever know. Nikita Khrushchev's fate was not as brutal as the Kennedy brothers; however, he lost his position as Premier the year after Jack was murdered, in 1964. He spent the last seven years of his life under the close supervision of the KGB. We have tried to re-establish communication with both the United States and Soviet governments to no avail, and not without cost. We have lost many people in doing so. We know that we are at risk from these secret societies and from the World's governments which is why I have told you all of this."

"That is so incredible! Can I tell anyone about Kennedy?"

"You must not speak of these things to anyone. It would be easily tracked back to you, faster than you can possibly imagine. I tell you these things because you are leaving your home. These people have killed world leaders, they would not think twice about killing you or your loved ones."

"Ok, I won't say a word!"

"To anyone!"

"No one, except Sam," I assured him.

"These secret societies you spoke of, Majestic Twelve, who are they?"

"We must have that conversation at another time."

# MENAGERIE

As we walked up through the forest, I noticed that the last signs of autumn were disappearing. The autumn leaves had almost completely gone, soon only the evergreens would be left retaining their dull green winter needles. The air was cold but there was no wind, the sun felt warm on my neck as we walked northwards into the woods. The silver trunks of the birch trees stood like stone skeletons, each holding up hundreds of vibrant mauve coloured twigs that seemed to pulsate with the hope of new life when spring returned.

We stopped at the old railway line to survey the scene. The reeds in the marshland shone brightly in a long golden-brown band, like the colour of a palomino horse, stretching to the east as far as the eye could see, beyond that the dark brown heather and the copper coloured bracken formed two more textured bands. At the top of the hill the holly was laden with clusters of deep red baubles, the yew trees too had an abundance of translucent scarlet arils.

It occurred to me how lucky I was to live there and how fragile our existence was. That wintery scene stark as it seemed, would surely have been only shades of grey, completely devoid of any sign of life in a nuclear winter.

"I have made contact with Paul and I know now that he is Malakh," said Victor.

"I know, I was about to tell you I met him last week. He's so old though! He gave me these," I said, showing him the Tarot cards that were in my pocket. "They're like the cards he used on the Worcester."

"I have seen such cards many times before."

"Are they old?"

"No," he smiled, "I believe they are the work of Pamela Colman Smith and A. E. Waite known as the Rider-Waite Tarot. Such cards are known to have existed since the fourteenth century, but these are contemporary my friend."

"Paul suggested I study them."

"I believe they represent a journey of some kind," said Paul.

"That's what I thought. I think that I am the Fool, and I believe you are the Magician."

"Perhaps, perhaps it is Paul," he suggested.

"No, you are the Magician, I know it."

I did not know what place if any Paul had in the cards, but I was certain about the emphasis of the first two, I saw Victor in that card just as plainly as I saw him there in front of me.

"What exactly are the Malakhi? Oh, and he told me to ask you about the Greys and their masters."

"Paul will tell you everything you need to know about the Malakhi, I can only repeat what he told me. I believe he is your friend and all will be made clear before we leave. Be patient for the time being."

"You know more than you are saying, but I can't read your thoughts."

"You can read my thoughts, as I said, I can only tell you what he told me, but please understand, I do not want to pre-empt the discussion he will have with you."

"Well what about the Greys, and their masters, and the other aliens visiting Earth?"

"I have told you what the Greys look like, short bipedal humanoids, grey skin, approximately four feet high, with distinctive sloping almond shaped black eyes.

"Their masters, if indeed they are their masters, are grey skinned but much lighter in colour than the Greys, tall, over seven feet, with long necks and with an extremely lean, almost wasted form, but with large distended stomachs. Their eyes are like Sapiens' except bigger, always with a blue iris and pale blue sclera; we call them 'Tall-Whites'.

"We know of them, and we believe they are working with the secret societies and the government agencies that we just discussed. We know they have been here since September 5th, 1945, three days after Japan surrendered at the end of your second world war. My son and his colleagues had no idea about their existence until they arrived here and met at council."

I understood that council was a gathering of Erateans starships.

"When I met Paul for the first time in 1961, I asked him about them, but he was reluctant to discuss them. We do not know exactly when they began working with the secret societies, but it became clear by 1964.

"In what way?"

"It's probably best if I show you."

"When?"

"Soon. We know they have an ambassador here, a liaison known as Krel, he is a Tall White."

"So there are three alien species of alien visitors here, or four if you count Paul."

"Paul has warned me not to seek out Krel's people. He said that they may present a danger to both Terrans and to Erateans alike. They have always avoided communication with us, and the others here."

"Others?"

"The Amorfons; a warm blooded oviparous race, Terrans call the Draconians or Draks, tall reptilian like with armoured scaly skin, tall like the Tall-Whites.

"Klingons eh?" I laughed.

"You may laugh now, but you were frightened enough when we first met," he reminded me."

"There are also the Hittites, known by the same name to Terrans. They are Sapien-like, but shorter, between four and five feet tall, with a wider skull and a much wider neck. They are a prototherian, oviparous race, with little body hair but both male and female have significant facial hair.

"Finally, there are the Yowies, again known by the same name to Terrans, Sapien-like, slightly shorter, four and a half to five and a half feet tall, with long arms reaching halfway down their thighs, and with short furry hair covering their entire body."

"And you communicate with all of them?"

"All except the Tall-Whites and The Greys."

"Will I get to meet any of them?"

"I think we should meet with Paul before we do. Since the governments have refused to disarm when we offered them help, it is reasonable to assume that Krel's people have not requested it; if that is so, it is possible that they are an aggressive race. As I said, judgement is a sin for Eratean people. We have no right to judge either the Krel's kind or the secret societies on Earth."

"Aren't you judging the people of Earth by denying them help?"

"We will not help them destroy each other, nothing is worth killing for."

"You mean you wouldn't defend yourself?"

"Sapiens are the only advanced race we have encountered who no longer use their telepathic abilities, as a consequence, they are also the only race who exhibit paranoia. Your people are frequently blessed with great wisdom, but they no longer possess the ability to see into each other's hearts, they are cursed with the pride of the ancestors. Pride as we see it is simply misguided adherence to ethical principles and values. None of us has the right to judge others, not even ourselves. There is no love in pride, not even the pride in another, it is merely an arrogance which divides and sets people apart from one another. To be proud of oneself or another implies in its words that one is less proud of another. Where pride exists, it gives life to its alter ego fear, fear in one and envy in another, fear of loss, loss of status or loss of material wealth. Fear has only one path that leads to secrecy and deception. Avarice inevitably follows and with it, anger, sloth, lust and gluttony the remaining deadly sins as your people refer to them. Each feeds upon the others until the virtues of love, hope and faith dwindle and die."

I will never forget the first time I heard those words.

"We know that the secret societies we discussed have endeavoured to pursue what they collectively believe to be the best course of action. Many of the members are great philanthropists, great thinkers or scientists. They consider their self-elected bodies to offer a feasible way forward. There has always been great fear that the discovery of intelligent alien life would cause mass hysteria and the breakdown of society and that is why our presence has not been made public."

"I have spoken with my people and agreed to meet in council tomorrow."

"How many of you are there here?"

"There are more than five hundred thousand of us living on Earth, some like me hoping to find the Malakhi and others hoping to witness a revolution."

"Revolution?"

"You will understand when you come with me to Erato."

Telepathy had become so much clearer than oral speech, it was much faster and conveyed with it an understanding of every subject and every word which would otherwise have required further explanation.

It seemed natural to speak that way, especially since we were alone on the forest; but I made a conscious effort to speak orally rather than use my newly acquired skills, I could still read his thoughts as he educated me in everything we discussed, in a parallel harmony with his words; however, I feared the possibility of becoming too addicted to telepathy and giving myself away.

# THE PLAGUE

Once again, he was silent for a while, enjoying the flora as we walked through the Redwoods, Douglas Firs and wild rhododendrons. We turned right towards Brockenhurst cutting across the plain rather than following the road.

"Sadly, we expect to see your people destroy themselves before the end of the next century unless there is a radical development in Sapien culture. If Sapiens are to survive it will probably require a transformation or intervention of some kind."

"Christian peoples believe that Christ will return after two thousand years," I suggested.

"The Erateans who heard the words of Jesus speak very highly of him, but alas your world has changed significantly from the days of the Roman Empire. Do you believe that the world would rejoice if he did? Would you recognise him as the son of God if he did return?"

"That is a very good question," I answered. "What chance would he have in the modern world amongst these secret societies you speak of?"

"We have become aware that operatives of the secret societies we spoke of, are actively deploying a deadly virus amongst the peoples of the African Nations. The most significant problem the people of Earth face is over-population. We believe that this virus is intended to cause the genocide of the African people.

"The virus is a modified strain of a naturally occurring simian virus. The new strain virus is slow acting and will probably reach pandemic proportions before it is even realised. It attacks the immune system and will eventually leave the body unable to fight infection."

"Is this some sort of plague? Could it destroy human life?" I asked.

"We believe there is already large-scale infection spreading across Africa and Asia as well as Europe and North America. We estimate over five million people are already infected."

"Is there a cure?"

"There is always a cure, and even a vaccination before such weapons are used. Since this is being deliberately deployed, logic suggests that neither will be made public. Developing a cure could take years for your people, it may not be a simple matter even for the Erateans. The virus is unknown to us and we do not know what effects it may have on my people."

"Do you think they intend to use it against your people?"

"We do not fear the virus since we know of its existence, but it is important that we understand it."

"Are my family at risk?" I asked.

"I do not believe so, at least not in the short term."

# GRATITUDE

W e reached the outskirts of Brockenhurst before I realised that we had walked further than I ever had as a boy. Perhaps I was leading him to my brother or perhaps he planted the seed in my subconscious mind and steered me in that direction.

"When you meet John just speak normally. He doesn't like me using my mind to communicate and I want him to feel comfortable. And don't say anything about the other aliens here either or you'll confuse the hell out of him," I said vocally.

We walked through the village up to the Morant Arms and across the road to Dory's Garage where my brother worked. John was outside talking with his friend Steve.

"That's John there with his mate Steve the motorcycle cop."

Steve would often stop by for a chat with my brother. John loved Steve's Norton Commando and Steve seemed to enjoy showing it off.

"John," I called out as we crossed the road.

"Hello Higgs," he replied. "You know Steve," he said.

"Yeah course I do," I answered shaking his hand briefly. "This is my friend Victor."

"Pleased to meet you Victor," said John.

Steve put out his hand and shook Victor's and nodded a gestured hello.

"I've heard all about your accident," said Steve. "Glad to see you're ok. John tells me he may soon be following you and joining himself."

"I know that's what he wants, I'm just not sure what I want right now," I answered.

"I can imagine. I see a hell of a lot of accidents and I know how much it shakes people up. People frequently say they will never drive again, but they usually do given time."

"I guess so. Shall I put the kettle on John?" I asked.

"Reckon so. You want a quick cuppa Steve?"

"Could do," he answered. "It's quiet enough at the moment."

I left the others on the forecourt and picked up four dirty mugs from John's desk, he always let them accumulate before washing them in bulk."

"Where are you from?" asked Steve.

"Alton," said Victor calmly.

"How long have you known James?"

"Not long, I only met him at the weekend. He's courting my little girl," he explained with a smile. "I said I would be in the area this week and he offered to show me around. We've just been for a long walk across the forest and made our way here."

Victor sensed Steve pondering the way I had introduced him as my friend rather than Sam's father, in the way nosy policemen do, but Steve dismissed it.

"John tells me she's a very pretty girl."

"She probably takes after her mother," said Victor and they all laughed.

"I'll just give Jim a hand with the tea," said John.

He left them outside on the forecourt and walked over to the sink at the back of the workshop where I was making the tea.

"What is all this about Victor being Sam's father?" he asked.

"Well he is, was, her father. Give us a hand with the tea and let's get rid of Steve then we can talk."

"I hope he doesn't stay long, he never normally stops for a cup of tea. He's just being nosey that's all,"

"Victor doesn't look old enough to be Sam's father," said John, as we walked back outside.

"I know"

"There ya go mate, that'll warm you up a bit," said John, offering Steve his tea.

It wasn't a cold day, but Steve was wrapped up well in his motor cycle gear and long leather boots.

Victor took the other cup from me but didn't drink. Steve drank his tea straight down despite it being piping hot, then said he should be getting back on the road. He said goodbye, shaking Victor's hand, then put on his helmet and gloves and rode off.

"God I love the sound of that bike," said John.

When he was out of sight John closed the workshop doors and the three of us sat in his little office.

I explained that Victor's appearance was an illusion before Victor revealed his true appearance to John, in order to convince him that he was indeed an alien. When John recovered from the shock I explained how Victor was Sam's father in her previous life."

"So you're telling me we have all lived previous lives, like you?" asked John hearing the revelation."

"Most of you," answered Victor without further explanation.

"Jesus!"

It was too much to fully comprehend.

"Hey, I wish I was going with you," he said, fully grasping that I was really going to see a new world.

"You have a family here and a life of your own," said Victor. "Much as I would like to take you, we do not like to break up families. James has a life with my daughter and she wishes to return to her home, in a way his life here nearly ended in Dubai."

"He's right mate," I said. "You could never leave Mary and Jane behind, and you couldn't take them from Mary's parents either. You would be gone for years."

"I know. I wasn't really serious any way. I had to think long and hard about the Merch', leaving here all together is not really an option. You'll be here for Christmas though?" he asked.

"That's the plan, Christmas and New Year."

"Where is your ship now?"

"It's out in space," I said.

"We find the best way to confuse those searching for us is to land right under their nose, on or near a top-secret military base, then send our ship away out of reach as it were. That way they have no idea why we are here and where we are going."

"Makes sense I suppose," said John. "I can't think of any secret bases around here though," he laughed.

"Oh you would be surprised. Early this morning I came down in the Solent as HMS Dreadnought was leaving Portsmouth harbour, before flying very low across the forest over Norleywood to Sway. Any nuclear target gets them excited. They will have tracked the ship going back up, so they know where it's parked. They'll be tracking it constantly waiting for it to return."

Victor told John more about the world I would be going to, and how his people could revisit the people they loved after their life ended, how heaven was actually a doorway to all the previous lives they had lived.

Eventually it was time to leave, we had talked for most of the day and John said he had work to finish. He could have listened all day and through the night.

360

"Do not worry about your brother John, he will be safe with me, and I give you my word that I will bring James back to you and your family one day, perhaps with a family of his own."

John's eyes welled up as he shook Victor's hand and he did his best to shrug it off with a smile, rubbing a tear away with the back of his hand. As we walked out of the office past the Morris Minor that he was about to work on, Victor ran his hand across the damaged wing. The damage was gone.

"That's incredible!" said John.

"Elementary telekinesis," he laughed.

"I thought that was moving things around?" I said.

"You mean levitation. In its simplest form it is. That little trick was nothing more than a demonstration of the mind control we use to travel across the galaxy, for that we need to manipulate the physical structure of space.

"Well if you ever need a job let me know," laughed John.

We all smiled, and I shook John's hand as we left.

"Thanks Victor, for dad. I saw him this morning." he explained.

As he said it his face turned red and I could see more tears running down his face.

"Guess I'll close up early and go spend some time with Mary and Jane. Do you guys need a lift?"

"No thank you," said Victor. "Go and spend time with your wife. I too must see my daughter."

"John, will ya call ma and tell her I have come back to stay with you tonight."

"Yes mate, no problem," he laughed.

# HARMLESS

V ictor and I walked across the road to the station and boarded the
next train to Waterloo. We took the tube to Highgate and walked
to Sam's flat. As soon as she saw me she threw her arms around me and
we kissed frantically.

"Ok you two, you'll have time for that later," joked Victor.

Despite knowing that he had once been Sam's father he still seemed
just like a friend to both of us.

"Tonight, you can meet with my people," said Victor, looking at me,
"and in the morning we will return and talk with you," he added looking
at Sam. Before we leave I have something for you. It will boost your
thoughts and allow us all to communicate with each other."

Don't worry, it won't hurt," I said.

He placed the small device in the back of Sam's neck in the same way
he had with me. Despite the fact that she had once been his son, Sam
was Earth-born as Victor had said and had the same limited powers as I
did, although my own seemed to be growing stronger every day.

"I will leave you both now for two hours while I make contact with
my people and arrange the meeting."

We both grinned as he left, realising he was simply giving us the
benefit of some privacy, while he communicated with his people. Sam led
me to the bedroom where we forgot the world around us for a moment
and gave time to sate our hunger for each other.

# BOAC 777

Sam and I were both asleep when I heard Victor's voice.

'I'm outside,' he said waking me.

'I'll be there in two minutes,' I replied silently.

It was hard to leave the comfort of Sam's warm body, as I took one last sniff of her hair, she lifted her head and turned around to kissed me, making it even more difficult to leave.

I reminded myself I was about to see Victor's ship and go into space; knowing Sam would be there when I returned, the excitement was more than enough to swing the balance. I pulled the quilt around Sam and left her to sleep, dressing in the living room in an attempt not to wake her fully. As I opened the front door, I felt her hand on my shoulder and then her soft lips found my own once more.

"Be careful," she said, "you know it will be dangerous!"

"I know, but I must go with him. I'll be back before you know it," I said, kissing her goodbye.

"Boys and toys, hopeless," she said. "So should I conclude that I am not exciting?"

"What can I say?" I answered, still grinning when she punched me in the stomach.

I opened the front door and Victor stood waiting for me in the cold night air. It was 8.30 and once again there was already a light frost forming.

"Good luck and be careful," she said to both of us.

"Of course. We will be safe enough," answered Victor. "Now go back inside, it's cold out here."

Captain Le Fevre was expecting Sam to work the following day and she had no intention of letting him down, besides it made no sense to risk three of us trying to board the ship in London.

"Where are we going?" I asked, as we walked away.

"Right under their noses," said Victor, "Heathrow airport."

"Heathrow!" I shrieked. "Are you insane?"

"I will bring my ship in at high velocity, above and behind a landing 747 jet. The military will track its descent but will have only moments to do so. The Air Traffic Controllers will probably rub their eyes in disbelief and call an observer if they spot my ship. We must be ready to board the ship within seconds or we will cause a major incident."

"No problem, sounds exciting!" I said.

"We will have to be inside the airport perimeter to board the ship. There is no other way we can be out of public view. We will be vulnerable having broken through the perimeter wire."

We took the tube back to Euston Station and picked up a cab outside.

"Stanwell Hall Hotel please Cabby. That's Town Lane, Stanwell near Heathrow," said Victor.

"Ok Gov, I should sit back and relax if I were you, it will take us nearly an hour in this traffic."

"No problem," answered Victor sitting back.

The cab dropped us at the hotel and Victor paid him.

"Keep the change!" he said, before turning towards the hotel.

'That was very generous of the banks,' I grinned. 'Why Stanwell Hotel? Why don't we just go to the terminal?' I asked silently.

'We are not taking a flight to New York my friend. Firstly, we have no luggage, and cab drivers are naturally suspicious people, they rarely take people to the airport with no luggage. We don't want him reporting us to the police later, that's why we picked up the cab at Euston Station, no connection to Highgate, and lots of people picking up a cab at the stations; secondly, we need to get to the western side of the airport and Stanwell Hall is only a mile walk from there. The western end is the most deserted, and fortunately for us it is also the end where the aeroplanes are making their approach tonight.'

As soon as the cab was out of sight we set off towards our true destination at the edge of the airport. The path around the western perimeter was quiet, the occasional car passed but there were no other pedestrians.

We arrived at a spot just to the right of the runway where the planes flew in above us, it was the quietest corner of the airfield as Victor had said. He told me that his colleagues were monitoring the air traffic control radio communications, and that BOAC flight 777 suited our needs. He said that the plane was now about to make its final approach for Heathrow, coming in from the west between Windsor and Heathrow at approximately 160 knots, flying at 1500 feet with wheels and flaps down.

The sky was clear with not a single cloud in sight and I could see the distant landing lights as Victor pointed them out to me.

'There are two planes behind flight 777, but neither are suitable for our purpose, they are smaller aircraft. The 747 is two hundred and ten feet long, and just as importantly the cabin width is twenty feet. My ship is nearly thirty feet long and fourteen feet wide, so it can nestle in just above the main fuselage keeping clear of the tail and concealing its descent from the ground detection equipment.'

Victor's concentration focused while he guided his ship down.

I studied the distant flickering lights, moments later I saw a faint blue light appear, descending at high speed, then abruptly slowing and nestling down above BOAC 777, as it did so it disappeared from view.

'They have already spotted my ship. The plane behind has queried Heathrow Tower and Air Traffic Control at West Drayton about an unidentified blue light above BOAC 777.

'They have requested the pilot on board PAN AM flight 101, the aircraft behind, to abort his landing, and instead increase speed, and visually confirm the unidentified light above BOAC 777, then circle.'

As we watched the sky PAN AM 101 edged slightly closer to BOAC 777.

'PAN AM flight 101 confirmed a small silver-blue aircraft flying immediately above BOAC 777, and is breaking off to re-queue for landing.'

We watched as the aeroplane behind turned away to starboard.

'Now they have asked BOAC 777 to make some small manoeuvres to see if they can pick up my ship with radar, but my ship is now locked onto BOAC 777 and will simply follow it where ever it goes.'

'Shouldn't we make our way inside the perimeter now?' I asked.

'Not yet.'

'West Drayton and the Tower can see nothing except BOAC 777 and are discussing final clearance for landing.'

As we waited anxiously for flight 777, I noticed a police car with a flashing blue light making its way around the perimeter towards us. It had two spotlights above the windscreen, which seemed to be tracking along the fence.

Before it reached us, Victor made a large circular stroke against the fence using his forefinger. I was not surprised to see the circle of fence fall away into the airfield. Victor hurried me through the hole and he quickly followed. I watched the police car draw closer as Victor picked up the broken fence wire and place it back where it came from. Running his palm around the circumference, he quickly fused the wires where they touched, sufficiently well enough to hold it in place.

We scurried across the airfield towards the runway watching the police car pass the place where we had entered and continue on its way.

As BOAC 777 approached the runway, we heard the sound of fire engine sirens then saw some engines heading down towards where we now stood. They were still a mile away when BOAC 777 dropped in over our heads.

Victor's ship left its concealment above the aeroplane and landed in front of us. I had little time to examine it but appeared to a shining metallic blue triangular craft with no apparent windows or doors. It glowed in the dark and must have been visible to both the fire engine crews and the tower.

Before I had time to think, a door opened in front of me and Victor pushed me inside. He stepped in behind me and the door closed silently behind him.

# BIG STEP

$I$nside the ship there was nothing except two very comfortable silver coloured chairs facing the aerodynamic end of the ship.

'We are clear,' said Victor.

"What?" I said in disbelief, having experienced no sensation of movement.

He had dropped his Terran like appearance and my eyes saw him as he was, his large black eyes shone eerily in the dim light of the ship. My brain had become accustomed to seeing him differently with my eyes and my mind.

'I expect you would like to see this,' he said, as the view behind me was exposed.

My surroundings began to spin with vertigo as my balance was questioned. I staggered across to one of the two chairs and sat down.'

'I'm sorry,' said Victor. 'You get used to it.'

I put my head between my legs and vomited, then seeing my stomach contents spread on an invisible floor made me feel even worse. I shut my eyes and sat back to regain my composure. When I opened them again the mess in front of me was gone.

Both chairs rotated 180 degrees to face the stern and I looked in awe at the Earth below me, gripping the arm rests in an attempt to push myself back into the seat.

'We came up vertically, Heathrow is now a thousand miles below us,' he explained, still standing to my left. 'It was a risk to land there, but pilots and Air Traffic Controllers don't like reporting UFO sightings, it tends to affect their promotion prospects. Close your eyes and imagine you are at the cinema watching a film.'

I did as he suggested and then opened my eyes again.

The Earth filled my field of vision completely, I could just make out both poles simultaneously without moving my eyes; Antarctica on my right, and the Arctic on my left; at the bottom of my view, South America on the left and Antarctica on the right; at the top, Europe on the left and Africa on the right. The line separating daylight from darkness rose from left to right, South America and Antarctica were still in day light, while Europe and Africa were in darkness with only the lights of the cities suggesting vague coastlines.

I stood up and moved closer to the window; there was no sense of any barrier between me and the Earth. I realised that I had been disorientated. I was standing on the floor with no sensation of weightlessness. The Earth's gravity had no effect on me, somehow the ship had its own gravity field.

I looked around me; there were no instruments, no control mechanism, not even any light source that I could see, but there was internal light, even if it was dim compared with the reflected sunlight on the Earth. The walls around the rest of the ship were all silver in colour, just like the two chairs.

'Would you like to see the Apollo 11 landing site on Luna?'

"Are you serious?"

He had already read my subconscious thoughts.

'Take a seat,' he said.

The two chairs rotated again, and I sat down beside Victor. The front of the ship became transparent, and as I looked ahead the moon grew rapidly in front of me, faster than a man can blow up a balloon. It was in the first quarter, with just over half the moon lit by the sun as we approached. The Sea of Tranquillity was half way down on the side in sunlight. In three or four seconds we were there, hovering above the surface.

"There!" he said pointing directly ahead.

No more than thirty yards in front of me stood the descent stage and launch platform of Eagle, the Lunar Module used on the Apollo 11 mission, beside it stood the American flag, eerily motionless, draped from its pole.

Victor edged the ship sideways towards the platform. I flinched, expecting an impact as one of the legs of the platform appeared through the side of the ship. He manoeuvred around until the leg was at the taller end of the ship, so that most of the leg was inside.

I got out of my chair. In front of me, attached to the leg was the same ladder that Neil Armstrong used to make his descent to the moon's surface, on the 16th July just four years before. Most of the chassis was covered in gold foil.

"Would you like to try the ladder?" asked Victor.

"How can you do that?" I asked, still stunned by the appearance of the Lunar Module leg inside the ship. "What is this ship made of?"

I glanced down before he answered. Below the ladder I could actually see the lunar surface, it sparkled as though there were thousands of tiny diamonds scattered across the surface.

'The ship is a water cerium thorium gravilux, a mixture of chemical compounds bonded through graviton alignment. A sophisticated metal alloy,' he explained. 'It is completely flexible and adaptable to any environment, able to move from gaseous state to liquid and to solid by realigning the gravitons,' said Victor.

"Water? How ..."

'A water molecule consists of two atoms of hydrogen bonded to one atom of oxygen held together by covalent bonding. Both of these elements are normally gaseous and possess very different qualities to water. To exist as a liquid, hydrogen must be pressurised and cooled to -252.88, oxygen to -182.96 degrees centigrade. Consider another common compound, salt. Table salt is the compound...'

"Sodium chloride. Yes, I know."

'Each molecule of salt is composed of one atom of sodium bonded to one atom of chlorine. Once again, the molecule has completely different chemical properties than the two elements. Salt is a solid material and is relatively non-toxic. We can mix it with food or water with little consequence. Sodium is a metal solid that is violently reactive with water. If sodium is exposed to water, the hydrogen gas that is released will burst into flames. At room temperature, Chlorine is a highly toxic greenish-coloured gas. In a similar way a gravilux produces a material with totally different properties to its original constituents. A gravilux can be manipulated through all three states at will.'

'And what the hell are Cerium and Thorium?'

'Cerium is a silvery metal element, belonging to the lanthanide series. It looks much like iron but is soft, malleable and ductile, it is the most reactive of Earth metals, naturally it would decompose in water. Thorium is a slightly radioactive metal which provides the energy required to form a gravilux, which prevents the water cerium reaction and produces a material with these extraordinary properties.'

I moved towards the ladder without any more thought of what he had said.

"Wait a moment," he said moving between the platform and me. He pointed down at the last footprints left by Armstrong and Aldrin then without disturbing them he moved his palms across the structure and the lunar surface at his feet.

"It was probably a little warm for you with the sun still up. I estimate close to one hundred and eighteen degrees centigrade."

"Good guess," I answered with a grin. The ladder? Is it okay now?"

"Yes, it's safe."

As I moved forward, I stepped down from the ship's hull onto the lunar surface. Keeping my feet behind the last footprints, I placed my hands on the ladder and pulled myself upwards towards the first step. I rose quickly past it and pushed my foot under the second step to stop myself from rising.

"There is no gravity," I said.

'Yes, there is gravity but only one sixth that of Terra,' answered Victor, 'your mass is constant, but you probably weigh about twenty-five pounds here.'

"I didn't notice it until I stepped up."

'The exposed field you are now in is in effect a protective bubble stretching beyond the normal contour of the ship. We have atmosphere inside; however, I have disabled the gravity field and we are now at

Luna's natural gravity. You will learn the significance of manipulating gravity fields when we reach Erato.'

I pushed myself away from the ladder and down onto the lunar surface mimicking Armstrong's steps.

"Hell, it seems like a pretty big step to me Neil," I said.

The ladder stopped well short of the surface to allow for the dampening of the landing structure.

"Can I touch the dust?"

"Yes you can, it will do you no harm."

I reached down taking care not to disturb the footprints left by my predecessors and ran my fingertips through the surface dust until I felt a small lump. I grasped it between my fingers and pulled it out of the dust. It was a shiny black crystal about one and a half inches across at its widest.

"I'll keep it for ever," I said looking at Victor.

"I was here when they landed," said Victor, "there were many of us, my Eratean colleagues, Amorfons, Hittites, Yowies."

"Really?"

"Wouldn't you have been here to witness it if you could? Yes of course really!"

"What about the Greys, and their masters, the Tall-Whites?"

"Not here. I told you they keep themselves to themselves. Come," he said, "we have much to do."

Before moving back to my seat, I turned back to brush away my footprints from the scene and I noticed how small they were compared to the huge boots that Armstrong and Aldrin had worn. When I was happy that there was no visible contamination of that historic site I moved back to my seat.

"How come there's no blast hole under the platform?"

'The mass of the Eagle's ascent stage was around 5400lbs with almost the same again in fuel. Here on Luna, it would have weighed about 1800lbs, the weight of around nine men, on Earth. The thrust of the ascent module was around 3500lbs, on Earth it would have required over 20000lbs of thrust, compared with 7.5 million pounds of thrust on the

Saturn V rocket to get it there. The initial burst of ascent thrust was dispersed laterally, remember that the descent engine was directly below it.'

The ship moved away from the platform, rising just a few feet above the surface, and I watched as it rushed beneath us through the front of the ship. Victor pointed out a second site on the far side of the Sea of Tranquillity and we slowed to a near stop.

"This is the landing site of Apollo 17 where Eugene Cernan left the last footprints on the moon, in December last year," he said.

"Were you here too?" I asked.

"I was, and so were many others, on all the landings."

We moved around the platform and then Victor moved the ship away to show me the Lunar Rover, intentionally left almost a mile away to film the lift-off of Challenger. The ship swung around, and I could see enormous mountains rising around us.

"Where are we going?" I asked.

"You wanted to know about the Greys and their masters, didn't you?"

"Yes, but you said they weren't here."

"No, I said they weren't at the Apollo landings."

We flew low across the moon surface at extremely high speed, which was emphasised by the surface rushing under us.

"What about Apollo 13?" I asked.

"After the assassination of Kennedy, Vice President Lyndon Baines Johnson was sworn in as his replacement, becoming the 36th President of the United States. Johnson pledged to carry out Kennedy's policies; civil rights, the space program, nuclear de-escalation in the Cold War, but Nikita had lost the man he trusted, and the Cold War became significantly cooler again.

"Image, as much as anything, became a significant part in the game of continental chess they played, the lies both sides had made about our existence had become a feral monster with a life of its own. Owning up to the cover-up in the midst of such global tension would spell disaster for both sides.

"American astronauts and Russian cosmonauts had reported UFO sightings on their early missions and containment was becoming more and more difficult.

"Kennedy's commitment to landing in the moon had been a bold one; however, it may have been over optimistic, time was running out and they could not afford to fail. NASA's courageous missions pushed American technology to the limits and there were serious fears that the Lunar landing may fail, and failure was not an option. Departments in the CIA and NSA worked in parallel with NASA to ensure that if the unthinkable happened, all would not be lost.

"Scripts for every mission written by scientists and engineers, politicians and even science fiction authors; photographs, film clips and voice recordings were prepared in advance so that provided the Saturn V launch was successful, a moon landing could be aired to the public. In the worst case, the heroic astronauts would never return, the command module would burn up in the atmosphere and no one would be the wiser.

"With the exception of Harrison Schmitt, all the Apollo astronauts were ex US Navy or US Air Force, prepared to give their life for their country; Schmitt being a geologist was the first scientist to fly in space; all knew the risks that they were taking.

"With so many of we visitors taking an interest in the project, there were great fears that the cover up would be exposed. Photographs and films were crudely edited to hide images of our ships, but careless radio messages from the astronauts to Mission Control were picked up by radio enthusiasts around the world, and containment became an issue.

"The Apollo mission was a success, Neil Alden Armstrong and Edwin Eugene Aldrin Jr, or Buzz, walked on Luna, while Michael Collins orbited above in the Command Module. First Collins, then after recovery of the Lunar Module, Armstrong and Aldrin saw what you are about to see.

"Mission debriefs after their return, caused great concern as it became evident that senior NASA officials only know half the story. Apollo 12 repeated the success four months later, landing in the Ocean of Storms. Charles Conrad Jr. became the third man to walk on Luna and

Alan LaVern Bean became the fourth, with Richard Francis Gordon Jr. as Command Module Pilot."

"Meanwhile the political storm between those who knew everything, and NASA officials, caused a re-evaluation of the Apollo 13 mission, long before Apollo 12 launched. On one side, keeping the alien presence a secret, and on the other, the safety of the astronauts, not just on their missions, but also when they returned in full awareness of the truth.

"The script writers went to work to create yet another cover-up, while future missions were put on hold. The script, probably written by filmmaker Stanley Kubrick, who had directed the science fiction file '2001: A Space Odyssey', was so well written, that everyone at NASA became heroes and the image was preserved."

"I saw the film, at the cinema. It was pretty weird at the end."

"Indeed," he smiled. "On January 30th, 1971, Apollo 14 launched taking Alan Bartlett Shepard Jr., Stuart Allen Roosa and Edgar Dean Mitchell back to Luna; Alan Shepard became the fifth man to walk on the moon, Ed Mitchell the sixth and Stuart Allen Roosa the Command Module Pilot."

"I was eleven years old when Apollo 8 went around the moon and I remember all the missions that followed. I was twelve when Armstrong and Aldrin landed on the moon, and almost thirteen when Apollo 13 had everyone glued to the television and radio. 'Houston, we've had a problem.' Now you tell me it was a set up!"

"They were all brave men."

"Yes, they were."

It was still light when we slowed down and eventually stopped behind a range of hills.

Very slowly the ship rose until we could see over the crest.

"There, this is just one of the bases the Krel's Grays have built with the full knowledge of the secret societies I spoke of."

"Who are these people?"

"It began in 1947," he answered, "but we must leave here now, my friends await our arrival, and Paul has told us not to approach them," said Victor.

We flew away, low and fast, heading back the way we had come.

"Can't people see that base with a telescope?" I asked, and Victor smiled.

"It is too far away to see such detail on the lunar surface using current technologies and besides it's on the dark side."

"Sorry?"

"Your moon is very special because it orbits Earth in twenty-seven point three days and the Lunar day is also twenty-seven point three days.

"Imagine a plate as the Earth, then picture a cup beside the plate with its handle pointing towards the centre of the plate. As the cup moves around the plate the handle always remains pointed to the centre of the plate. So as it travels around the plate, the cup is also turning in the opposite direction. Because the time Luna takes to turn on its axis precisely matches its orbit around Earth, you always see the same side. So, there is a near side and a far side, or dark side as your people call it. Luna's phases are caused by its position relative to the sun. Light or dark, you still only see the same side of Luna from Earth."

"Yes, I remember hearing about it during the Apollo missions now."

"Indeed they did. There are no radio communications to Earth from the far side of Luna, so no communications would be possible without a Lunar satellite to bounce the signal back to Earth. The other interesting fact about Luna is its size relative to its distance from Earth and Helios, Luna's size is identical to that of Helios during an eclipse, providing an excellent opportunity to study the corona."

"That's interesting. Has that always been the case?

"No, Luna is very slowly moving away from Earth, currently one point six inches a year."

Ahead of us, Eratean ships were beginning to gather.

"I warn you now, the meetings at Council, and indeed at the Eratean Forum on my home world, are very formal structured gatherings. I know you will find it amusingly fastidious, but please understand that in serous matters my people adhere to our ancient customs rigidly. Think of the meeting as a military briefing or even court proceedings, clarity is essential, and I know you get frustrated with me sometimes. You really don't like rules."

"I'm sorry if I have offended you."

"I know no offence was intended. You are a Maverick, an individualist nonconformist free-spirited unorthodox unconventional original bohemian eccentric outsider rebel dissenter dissident informal, bad boy!"

"I know, I know."

I laughed about our differences with him.

# THE ERATEAN COUNCIL

I watched as other ships identical to Victor's came together to form one much larger circular ship, high above the Earth. We moved into the last segment closing the circle.

"That was so fast! It's incredible!" I said.

"Not really, we didn't even reach light speed. Light travels from Earth to Luna in 1.28 seconds," he said with a smile.

The chairs remained rotated facing the aerodynamic end of the ship, while above and beside me the hull disappeared to reveal the occupants in the circular vessel, sixty feet in diameter. I looked around at the other inhabitants who were all Eratean. Sixteen ships made up the circle and I was the only Terran there. For the first time I realised I was the alien. There was little if anything that I perceived as different about the other Erateans, who all appeared to be dressed in the same type of loose fitting white himations.

There was a chaotic sense of chatter in my mind, clearly the Erateans were welcoming each other. I turned to focus on Victor and became aware of more ships arriving around us. As each ship merged with the circle, its occupants were revealed. They sat slightly above and behind the first circle of Eratean ships, forming another tier.

More and more ships arrived until I lost count of the rows of seats that formed one huge ship. Looking around the ship I saw that there were two other Terrans on board. One of the Erateans in the front row stood up and looked around what had now become an amphitheatre-like auditorium with perhaps two hundred thousand Erateans.

'People of Erato, friendship, I am known here as Bernd. We have been called to Council by he who is known here as Victor. We welcome his guest James and also our guests Susan and Sital, who have been invited to our home and whom we henceforth regard as denizens of Erato. I stand down to allow Victor to begin the debate by informing us of all that he knows about the Malakh.'

Victor stood up and looked around circle turning his head as far back as he could, first to the left and then back around the room, completing the circle behind his right shoulder.

'People of Erato, friendship, I am known here as Victor. It is with the greatest joy that I am able to tell you that I have met with one who I am almost certain to be Malakhi. I first met briefly with one, who uses the name Paul Caveat, six years ago, at which time he was able to foresee a way that I would find the reborn soul of my son, who was taken prisoner by the US Air Force after the crash at Corona in 1947. I am certain that I have done so with the help of my companion James Alexander Cummings who sits with me now, as he predicted. I met again with the one name Paul eight days ago and he enlightened me with the history of the Malakhi, and how his people had once been known to us on our home-world. I expect to update the counsel as soon as I can confirm what I have been told.

'So it is with equal joy, that I can confirm I have found the living soul of my son, who ended his life after four years of torture by the US Military. He has been reborn as a Terran Sapien and is known here as Samantha Dee Cooper. It is Samantha's wish that she return to Erato in thirty-three days' time, together with James whom I have invited to our world.

'I therefore ask the Council that we obtain updates on the following, so that I can relay these at the Eratean Forum when we arrive.

'I ask you now;

'What is the current status of the United States government groups established to conceal our presence after the Corona incident, the Majority 12 group, its predecessors and successors?

'What high level secret societies exist, what influence if any do they have over Earth's governments, and what is the membership status of each.

'What update do we have on the modified simian virus strain we discussed at our last council meeting?

'What information do we have on the Greys and the Tall-Whites?

'What other significant information do we have?

'Please prepare any personal messages you wish me to take back to our home-world.

'I volunteer myself for post-debate tasks.'

# MAJORITY

Victor sat down beside me.

'Who the hell are the Majority 12?' I asked with my thoughts, assuming only he would hear. Instead everyone in the ship heard my question and it was answered by Bernd, who once again stood to do so.

'The Majority 12 origins lay with the Majestic 12, also known as the Majic 12, MJ 12 or MJ XII. Majestic 12 was the code name of a secret committee of government officials, military leaders, and high-level scientists. It was originally formed in 1947 at the direction of U.S. President Harry S. Truman, representative of the Democratic Party. Their mandate and immediate objective, to contain and control all aspects of the Corona incident, the ships and their crews, Eratean or Greys, dead or alive.'

'Friendship, I am known here as Martin. May we know the significance of the letter 'S' used in President Truman's name?'

'President Truman died on December 26th last year, his middle name was simply the letter 'S', perhaps honouring maternal grandfather Solomon Young or his paternal grandfather Anderson Shippe Truman, probably both.'

'Thank you. I volunteer myself for post-debate tasks. Please continue,' replied Martin.

'To continue. The ongoing mission of the group was to investigate alien activity in the aftermath of the incident, in which as we know two Erateans were killed, the daughter of Václav, and the daughter of Pietro.'

Václav and Pietro stood up to make themselves known.

'Friendship, I am known here as Václav. Sadly, the search for my daughter's reborn soul goes on. I would therefore ask Victor if it would be possible to meet with the one who calls himself Paul, in the hope that I also may find help with my search.

'Friendship, I am known here as Pietro. It is with great joy that I too have found the reborn soul of my son, he is reborn a Terran female known here as Marie Ava Falkenstein and she will be returning to Erato with me,' said Pietro.

'I will put this to Paul when I next meet with him Václav, I share your pain, and your joy Pietro,' said Victor, standing to do so.

Bernd rose again to continue his monologue.

'A third, son of Amulya was critically injured in the crash and died 3 days after being taken prisoner by the US Air Force,' he continued.

'Friendship, I am known here as Amulya. It is with great joy that I can confirm, that I too have found my son known here to the Sapiens as Ebe, he is reborn a Sapien female known here as Suzanne Jayne Pope or Suzy, she sits with me now,' said Amulya, standing to do so. 'Suzanne has told me that she wishes to live out her Sapien life here, at least until her parents and sister have died. I will remain here on Earth with her until that time. I ask therefore for a volunteer to be my second in case anything should happen to me.

'I will be your second,' said Václav, rising from his seat again, 'at least until my mission is completed.

'Thank you Václav,' said Amulya.

Both sat down allowing Bernd to continue.

'The fourth, the son of Victor, survived the crash and was taken prisoner, as Victor has told us.

'To continue. President Truman effectively created the Central Intelligence Agency a month after the crash, on July 26, 1947 by signing the National Security Act of 1947 into law; five years later he created the National Security Agency by secret Executive Order on November 4th, 1952. We believe its primary purpose was to monitor all communications and emissions, from any and all devices worldwide, for the purpose of gathering intelligence, both human and alien, and to contain the secret of our presence. We know that numerous covert projects followed, directed by select personnel of the CIA and the NSA.

'As you know the Eratean delegation which arrived here in 1954, made direct contact with United States President Dwight David Eisenhower, at Edwards Air Force Base in California. The meeting was planned after our initial landing at Holloman Air Force Base in New Mexico.

'In preparation for the meeting at Edwards Air Force Base, President Eisenhower established a permanent committee to be known as Majority Twelve. Their mandate, to covertly control and conduct all activities concerned with our presence, without the knowledge of the US Congress.

'In answer to your original question James, the Majority Twelve group was made up of the following members; Nelson Aldrich Rockefeller, Governor of New York; Allen Welsh Dulles, Director of the CIA; John Foster Dulles, Secretary of State; Charles Erwin Wilson, Secretary of Defense; Admiral Arthur William Radford, Chairman of the Joint Chiefs of Staff; and John Edgar Hoover, the Director of the FBI. Admiral Radford died in August this year, and J Edgar Hoover as he was known, died in May last year.

'They were assisted by six men from the Executive Committee of the Council on Foreign Relations, known as the Wise Men'.

'I am known here as Declan. What was Mr Rockefeller's position at that time?'

'Mr Rockefeller, already heavily involved with the CIA, became Special Assistant to President Eisenhower for Foreign Affairs in 1954, sometimes referred to as Special Assistant to the President for Psychological Warfare. His duties frequently found him supervising secret operations of the CIA. He is currently the Governor of New York; however, we know that his ambition is the Presidency. He has already spent several millions of dollars in attempts to win the Republican primaries in 1960, 1964, and again in 1968. He is the son of John Davison Rockefeller Junior and the grandson of oil tycoon John Davison Rockefeller, founder of the Standard Oil Company, both of whom are known to have been great philanthropists. His other grandfather was Senator Nelson Wilmarth Aldrich.'

'Thank you. I volunteer myself for post-debate tasks. Please continue,' said Declan.

'Allen Welsh Dulles was the first civilian Director of the Central Intelligence Agency between 1953 and 1961. He was also a member of the Warren Commission that investigated the assassination of President John Fitzgerald Kennedy. Allen Dulles was the younger brother of John Foster Dulles and died in January 1969, as a result of influenza, complicated by pneumonia.

'John Dulles is thought to have been a man of strong conviction who was prepared to pursue his ideals, regardless of the opinions of his peers. He died of cancer ten years before his brother in May 1959.

'Mr Wilson also known as Engine Charlie, was United States Secretary of Defence from 1953 to 1957, and formerly President of the General Motors Corporation.

'Admiral Radford was Chairman of the Joint Chiefs of Staff between 1953 and 1957. We believe he died in August this year at Bethesda Naval Medical Center; however, we have no confirmation of his death, nor are we aware of the circumstances of his death.

'John Edgar Hoover was the founder of the Federal Bureau of Investigation in its present form, and its director from May 10, 1924 until his death last year. Mr Hoover was appointed acting director of the FBI by President John Calvin Coolidge to reform and clean up the Bureau. There have been allegations that Mr Hoover was in fact a homosexual, indeed there were also allegations made that Admiral Radford had homosexual relationships; however, we have no evidence to support either case.'

'Friendship, I am known here as Angelika. Why is the sexual preference of relevance to this debate?'

'I mention it because it is a matter of strong opinion amongst the Terran peoples. We know that the major religious and social groups consider homosexuality to be abnormal or sinful, in some countries it is punishable by death. We should perhaps remind ourselves of the fundamental and instinctive desire of developing civilisations to procreate. We also know that the majority of Terrans believe in monogamous relationships with members of the opposite sex despite the fact that multiple procreation with one partner has a negative impact on the gene pool and gives rise to sibling rivalry. The risk of sexually transmitted disease would be significantly increased in these people due to their overwhelming instinct to couple, therefore such religious beliefs would appear to be consistent with a protective regime.'

'I volunteer myself for post-debate tasks. Please continue,' replied Angelika.

'I am known here as Rafael. It is possible that a man in Mr Hoover's position, may simply have felt that a relationship of any kind may provide members of organised crime with an additional target, and threat to his determination to succeed in his position.'

'The possibility is made more plausible due to the fact that the birth certificate for Mr Hoover's birth was not registered until 1938, some forty-three years after the seemingly absurd birth date of January 1st, 1895. It would seem logical that Mr Hoover would also have wishes to protect the identity of his family, therefore selecting a new date and place of birth at random would be a logical move.'

'Absurd? In what way?' asked Rafael.

'Aside from December 25th, there are few dates in the Gregorian Calendar that have more significance in the western world. I should add that his characteristics are typical of a Sapien of Cardinal birth, he was almost certainly born under the sign of Capricorn,' answer Bernd.

'I volunteer myself for this or other post-debate tasks. Please continue,' said Rafael.

'Sorry, I am Sital,' said my fellow Terran, bravely standing up to do so. 'Why should a man in his position have registered his birth 43 years after he was born?'

'Welcome to our council Sital,' said Bernd. 'The intention would appear to be the creation of a new identity and the destruction of all evidence of the original man, so that no one can apply pressure to Mr Hoover by attacking his family. I should add that there are also claims that Mr Hoover had some African American ancestry, which he may have wanted to conceal. Further, all the members of the Majority 12 since its inception were of white, male, Caucasian origin; however, given the level of racism and sexual discrimination still apparent on Earth this is not necessarily surprising.

'We know now that John Edgar Hoover's father was Dickerson Naylor Hoover, born in Washington D.C. on November 21st, 1856. Dickerson Naylor Hoover died of melancholia in Washington DC on the 30 March 1921, and was buried in the Congressional Cemetery, Washington DC. His mother Anna Marie Scheitlin was still alive when he took office in 1924. Again, born in Washington DC on September 12th, 1860, she died in Washington DC on February 22nd, 1938, the year John Edgar Hoover's birth was registered. She too was buried in the Congressional Cemetery, Washington DC. Perhaps his original records were destroyed to protect her or his siblings. John had a brother, Dickerson N. Hoover Jr., and a sister Lilian, who were both over 10 years older than him. He also had another sister who was 5 years younger than him, Sadie Marguerite, but she died of Diphtheria.'

'Ok, I understand,' said Sital, apprehensive about his need to follow the apparent Eratean protocol.

'The remaining six members of the Majority 12 consisted of men from the executive committee of the Council on Foreign Relations also known as the Wise Men: John Jay McCloy, also known as Jack McCloy; Robert Abercrombie Lovett; William Averell Harriman; Charles Eustis Bohlen, also known as Chip Bohlen; George Frost Kennan; and Dean Gooderham Acheson, who died in October 1971.

'These men were all members of a secret society, known to themselves as The Jason Scholars who in turn recruited their members from the Skull and Bones society of Harvard, and Scroll and Key society of Yale.'

'Why Jason?' I thought.

'We believe the Jason Scholars derive their name from the Greek mythology. Jason, the rightful king of Iolcus was sent by his half-brother Pelias to search for the Golden Fleece, a challenge he undertook in the Argo with his crew of Argonauts.'

'Thank you,' I answered, allowing Bernd to continue.

'Mr McCloy is an American born lawyer and banker who later became a United States presidential advisor. He graduated from Amherst College in 1919, and then received a Legum Baccalaureus, Bachelor of Laws, from Harvard Law School in 1921. He was the Assistant Secretary of War from 1941 to 1945, during which he was noted for opposing the nuclear bombing of Japan. As assistant Secretary of War he was a key voice in setting United States military priorities.

'Mr McCloy was repeatedly asked by the War Refugee Board, the Emergency Committee to Save the Jewish People of Europe, and indeed by other groups, to order the bombing of the railroad lines leading to Auschwitz; however, Mr McCloy refused the requests, claiming the target was outside the range of United States and British bombers.

'Mr Lovett is a US Democrat politician, businessman and diplomat. He was United States Secretary of Defense, serving in the cabinet of President Harry S. Truman from 1951 to 1953 and in this capacity, directed the Korean War. He graduated from Yale University in 1918 and took postgraduate courses in law and business administration at Harvard University between 1919 and 1921.

'Mr Harriman is a US Democratic politician and the son of railroad baron Edward Henry Harriman, a financier and executive of the Union Pacific Railroad and the Southern Pacific Railroad. He served as the US Ambassador to Soviet Union between 1943 and 1946, later that year as Ambassador to Britain. He was later appointed the United States Secretary of Commerce under President Harry Truman between 1946 and 1948.

'Mr Bohlen is a United States diplomat and Soviet Union expert, serving in Moscow before and during World War II, succeeding Mr Kennan as US Ambassador to the Soviet Union from 1953 to 1957. He then moved to the Philippines from 1957 to 1959, and later to France from 1962 to 1968. I will discuss Mr Kennan after Mr Acheson because he seems to be the odd man out in the group.

'Mr Acheson was educated at Yale University, and later Harvard Law School. He was United States Secretary of State under President Truman between 1949 and 1953. Mr Acheson was a supporter of the Democratic Party. Although he developed anti-Communist views early in his political career, he was a prominent defender of State Department employees accused during anti-Communist investigations led by Senator Joseph Raymond McCarthy. Mr Acheson died in October 1971, we believe as a result of a heart attack.

'I return to Mr Kennan, who is an American advisor, diplomat, political scientist and historian, also known as the Father of Containment and as a key figure in the emergence of the Cold War. As I said earlier, he would seem to be the odd man out here, because of strong disagreements with other members of the group. Considering the normal Terran inability to trust implicitly those with a strong difference of opinion, this seems odd for such a secret organisation. Mr Kennan regarded himself as an outsider and had little patience with critics.

'William Harriman was the U.S. Ambassador in Moscow when Kennan was deputy between 1944 and 1946. He remarked that Mr. Kennan was 'a man who understood Russia but not the United States'. Mr Kennan was born on February 16, 1904 in Milwaukee, Wisconsin. Unlike the majority of his counterparts in the group, he did not study at Yale or Harvard, he attended St. John's Military Academy in Delafield, then studied at Princeton University. He was unaccustomed to the elitist atmosphere at Princeton and found his undergraduate years difficult and lonely; however, he graduated in 1925.

'We believe he considered law school after graduating but instead applied to the Foreign Service, entering a year later with early postings taking him to Switzerland, Germany, Estonia, Latvia, and Lithuania, mastering a number of languages, including; Russian, German, French, Polish, Czech, Portuguese, and Norwegian.

'When the United States opened diplomatic ties with the Soviet Union in 1933, he accompanied the United States ambassador, William Christian Bullitt, to Moscow. By the mid-1930s, he was among the core of professionally-trained Russian experts on the staff of the U.S. Embassy in Moscow, along with Mr Bohlen. At that time the general consensus of the group was that there was little basis for cooperation with the Soviet Union, even against potential adversaries.

'At the outbreak of World War II in 1939, he was assigned to Berlin and later interned there for six months, after the United States had entered the war in 1941.

'During late 1943 and 1944, he was counsellor of the U.S. delegation to the European Advisory Commission, which worked to prepare Allied policy in Europe.

'It was Secretary of the Navy James Forrestal that helped bring Mr Kennan back to Washington. We believe Mr Forrestal was killed by the members of the Central Intelligence Agency, the facts as we know them I will discuss later.

'Soon afterwards Mr Kennan became the first head of the new State Department policy planning staff, a position that he held from April 1947 through December 1949. Between April 1947 and December 1948, when General of the Army George Catlet Marshall was Secretary of State, Kennan was more influential than he was at any other period in his career. Marshall valued his strategic vision, and had him create and head what is now called the Policy Planning Staff, the State Department's internal think tank.

'Kennan became the first Director of Policy Planning. Marshall relied heavily on him along with other members of his staff, to prepare policy recommendations. Mr Kennan's opinions about the Soviet regime did not reflect the consensus of the Truman Administration, as a result Kennan's influence was increasingly marginalized, particularly after Mr Acheson was appointed Secretary of State in 1949.

'The following year, Mr Kennan left the Department of State and accepted an appointment as Visitor to the Institute for Advanced Study from fellow moderate Robert Oppenheimer, then Director of the Institute. Mr Kennan opposed the building of the fusion bomb, also referred to as the H bomb or Hydrogen bomb.

'During the Korean War, rumours started circulating in the State Department that plans were being made to advance beyond the 38th parallel into North Korea, a move that Kennan considered highly dangerous, he engaged in intense arguments with Assistant Secretary of State for the Far East Dean Rusk, who apparently supported Mr Acheson's goal to forcibly unite the Koreas. Despite his influence, Kennan was never comfortable in government.

'In 1951, President Truman announced the nomination of Mr Kennan to be the next United States Ambassador to the Soviet Union. The United States Senate approved this appointment at a time when tensions between United States and Soviet had moved beyond the point at which diplomacy could play any significant role.

'In September 1952, Kennan made a statement in which he compared his conditions at the Ambassador's residence in Moscow to those he had encountered while in incarceration in Berlin during the first few months of the Second World War; the Soviets took the remark as an implied analogy with Nazi Germany. The Soviets then declared Mr Kennan persona non grata and refused to allow him to re-enter the Soviet Union.

'Mr Kennan returned to Washington where he soon became embroiled in strong disagreements with Dwight D. Eisenhower's hawkish secretary of State, John Dulles. Even so, he was able to work constructively with the new administration. In the summer of 1953, President Eisenhower asked Kennan to chair the first of a series of top-secret teams.

'Under President Eisenhower and President Kennedy the Majority 12 group was also referred to as the '8412 Committee' and additionally the Special Group. Later under President Johnson it became known as the '303 Committee' and under President Nixon it is also known as the '40 Committee'. We have limited information about the current activities of the group since all attempts in communication have led to the incarceration of our representatives. We know that the group is now aware that they can prevent our escape by containment within a crude electromagnetic field.'

'Friendship, I am known here as Mohammed. Why have you singled out this man with such detail?'

'If we are to obtain more information about the new visitors we need to establish communication with one of the group. Since Mr Kennan has been marginalised in the past it would seem logical that he would be the most likely member to break silence.

'Thank you, I volunteer myself for this or other post-debate tasks. Please continue.'

'Thank you, Mohammed, I assign you to select and lead a team to establish communication with Mr Kennan and report back at the next debate. I suggest you use a Russian facade and name to draw on Mr Kennan's intellect.'

'I will use the name Mikhail.'

'Were these the men that conspired to kill Kennedy?' I thought.

'Perhaps. They, their successors, key military men and probably members of the American Mafia, brought to heel by the NSA, CIA and perhaps even the FBI; almost certainly funding the group's operations with a percentage of funds raised through drug trafficking and prostitution,' answered Victor.

# MAJESTIC

'Returning to the Majestic 12 group, the committee was originally formed on September 24th, 1947, and chaired by Vannevar Bush, Julius Robert Oppenheimer and Albert Einstein.

'Mr Bush is an American engineer, a scientist and a technocrat, believing in a government led by technical people, experts in their field,' explained Bernd.

'Mr Oppenheimer, who died of throat cancer in 1967, was an American theoretical physicist. Mr Bush and Mr Oppenheimer worked on the development of the atomic bomb.

'Mr Einstein was a Jewish theoretical physicist, born in Ulm, Germany. The American government declared that Mr Einstein died peacefully in his sleep on April 18th, 1955, in Princeton New Jersey, after a long illness. The listed cause of death stated that his death was caused by a ruptured artery in his heart; however, it was actually caused by internal bleeding due to an abdominal aortic aneurysm. He refused surgery, saying, 'I want to go when I want. It is tasteless to prolong life artificially. I have done my share; it is time to go. I will do it elegantly.'

'The Majestic 12 membership at the time of inception consisted of the following people; three Directors of the Central Intelligence Agency, Rear Admiral Sidney William Souers, Rear Admiral Roscoe Henry Hillenkoetter and General Hoyt Sanford Vandenberg. Government Officials, James Vincent Forrestal Secretary of Défense and Mr Gordon Gray Assistant Secretary for War, at thirty-eight years of age the youngest member of the group. United States Air Force Officers, Major General Robert Miller Montague Commanding Officer of the White Sands Air Base and General Nathan Farragut Twining the United States Air Force project leader for investigation into Unidentified Flying Objects. Finally, the scientists and engineers, Doctor Detlev Wulf Bronk neurophysiologist, Doctor Jerome Hunsaker aeronautics specialist, at sixty-one years of age the eldest member, Doctor Donald Menzel astronomer and astrophysicist, Doctor

Vannevar Bush specialist in computing and Doctor Lloyd Berkener specialist in aviation systems.'

Bernd paused briefly for questions, but there were none, so he continued his monologue.

'James Vincent Forrestal was Secretary of Defence until he resigned on March 28, 1949, apparently due to a mental breakdown. He was admitted into the Bethesda Naval Hospital five days later with a condition officially announced as nervous and physical exhaustion. His physician, Captain George Raines, diagnosed his condition as depression or reactive depression. We believe that CIA agents killed Mr Forrestal in the early morning hours of May 22$^{nd}$. His body was located on the third-floor roof below the 16th-floor kitchen, which was across the hall from his room. The Montgomery County coroner declared the incident suicide within hours of the death.'

'Friendship, I am known here as Clay. Why do we believe the Mr Forrestal was killed by the Central Intelligence Agency?'

'According to Mr Einstein, Mr Forrestal was unhappy that our presence here on Earth was being withheld from the public. All other members of the group were in unanimous agreement that confirming our presence could destabilise the governments of the world and cause mass hysteria, which could lead to a total breakdown of the economy, social structures, and even the religious establishments. Mr Einstein believed that Mr Forrestal was ready to pass on full details of the Majestic 12 and its reports about our presence and was therefore considered to have been a significant threat to the survival of the human race.'

'I volunteer myself for post-debate tasks. Please continue,' replied Clay.

'Mr Forrestal was replaced after his death by General Walter Bedell Smith, also known as Beetle Smith, then US Ambassador to the Soviet Union. He also replaced Rear Hillenkoetter as Director of the CIA on October 7$^{th}$, 1950. General Smith died on August 9, 1961 at Walter Reed Army Hospital in Washington, we believe as the result of a heart attack. The group also included Edward Teller a Hungarian-born American nuclear physicist who worked on the development of the atomic bomb. We believe Admiral Souers died in January this year.'

'Friendship, I am known here as Samer. Can we confirm Admiral Souers death?'

'We must allocate the task after the debate. We have no confirmation of the Admiral's death at this time, no information has been disclosed to the public.'

'I volunteer myself for this or other post-debate tasks. Please continue,' replied Samer.

'Thank you Samer, I assign you to select and lead a team to investigate the death of Admiral Souers and report back at the next debate.

'General Hoyt Sanford Vandenberg died of prostate cancer at Walter Reed Medical Center, Washington D.C. April 2, 1954.

'Mr Gordon Gray was Secretary of the Army between 1949 and 1950. President Dwight David Eisenhower appointed him his National Security Advisor from 1958 until 1961. He served on the President's Foreign Intelligence Advisory Board under Presidents John Fitzgerald Kennedy, Lyndon Baines Johnson and currently Richard Milhous Nixon.

'Major General Robert Miller Montague was Head of a secret project at the Atomic Energy Commission installation of Sandia Base in Albuquerque. We believe that General Montague was the Senior Officer in control of the recovery of the Corona site. The United States Government reported that General Montague died as the result of a cerebral haemorrhage in 1957; however, we believe this to be incorrect. The Eratean known here as Lorne, was killed while investigating his death but not before he managed to communicate the fact that the circumstances of the General's death were inaccurate.

'General Nathan Farragut Twining was Chairman of the Joint Chiefs of Staff between August 15th, 1957 and September 30th, 1960.

'Doctor Detlev Wulf Bronk presided over the autopsies of the Eratean bodies recovered at the Corona crash site.

'Doctor Jerome Hunsaker was an American aeronautical and officer in the Construction Corps of the U.S. Navy, more significantly he was

393

Chairman of the National Advisory Committee on Aerospace between 1941 and 1957, and Head of the Department of Mechanical Engineering, MIT, between 1947 and 1951.

'Doctor Donald Menzel is an American Astronomer and was President of the American Astronomical Society between 1954 and 1956.

'Finally, Doctor Lloyd Viel Berkener was an American physicist. Mr Berkner assisted in the development of radar and navigation systems, naval aircraft electronics engineering, and studies that led to the construction of the Distant Early Warning system. He died of heart failure in June 1967.

'In 1961 another Eratean Delegation met with President John Fitzgerald Kennedy and Nikita Sergeyevich Khrushchev, General Secretary of the Communist Party of the Soviet Union, in an attempt to persuade both to destroy their stockpile of weapons.

'We reaffirmed the assurances made to President Eisenhower that we would not enter into a strategic allegiance with any nation on Earth, in order that they as the leading Terran super powers, should not fear the transfer of technology to a potential aggressor.

'In October 1961, the Soviet Union exploded the Tsar Bomba, tested in a reduced state it produced a yield of around 50 megatons and was estimated to have been around 100 megatons in its full state.

'In 1963, the United States, the Soviet Union and Great Britain signed a Limited Test Ban Treaty, by which time the British and the French had already tested their own nuclear weapons.

'We believe both President John Kennedy and his brother Robert were assassinated for the same reason as James Forrestal, to prevent the destabilisation of world governments, breakdown of the economy, social structures and all powerful religious organisations. We have been unable to make contact with leaders of the major powers since that time. This is the most up to date reliable information we have.'

'Friendship, I am known here as Michelle. Why have we not made contact with the Greys and Tall-Whites? We coexist here with the Amorfons, the Hittites and the Yowies. Are we to assume that these visitors are more advanced than ourselves and our technology,'

'As with all the species we encounter, we do not attempt to force communication,' said Bernd.

'Friendship, I am known here as Yuri. Should we attempt contact with the Soviet or other governments to determine their knowledge of the visitors?'

'That is a question we must debate now,' answered Bernd. 'Originally we avoided communication with other governments in order not to fuel United States fears of a pre-emptive strike of any kind by another power. Since bringing together President Kennedy and Premier Khrushchev, we have been unable to regain contact with either power. If we establish communication with other governments, we risk destabilising what is already a very precarious situation. China, Great Britain and France already have nuclear capability. We should consider that the United States government is likely to assume that we possess the technology to empower any nation with superior weapons. I suggest we initially confine ourselves to the United States government and its secret societies. It appears that there is no opposition,' said Bernd.

There was no voting, each and every one of the Eratean council was aware of the opinion of the others and perhaps more significantly no to thoughts the contrary.

# CHARGED

Bernd remained standing to coordinate the list of requests and agree their mandates.

'Victor, I ask you to select and lead a team to re-establish contact with the Malakh known here as Paul. I suggest you involve Václav, since he seeks an audience with Paul.'

Victor rose to give his response.

'I am uncertain when I will next meet with Paul; however, my colleague James has spent much more time with him than I and is much more likely to meet with him sooner. I suggest that James may be more productive than I in discussing the Malakhi, the simian virus, the Greys and the Tall-Whites with Paul. I would however, like to lead a team to investigate the nature and proliferation of the simian virus. I was told that there are more than five million people on Earth who have been infected and carry the disease, mainly in central Africa but also with small but growing numbers in Europe, Asia and North America.'

'James, you are in no way obliged to do as Victor asks, should you decline, it will have no bearing on your invitation to go to Erato with Victor.'

'I accept the request. Václav, I will do my best to help you find the reborn soul of your daughter.'

'I thank you for your kindness,' said Václav.

'Very well. Then I ask you to report back at the next debate. Victor will bring you. Victor, you are aware of the risk to yourself in undertaking such a task.'

'I am.'

There was no objection from the Council.

'So be it,' said Bernd. 'Would you select a team before we move on?'

'I ask the following if they will work with me on this undertaking; Piotr, Slobodan, Kez, Yasin, and Amulya, since I am well acquainted with all; however, I will need five more volunteers.'

All five acknowledged and accepted Victor's request.

'People of Erato, friendship, I am known here as Juma. With respect, since the majority of infected people here are African, I would like to volunteer to assist Victor. My visit here has been spent studying in central Africa.'

'Agreed,' said Victor.

'Before we continue to assign tasks does anyone else wish to join Victor in his undertaking?' asked Bernd.

'No more who have lived and studied in Africa,' said Victor. 'I will need one who has lived in the United States, one who has lived in the Soviet Union, one who has lived in China and one who has lived in India.

'Clay, I have lived in California and have already volunteered for post-debate tasks.'

'Friendship, I am known here as Olga. I have lived in Moscow'

'Friendship, I am known here as Jenlong Wu. I have lived in China and many other eastern countries.'

'Friendship, I am known here as Sunil. I have lived in India.'

'I thank you for your support,' said Victor.

'Agreed,' said Bernd. 'Victor, please report back at the next debate.

'Martin, I assign you to select and lead a team to provide an update on the Majority 12 group, its members and any relevant new groups. I suggest at least twelve assistants.'

'I accept and select Pierluigi, Joette, Vor, Irina, Esther, Jeff, John, Zoe, Darren, Bhaskar, Colleen and Orlin.'

Again, all acknowledged and accepted the task as requested.

'Agreed,' said Bernd. Martin, please report back at the next debate.

'Samer, I assign you to select and lead a team to provide an update on the Majestic 12 group, establish the cause of death for Admiral Souers and General Robert M Montague.'

'I accept and select Jeorg, Ngurah, Jan, Joanna, Greg, Maarten, Catherine, Divya, Karen, Tina, Ken and Heidi.'

All acknowledged and accepted in the same ritualistic way.

'Agreed,' said Bernd. Samer, please report back at the next debate.

'Pietro, I assign you to select and lead a team to investigate the existence of any high level secret societies, determine what influence they might have over Earth's governments, and the membership status of each.

'I accept and select Nicole, Charley, Sheena, Ray, Giles, Sylvia, Carole and Adam.'

All acknowledged and accepted.

'Agreed,' said Bernd. 'Pietro, please report back at the next debate.

'Václav, I assign you to select and lead a team to investigate the origin of the Greys and Tall-Whites. Avoid direct contact with any except the Ambassador Krel. We know he has met with representatives of the US government, but take great care and do not expose yourself to unnecessary risk.

'I accept and select Michelle, Christopher, Guy, Pamela, Joan, Brian and Ahmed.

Again, all acknowledged and accepted.

'Agreed,' said Bernd. 'Václav, please report back at the next debate.

'People of Erato, if you have any projects or experiments in progress here on Earth please complete them as soon as possible. If there are Terrans you wish to invite to join us on Erato please do so urgently. If there is any threat to our presence here we will leave.

'I ask you all to discuss our concerns with your Amorfon, Hittite and Yowie contacts. Team members should meet immediately to discuss your charges, please adhere to them and avoid contact with Earth governments. We will all meet here in five days to continue the debate. Thank you all.'

# COMRADES

When the outer ships had all broken away from the auditorium the ship's hull took shape again. Moments later we reunited with the team Victor had selected, forming another smaller circle of ten ships.

'People of Erato. welcome and thank you for volunteering for this mission,' said Victor silently. This is my guest James whom I have invited to join us on Erato.

'I am privileged and honoured to be your guest here,' I replied in silence.

'Friendship,' the group echoed as one.

'We need to establish the truth about the virus, its origins, the extent and consequences of infection to both ourselves and to the Terran people. Your first assignment will be to observe all that you encounter to identify the virus and its effects. Use your life force to affect a cure if possible on any willing infected subjects.

'Secondly, we need to understand how the virus is transmitted, that will help us determine when the virus evolved or was released. In addition, search for any person or body that is aware of the virus.

'I will infiltrate the CIA and NSA to investigate biological research programs.

'Clay, focus on The United States, Olga on the Soviet Union, Jenlong on China, Sunil on the Indian subcontinent. The rest of you will focus on the African countries. Yasin, take North West Africa as far as Tunisia, Algeria, Niger and Nigeria. Amulya you take the north east as far as Libya and Sudan, Kez on the south as far as Angola, Zambia and Mozambique. Piotr on West and Central Africa from Chad, the Central African Republic and Zaire to the west coast and Slobodan on East Africa as far as Eritrea,

Ethiopia, Uganda, Burundi, Rwanda and Tanzania. Juma you will coordinate the work in Africa.

'Since none of us has any experience of the virus and we have been warned that infection could be fatal, we will maintain hourly contact with each other. If any of us is infected isolation procedures must be established and we will reconvene here as soon as possible.'

He paused for a moment.

'There are no questions, so we will close the meeting and begin our mission. We will meet here in seventy-two hours.'

Understandably the whole experience had been a very sober one due to the circumstances of the meeting. To anyone unable to hear the telepathic debates that had taken place the scene would have seemed like some silent and ghoulish monastic gathering.

'We will meet here in seventy-two hours.

\* \* \*

The other nine ships broke away one at a time as they had before and once again we were alone.

"These men, the MJ12 groups, they sound very sinister and capable of anything. Are they dangerous?" I asked.

"In short, yes, they are dangerous. These men were chosen to protect the American people, and as the major world power, in some respect the people of Earth. They are military leaders who have pledged their lives in defence of their country. They are used to giving and carrying orders and will not hesitate to act in any way that is necessary.

"My people have refused to provide them with new technologies while they continue to develop weapons of mass destruction; however, we do not judge them. They play a life and death game of chess, playing out the various possibilities, always looking several moves ahead, they make their decisions based on their analysis; they care nothing about the loss of pawns, and are quite prepared to sacrifice even key players in order to stay ahead. Of course, we have the advantage of shared thoughts, nothing is hidden from any one so there are few surprises."

"You said that the CIA killed Forrestal!"

"Yes possibly, but if it is true, I believe it was done in order to avoid panic and chaos amongst the public.

"On Sunday, October 30th, 1938, a man called Orson Welles gave a special radio broadcast of a relatively well-known novel by Herbert George Wells, 'The War of the Worlds'."

"HG Wells, yes I've read many of his books. So?"

"The broadcast was performed as a series of breaking news interruptions interwoven into the scheduled program of evening music. Many of the listeners missed the opening of the program and thought the news items were genuine. The result was blind panic on an unimaginable scale. Thousands of families left their home in fear for their lives. Who knows what might have happened if Mr Forrestal had leaked the secrets of our presence here?"

"Crazy!"

"They were difficult times. 1934 was probably one of the worst years of the Great Depression, unemployment in the United States peaked at around twenty-two percent; the world's economy was at an all-time low. Many nations around the world fell into extremist political views; Fascism, Nazism, and extreme Communism dominating the political landscape.

"We met separately with many world leaders at that time; Joseph Stalin General Secretary of the Communist Party of the Soviet Union, George V King of the United Kingdom and the British Dominions Beyond the Seas, Adolf Hitler Führer and Chancellor of Germany, Albert François Lebrun President of France, Lin Sen Chairman of the National Government of China, Haile Selassie Emperor of Ethiopia, Emperor Hirohito of Japan, Victor Emmanuel III King of Italy, Pope Pius XI Sovereign of Vatican City, and many others.

"We met with United States President Franklin Delano Roosevelt on the USS Pennsylvania, off the coast of Galeta Island Panama, on the July 11th, 1934. Our intention was to promote peaceful reconciliation and avoid a possible second world war. We made it clear to all, that we were a peaceful species and would not be drawn into their conflict.

"Mr Roosevelt was a very wise man. He told us, 'I cannot risk your existence and presence on Earth becoming public knowledge at this time', despite his wishes to do so, knowing that it could trigger a complete collapse of the economic structures he'd worked so hard to establish."

"On September 15th, 1938, Neville Chamberlain, Prime Minister of the United Kingdom, met with Adolf Hitler, Führer and Chancellor of Germany, at Hitler's summer retreat on the Austrian border, Berchtesgaden. With German invasion of Czechoslovakia looking imminent and a future European war a very real possibility.

"On September 30th, 1938, Hitler signed the Munich Agreement, permitting Nazi Germany's annexation of portions of Czechoslovakia.

"The likelihood of war in Europe looked beyond doubt. The United States had lost over four million men in World War I, and the American people had no desire to become involved in another European war.

"Roosevelt realised disclosing the existence of a technically superior and enlightened race, capable of traveling across the galaxy, could have several possible outcomes.

"It might be seen as an eleventh-hour wake up call for humanity, who like he, might embrace the knowledge that they were not alone; it could equally unite mankind in perceiving another species as a potential aggressor, and of course it could cause uncontrolled panic and the complete collapse of civilisation; most likely some combination of all three.

"Relations with Japan, at war with China, were increasingly strained, and an attack on the west coast of the United States was not beyond possibility.

"Roosevelt had received prior warning of the planned Welles radio broadcast, flagged up and escalated through the normal channels; having discussed the matter with his advisors, he considered cancelling the broadcast, but he decided it would be worth the risk to test the water and see how the American people would react to news of a superior alien race.

"The flaw in the exercise was that it had to follow Wells' disturbing storyline rather than a prearranged peaceful meeting of species. The result was the blind panic I spoke of."

"You think he would like to have told the truth?

"As I said, he was a very wise man, as President of the United States very accustomed to negotiation; he would have told the world about us if he could, but he had a responsibility to the American people and indeed to the people of the world.

"What about this disease?" I asked moving on.

"Until we have found evidence that the disease exists and understood its effects we know nothing. Whether anyone has been deliberately infected cannot be determined until we know more."

"If you say so! So where are we going to land?"

"The next few days will be extremely dangerous, so I'm afraid that I must take you home. I must work alone in order to infiltrate the CIA and NSA, and I cannot risk exposing you to the virus until we know more about how it is transmitted. I will take you to the forest where we walked together and then I must return to London to begin checking the Ministries of Defence and Intelligence before I leave for the United States. You will need to meet with Paul before we meet again."

"What about checking the hospitals for infected people?"

"I could, since access to the Ministry buildings will be less conspicuous during the day, though I suspect that the task of finding infected people will be more fruitful in Africa and India."

# PERSPECTIVE

**D**espite the sombre mood, I was in awe, looking down at the Earth from space. Having walked on the moon just an hour before, I was not yet ready to go back.

"So, you have a few minutes to spare?" I asked.

"For what?" asked Victor.

"Well just in case anything goes wrong, it would be great to see the solar system before we go back. Seems silly to miss it now we're here," I said with a grin. "Besides you could drop me in London when you go back, and I could spend the night with Sam."

"I suppose that one landing would be safer than two. What would you like to see?" he asked.

"Pluto?" I suggested tentatively, assuming it was the outermost planet.

"Well there are three more planets beyond Pluto and they are just as small and uninteresting. Your scientists have not yet discovered the outer planets, and for your information Pluto is not always the outer most planet of those which have been identified; it will pass inside Neptune's orbit in six years' time and remain there for twenty years.

"Well; Neptune is in Sagittarius, way out there beyond Helios, Uranus and Pluto, to the right at one o'clock, just about as far away as they ever are, Mercury slightly further to the right in Scorpio, but it's really not very interesting, Saturn is in Cancer at four o'clock," he said, turning the ship around to face it. "Mars is in Aries around at seven o'clock, way out behind the moon," he continued, again turning the ship towards it. "There," he added magnifying the view ahead. "The infamous Red Planet.

At first, the moon looked slightly larger than normal, about the size of a dart board, while Mars appeared less than half the diameter of the bull's eye; as the view was magnified, the moon in the foreground filled the right side of vision in comparison to Mars.

"Moving around, Jupiter is in Aquarius at nine o'clock, on the opposite side of the solar system to Saturn, and finally Venus is in Capricorn, just to the right, close to Helios.

"Pluto is almost five billion miles away, at sub-light speed it would take us over six hours to reach it. Uranus, Neptune and Pluto are all in the same quadrant beyond Helios; Jupiter and Saturn are probably the most interesting, but they are on opposite sides of the solar system, Jupiter fifty minutes away and Saturn ninety, so you could choose either; the rest we can reach in less than fifteen minutes at sub-light speed. So, what is it to be?"

"Which do you recommend?"

"Well Saturn has its rings and many moons including Titan, but most are little more than misshapen asteroids. Jupiter is closer and has four interesting moons; Io, Europa, Ganymede, and Callisto; Ganymede is the largest moon in the solar system, larger than Mercury. Jupiter does have rings, but essentially just dust from its moons Metis and Adrastea, it is the largest of your planets, and it does have its huge red storm.""

"That's either a two or three hour round trip," I thought.

"Well, I should make at least one warp trip as a precaution."

"You're kidding," I laughed. "Warp drive?"

"Yes, if you like warp drive," he answered. "Why should that be funny?"

"I don't suppose you have watched Star Trek!" I said.

"The television program, Captain Kirk and Mr Spock. Where do you think Gene Roddenberry got the name?"

"I have no idea, but I suspect you are going to tell me."

"I believe one of my colleagues mentioned the word in his presence."

"You mean Gene Rodenberry knows the Erateans exist?"

"No. I believe my colleague may have infiltrated the production crew simply out of curiosity. We use the word 'warp' simply because there is a time distortion. 'Warp' is just an English verb describing the act of distortion."

"I don't understand?"

"You understand mathematics, don't you?"

"I'm pretty good," I boasted naively.

"What can you tell me about pi?" he asked.

"Pi is a constant, the ratio of the diameter or a circle to its circumference, three point one four one ..." I replied sneeringly.

He interrupted me before I could say six.

"Five nine two six five three five, blah blah blah, blah blah blah. Constant," he mocked rhythmically. "Nothing is a constant!"

"What about the speed of light?"

"Tell me, at what point pi is equal to one?"

"I don't know what you mean. I think we can discuss pure and applied mathematics at another time," I said laughing.

"It's neither, think out of the box, let's call it abstract maths."

I changed the subject having more exciting things to think about.

"So how long will it take to get to Jupiter using warp drive?" I asked.

"If we use warp flight for the whole journey it will take us less than a minute each way in real time. In Terran time there will be a time distortion, or warp, and we would be gone for over an hour."

"An hour!" I blurted aloud. "But we got here so quickly!"

"There is a significant difference in distance to consider, the trip to Jupiter is much longer than our trip to the moon, but much shorter than the trip to Erato. We will only be able to accelerate to Warp Factor one," he grinned. "Oh, I see. You're in a hurry to get back to Sam. Very well, I suggest Jupiter."

"How long will that take?"

"Each trip will take forty-five seconds. You will have a brief opportunity to find yourself in an earlier time."

"Find myself?"

"Unlike your Star Trek television series, we suspend all neural activity during warp travel. Our bodies are sustained by the ship's transcriptor, which also controls the flight during suspension, the consequence is that our life force is then released to travel backwards in time, like being in the state of heaven for a brief moment.

"Time becomes fluid, your entire existence becomes accessible in the same moment. On this occasion you can follow me, I need to establish a link with you that will allow me to find Sam. You will have only seconds on each trip. I suggest we seek out the time we first met in the water. It will calm you when you most need reassurance, you will know who I am; whilst I will know I have found the man I am looking for. If you are ready we will proceed."

"I'm ready when you are." I answered.

"Remember do not stop for anything until your accident. Now sit back and relax."

I sat back in the chair and was aware of a smothering sensation as I was enveloped by the ships form. At first, I fought against it, in the way we have a natural instinct not to breathe in water, but almost as though I needed to draw breath I relaxed, and I felt myself sinking into my subconscious mind.

Suddenly my mind and soul were released from my body. Around me, I could see images of our encapsulated bodies on the ship, of Sam at her flat, of my family and of the other Erateans leaving their ships on Earth. It seemed that any location in the three-dimensional world was available to me.

I followed Victor as the images before us accelerated backwards in time, discovering I could vary the speed at which time moved backwards. We skipped through the events of the last few days until I saw the moment when Sam and I had bonded for the first time. My instinctive desire was to stop, but remembering Victor's words, we continued our journey.

It seemed strange to see my life replayed in reverse, seeing Sam and my family. We were back in Dubai, back to the Consulate building and still further, back to my second trip on the supply-boat.

Again, I hesitated, wishing to stop when I saw Sam crying in Captain Le Fevre's office, suddenly aware that he had just told her about my accident.

I had no idea of how much time had passed but it seemed I have been travelling backwards for over an hour. Soon we were back in the hospital where I lay in bed beside my murderer friend and I felt so sad for him. Eventually I was in the supply-boat, having been plucked from the water.

As I approached the point where I first became aware of Victor, I instinctively moved towards my own body and merged with the life force that was there.

"Victor! You are Victor!" I said softly.

"Yes, it is I," he grinned. "You are not in danger now."

Before I could say more, I felt myself pulled back to the present. I opened my eyes to see the cocoon that had enveloped me disappear. I sat up quickly and immediately regretted it.

"Patience," said Victor. "You have just risen from the dead!"

"Bloody hell! It feels like it," I replied, shaking my head.

The world around me was spinning and my vision was blurred, I felt like I had another hangover and came close to vomiting.

"Focus your mind," said Victor.

I did as he suggested and within second my senses were restored to normal.

"Wow! Some trip!"

"The first experience is always a momentous one," said Victor.

"I lost you. Were you successful?"

"Yes. I went back to my ship at the time we met in the water, to tell myself you were the one I was looking for."

I looked around me and once again the ship's hull disappeared from view, revealing a ghostly black silhouette of Jupiter, surrounded by a thin grey band of rings that I had not known existed.

"I have bought you to the far side to see the rings," he said.

"It's beautiful!"

We moved around the planet towards the sunrise and as it rose above the horizon I was shocked at what I saw.

"It's so much smaller from here!"

"Well we are over five times further away from the sun than Earth."

"The Earth is out there, as are Venus and Mars. They are all relatively close together now, but far too small to see from here."

Without a word, he magnified the image in front of me again, suddenly the left side of the sun filled the entire view in front of me. There was a cluster of small planets in one area.

"That is Earth on the right, Mars on the left and Venus nestled between them."

"My god it's incredible!"

Seeing the Earth so insignificant against the Sun emphasised just how far away we were. At first, the Sun had appeared much smaller than our moon and had no significance. Now with the Earth beside it almost touching the other two planets, I realised just how enormous the sun was in comparison, and how far away they all were.

"Helios is over a hundred and seventy times the size of the Earth," he said.

The views changed as Victor applied different filters and I could see the wild power of the Sun, with jets of fire emanating from its red and yellow surface.

"So back to Jupiter and its moons," said Victor turning the ship. "There actually over one hundred moons around Jupiter depending on how you classify them; however, most are as insignificant as Terra's secondary moons."

"Secondary moons?"

"By the same classification, Earth has several other moons, none of which have been discovered by your people. The most significant is approximately three miles in diameter. It takes seven hundred and seventy years to complete a horseshoe-shaped orbit around Earth, and it will remain in a suspended state around Earth for at least five thousand years. Now you can see the four Galilean moons, Io, Europa, Ganymede, Callisto. First seen by Galileo Galilei in January 1610," he added.

The small moons looked like footballs hovering around the huge planet Jupiter.

"A Danish astronomer named Ole Romer was the first Sapien to demonstrate that the speed of light is finite in 1676."

"You said nothing was constant?"

"I said he demonstrated the speed of light was finite, not constant, not even through a vacuum. Did you not study refraction? Have you not seen the distortion it causes when looking through a glass of water?"

"Of course," I recalled, "your Pink Floyd T-shirt, the prism."

"Indeed. Mr Romer observed eclipses of the closest moon Io, as Jupiter's distance from Earth varied through the year. He noticed that the observed period of Io's orbit differed by about twenty minutes and concluded that this difference was due to the extra distance that the light had to travel to Earth. His calculations determined the speed of light to be around one hundred and forty thousand miles per hour, some forty-six thousand miles per hour too slow."

As he spoke orally, his thoughts explained Kepler's laws of planetary motion.

I could clearly see a giant red spot on the surface of the planet with a smaller white one close by.

"The red spot is the huge storm I spoke of; it has existed for almost two hundred Terran years, the smaller white one is less old. The swirling stripes around the equator are winds that blow at over four hundred miles per hour. The planet is a gas giant over ten times the diameter of Earth, but it rotates on its axis in less than ten hours which is why it bulges at the equator."

"Sure beats any geography trip I ever had," I said with a grin.

"We should continue our journey now if I am to get you back to London."

"I'm ready! How far back in time can we go doing this?" I asked.

"On a long trip, beyond our lifetime and all of the lives we have ever lived."

I relaxed and waited to be enveloped by the cocoon. Back again I went, faster than before, beyond the accident to the classroom where I first fell in love with Sam. I slowed as I watched myself stare into her eyes, moving backwards to the point before she entered the room. I moved towards myself and merged again as I had before.

'Sam, she is my destiny and I hers. Miss Cooper is Sam.'

# EAU DE VIE

J ust as before, I was pulled back to my body on the ship, but this time I was in no rush to sit up as my cocoon retracted. I focused my thoughts and took a look around me.

"The red planet," said Victor.

"Mars!" I gasped.

The planet below me looked very much like the moon except for its rusty brown glow. The cratered surface was clearly visible unlike the gas giant we had just left.

"Does it have any moons?"

"There are several small asteroids similar in size to Terra's second moon but nothing of any great significance," he answered.

We moved down to the planet surface and flew at low level across the Martian landscape. With the entire hull in its transparent form it felt like some kind of high speed fairground ride. A flat mountain top appeared over the horizon and grew until it dwarfed anything I had ever seen or even imagined.

The ship halted all forward motion without warning and we dropped down to just above ground level, then moved slowly sideways.

"What's wrong?" I asked?

"It appears we have visitors," he answered.

"The other aliens?"

"No, these people are Terran, I can feel their confused thoughts" he said. "We were not aware that your people possessed the technology for interplanetary flight."

"How many are there?"

"I am not sure but at least a thousand, perhaps two, and they have been here for some time."

"Two thousand!"

"They seem to be constructing some sort of base."

Once again, the view in front of me was magnified and I could see several buildings, clear glass dome like structures and vehicles at the foot of the mountain, dwarfed and almost inconsequential in comparison to the titanic mass behind them. As we moved around further a huge Zeppelin shaped craft came into view, then a second and a third.

"These ships are identical to a type used by the Greys and the Tall-Whites I am certain, though I can detect no alien presence here."

"Does that mean there are no aliens here?"

"Not necessarily. We have never heard the thoughts of the Greys or the Tall-Whites as you know. The buildings are too small to contain that number of people, there must be an entrance into the volcano."

"Volcano!"

"Yes, Olympus Mons or Mount Olympus."

"Like in Greece,"

"Indeed. Your people know of its existence, hence the name. It's seventy-two thousand feet high, two and a half times as tall as Mount Everest's height above sea level, and Everest sits on the Tibetan Plateau at seventeen thousand feet, so if you stood it beside Olympus Mons, the latter would be more like five times higher; its base would almost cover the whole of France.

"If they have created a void inside the volcano it may be shielded, or if as we believe the visitors are more advanced than us, they could perhaps shield their thoughts from our detection."

We circled the base of the mountain at high speed and extremely low altitude for what must have been hundreds of miles, eventually we discovered another similar base or entrance, this time with two of the huge alien craft nestled alongside.

"Enough," said Victor. "We must leave here now."

I sensed his message to his Eratean colleagues warning them that there were bases here on Mars, apparently constructed by Terrans using alien space craft.

413

"We should check out the far side of Luna before we return, if there are Terran bases here on Mars, there are almost certainly Terran bases there. There is little of interest to us on Luna or the other planets, they were studied in great depth when our ancestors first visited the Helios system. I have no idea how long these bases have been here.

"We will fly back at sub-light speed. Warp acceleration creates a warp pulse when light speed is reached, that would be detected by the visitors if they are here."

"Like breaking the sound barrier?"

"Yes, exactly like breaking the sound barrier, but a gravitational and electromagnetic pulse rather than a sonic boom. Like a sonic boom, it only occurs on acceleration not deceleration. The journey will only take four minutes."

We moved away, and Mars began to shrink behind us.

\* \* \*

"If you can travel back in time, how come you had to find Sam through me? Surely there was an easier way to find her?"

"I should have explained we cannot travel into the future except by visiting ourselves in the past. Only one future and one past exist, there are no alternatives. Paul told me I would find Sam, my son's reborn soul, through you."

"Yes, Paul warned me about my accident, or tried to."

"That is why I believe he is a Malakh."

"You said I could go back to a time before all the lives I have lived."

"Of course! You know Sam was my son in a previous life. We have lived many lives."

"And before that, before the first life?"

"Before that our life force was a part of Erato's life force. We were born Eratean, of Erato."

"And in between lives, you can revisit any life you have ever lived, see the people you loved and interact with them."

Having experienced the brief periods in suspension it suddenly made much more sense.

* * *

Three minutes after leaving Mars, the Earth began to grow more and more rapidly in front of us. I was staggered at the speed at which we circled behind the Earth, it was like swinging around a vertical bar, in less than a second, pivoting with one hand. It took no more than three seconds to reach the moon surface; there was no deceleration, one moment we were travelling just below the speed of light and the next we were hovering a few feet above the surface. There was never any sensation of acceleration, deceleration or changing course.

Once again, we travelled low across the surface at high speed and before long we had discovered another base on the far side of the moon. The base appeared to be similar in construction, smaller than those on Mars, Victor estimated two or three hundred Terrans. We moved on as we had on Mars and found yet another base, this time there was more activity, perhaps five hundred Terrans. Here again there was another of the long Zeppelin shaped spacecraft. Victor moved us quickly around the base as the ship began to move.

"Can they see us?"

"Terran radar will not detect us so low on the horizon, but I have no idea whether alien technology is capable of detecting our presence. If we assume that they have detected our starships before and not made contact, it is logical to assume that our discovery here will make little difference to their plans."

"But if this is a secret base they may not want us to leave here knowing of its existence," I said.

"They would surely know that I have passed on the information regardless. We will wait and follow a leaving ship."

Paul passed on the information to his colleagues and asked them to observe the skies for returning ships.

"These ships are clearly piloted by Terrans and not by technically advanced aliens. They move so slowly," said Victor.

As the ship faded into the distance Victor moved his ship away from the base and then back towards Earth.

"They are taking a wide flight towards Terra, probably to avoid detection. A ship of that magnitude could easily be seen as a moving dark spot between Earth and Luna."

"How long will they take to reach the Earth? The Apollo flights took over two days to get to the moon."

"Don't be so impatient, I will get you back to Sam before the night is over. They move slowly but not that slowly," he grinned. "I estimate this will only take fifteen minutes."

He was right, the Earth was growing steadily closer. I looked at my watch, it was four thirty. Victor said we would lose an hour of Earth time on each trip, so perhaps five thirty on Earth.

The alien ship eventually made it back to Earth and to our surprise moved straight down towards the Pacific Ocean. We watched it move south to the vast dark emptiness between New Zealand and Chile, on the borders of the Pacific and Southern Oceans. It landed in darkness on the surface of the sea, and within minutes, all but disappeared below the surface, then rose into the sky and began its return trip to the moon.

"They are transporting water to Luna, and probably Mars too," said Victor.

'Water tankers?"

"Yes, I estimate ten million gallons of water per trip. There is water on Mars, but difficult to extract in such quantities. Mars has just passed its closest point to Terra, on the 18th of October. These ships would take around three days to make that journey. These are vast amounts of water, much more than that required to support four hundred people. Each of those tankers contains enough water to easily sustain at least one hundred thousand people if the water is recycled. Of course the ships could easily be transformed to carry other cargos."

"Now what? I asked.

"Now I get you back to London."

"Sam, I'm coming back to you now."

"I'm here waiting for you my bear! I have heard Victor's messages about the bases, so I know you have been gallivanting around the solar system like a spoilt little boy," she answered.

"Well it's just as well we did, or we wouldn't have known about them," I said justifying the trip. "Besides I went back to see you on the Worcester, I'll explain later."

"Where are you going to land?" she asked.

"The north lake on Parliament Hill, at the top of Merton Lane," answered Victor.

"I'll come to meet you," said Sam.

"Too late, I'm just about to leave Victor," I answered.

"I will leave you with Sam now and catch the tube back into the city?" grinned Victor.

"When will we see you again?"

"Assuming you talk to Paul, in two days' time, Friday evening. I have a great deal to do as I'm sure you can imagine."

"Is there anything I can do to help?"

"Not really. Look after Sam and get ready to leave. A hundred yards in that direction and you will come to Merton Lane, follow it to the end and then turn left down Highgate Hill, turn right onto South Grove and right at Highgate High Street," he explained as the door opened.

He had landed on the water at the edge of the lake.

"When the circle is laid flat," I cried triumphantly, as I stepped off onto the grass.

"Very good," he answered, stepping out behind me. "You're half way there, but as the circle approaches the horizontal, pi draws closer and closer to two not one, up one side and down the other; we are talking about moving along the circumference until we return to the starting point. Consider then that we now fold the flat circle to form another circle, then pi would equal one; that in essence explains how we warp space and time."

"Like the infinity sign on the Magician card!"

"Go before we create an incident here."

417

"Good luck," I said.

The starship was gone in less than a second, high into space, and I watched him disappear into the trees.

# CLOSE ENCOUNTER

Wednesday ~ 5th December 1973

I looked at my watch, it was five minutes past five, five past six back on Earth. I started off towards the lane as Victor had instructed me and walked straight into a couple who had obviously seen us land. The man stared at me with his mouth wide open in disbelief, while his partner pulled desperately at his arm.

"Derek, come on! Let's get out of here."

"Ah... ar... Are you from space?" asked the man.

I raised my arms straight out in front of me and began to walk towards them, imitating the menacing slow zombie-like step of an Egyptian mummy who has just risen from the dead.

"Food!" I thought, and he heard it as clearly as if I'd said it.

The woman screamed loudly in panic.

"Stop it Jean," said the man trying to cover her mouth. "Have you come to take us?"

"You are needed for our experiments!"

"Yes. Yes of course," said the man bowing his head in some passive gesture, then he turned and began to run. "Run Jean! Run!"

"There's no need to be afraid," I thought, but fear had been instilled in them. Despite the sincerity in my thoughts it was too late to reassure them.

"Come on Jean! Quickly!" he shouted.

I walked quickly down the lane as they ran off, left along Fitzroy Park, and met Sam running towards me at the top of South Grove. She wrapped her arms around me and we kissed as though we had been apart for a month. As we began the walk back to her flat, a police car drove past with its siren wailing heading back the way I had come, a second followed two minutes later.

By the time Sam opened the door, I had explained how I was able to go back through time and join with myself in the sea, recognising Victor, then again on the day we met on the Worcester.

"That doesn't explain how I knew about you," said Sam.

"Yes it does, it just means that you will do the same thing at some point in the future.

"Had enough fun for one night have we?" she asked.

"It's not quite over yet!" I answered hopefully.

"Oh yes it is my poor sex starved young bear. I have to be at work in two hours, I leave home at eight!"

"Bollocks to work! You're leaving aren't you!"

"Well let's see how long it takes for you to make me forget all about space ships my gullible little slug," she said running up the stairs.

"You bloody teaser!" I said running up behind her.

# BLISS

I woke up to the smell of fresh coffee. Sam walked into the bedroom already dressed for work.

"Coffee!"

"What?"

I had only been asleep for ten minutes.

"Milk?"

"I'm not going to drown it milk, you'll miss the flavour!"

"What time is it?" I asked.

"Ten to eight. I normally have my coffee and croissant at work, but I wanted to have breakfast with you before I left."

She went back to the kitchen and reappeared with two warm croissants.

"This will taste a little different to anything you have had before. Yours has no sugar in but let me know if you want some."

"Jesus, no milk and no sugar!"

"Try it. I like my tea sweet and my coffee strong and black without."

I tasted the coffee and recognised the flavour.

"I can't get used to knowing everything you know," I said. "I like it! I grinned after tasting it.

"Good morning Bear," she said, as though it were the first words of the morning.

She gave me a long lingering kiss.

"Freshly ground Jamaican coffee with warm butter croissants."

"They're wonderful," I answered with my mouth full.

The coffee had been brewed in a simple Italian espresso pot, it was rich and strong, bursting with flavour.

"Are these from downstairs?" I asked holding up my half-eaten roll.

"No, there is a French baker around the corner. Are you going to hang around today? You could meet me for lunch and we could have a cosy night together. You don't have to be back till Friday, do you?"

"No, I suppose not."

"There's plenty to do around here or in the city. I have to leave in a while, but you can follow me in later. Would you like another croissant? She asked watching me push the last piece in my mouth.

"Sorry I was starving, I didn't eat last night, there was so much going on I just forgot."

She reappeared with another warm croissant and sat down beside me again.

"So, will you stay?"

"Of course I will, but there is a small problem, I'm running very low on cash and my account is empty."

She walked around the bed to the chest of drawers and picked up her handbag.

"Here, this should keep you going," she said, handing me a crisp new ten-pound note.

"Thanks, I will pay you back."

"When?" she laughed. "What does it matter, it's no use to me on Erato."

"No, I suppose not. What time do you have lunch?"

"One. I'll meet you in the Globe?"

"Sure, I'll be there."

"If you leave here at twelve thirty you'll be there on time. Here's a key to the door. There are clean towels in the bathroom smelly, yours are blue, they're Kevin's, mine are white. There's a new toothbrush in the cupboard. I have to go now, don't be late."

I put my empty coffee cup down and she gave me a last hug and an arousing kiss.

"Behave!"

I looked at the alarm clock on her beside cupboard, it said eight forty-five; my watch said seven thirty, so I took it off and correct it.

# REVELATION

After my bath, I decided to go back to the park where we had landed the night before, to see if there was any indication of what took place.

When I arrived, the park was crawling with police, the area beside the lake was surrounded by tape and keep out signs. The people inside the cordon wore dark blue boiler suits with hoods and gas masks. Some walked slowly around the area, turning every blade of grass as they went, others probed the ground with instruments attached to small boxes which they carried over their shoulder. There were frogmen standing at the edge of the lake where we had landed.

I caught sight of the couple I had frightened early that morning, talking to what appeared to be two plain-clothes policemen in dark blue suits.

"You should be more careful," said a voice behind me.

I turned around to see Paul standing behind me, dressed in his B.P. uniform, looking exactly as he did when we first met.

"What are you doing here?"

'Looking for you! I think we should find somewhere a little quieter to talk,' he said silently.

'Yes, perhaps we should! Let's go back to Sam's flat,' I answered in the same manner.

'Ah yes, Sam! We're a little more experienced in life than when we first met,' he smiled.

'Yes, I suppose a great deal has changed since then. But you, I don't understand, you're young again. What exactly do you want with me?'

'To prepare you for your destiny.'

'Destiny?'

'Be patient, wait until we get to Sam's flat.'

'Okay, I have to meet Sam at one o'clock though.'

'You have time.'

We continued our walk back to Sam's flat in silence and with no exchange of thoughts.

When we entered the flat, the same white haired old man I had met in the cottage replaced the young cadet.

"Can I get you a drink, tea, coffee, water?"

"No thank you, my time here is brief.

"I told you once, your destiny is preordained. What must be must be. You will leave here soon for Erato where you will come to understand that which you will need for the future. You will learn everything about the way of life on there."

"Why?"

"Because you are Malakhi."

"What!"

"Victor has told you about reincarnation, he has explained heaven and you have experienced your free spirit, if only briefly."

"You mean I was Malakhi in a previous life?"

"No, precisely the opposite. You are New-born, born of the Earth. Victor knew you were New-born, and I told him you were Malakhi."

"He didn't tell me!"

"I told him not to. You died on November 14th, you drowned, and your body was never recovered."

I laughed nervously.

"I'm dead?"

"No, you're alive."

"I died but I'm alive. I thought heaven was a gateway to all our previous lives?"

"What previous life? You are New-born. You can revisit the life that you had if you wish. You chose not to die and be reborn as a mortal and now you will live forever."

"Forever?"

"Like me, you will live until the Earth is consumed by the Sun, and then everything that you are will exist in the Sun, until the Sun itself is consumed by the Black Hole at the centre of the galaxy, and beyond, when the Black Hole explodes scattering its seeds into the void, you will exist in every seed, and every seed will become a new universe and time will begin its cycle once more. You will exist in different timelines and the ability to change what was. But you are young and have much to learn."

"Forever!"

Suddenly, I grasped the meaning of eternity.

"My name is Saul of Tarsus, I was beheaded and died in Rome during the reign of Nero, the same day that Peter was crucified. Like you, I was New-born and chose not to be reborn in another life, but to return. The body you see before you is the physical manifestation of what was.

"My mentor was Jesus of Nazareth, he also chose to return as did his mentor and all of those that came before him. All the Earth's religions are based on the teachings of Malakhi, each for its time, and the needs of the people; prophecy and religion are one of many ways by which we can guide those we watch over.

"I exist as a Trinity, I am the New-born, Saul of Tarsus; I am the mortal who lived his last life as Luke the Evangelist, disciple of Paul; I am also the mortal who lived her last life as Mary wife of Clopas, mother of James the Less and Keeper of Knowledge. My mentor was the New-born Jesus of Nazareth; he was also the mortal who lived her last life as Mary Magdalene, wife of Jesus; he was also the mortal Judas Iscariot, disciple and betrayer of Jesus.

"You are still one, you have not yet evolved, before you can follow your destiny you must become three in one, but you must choose wisely, because the three of you will exist together for the eternity I speak of.

"It is important that you know more about our world before you learn the ways of another."

"What about Sam? And Victor?"

"Sam is a mortal, her spirit and lifeforce are Eratean, but her physical being is of Earth. She knows nothing of what I have said, and she must not.  Victor is Eratean, his spirit, lifeforce and physical being are Eratean."

"Sam can read my thoughts, she knows everything I know."

"Sam knows what is in your mind.  You can conceal what you do not want her to know just as I have concealed things from you.  You are Malakhi, unlike the Erateans it is essential that you do so."

"I'm sorry but I won't hide this from Sam.  I want to be with her.  I want to live my life with her on Erato."

"She is mortal, and she is of the Earth.  She will not live more than two hundred years even on Erato.  Her lifetime will be as a dying star in the universe that is you."

"I don't care, I will not deceive her."

"As you wish, it is your choice."

"What does it mean?  Do I have the same powers as Victor?"

"You have studied the cards I gave you?"

"Yes, I have."

"And what have you learnt?"

"I believe that the Fool is a depiction of me and Victor is the Magician that will teach me the ways of Erato."

"That is good.  You are the young fool," 'Le Mat,' he thought, showing me the card.  'From the Tarot of Marseilles, given to me by my Erudita, Mary Magdalene.'  "You are at the beginning of a journey that has no ending.  Victor is your magician." 'Le Bateleur,' showing me the second card, "as you correctly determined.  His powers are no more than that of an illusionist in comparison with the powers you will develop.  You fell in love with Sam's beauty, her knowledge, her wisdom, and the mystery that she was," 'La Papess, your High Priestess,' "she will soon recall her past life and the same powers that Victor has."

He showed me the third card.

"I see now that she will bear your child and I suspect she will become your Empress.  It is time for you to grow and become the Emperor," he said showing me both cards.  'L'Imperatrice and L'Empereur'

"And you?"

427

"I am your hierophant," 'Le Pape,' your friend and ally, your spiritual counsel and guide, a father and a brother, a mother and a sister, I am both male and female.

He showed me the fifth card.

"And me?"

He laughed.

"You were born male, when you make the metamorphosis to become a Trinity, you will choose mortals, they will have lived as both."

"The Eratean Council has asked me to ask you about the Malakhi."

"And about the Greys and the Tall-Whites and a deadly virus. There is nothing that the Erateans can do to influence what is happening here and nothing to prevent you from joining them. When you return we will discuss the Greys and the Tall-Whites. All you need do is observe what is happening here. If you intend to tell Sam the truth you may tell the Erateans you are a Malakh, a Messenger, and that when the time is right, you will return to Earth having made the metamorphosis and become Trinity."

"I was also asked if you could help an Eratean who is known here as Václav, he has asked if you can help him find his daughter's reborn soul"

"Then that will be your gift to the Erateans. Use the cards and you will find her spirit. Have faith, all will become clear. In the words of the Malakh Khalil Gibran, 'Faith is an oasis in the heart which will never be reached by the caravan of thinking'."

"Judge no one, no one has the right to judge another, do what good you can, in any way you can, to all life, and in all places."

He paused and smiled at me.

"You can begin by not frightening your fellow men, telling them you are an alien! Have you forgotten how afraid you were when you first realised Victor was an alien?"

"Yes, I'm sorry, I suppose it was cruel, but it seemed funny at the time."

"Laughter is fine, but never at another's expense.

"When you act, do it without malice, you will become a surgeon of time. We cannot end a timeline, but we can create a new branch. You created a new branch on mine when you chose to live.

"You want to know who killed Jack Kennedy? I did. I entered the body of Secret Service Special Agent, George Warren Hickey Jr. and shot Kennedy in the back of the head. Hickey thought he had stumbled, being off balance, and those that planned the assassination were grateful.

"In the alternate time line his assassination was botched, he was shot through the neck, but he survived. Outraged at those around him, he did what many before him have considered, he told the world about the Erateans, and the Amorfons, the Hittites and the Yowies."

"Not the Greys and the tall-Whites?"

"He didn't know about the Greys and their masters."

"You murdered Kennedy?"

"In this timeline? Yes, I killed Kennedy. The alternate time line still exists where I did not. In that timeline, Kennedy's revelations began a sequence of events that ended in Armageddon, a nuclear holocaust that wiped out another civilisation. After the bombs, the air was filled with radioactive dust and ash. Those that didn't die in the explosions died of radiation sickness, starved to death or killed by murdering gangs of scavengers. Animal life suffered in the same way; the world's forests burned away by the rising temperatures under the radioactive clouds that filled the skies. You existed in the timeline, and died as did almost all mankind."

"Can I see this alternate timeline?"

"Yes, you existed there before the branch in time when I killed Kennedy."

I stood with him in another time, the stench of death was everywhere, the skies thick with dust and ash. There was no sign of life, even the rotting bodies of men and women on the streets were devoid of flies. Only remote aboriginal groups survived.

"Over three billion people died, less than two hundred thousand survived."

We were back in my room and he was young again wearing the pale grey suit and waistcoat he had on the Worcester.

"Lawd above! Who'da thought ter me dressed like dis?"

I smiled.

"Maybe. Why the uniform earlier?" I asked.

"It wus what yew expected ter see. Nuff said.

"I don't take any pride in killing a man, as I said there are many ways we can guide our flock; and our lives are not monastic. The women here, they like a cheeky young cockney sparra!" he grinned.

The old sage appeared before me in the blink of an eye.

"Now I must leave you. Consider my words and have faith. There is nothing hidden that will not be revealed. I suggest you say your goodbyes and leave this place as soon as you can, every day you spend here will put you more at risk."

"At risk? Form who?"

"Until you have mastered your powers and become Trinity, you are as vulnerable as a new born gazelle surrounded by lions and hyenas. You are not ready to face this world. Enjoy life on Erato, I will meet you there. You wanted to be a sailor, learn to sail when you get there."

He took both my hands and placed them together inside his and then left.

* * *

"No coffee for you this morning?" said Le Fevre.

"No, I had breakfast at home this morning," said Sam.

"Oh, he's back is he?"

"Who is?"

"Cummings! You can't fool me! You have had coffee and a croissant for breakfast here every day since the day you started."

"Yes alright, he's here."

"And it is he that you intend to go travelling with isn't it?"

His tone befitted a member of the bar cross-examining a witness.

430

"Ok it's James, does it make so much difference?"

"Only that you know nothing about him, he's very young and he's just had a terrifying experience. He could change his mind this afternoon and go back to sea."

"You can't possibly understand how wrong you are. I know more about James than his brother does, and he has more experience of life than people twice his age. There is absolutely no chance he will change his mind."

"Well if you're so sure ask him to come and see me this afternoon and we will discuss it. I'd like to get the issue sorted out as soon as possible if your minds are made up."

"Oh yes," she said. "Our mind is made up."

The significance of the plural was lost to him.

"Well I will be extremely sorry to see you go, you know that. We will discuss it together, after I have spoken to Cummings this afternoon. I assume you will be meeting him for lunch?"

"Yes, he's meeting me in the Globe at one."

"Well don't come back sozzled, there is still work to do young lady. Go on, be off with you. I have work to do."

"Certainly Sir," she said, mocking his paternal instincts.

He picked up his morning paper and feigned a swat at her.

# POCKET MONEY

"James, where are you?" she thought.

"At the flat," I answered.

"Le Fevre wants to speak to you this afternoon."

"What about?"

"He knows it's you I'm leaving with and he wants to get your situation resolved."

"My Dad will be furious!"

"You know as well as I do that it makes no difference. We are not going to be here for a very long time."

"I know, Paul was here. Don't ask, it's a long story. I'll tell you all about it at lunch."

"Ok, I've washed your shirt by the way. I thought you may need it on Friday, so it's ironed and hanging in my wardrobe."

"I know, I found it, and my clean underpants, looking for some clean clothes. Thank you."

"You're welcome. Don't be late"

\* \* \*

Sam met me in the Globe as planned, and we hugged and kissed with our usual passion.

"Where did that come from?" she asked, in surprize.

"I found it hanging in your wardrobe beside some of my other clothes. I know you like me in uniform," I said with a grin. "Dry white?"

"Please, a small one, Stuart and I had a little chat and he told me not to come back sozzled.

I bought her a glass of white wine, and the barman handed me the sandwiches I had already ordered.

"Well tell me about your talk with Paul," she said urgently.

"Eat your sandwich," I said.

While we ate, we exchanged thoughts silently. I told her everything I knew about Paul, the Malakhi, Kennedy, my destiny and her life expectancy; that Paul told me not to tell her that I was Malakhi, and that I could not do that; I told her that he foresaw a time when she would bear my child, and that Paul had told me to leave and go to Erato as soon as possible, that I was vulnerable here; she listened in silence.

"James, I'm glad you told me, but none of this makes any difference. I am going back to my home-world with the man I love. I love my life here, but I don't want to die and not remember the lives I have lived before. I want to have children with you and bring them up in a world without repression, poverty and starvation. I want my life with you to be the holiday of a lifetime. I am not sure that I want to spend eternity with you, yet, but I want us both to have an oasis of love that we can visit from heaven. If you are vulnerable here we should do as Paul suggested and leave here as soon as we have said our goodbyes."

"There is no heaven for me, I died and now I will live for eternity."

"But you can be anywhere, at any time. Who knows? I might consider it myself in time," she said smiling.

"Of course, that's how it got there. I must have brought my clothes here in a different time, but I don't remember doing it."

"Do it when you go home," she said, giving me a wink and sipping her wine.

"What do you think Le Fevre is going to say?" I asked.

"I have no idea. Does it matter? Don't be frightened of him, his bark is worse than his bite."

"I'm more concerned about what my dad will think when he finds out!"

"Well, I will see to it that he doesn't, at least until Friday."

We finished our drinks discussing the remaining time we had left on Earth, what had to be done before leaving for Erato. The biggest priority was to see Sam's parents, so we agreed we would do that first thing Saturday morning. We would catch a train from New Milton to London straight after my prize-giving and travel to Alton the next day. There was no chance that my mother would allow us to share a bed at home.

Sam looked at her watch.

"Okay, I'd better get back now, he will blame you if I'm late. Come over when you've finished your beer."

She gave a me a kiss as she left.

* * *

Sam showed me into le Fevre's office and I closed the door behind me.

"James, how are you?" he asked.

"Very well thank you Sir."

"I hadn't expected you to be in uniform today."

"Sam called to tell me you wanted to see me, we had planned to have lunch together. The only other clothes I have with me are jeans and T-shirts."

"Well it's nice to see you're still proud to wear it. Let's not beat about the bush, Samantha has told me that it is you she intends to go travelling with, and insists that you have made up your mind about your immediate future."

"Yes Sir, that's correct."

"You know I feel very paternal where Samantha is concerned, she's a delightful girl and very good at keeping me on top of things. I shall be very sad to lose her. Are you sure you know what you are doing? I know I have been trying to get you back on a ship as soon as possible, and I know you have had little time to consider your future."

"We both feel this is something we have to do Sir. It's hard to explain but we both know it's right."

"What about your father? What does he have to say about this?"

"My father thinks I should use all the time I have to make a decision Sir"

"Very wise. You should listen to him you know."

"Yes Sir."

"Well if you're determined to do this, the best I can do is to offer you three months to reconsider and three months' salary to help you with your plans."

"I'm not sure three months would be long enough Sir," I said without thinking.

"Well, you certainly have brass!" he said with a smile. "Very well, six months' salary but if you come back early you'll be on half wages until you repay the other three months."

"I meant to reconsider Sir, not the salary."

"Oh well I've made the offer now, I can hardly retract it can I?"

"No Sir, I suppose not Sir. Thank you Sir."

He picked up the phone.

"Samantha would you like to join us?"

"Certainly Captain."

Sam entered the room and sat down beside me.

"Well here's the score. I have offered young Cummings six months to reconsider his position with six months' pay in advance. I would like to do the same for you but alas the circumstances are slightly different, and I cannot offer you any salary. What I can do is offer to hold your position for six months and use a temp in the meantime. Hopefully you two will come to your senses and accept your positions back after a few weeks back packing!"

"That's very kind of you Sir and most gratefully accepted," she said.

"Would you mind not speaking to my father Sir until I have had time to speak to him myself?" I said.

"Of course not, I quite understand," he answered, "although I think he would be proud of your negotiation skills; and that you haven't dismissed the idea of going back to sea."

"Samantha, will you please make the arrangements with the wages department to make an immediate six-month payment to Cummings and type up an agreement for him to sign before he leaves."

"Yes of course Captain."

"Three months to be deductible from his future salary if he comes back early. He'll go on half pay till it's recovered."

"Certainly Captain, I understand"

"Well then, off with you both," he said, looking down to his desk and shooing us away with his outstretched hands.

Sam closed the door behind us and sat down at her desk to type.

"He's so sweet. You know I wouldn't be surprised if he was shedding a quiet tear in there. He's been so kind to me."

"Well I can pay you back the tenner you gave me as soon as I get paid."

"Forget it! I don't need it. Give it to you mother when we leave if we have anything left. Tell you what, buy a couple of bottles of fizz for tonight, we'll celebrate in front of the fire.

"What flavour?"

"Champagne dummy, not Corona!"

"I've never had champagne before."

"I know. Don't worry! I'll get it on my way home, and I'll grab a small tin of caviar to go with it. Now I have never had that!" she said, stressing the first person.

"I know!" I said, poking my tongue out at her.

Sam finished her typing and rolled out an identical copy of the first draft.

"Sign here and you will be two hundred pounds richer by this evening after tax and National Insurance. I'll get Le Fevre to sign a petty cash advance for fifty pounds."

She wrote out a petty cash slip in lieu of salary advance and took it in with the agreement for Le Fevre to sign. He looked up at her with an expected raised eyebrow.

"There are a few things we need to buy before we leave Captain. I have allowed ten percent for tax and National Insurance deductions. Twenty-six weeks at £8.62 per week comes to a total of £224.12, minus ten percent for tax and national insurance at £22.42, leaving a total of £201.71; £50 to be paid in cash and the remain £150.71 as an open cheque."

He signed the papers in silence and shooed her away, then followed her out to shake my hand before I left.

"Good luck James," he said. "Make sure you take good care of my secretary!"

"Yes Sir. Thank you for everything."

He went back into his office closing the door behind him, leaving me to wait in Sam's office while she went to the accounts department and collected my advance.

"I'll bring the cheque back tonight and we can cash it tomorrow morning," said Sam.

"At least I won't have to ask you for money now," I said.

"You're mad! Whatever I have is ours to share!

"I need to do some Christmas shopping before the weekend. I could come back when you finish work and we could do it together. I'm hopeless about choosing presents."

"I'd love to... but if I help you choose they would know. It's not the gift that matters, it's the thought behind it. They will treasure whatever you buy them. No, you go this afternoon. I have to do my shopping too, so I'll be late back tonight, I'll try to be back before eight. Just make sure you have made the bed and lit the fire."

"Yes Ma'am," I said curtsying.

I spent the afternoon around Regent Street, searching for presents for my family; there was so much to choose from, but I wanted something practical for them all, something that would be a part of their daily lives. There were things I wanted to say to them, especially to my brother who was the only one who really knew what we were intending, and I realised I would have to go back on Friday morning ahead of Sam and stop off at Brockenhurst on my way back.

# SIMPLE PLEASURES

Sam arrived home just before eight o'clock, struggling with several very posh looking carrier bags.

"Two bottles of 1969 Bollinger Brut, an ounce of Beluga Caviar and a slice of pâté de Fois Gras. Not bad for thirty pounds," she said.

"Thirty quid! Have you gone mad?"

"There are a few things I would like to try before I leave this place and caviar is one of them. The woman in Harrods reckoned I should try the pâté too if I wanted something special. In fact, she recommended the Fois Gras livers if we could find a restaurant who knew how to cook them properly. But I know you're not very fond of liver."

"No sorry, but I'm happy to try this."

"Well I'll pop the fizz in the fridge to chill, not that it needs it, it's freezing out there. You can open this," she said, handing me a bottle of French Chardonnay. "Pour us a couple of glasses, I'll run us a hot bath if you'd care to join me."

"Sounds good to me! You know with all these new experiences I'm not sure I want to leave here," I shouted.

"Don't you even think about it," said Sam, coming out of the bathroom.

"What was that word you used? Gullible, yes that was it gullible!"

She walked up to me as I stood defenceless, holding the two glasses of Chardonnay out towards her, she gave me a kiss and squeezed the sensitive region between my legs.

"Now that... my little slug... is gullible," she said.

"Very funny!" I answered sipping my wine and holding her glass high in the air.

"Don't be a silly bear!" she said, and in anticipation of a more vicious attack I surrendered her glass.

We undressed and stepped into the hot foamy water, Sam sat in front with her back towards me.

We sipped our wine and talked about the gifts we had bought.

"So, what is all this about your destiny?" she asked.

"The Malakhi..."

"*We* Malakhi! You are a Malakh," she said, correcting me.

"*We* Malakhi... Messengers, are apparently some kind of guardian angels that can change time. Paul said 'all of the world's religions are...'"

"...'based on the teachings of Malakhi, each for its time, and the needs of the people; prophecy and religion are one of many ways by which we can guide those we watch over.'" Yes, I know.

"We...the Malakhi, can move between different timelines, but I don't know how. What I saw of the world where Kennedy survived was heartbreaking; I don't have the words to describe the emotion, pain... grief... sorrow... sadness... stupidity..."

"I feel what you feel, words are not needed," she said.

"Paul said that the Kingdom of God was within me, you, all of us I guess, and all around us. What do you make of that?"

"It's a quote from the bible, Jesus said something along those lines as far as I recall. I don't know what *they* meant, but *I* am in heaven right now. Well I will be if you would pour me a glass of that fizz. You'll find two flutes in the cupboard."

"*I* know," I said.

"Bring the caviar too, it's on a plate in the fridge, a tea spoon and the little biscuits."

"Ma'rm," I answered in my more rustic voice.

"Now twist the bottle not the cork," she ordered.

"What's the difference?" I asked, knowing full well why.

"We won't lose half the bottle if you do it properly. We don't want the cork coming out with a bang. It should come out as quietly as a nun's fart."

"Charming!" I said, shocked at her choice of words.

I managed to do as she said. There was a disappointing fut sound as the cork came out and I laughed at the impression she had planted in my mind.

"Now put the bottle back in the fridge to keep cold."

"Ma'rm."

It was the most decadent night of my life. We finished the caviar in the bath and ate the pâté in front of the fire drinking champagne, showing each other the gifts we had bought and making love in between. The combination of champagne and caviar was a wonderful aphrodisiac and a wonderful aperitif to her essence.

### Thursday ~ 6th December 1973

Once again, I was woken to the smell of fresh coffee, but this time it was accompanied by the smell of smoky bacon.

Sam walked into the bedroom with the breakfast tray, placed my coffee and fresh warm bacon roll on the bedside table beside me, and took hers to the other back to her side of the bed.

"You are beautiful," I said.

"Thank you. So, do you intend to desert me today or can I count on your company this evening?

"Well I could do with some of mother's cooking," I teased.

"Now if I didn't know without doubt that you were joking, you would be wearing that hot coffee."

We ate breakfast together and I promised to meet her for lunch.

* * *

At nine o'clock I was happily soaking in another hot foamy bath wondering how to spend my day when Victor knocked at the door.

"Why didn't you warn me you were coming, I would have got dressed."

"Relax, there is nothing you can do at present. I just came to see you and Sam before I leave for the United States. I have discovered the origin of the simian virus. Piotr has identified cases in the Democratic Republic of Africa, Slobodan likewise in Burundi and Rwanda. The virus was developed in England in 1952, at the Porton Down Chemical Defence Establishment in Wiltshire. I found records there that suggest the virus was developed from a naturally occurring virus in apes. The virus attacks the immune system over a period of approximately ten years and eventually the ape succumbs to infections or cancers and dies. The virus is relatively safe to handle, since it is not airborne and dies outside the body. It can only be transmitted in blood and bodily fluids."

"So, is there an antidote?" I asked, expecting confirmation.

"There are no records of any antidote, and neither Piotr nor Slobodan has had any success in attempts to destroy the virus in infected subjects."

"What does that mean?" I asked, anticipating the worst.

"Exactly what you are contemplating. They will all die, and millions more will also die, unless the virus is contained."

"My god, is this to be the end of the world?"

"I do not believe so. This appears to be part of some organised strategy. Precautions can be taken which prevent the spread of the virus. I need to join Clay in the United States to follow up what I have already discovered. I will be leaving shortly for New Mexico."

"I thought you said the United States."

"New Mexico is a state in the United States north of Mexico," said Victor grinning. "Corona, the place where my son crashed is also in New Mexico, to the east is Texas, to the west Arizona. The virus was passed to the United States Government in 1953 for further testing in a 'Special Cancer Virus Program', under the direction of the Central Intelligence Agency. Clay believes this testing was performed at the Chemistry Division Laboratories at Los Alamos Base, where the Atomic Bomb was developed during the Second World War."

Victor's news disturbed me immensely. I remembered what Paul had said the day before. I felt somehow that by leaving now I would be deserting my family and all the people I loved. 'How would Sam feel now?'

"Paul was here yesterday. You took me off guard arriving unexpectedly. He told me I am Malakhi... and he said you knew."

"He told me not to tell you."

"I know. Considering what you've just told me, what he said makes sense. He told me to have faith and go with Sam to Erato."

"He is right, you can do nothing here. If we are unable to help, what could you possibly do yourself?"

"I don't know. I suppose you are right.

"I will meet with the team as planned."

"I will be here until Friday. Friday, I have to go home with Sam. It's my school prize-giving evening in New Milton."

"I know. I will contact you after that. Now I must join Clay."

\* \* \*

I deposited the cheque for £150.71 into my account, using the Barclays Bank just a hundred yards from Moorgate tube station in the opposite direction to the Globe, then walked back to the pub. Sam and I met at lunchtime as planned. I was subdued by the news Victor had given me that morning, Sam knew everything of course. She told me that Spanish Flu had killed almost a hundred million people around the world between 1918 and 1920 and reminded me that our destiny was Erato, the birthplace of her soul. Even though she had never consciously known of its existence, her deep subconscious possessed the memories of a thousand Eratean life times.

Still, the thought of the unimaginable suffering that awaited millions of people across the world seemed terrible. I felt my throat constrict as I tried hard to suppress my emotions, but I was unable to stop the tears form in my eyes. I tried to dry them with the back of my hand, but it would have been obvious to anyone that I was crying. Sam sensed my emotions as clearly as if they were her own, and I was aware that by sharing it, she was easing some of the pain I felt.

"You know there are millions of people out there who are trying to change the world. Just because some lunatics want to keep fighting doesn't mean they are going to destroy the world," said Sam. "I want to go home, and I want you to come with me. Even Paul has told you it's your destiny too."

"I know you're right, I just don't understand how people can plan to murder millions of innocent people."

"We don't know that is the case."

It occurred to me that she may have felt less of me for crying, but I knew that she thought the opposite. She too shared my opinion about the virus but dealt with her feelings realising that there was nothing she could do. She reminded me that I had cured my father's arthritis and that he would regain his strength and mobility. Thinking about my father only produced more tears, this time caused by relief and joy that he was no longer suffering.

"Stuart has offered to throw a leaving do for me tomorrow. I told him we would be at your prize-giving, so he suggested tonight. I know it's short notice; shall I say yes?"

"Of course! It's your last chance to say good bye to all your friends. You know they are going to raise an eyebrow when they see me."

"Who cares?"

"Not me! I'm the lucky bloke who is taking you away to the stars."

"That's my Bear," she said tenderly.

"I'd better buy myself some smart clothes."

"Wear your uniform silly, I put your shirt in the machine last night, it's hanging up in Kevin's room, you'll need to iron it. I'll get away as soon as I can, Stuart suggested meeting at seven."

"Okay I'll get back and sort out my shirt. I have a spare at home for tomorrow night.

* * *

Thursday night was her night, mine would follow, I was happy to see her enjoy herself. Despite her desire to leave there were the inevitable tears when it came to saying goodbye to the people she had become close to in her first job. The Captain had become her second father and presented her with a parting gift from everyone at the party. It was a very beautiful gold Saint Christopher 'to protect her on her travels and bring her back safely', saying which left him embarrassingly emotional. There was also a very expensive looking rucksack which seemed to be the obvious gift to her friends.

The word that we hardly knew each other had already spread around the office. Everyone wanted to know where we were going and when we were leaving, and we told that we would be going to Jerusalem on the twenty-first, spending Christmas in Bethlehem. It seemed to have the desired effect in convincing her friends that Christmas would be exciting for us, despite serious concerns about the Arab Israeli conflict.

Eventually we caught the tube back to Highgate and opened the second bottle of Bollinger in front of the fire.

"What will you do with the rucksack?" I laughed.

"You may well laugh but a girl needs clothes you know. What exactly do you intend to pack your belongings in, that huge blue suitcase you took to Dubai?"

She had a point, I hadn't even considered what I would take with me, not that I had a great deal if you excluded my uniforms.

"I need to see my brother and my family tomorrow before the prize-giving. I'll leave in the morning and meet you at Sway station; okay?"

"No problem. I'll have to leave early to catch the train, I know Stuart won't mind, it's my last day and he knows it's your prize-giving tomorrow."

I was beginning to love being in London and more importantly sharing Sam's bed. Because it was her home it was also mine, I knew where everything was and where everything had come from. Sam loved to decorate the flat with white candles and oriental nick knacks. I loved the lotus flower joss sticks she burned and the Van Morrison music she played. His timing and phrasing took the music I had grown up with to a different plane, I recognised his talent with enthused envy.

I put the record player on and sat down with Sam to listen to her Astral Weeks album.

"Just as well smoke this before we leave. Shame to waste it," she said.

"Let me," I said, and she passed me her special tin. "Take a look at this."

"What is it?" she asked.

I passed her the black moon rock and rolled a little trumpet shaped cigarette with all her expertise.

"Moon rock," I answered.

"It's beautiful."

"It's yours."

"Mine? Really?"

"To remind you of Earth and the Moon," I laughed.

We smoked it together sipping the champagne, losing ourselves completely in the music. Eventually the music ended but we continued our soporific small talk oblivious to the crackle of the looping stylus for what might have been hours.

Eventually Sam got up to use the toilet and I became aware of the mindless crackle.

Taking a look through her albums for the first time I came across a familiar face.

"What's that you're putting on?" she asked returning to the sofa.

I threw her the Album cover.

"Hey Arlo!"

"John has the same album. He told me it was him singing when the first time he played it to me; he said he'd been and made his own record with his mate Ron, who played the guitar."

'I don't want a pickle. Just want to ride on my motor-cickle. And I don't want a tickle...'

Arlo Guthrie opened his Motor-cickle song in the style of an intoxicated hillbilly, then began his dialog about 'How he came to write the song'.

"I love this bit," I said quietly as we listened.

'I knew it was the end. I looked down, I said Wow! Some trip. I thought it...well I knew it was...I knew it was my last trip,'.

We listened to the end of the track, when it had finished we moved into the bedroom.

"I will remember this night for ever," said Sam.

"It's not over yet," I said.

# BEARING GIFTS

I had intended to get up when Sam did, but once again I awoke to the smell of fresh coffee and croissants, delivered to my bedside and accompanied by a long playful kiss.

"Sorry Bear, I'm late and have to rush, have to go if I'm to get off early. I'll see you tonight at half six. Don't forget your uniform. Oh, and I know we're planning on coming back but I am taking clothes for the weekend, just in case. Our plans have a habit of changing. Here; it's a beautiful gift, give it to your brother, it might prove that you've been there one day.

She handed me back the black stone and walked off towards the door.

"Hey," I called her back, "I love you."

She gave me one more kiss then turned back to the door.

"I know," she said smugly. "I love you too."

She blew me one last kiss and scuttled off down the stairs.

I packed my uniform and what other clothes I had, which had mysteriously appeared in Sam's wardrobe in what appeared to be my grandfather's old suitcase, along with the Christmas presents bought with size in mind, inside the carrier bags they came in.

\* \* \*

John was working on Charles' car when I arrived at the garage.

"Hiya mate, how's it goin?" I said.

"Hey Higgins; not bad, what's with all the bags?"

447

"I'll explain later. What's wrong with the motor?'

"Nothin'. Andy wants me to check it over and put it through an MOT for him. I thought you would be in this week, s'pose you had better offers," he said smiling."

"Yeah could say!" I laughed. "I'm not going to be here for much longer and there are things I need to tell you before I go."

"You won't be here for Christmas?"

"No mate, I have to go. I'm not sure how long we have here now."

"Put the kettle on and make us a cup a tea; I'll just finish this off. I have to take it round to Gates' garage to get the MOT, but we can have a pint at the Morant after we drop it off."

I drank my tea while he removed his boiler suit and washed his hands, then he joined me in his little office and drank his down quickly. We drove around the corner and dropped off Charles's car. I told him all about my trip into the solar system on our walk back to the pub, taking care to avoid anything related to the bases on Mars and the moon.

"My little brother, an astronaut. Sorry mate it's just sinking in. Erato was some place that didn't exist in my mind, whereas the moon, Mars and Jupiter are... real... you know!"

Somehow the reality of our own solar system had more effect on him than talking about leaving for Erato.

"Here, take a look at this," I said showing him the shiny black moon rock.

We looked around the sky, the ghostly image of the moon, now almost full, was just rising above the trees.

"Is this really from the moon?"

"Sure is mate. Keep it, it's yours!"

I put it in his hand and as he gazed at it, I sensed his growing sadness at the thought of me leaving.

"Where are Mars and Jupiter now?" he asked.

"Well the Sun was beyond the Earth when we came back from Mars, so I guess you should be able to see it tonight. It is a glowing rusty red colour, well brown really and Jupiter...," I paused for a while to get my bearings. "The Earth was on the right side of the Sun with Mars and

Venus, so with the Sun on my left Jupiter should be out to the east beyond Luna somewhere."

"Luna?"

"The moon!"

"And where is Erato?"

"Haven't got a fuckin' clue mate. On the other side of the galaxy, but I'm not even sure which way that is."

Our outburst of laughter was mixed with the sadness of my imminent departure.

We stopped at the garage where I unpacked one of the carrier bags from my suitcase and took it with me to the Morant Arms across the road. For the first time in my life I bought my big brother a beer, and another for myself. George, the landlord's brother, knew I wasn't eighteen, but he turned a blind eye.

John got out a cigarette as he always did with a beer, and asked George for a box of matches.

"Here," I said. "You'd just as well have this now! Sorry it ain't wrapped up."

I handed him a gold-plated Zippo lighter, a small but very cute and expensive teddy from Hamleys for Jane, and a pair of gold star-shaped earrings for Mary.

"Bloody hell Higgs! he shrieked. "Have you robbed a bank? This must have cost a bloody fortune!"

"I got the money from Le Fevre, he asked to see me when he found out I was staying with Sam. Sam told him that we are going away together, he just doesn't know where. Anyway, we had a chat at the office, and I told him I wasn't sure I wanted to go back, so he's given me six months to reconsider, with six months wages up front."

"Oh well, don't s'pose it really matters much now. Thanks Higgs, that's really very kind of you. Mary will love these."

"The stars are to remind you both where I have gone."

"I wanted to give everyone something that would last after I've gone. I bought the old man a tankard and our Mother Teresa a crucifix necklace." I pulled them out of the bag to show him.

"They're lovely Bro. Here, you keep this, to remind you where you came from," he said, placing the moon rock back in my hand."

It was the first time he had used that epithet, and it seemed to put us on equal terms, our seven-year age difference forgotten.

"I've heard back from Le Fevre already, I have an interview next Thursday for a chance to join as a JE, Junior Engineer."

"That's great news Bro, he didn't mention it to me. I'm really pleased for you; just be careful with those ladders!" I joked, using the same brotherly epithet he had.

"Reckon I'm done with crawlin' around under cars."

I put ten pence into the jukebox and selected three records, to prevent our conversation being overheard, then told him what I knew about the virus and the secret societies. He was stunned by what I said, but much more pragmatic about the impact on his life.

Like Erato, the virus was unreal to him as indeed it had been with me. The effect was that it lifted the burden on me, the feeling I was deserting a sinking ship evaporated, it was my family I felt most concern for.

I realised it was probably the last time I would see him for a very long time. Before I could make my departing speech my eyes filled with tears, which had the same effect on him. I struggled to speak, my throat was blocked, I tried hard to clear it but couldn't. I didn't have to say anything because my thoughts had been clear enough for him to hear. He laughed away his tears and wiped his eyes.

"There is no way I'm not going to see you off, I don't care what you say. When are you leaving?"

"We still have to see Sam's parents, I haven't even met them yet. We'll be catching the train to London after my prize-giving tonight. I need to say goodbye to Mum and Dad, and the rest of the family."

"Sure, I'll take you home now, then I'll go and get Mary and Jane. Jane and Charles are catching the train over here after work to collect his car, so I'll drop Mary and Jane at Sway and come back over here to meet them. We'd better get out of here now before someone notices we are both blubbering."

"Hey, do you still have your old rucksack?" I asked.

"It's not very big but it's yours Bro! I'll bring it with me when I pick up Mary."

We collected my bags from his office and set off to see Mum and Dad.

* * *

My eldest sister Jean lived just across the road from my old school, I had planned to pop in and say goodbye to her and Richard before going to the prize-giving. When I got home, she was already there with her daughter Clare. She was expecting another baby in the spring. I gave both Mum and Jean a kiss and sat down at the table.

"Your dad was getting flustered about tonight, you should have called to let us know you were alright," said Mum.

"Course I was alright Mother. Sam doesn't have a phone."

"Don't give me that rubbish. You expect me to believe there are no phone boxes in London?"

"No Mother, sorry. Here this is for Christmas, sorry it's not wrapped up."

I passed her the small blue box and she opened it up and started to cry.

"It's not Christmas yet. What ya go an' do that for?"

"Stop blubberin' or you'll make Clare cry. We won't be here for Christmas Mother, in fact this is probably the last time I will see you all before we leave. We've got some cheap tickets, but we have to leave on Sunday and we haven't seen Sam's parents yet."

The shock only worsened her crying; I gave her a cuddle and assured her we would be back very soon.

"Where's Dad?"

"He's in the bath getting ready for tonight," said Jean. "He really is so much better than he's been for years. He's thrown his stick away but he's still not really steady on his feet," she laughed.

I took the necklace from Mum and put it around her neck doing up the clasp from behind her.

"Is Richard going to pick you up later?" I asked.

"Yes, he'll be here about half past five."

"Great. This is for you, and this is for Clare," I said, giving her an identical pair of star-shaped earrings and teddy bear.

"Oh Buggs, they're lovely. Are you really leaving us again already?"

"Well I really wasn't meant to be here any way so what's the difference. I'm just sorry I won't be here to see him," I said, touching the big round bulge she carried.

"Yes, but you'll see him when you get back. Anyway, what makes you think it's a boy?"

I realised I knew.

"Do you know anyone called Esther Ma?"

"Course I do, she was my grandmother, she died in 1939, why?"

I nodded towards Jean's stomach.

"Whoa!" scoffed Jean sensing my thoughts. "You said it was going to be a boy."

"He is a boy, take my word for it!"

"We'll see," she said.

The Christmas tree had been put up in the sitting room while I had been in London with Sam, along with all the familiar decorations. Jane was the third to leave home when she married Charles, since then the job had been passed to me. I could not recall Dad ever doing the job himself, even before his arthritis; it was a task I relished. I know that he loved Christmas when we were young, he would always do his utmost for us all. I had vague memories of the sit-in train he made for me when I was three or four years old; woodwork and painting had been his lifelong career. Somehow Mum and Dad had managed to do it together while I was away, and I realised that life would go on without me.

I hadn't planned on Mum and Dad going to the prize-giving, but I should have realised they would want to go, especially now Dad was no longer in pain. Five O-levels was not going to make me stand out from the crowd, it had been all I needed so it was all I took, I did get Grade 1 in both Maths and Physics. Aside from being the school chess team captain, there was nothing else worth mentioning about my school days.

452

I had a few minutes to sort through my belongings, but no idea what either of us would need on Erato; I would need a change of clothes for the weekend. There was little else I would take except for a few photographs and of course my Tarot cards; sadly, there weren't many photographs.

Seeing my white and khaki uniforms hanging in the wardrobe, I realised that the monthly payments would continue as scheduled. Merchant Navy Officers had to purchase their own uniforms, only the company cap- badge was supplied by B.P.

There was now more than enough money in my account to pay for them, but I didn't have time to deal with it myself. It seemed such a waste, most of the clothes had never been worn except to try them on.

"Hello son, what are you up to?" he said, standing in my bedroom doorway with a towel around his waist.

There was a sparkle in his eyes and a smile on his face that I hadn't seen for a long time.

"I'm leaving Dad. Sam and I are leaving tonight. I've seen Le Fevre and he's given me six months to reconsider, but I won't be going back."

"I know son," he said. "I knew the moment you got home from Dubai; you'd changed."

"The loan for my uniform will have to be paid, but there's more than enough money in my bank account to cover it thanks to Le Fevre."

"Don't you worry about the uniform, I'll take care of that son. Most of it has never been used and can simply go back to the outfitters, and I'll see to it that B.P. takes care of the rest."

"Le Fevre has already given me six months' pay."

"I should bloody well think so! You were nearly killed out there! You just forget all about the uniform and do what you have to do. I have a little put aside I can give you, it's not much but it'll help."

"There's no need dad, we'll be working our way around. Here, I bought you a Christmas present."

I watched him open the box, a simple enough task, but something he wouldn't have been able to do two weeks ago. He pulled out the pewter tankard and his smile was replaced by a much more solemn face. He opened his mouth in an effort to speak but couldn't.

"Sorry it's not engraved, I never had time. Anyway, I know you hate the name Adam and Jock seemed a bit odd, even if it is what everyone calls you."

"What are you talking about, it's beautiful."

It was a beautifully shaped Georgian style vessel, unbeknown to me it had been engraved with the Scottish thistle and the word Courage, which I knew to be the Cummings Clan motto.

"I thought you could leave it at the club."

"Thank you son, I will." I felt the deep emotion in his heart. "I suppose I'd better get dressed."

Normally Mum would have had to get him out of the bath and dress him. Part of me wanted to stay and see him make a full recovery, but then he was probably just as pleased that most of us had flown the nest to let him have some peace.

Soon the house was filled with people; first the twins came home from school, then John arrived with Mary and Jane, then onto the workshop to await Charles and Jane, shortly afterwards Richard arrived to collect Jean, and finally John returned with Jane and Charles.

It was the second time I was leaving home in less than a month, so things were much less stressful than I thought they would be. Only John knew I would be gone for a very long time.

Mother performed her usual miracle, producing enough food for the masses before getting herself ready to leave. I smiled to myself as it crossed my mind that whenever she did, it reminded me of the Sermon on the Mount story, two small fish and five barley loaves; there was never an abundance of food in the house, but somehow, she always managed.

By the time everyone had arrived there was very little time for goodbyes, Sam's train was due at six thirty-three. I handed out the remaining presents and went through the hugs and kisses. Jane had the same star-shaped earrings, Richard and Charles the same gold-plated Zippo, and the twins, Julie and Jenny, both had a silver bracelet.

It had always been that way when I went carol singing with my sisters, all the boys would get a packet of cigarettes, and the girls a selection of bath salts and bubble bath; whatever it was, they were all treated the same way.

There was a mass exodus at twenty past six, only John stayed with Mary and Jane to keep an eye on the twins; he would take Sam and I back to the station after the prize-giving.

I climbed into the back of Dad's little yellow Fiat 500 almost filling the back seat, and Mum got in the front beside Dad.

I wore my uniform as planned, despite knowing I would not be going back to sea. My life had changed beyond any imagination, and that was all due to my joining B.P., so it still seemed appropriate. I also felt that having survived the accident, I had earned the right to wear it to the prize-giving.

While dressing, I communicated with Sam to confirm that we would be picking her up at the station, her last day had gone well, she had shed a few tears saying goodbye to the Captain and would miss him. She told me that Victor was in Maryland at the National Security Agency campus at Fort George G. Meade. He told her that the CIA, NSA, MI5 and MI6 had all been alerted to recent activities, and that surveillance had been stepped up. He suggested we go straight to her parents after the prize-giving to be sure she had a chance to say goodbye. He would meet us on the forest at ten o'clock at the site of the Naked Man where he and I had walked at Wilverley Plain.

After I had finished dressing, I took my cheque book from my bedside table drawer, signed every cheque, and put it in my jacket pocket.

\* \* \*

I was waiting on the platform when Sam arrived, and helped her off with her rucksack and large holdall. She was dressed in an extremely attractive black business suit with her hair tied back behind her head. Her skirt was long enough to be elegant, but short enough to show off her lovely legs.

"You look so sexy," I said, holding her in my arms.

"Behave yourself, you're such a naughty bear. And please don't smudge my lipstick," she pleaded, offering me her cheek instead.

She smelled every bit as good as she looked.

"Chanel," she said sensing my thoughts. "Do you like it?"

"It's nice, but I like your other perfume too," I answered.

Mum was standing beside the open door of the car, waiting for us to climb into the back seat.

"Hello Mum, merry Christmas," said Sam.

"Merry Christmas to you too Sam, you look beautiful," said Mum.

"Thank you and so do you. And how are you Mr Cummings?"

"Better every day lass, and call me Jock," he said, looking across from the driving seat.

She knew it wasn't his real name, and that he really hated being called Adam. It was his father's name, nobody used it, not even Mother.

"This is for you Mum," she said, handing her a gift from inside her handbag.

"Oh thank you Sam, I'll put it under the tree when we get home," said Mum graciously.

"You can open it now, it's our Christmas tonight," said Sam.

Mum opened the beautifully wrapped gift; dressed in ribbons and bows it looked too good to open.

"Oh my word," said Mum, "Thank you so much Sam."

She was overcome with such an extravagant gift. It was the same Chanel that Sam had bought for herself.

Sam took another gift from the holdall.

"And this is for you Jock," said Sam, walking around to his door.

He opened it up, smiling with excitement. It was a bottle of 10-year-old Glen Turret malt whisky.

"Och lass, ye shouldna done tha'" said Dad, his Scottish accent all the stronger at the sight of her gift.

Sam gave him a kiss on the cheek, then climbed in through Mum's door and sat in the back seat, while I put her rucksack into the small boot.

"Not enough room for the holdall I'm afraid. I'll hold it on my lap." I said.

I climbed in beside Sam along with her holdall, then mother folded back the front seat and climbed in beside Dad.

My hand brushed against the silky black stockings that Sam wore. The silkiness of the stockings produced a highly arousing sensation, which intensified when I sensed the effect my uniform was having on her.

Dad now drove the little car like a sports car, rocking his shoulders, audibly urging the little engine to produce more power.

We arrived at the school at ten minutes to seven and Dad drove straight into the small car park. He could park anywhere given the protection of his disabled sticker in the back window.

The school hall was already full of my old friends, most of whom were accompanied by their parents. It felt good to be dressed so smartly in my uniform with Sam on my arm. I looked around wondering if any other Cadets were there, three other lads in my year, Paul, Wiggy and Sainty had also joined the Merchant Navy but with other companies. There were a few other lads in uniforms, three in the Army and one in the Royal Navy.

As I looked around, I noticed some of the girls that I had so desperately wanted to date during my school years. I'm not sure if any of them knew, but they all made eye contact and I sensed a mixture of surprise, affection and envy from all of them, and others around me; I had never been a heartthrob, or part of the trendy cliques, but that evening, dressed in my uniform with a beautiful nineteen-year-old woman on my arm, we both stood out. I was happy with Sam, very happy, and yet I still had pleasant recollections of dreams gone by and what might have been. There was no feeling of smugness, that I had done better with Sam, it was simply a new beginning and what fate had bestowed on me. Sam knew each of them and of course all my other friends.

We met Bogie talking with Martin and I introduced Sam. Seeing Martin again reminded me of the séance he had held with his circle of friends, and the prediction the following day that Arsenal would win the FA cup. It had always intrigued me, and I made a mental note to check out the mysterious séance when I next entered the time warp on my way to Erato.

"Have you done anything exciting since you left," asked Mark.

Looking around at all my old friends emphasised just how much had happened to me since the last days of school.

"Not a damn thing mate! Just waiting for my first ship," I said. Bogie gave me a puzzled look, fully aware of my trip to Dubai and the accident but said nothing.

The presentation didn't actually begin until eight o'clock, so I was getting anxious about time, then the CSE certificates were dispatched before the GCE's, both in subject order, handed out by the various subject Heads, so I had to wait for my last certificate before telling Dad we had to leave.

We waited for a natural break between subjects and then made our way to the exit.

"We have to get back to London tonight to collect Sam's belongings before going to Alton tomorrow to see her parents," I explained to them both.

"We can drop you at the station son," said Dad.

"No, I have to go home to pick up my case first, John and Mary are waiting to take us to the station. By the way, I hope you don't mind if I take Grandad's case Mother."

"Of course not," said Mum.

"Ok but I'm coming with you to see you off," said Dad, determined he would be there. "Mary will understand."

"Don't worry there is nothing we can do to stop him. Does it matter so much that he knows the truth," thought Sam.

"I suppose not," I replied silently.

We arrived home at twenty minutes to ten, and I was anxious to be at the meeting point on the hour as planned. Victor would not land until we got there but everyone knew the train for London left at seventeen minutes past the hour. I rushed in and collected my case and came downstairs to say my goodbyes to Mum, Mary and the twins, little Jane was fast asleep on the sofa.

"I have the rucksack in the car if you still want it Higgs," said John.

"No time Bro, I'll take the case and pack the rucksack later," I answered.

"Why are you in such a hurry, the train doesn't go till quarter past?" asked mum, not really expecting and answer.

"We can pick up the fast train in Brock' at twelve minutes past if we hurry," I explained. Brockenhurst would take at least ten minutes across the forest by car.

"Well make sure you write," she said, giving Sam a final hug and kiss.

"As often as we can," I said, giving her one last hug.

We all climbed into John's Cortina, his latest car had much more space than Dad's Fiat. John took the left route at the end of the road, maintaining the appearance that we were going to Brockenhurst; it made little difference which way we went any way.

Dad said nothing when John turned left at Marlpit Oak crossroads instead of going straight on. We drove past Longslade to the end of the road and turned right, down the back road to Brockenhurst a short distance before pulling off onto the forest.

It was always deserted at that time of night, with just the ponies trying to find shelter from the cold December wind that blew across the plain. John drove along the edge of the enclosure, down the gravel track that was once the main road to Burley and Ringwood until we reached the Naked Man. The old oak tree was once the local hanging tree where highwaymen and serious criminals met their end.

"Someone want to tell me why we are in the middle of the forest?" asked Dad.

"Seems you and I are going to see something out of this world!" said John.

"We're not going to Israel Dad, not even to Egypt. It's a long story and John will have to tell you all about it in detail, but at least you will know the truth. All I can say is Sam is going home and I am going with her. We'll be gone for a long time, fifteen years, perhaps more, and we won't be able to write."

"I knew something was going on, I'm not daft ya know. The doctors have no idea why my arthritis is in remission, but I guess it's got something to do with this."

"Yes it has Pop," said Sam, using the same affectionate name she used for her own father. "It's important that you know we will be safe."

"Our friend will be here soon to pick us up; it's him you can thank for saving me, I might not have been here without him," I said.

"Not so and you know it," said Victor silently. "Prepare your father and brother for my appearance."

"Prepare yourself for a shock Dad. Time to get out of the car," I said.

Victor's holographic image appeared before us in his Terran form.

"Mr Cummings, my apologies, time will be brief if I am to ensure your journey home is not delayed by the police. Please prepare yourself to see the image of my true form and do not be alarmed."

The ginger haired Terran dissolved and was replaced with Victor's Eratean image.

"Very shortly I will bring my ship down and your son will board the ship with mine. You see Sam was my son in a previous life."

"John will explain," I added.

"James has accepted my offer to join Sam and I on our home-world Erato. Be assured he is free to return whenever he wishes; however, the journey will take several years of your time. James will be gone for at least fourteen years, probably significantly more. Communication will not be possible when we leave, but I know that you have experienced similar difficulties, all be it terrestrial separation from your loved ones."

"I want to thank you for saving my son," said my father.

"That is not necessary, your son did as much as I did to save his own life; it would not have been possible if he had not wanted it. I am here to reassure you your son will be safe, and he will have the opportunity to see things far beyond your imagination."

"I thank you any way," he answered.

"If we are ready please stand still and I will land my ship."

"We're ready," I said.

I took my father's hand, then realising I could, put my arms around him and hugged him, man to man, then he kissed me on my forehead; when I had left the month before it would have been too painful for him. I did the same with John.

"Good luck Higgs, love ya Bro, goodbye Sam, take care of my little brother," said John.

"Good Luck to you too Bro, love ya loads. I hope the Merch works out well for you. It's a new chapter for us both.

"Love you Dad, you can tell Mother I love her too, and the rest of the family."

"Love you too son, thought I'd lost you when you were two. I'll be here when you get back."

Sam gave them both a kiss and a hug.

"Make sure you bring him back to us," said Dad.

"Promise," answered Sam.

"Oh, I almost forgot. There's over a hundred pounds in my account, we won't need money where we are going. I've signed every cheque so use it for whatever you need," I explained, handing my father my cheque book.

Victor's image faded away and a moment later his ship appeared in front of us in a streak of blue light, nestling softly and silently into the bracken.

The side of the shimmering blue ship opened, and Victor stepped out in his true form. He stood in his white gown and took my father's hands.

"I will personally bring him back to you, you have my word," he said.

He turned to John and took his hands.

"It is time for you to leave. Go quickly before the authorities arrive and say nothing to anyone of this to anyone outside your family."

We stepped into the ship and it rose slowly into the air. We waved goodbye for the last time and the doorway closed in a rippling wave.

"Very practical I'm sure but it could do with a woman's touch," teased Sam.

"There is everything here that anyone could need," answered Victor silently.

# ISV170

The hull disappeared from view and Sam gasped as it revealed the Earth below.

"Oh shit! We're flying! We're in outer space!" she shouted.

We stood together and looked at the city lights across Europe, trying to identify the cities below us. Victor moved the ship eastwards across Asia towards the sunrise, which swept down the China coast, with Japan and Australia basking in the morning sunshine. A huge swirling typhoon covered a large area of the Pacific Ocean to the east of Japan, in contrast to the bright blue seas that surrounded Australia.

"I can't wait to see Erato," she said. What is it like?'

"It is everything you can imagine and whatever you want it to be. You will see your home for yourself soon enough. There is so much here you should see first if we had more time," Said Victor.

Just as before the other ships formed around us one by one and the ship expanded as they did so. Soon the circle was complete, and Sam saw for herself the small group that made up Victor's team.

'Friendship, I have with me now my son reborn in Terran form known here as the female Samantha Dee Cooper,' said Victor in silence.

A unanimous welcome came back from the group.

'We have forty-eight hours to review and complete our task before we meet with the assembly again. Let us begin by understanding what the virus is and how it affects the Terran victims.'

'Friendship, I am known here as Piotr,' he began for the benefit of Sam. 'I return from central Africa having found many subjects infected with the simian virus, which I have logged as Immune System Virus 170. It appears to be a mutation of ISV88, which was identified by us in the Terran year of 1504. Cases exist in all of the countries I was asked to research. In some cases, I estimate one half of one percent to be in the primary stages of infection. I have found no indication that the virus or its symptoms have been acknowledged or classified in any way by

Terrans, neither has the ultimate cause of death been linked to a viral infection.'

'Have any of you discovered any awareness of the virus other than Clay?' asked Victor. Their response was a unanimous no.

'Please continue Piotr,' he said.

'ISV170 appears to infect cells in the immune and central nervous systems. The main cell that ISV170 infects is a T helper lymphocyte, which is a crucial part of both the Eratean and Terran immune system, its function co-ordinating the actions of other immune system cells. A large reduction in the number of T helper cells seriously weakens the immune system. ISV170 is able to infect the T helper cell because it has a protein on its surface, which ISV170 uses to attach itself and then enter the cell. It then replicates itself within the cell and continues to infect other cells. Infected cells are typically destroyed or malfunction. It appears the ISV170 infection can generally be broken down into four distinct stages, primary infection, clinically asymptomatic stage, symptomatic 170 infection, and progression from stage A to stage D. Stage one we have named ISV170A, lasts for a few weeks and is often accompanied by a short flu-like illness. A large amount of ISV170 can be found in the peripheral blood, the immune system begins seroconversion by producing ISV170 antibodies and cytotoxic lymphocytes. Stage two ISV170B is an asymptomatic stage that appears to last for approximately ten years, it is difficult to be more accurate without prolonged monitoring. The subject is free from major symptoms, although there may be swollen glands. The level of ISV170 in the peripheral blood drops to very low levels; however, subjects remain infectious and ISV170 antibodies are detectable in the blood. Despite the absence of symptoms, ISV170 is very active in the lymph nodes. Large amounts of T helper cells are infected and die and a large amount of virus is produced.'

'Have you found any evidence of vertical infection?' asked Victor.

'Without doubt there are high rates of vertical infection. I estimate that the occurrence rate lies between twenty to fifty percent.'

'If the virus is not passed on in all cases it would suggest that vertical infection can be eliminated,' said Victor.

'I would concur with your thoughts,' answered Piotr. 'It is possible that the infection is passed on during labour or delivery. I have also considered that the virus may also be passed on in milk from infected mothers.'

'I agree, please continue,' said Victor.

'Stage three is the symptomatic stage of the ISV170C infection. Over time, the immune system loses the struggle to contain ISV170 for three main reasons; firstly the lymph nodes and tissues become damaged because of the years of activity, secondly ISV170 mutates and becomes more pathogenic leading to more T helper cell destruction, and finally the body fails to keep up with replacing the T helper cells that are lost.

'Symptoms develop as the immune system fails, initially mild; however, as the immune system deteriorates the symptoms worsen. Symptomatic ISV170 infection is mainly caused by the emergence of opportunistic infections and cancers that the immune system would normally prevent. These can occur in almost all the body systems, but commonly in the respiratory system, the gastro-intestinal system, the central peripheral nervous system, and the skin.

'Symptomatic ISV170 infection is often characterised by multi-system disease. Treatment for the specific infection or cancer can be administered; however, the underlying cause is the action of ISV170 as it erodes the immune system. Unless 170 itself can be slowed down, the symptoms of immune suppression continue to worsen.

'At stage four, ISV170D, the immune system becomes more and more damaged, the illnesses that are present become more and more severe, leading eventually to one or more of a specific number of severe opportunistic infections or cancers.'

'Thank you Piotr,' said Victor. 'My own research suggests that there is no evidence that the virus is airborne. The virus exists in the victim's blood and sexual fluids, transfer of either into the bloodstream would seem to be necessary in some way for cross infection to occur. Is there any evidence that the spread of infection could have been caused by the mosquito or other biting insects?'

465

'Friendship, I am known here as Kez. My research in East Africa would suggest not. When extracting blood from its victim mosquitoes do not inject blood from any previous person. The only thing that a mosquito injects is saliva, which acts as a lubricant and enables it to feed more efficiently. Whilst other viruses such as malaria are transmitted in this way, I have found evidence that ISV170 is present in mosquitoes. I have also conducted preliminary examinations of mosquitoes that have fed on ISV170 infected hosts and the virus appears to have no effect on the mosquito. I should add that there has been a significant drop in the number of mosquito transmitted viruses since the World Health Organization commenced a program to eradicate malaria worldwide in 1955, reliant largely on dichlorodiphenyltrichloroethane.'

'Friendship, I am known here as Slobodan. It is clear that ISV170 cross infection is taking place at increasing rates since the virus has not yet been discovered, for example, when blood transfusion takes place or the use of shared hypodermic needles.'

The others all echoed similar findings indicating that the virus was spreading, undetected and unresearched. In South Africa and Rhodesia, the virus appeared to be particularly prevalent, and in the United States the virus seemed to be much more confined to male subjects.

'Thank you Slobodan,' said Victor.

'Friendship, I am known here as Clay. My conclusion regarding the spread of infection in the United States is that major causes of virus cross infection include sexual intercourse between homosexual males, and by the use of contaminated syringes in drug users. There is evidence that the virus is passed from men to women during sexual activity, particularly in cases where anal intercourse is practiced.'

'Thank you Clay,' said Victor. 'My own research in England uncovered evidence that the original virus was almost certainly developed in 1947 by the British Ministry of Defence, at the Porton Down Chemical Defence Establishment. Records there confirms that the virus developed from a Simian Immune Virus; however, they were also experimenting with ribonucleic acid in cancers. I was unable to find any records of testing or trials; however, I did find additional viruses designed to attack both Sapien and livestock.

'Clay contacted me with information that the Central Intelligence Agency in the United States received samples of the developed virus identified as SV71 from the British Government in 1948. Together we continued the investigation and discovered evidence that the results of testing at the Los Alamos base in New Mexico were dispatched in their entirety to the National Security Agency headquarters at Fort Mead Maryland.

'We can find no evidence of any antidote or cure for the virus. Despite this, we cannot overlook the fact that large-scale infection has occurred in a similar period. There is no evidence that ISV170 has been used by the United States or British governments; however, the scale and spread of infection would seem to suggest simultaneous mass infection by some means unless the virus existed in mass before 1949.'

'Friendship,' I said following Eratean protocol. 'Why can you not cure the infected people as you do with other illnesses?'

'Friendship, there appears to be no way we can destroy the virus without damaging the immune system,' said Slobodan. 'We are able to correct damaged or mutated deoxyribonucleic acid structures, but not ribonucleic acid which is the basic component of ISV170.

'Limiting the replication of the virus could be possible by slowing down the replication of ISV170 in the body. When ISV170 replicates it often mutates, we know this because we have identified many different strains of virus within the same host. If levels of mutation could be increased by ensuring that the DNA copy is faulty, the process of ISV170 replication could not continue.

'Another possible way to deal with the virus might be to create bogus T Helper cells with the same protein covering that attracts the ISV170 cell. These bogus cells could be designed to self-destruct within the body simultaneously destroying any captured ISV170 cells. If large quantities of these cells exist in the body it might be possible to slow down or even eliminate the ISV170 virus.'

'So what would happen if you were infected? I asked.

'If our research is correct the virus would essentially work in the same way if an Eratean was infected. The effectiveness of the virus on the Eratean people would be somewhat different. Since infection requires the transfer of blood or sexual fluids there is almost no likelihood of cross infection, the virus would be detectable by the Eratean mind and this would necessitate self-imposed quarantine. The inherent desire for sexual intercourse in Eratean people is significantly different to that of Terrans and we have no need for blood transfusions. Do we have any estimates on death toll?' asked Victor.

I sensed a rapid exchange of figures and mathematical calculations between the group.

'So, we are agreed at a figure between twenty and forty million people killed by the end of the century depending on containment and the development of treatments. We have forty-eight hours to continue our research. Please focus on how the virus may have been deployed and possible methods of containment. Be prepared for departure to Erato when we next meet in Council.'

One by one the ships broke away until we were alone again.

# WANTED

## THE GREYFRIAR

---

"Now I should get you two to Chawton," said Victor.

"Couldn't we go back to London tonight?" asked Sam. It's late and we're not expected until tomorrow."

"It would be dangerous to risk another landing so soon and tonight is a busy night in the city, I would advise against it. Chawton is a quiet village and I believe the public house has not yet closed," said Victor.

"There's a grass area to the right of the pub where you could land," said Sam.

Victor zoomed in to survey the area and we could see the small village in detail. The pub appeared to be open and the street was deserted. I put on Sam's rucksack and she donned my smaller empty one in preparation for our transitory landing. I would carry my small suitcase, leaving Sam with only her holdall and handbag. When we were ready, Victor landed the ship and we ran off together towards the pub. A moment later Victor and the ship were gone.

"It's quarter to eleven," I said checking my watch. "Won't your parents think it's strange us arriving so late?"

"We'll just tell them your brother drove us straight here. I have plenty of clothes and toiletries in my rucksack, but I must get back to London before we leave to pick up all my treasured bits and pieces."

"Bugger!"

"What? Men! You're so bloody hopeless," she rebuked, reading my thoughts. "You can use my toothbrush tonight, you won't need anything else, there will be plenty of soap and shampoo."

Sam's father Peter Cooper was landlord of the Greyfriar Public House, and her mother Frances the landlady. The lower wall was painted white, and the upper floor had a terracotta tiled facia; it stood opposite the home of Jane Austin.

"Don't worry they won't bite," said Sam. "They're not expecting us until tomorrow though!"

Sam opened the bar door and walked in. Her father was in the middle of pulling a pint of bitter; seeing his daughter, he put the glass down on the bar and walked around to embrace her with a hug and a kiss.

"Pumpkin! We weren't expecting to see you until tomorrow! Never mind it's lovely to see you. I'll be with you in just one minute."

He stepped back behind the bar and finished pouring the beer, then popped around to the kitchen to call her mother and brother."

"Kevin has just arrived, he's with your mother."

"Pa, this is my boyfriend James."

"Very nice to meet you Mr Cooper," I said shaking his hand.

"Nice to meet you too lad, we've heard a lot about you from Sam. Call me Pete, James. Now what can I get you to drink," he asked.

"Give him a pint of bitter," said Sam before I could speak. "And I'll have a G and T please; a large one!"

"My pleasure poppet. So, you've come straight up from your prize-giving," he said looking at my uniform.

"Yes, my brother was kind enough to drive us up, we had planned to go back to London and catch the train down to Alton tomorrow morning."

"Has he gone?"

"Yes, he had to get home."

"He must drive like the wind!" he said.

"We left as soon as we could," said Sam.

He was a big man with an equally big smile on his face. His well-rounded belly lent itself well to the surroundings and I sensed a welcoming feeling drawing me to him like the pull of a warm fire.

"There ya go," he said handing me the beer.

"Cheers Pete," I said. "Wow that's gorgeous. Nothing like the keg I normally drink," I added, sipping the beer.

"Keg! That's a premium pint of best draught bitter! Keg be damned!"

"Sorry I've never tasted it before."

"Don't be such a bully Dad. Not everyone knows as much about beer as you do."

Frances appeared from the living quarters and rushed around the bar to greet Sam. She put her arms around her then stepped back and held her hands at arm's length.

"Let me take a look at you. You look beautiful my darling. Oh, it's so good to see you. You have a real glow about you."

"It's lovely to be home Ma," answered Sam, giving her mother another hug and a kiss."

"And this must be James. What a handsome young man he is in his uniform."

"Hands off Mater, he's mine," joked Sam.

"Hello Mrs Cooper, lovely to meet you at last."

"Call me Fran, Frances sounds so formal."

She moved towards me offering her right cheek.

'Give her a kiss,' said Sam silently.

I moved my head around her and kissed her lightly on the lips.

"Wow! I don't get many of those," she said.

'On the cheek Stupid!' Sam clarified silently.

"Fill your boots lad," said Pete grinning.

"Daddy!" snapped Sam.

Kevin appeared from behind his mother and gave his sister the kiss on the cheek I was supposed to have given her mother.

"Hi Sprout. So, you're all finished with B.P. then?" he asked.

"No! Le Fevre has given me six months to reconsider. Mean time he will make do with a temp from the pool."

"You're very lucky to have such a considerate boss," said Frances.

"Hey, I'm good at what I do, and he knows it. I made his life easy and everyone likes a stress-free life."

"He's just a dirty old man," said Kevin.

"Kevin!" snapped Frances.

"Joking, I was just joking," he said defensively. "He's a very nice guy actually."

"We weren't expecting you tonight. Space is tight, so James will have to share Kevin's room."

"Oh mother," said Sam.

"What you do in your own house is up to you but here you will sleep on your own until the day you are married. I'm sure James' mother would say just the same," she said, looking at me for confirmation.

"She certainly would Mrs Cooper. Well if Kevin doesn't mind me sharing?"

"No problem," said Kevin. "You get used to sharing your cabin on board ship," he answered. "I've heard a little about your accident, are you sure you two are doing the right thing?"

"Why don't we show James up to your room?" Sam butted in.

"Sure. Follow me," said Kevin.

I put my beer down on the bar and followed Sam and Kevin up the stairs at the left end of the bar.

"I have my own little den up here away from the rest of the house. They don't like my music," he explained. "There's more room up here and of course I can sneak down to the bar or kitchen without disturbing anyone, so it suits me."

We walked through the door and up the stairs, below us the beer cellar was on ground level and accessible only from the back of the pub. Upstairs there was a large room with two beds. Kevin picked up his bag from the bed on the right and moved it to a chair across the room.

"That one's yours," he said.

"Kevin, we need to talk but not now," said Sam. "There are things I must tell you that I couldn't discuss on the phone. Until this evening, I wasn't even sure that I wasn't in the middle of some wonderful dream. Don't say any more about us leaving in front of Ma and Pa, I don't want them worrying."

"What's in it for me then Sprout?"

"You get the flat to yourself and I will keep paying my share of the rent."

"But I'm never there. At least the place was occupied at night while you were there."

"You're such a whinger! Find yourself a tenant to share with and that way you'll pay nothing for it."

"Ok deal. I am your obedient servant!"

"Well leave us alone for a moment," she ordered.

"Certainly. You know Ma will be up here in a flash if you're up here on your own for more than a minute though."

"Go!" she shouted. "No wait, turn around."

He stopped leaving his hand still holding the door handle and turned to look at her.

'I wanted you to see this, just so you know how serious this is," she said silently.

'Don't worry, she is still your sister,' I thought, following her lead and sensing his concern.

His hand fell off the handle and he shook his head in disbelief.

'I am your sister, but in my previous life I was from another world. I died here on Earth and was reincarnated,' she explained in silence.

'And I am Terran, human, from Earth,' I added. 'Your sister is too, but her spirit is from a world called Erato. Her Eratean father found her through me and has invited us to return with him to Erato.'

'I will return, this is my home, but Erato is where my soul belongs. I must return there to relearn the Eratean way of life. We will explain everything later when we have more time.'

"I'm not sure who is safe with who here," he said.

"Don't worry," I said aloud. "She is the same sister you grew up with.

"Not a word to Ma and Pa you'll just frighten them," she spoke aloud, "And it's who is safe from whom!"

"Now I know it's my sister," he laughed.

He left us in the bedroom alone and my hand went immediately to her stocking tops.

"Don't be a naughty bear," she said, slapping my wandering hand. "You'll only get over excited. Shit! I just saw a police car go by outside. You stay here. I'll go downstairs before my mother knocks the door down, and I'll check outside to make sure the police didn't stop."

I stroked the front of her knickers defiantly and she moaned submissively before pushing me away.

"You are a very bad bear and I will have my revenge!"

She left me in the room and I considered changing out of my uniform but there seemed little point since it was so late.

# THE GOOD

I knelt on the bed and opened the front window above it. A moment later I saw Sam and Kevin step out of the door. To my left blue flashing lights lit the area at the end of the road, where we had landed. Sam walked down the road to investigate with Kevin following a few feet behind. They were met at the end by one of the police officers who stopped them from going any further and seemed to be asking them questions. A brown Rover 2000 arrived from the other direction and stopped in front of them. Three plain clothes men stepped out of the car, two of them moved out of sight in the direction of our landing site and the third joined in the conversation between Sam, Kevin and the two uniformed policemen. After a minute or two, the third man went off to join his colleagues and Sam and Kevin made their way back to the door.

"Close the window James, it's bloody freezing up there at the best of times," shouted Kevin.

Moments later the door opened and they both walked into the bedroom.

"Someone must have seen us land, but they're not saying anything," said Sam.

"Well they wouldn't would they," said Kevin.

"I suppose not. What did they say to you?" I asked.

"They wanted to know why we were there, whether we'd seen anything unusual tonight, where we were from and how long we'd been here. I said we been here since half past ten and Kevin said he had arrived about half an hour before," said Sam.

"Why? We arrived at quarter to eleven," I said. "And we are supposed to have driven up from New Milton, it takes almost two-hours to get here by car."

"I know, but now they think we were here before the ship landed."

"I did arrive at ten. Hopefully the Olds won't remember if they come asking questions," added Kevin.

It was their pet name for their parents.

"Perhaps we should go back down in case they come in?" said Kevin. "They will probably want to take names and addresses of everyone in the bar before they leave. I reckon there'll be a few taxis being ordered tonight!"

As he opened the door to go down the bar went silent. One of the uniformed policemen was standing at the door behind two of the plain clothes officers who had just walked in.

"Can I help you gentlemen?" asked Pete.

The man in front checked his watch as we reached the bottom of the stairs.

"Good evening Sir, Chief Inspector Connolly, Hampshire Police. Well I suppose you could pour me a Scotch to start with, a large one. There's been a reported incident just down the street and I just need to gather some details before any one leaves tonight.

"Show the gentleman your card Sergeant."

The other man took out his warrant card and showed it to Pete.

"Peter Cooper, landlord," acknowledged Pete.

"What sort of incident?" asked Fran.

"I'm afraid I'm not at liberty to discuss that Madam."

"Ice?" asked Pete handing over the whisky.

"I beg your pardon?" said the Inspector. "Oh yes, the Scotch. No thank you," he added shaking his head.

"Anything for your colleague," asked Pete.

"I'm afraid not. Sergeant Hodson here is on duty."

"That'll be twenty-two pence then please."

"Oh yes of course. Sergeant!"

He gestured with his left hand urging him to pay for the drink.

"Sergeant Hodson here will have to take down some details from everyone now, so I will have to ask everyone to stay until we have spoken to them."

"Well I was just about to call last orders."

"Oh were you, better have a top up then before it's too late."

"Last orders ladies and gentlemen please."

Sam and Kevin stepped behind the bar to help their father deal with the rush to refill empty glasses.

"That'll be forty-four pence then," said Pete.

The sergeant dipped into his pockets once more before handing over the money.

"Carry on then Sergeant, the sooner we get started the sooner we can let these nice people get home," said the Inspector.

Fran began to collect the empty glasses from around the bar, so I made myself useful and did the same thing. The sergeant sat down at the first occupied table and began taking notes, while the uniformed officer stood at the doorway preventing anyone from leaving until authorised to do so.

I followed Fran into the kitchen behind the bar and passed her the glasses.

"There's a good boy," she said. Would you mind just emptying the ash trays into this bin for me?'

"No of course not, I'm delighted to be of help."

"Bring the dirty ones back if there is no one using them, if they're clean just leave them be."

I did as she asked, beginning at the far end of the bar which was almost empty, working back towards the Inspector, who sat on a stool in silent oblivion at the bar, munching on a pork pie which he plied with English mustard as he ate.

"And what are you all dressed up for young man, not clearing up dishes I'm sure?" he asked, as I drew level with him.

"No Sir, I'm here with my girlfriend, I'm on leave and we were at my school prize-giving this evening."

"Aha," he said as best as he was able whilst eating another piece of pork pie. "And where would that be?"

"Arnewood School in New Milton."

"New Milton? Where's that then? It's not around here is it?"

"No, it's down on the coast. My brother drove us up here after I got my certificates."

"So, what's your name then Admiral?" he said with a friendly smile.

"James, James Cummings, and I'm a Cadet."

"Yes of course you are. And where might your girlfriend be now James?"

"There, that's Sam, Samantha Cooper," I answered, pointing towards her behind the bar.

"So, you would be sixteen, seventeen...?'

"Sixteen," I said.

"And would that be your brother?" he asked, looking at Kevin.

"No, that's Sam's brother Kevin, that's her dad, Mr Cooper, the landlord. My brother went straight back home to Ringwood after dropping us off."

"And what time would that have been?"

"Half past ten," I said, in line with what Sam had told him.

"Couldn't have been a little earlier or later?'

"No, I remember looking at my watch when we arrived. It was definitely ten thirty."

"And what time do you make it now?"

"I make it ten past eleven."

"Ah, mine says five to eleven, perhaps mine is wrong?" he said, lifting it to his ear to see if it was ticking.

The bar was still open, so something was wrong. I glanced at the clock on the wall and confirmed it matched his watch. I realised my watch was fifteen minutes fast; if I had looked at it when it said ten thirty it would actually have been ten fifteen, fifteen minutes before the ship landed, which implied that we left New Milton at around eight fifteen. I realised I'd scarcely looked at my watch since adjusting it after our time warp, using Sam's alarm clock for reference; on the occasions when I had, it would only have compensated for my tardiness.

"Well at your age you shouldn't be in the bar after time is called, but I want you to hang around until Sergeant Hodson takes down your details," said the Inspector.

"Yes of course. I was just helping to clear up."

"Yes alright son," he said, putting the last piece of pork pie in his mouth.

He lifted his glass just as Pete looked at the clock.

"No need for these nice people to rush their drinks until we have taken their details," he said to Pete. "One for the road and a packet of your finest cheese and onion crisps please landlord."

I finished emptying and collecting the ashtrays and took them through to the kitchen. Sam followed me in with her hands full of empty glasses.

"James is not supposed to be here after-hours Ma, so we'll pop up stairs to Kevin's room until this lot clear off. Give us a shout when they go, and we'll help you clear up."

"Don't worry love, there's not much left now. The cleaner will be in tomorrow morning to hoover and polish. Any idea what this fuss is all about?"

"No Ma, they wouldn't say."

I followed Sam back to the bar and she topped up our glasses.

"We will be upstairs in my brother's room at the end of the bar when you want us," she said to the Inspector.

"Fine, I'll talk to you a bit later. Any chance of a cup of coffee?" he asked.

"If you ask my mum she will probably get you one. If you follow me, she's in the kitchen."

She picked up our drinks and led the way back to the kitchen, nodding to her right as I opened the door to the bedroom stairs.

"Were does this door go?" he asked.

"To the garden and the cellar room" she answered.

# DARK SIDE OF THE MOON

Kevin was already upstairs looking through his record collection. He picked out a record and showed it to us for approval.

'Dark Side of the Moon, fine but not too loud so we can talk,' said Sam silently.

"Could we just talk normally please?" he asked.

"Yes of course, sorry?" said Sam.

"Well do you mind if I tape this, so I can listen again later."

"No of course not. It may help you explain to the Olds when I have gone."

"With the police downstairs?" I asked.

"You mean Einstein of the Yard down there? All he's interested in is a drink, his thoughts are a complete muddle," said Sam. "The man's as stupid as he looks!"

"What is all the fuss about downstairs anyway," asked Kevin. "You mentioned a ship landing."

"We left James' brother and father in the forest near his home in Sway. His brother drove us there after the prize-giving. We were picked up by Victor, my previous father, he brought us here in his spaceship and landed at the exact spot the police have cordoned off. Someone must have reported the landing and they've come out to investigate. They did the same thing on Wednesday when Victor landed on Parliament Hill."

"Which is why you told them you arrived at half ten," said Kevin.

"Yes, if someone saw us land they must know what time it happened."

"How do you know this Victor chap is really your father from a previous life?"

"I don't. I just feel I have to do this in the same way I knew James and I would be together."

"Yes, I did wonder what the attraction was. No offence James mate, just a bit jealous. Older women never throw themselves at me if you see what I mean."

"None taken," I said. "I would never have expected her to fall for me either."

He turned down the music to background level, put a new cassette into the tape deck and handed Sam a microphone.

I listened to her relate the story beginning at the point we first realised each other when we met on board the Worcester. What began as a romantic fantasy would soon have deteriorated to the apparent ramblings of a delusional nut case had it not been shared by the two of us. Hard as it was for Kevin to believe what he was being told he listened carefully without interruption.

She described my accident and how Victor had appeared in the water behind me, touched delicately on the experience that enabled us to share each other's minds, how she came to be reborn on Earth, our brief excursions into the solar system, the other visitors, the Martian and Lunar bases, the virus, and our plans to leave together.

"Do you have any more questions for me or can I put this thing down?" she asked.

"If you know everything Sam knows, you would know my dad's middle name," he said to me.

"He doesn't have one," I answered.

"Very Good! And you should be able to tie a bowline," he said throwing a piece of rope to Sam. She put down the microphone and picked up the rope.

"Oh well, I've never done this before but here goes, make a loop, the rabbit comes up the hole walks around the tree and goes back down the hole. Pull it tight. There you are! Is this what you want?"

"Not bad! Of course, he could have taught you to do that."

"Oh, come on! How many girls have you taught to tie knots?"

"Well two or three actually," he said smirking.

"You dirty little tow rag, and how many times did you teach them that one?"

"Ok, I'm done."

He stopped the tape and pressed the rewind button.

"What are you going to tell the Olds?"

"Just that we are going on a back-packing trip around the world. We told James' family and everyone at work that we were going to Israel. We said we wanted Christmas in Bethlehem to explain why we were leaving before Christmas."

"Oh, very smart, and the little disagreement they had with the Egyptians and Syrians six weeks ago is supposed to reassure them that you'll be safe is it?"

"Well we'll just tell them we have cheap tickets to go to Australia. The point is we'll be gone for at least fourteen years and probably more than twenty. We need you to tell them the truth after we have gone. As I said the tape will help."

He pressed the play button and the tape began to replay Sam's words.

"Seems ok," he said.

There was a brief knock at the door before Fran stepped into the room leading the Inspector and his sergeant behind her.

"Don't get up," said the Inspector. "I believe Sergeant Hodson has your details young lady."

"Yes, my brother and I share a flat in Highgate," she answered.

"I'm at Warsash College at the moment, down near Fareham. I came up the A32 through Wickham."

"And you arrived at ten thirty?" said the Inspector expecting confirmation.

"No, I arrived at ten. James and my sister arrived at ten thirty."

The sergeant flipped through his notes and nodded to the Inspector.

"Could I have your address please James?" asked the sergeant.

"37 Setthorns Road, Sway, Lymington, Hants."

"Post code?"

"SO41 6AG."

"Telephone number?"

"Sway 324."

"And none of you saw anything unusual this evening?" asked the Inspector.

We all looked around at each other shaking our heads.

"Well we will leave you to your music. Thank you for your time."

The sergeant followed the Inspector back down the stairs closing the upstairs door behind him.

"That could have been worse," I said.

"He just wants to get home," said Kevin.

"Who?" asked Sam.

"Chief Inspector Plod Connolly, who do you think?"

Shall we go and help the Olds get cleared up then?" I suggested.

"It feels a bit weird hearing someone else call them that," said Kevin.

"Sorry, can't help it. Its Sam's memories," I replied.

"Come on you two, let's go down and see them. That's what we're here for," said Sam.

# THE BAD AND THE UGLY

Sam led the way downstairs to the bar thinking her parents would be alone; we were surprised to see Inspector Connolly and Sergeant Hodson still there, sat at a table in the bar looking through the sergeant's notes.

Sam ignored them and set about wiping down the tables. Her mother had already cleared the last glasses and her father was using the time to restock the bar.

"Well gentlemen, it appears we're all done down here and would like to lock up if you've quite finished," said Pete.

"Yes of course you do, come along Sergeant. We must let these people get some rest."

"Seems my watch was right all the time James," he said, without divulging the relevance.

He handed back the notebook his Sergeant and rose from the chair, leading the way out. The uniformed officer was now standing just outside the door talking to two other men,

Before the Inspector could step through the door, the two men had confronted him.

"Connolly?" said one.

"Chief Inspector Connolly," he answered indignantly.

"Lyons," he said showing the Inspector his card and returned it to his pocket without showing it to anyone else. The Inspector stepped back inside and allowed them in. "This is my colleague Evans."

"Good evening Chief Inspector, Raymond Evans," said the second man offering his hand.

Like his colleague, Evans showed the Inspector his ID card and put it back in the inside pocket of his jacket.

"I'm very sorry Mr and Mrs Cooper, it appears my colleagues would like to ask some more questions if you don't mind," said the Inspector.

"Yes we bloody well do mind," said Fran, "It's late and we would like to get to bed."

Pete patted her on the arm to calm her down but said nothing.

"I'm afraid we've flown in specially to take charge here, so if you would bear with me for just a little while I would just like to establish what information the Inspector has," said Lyons.

He was more abrupt than his colleague who seemed to have a constant grin on his face.

"Bloody cloak and dagger brigade!" said Connolly.

I wasn't sure if the Inspector had spoken the words quietly or I had heard his thoughts, but it reminded me of the two men in blue suits I had seen on Parliament Hill. I knew as soon as I had made the connection it was them.

"Come on then Sergeant, let's not keep everyone waiting. Show the gentlemen your notes."

The sergeant offered his notebook to Lyons, but it was Evans who put out his hand to take it. He fingered his way through the pages then skipped back showing the first page to Lyons, then turned the pages back to the point is forefinger had marked without saying anything.

"Samantha Cooper I presume," said Lyons looking at Sam "and Mr Cummings," turning to me. "Is there somewhere we could talk in private?"

"What is this all about?" asked Fran.

"Just some routine questions," said Lyons.

"About what? I think we are entitled to know what about before you start questioning our daughter," Fran persisted.

"Connolly!" snapped Lyons.

"I'm afraid my colleague from the government has the power to make life extremely uncomfortable for all of us unless we cooperate Mrs Cooper," said the Inspector.

"You mean he's not even a police officer?" she asked with a raised voice.

"No, I am the senior police officer here," said the Inspector. "As I said, these gentlemen are from the government."

Pete pulled Fran towards him fearing that the men were actually Customs and Excise men who could cause his business serious damage, if only by making a nuisance of themselves.

"Do you or James have a problem talking to these men," asked Pete.

"Of course not Pops" she answered. "Let's go upstairs to my brother's room," she suggested.

Sam led the way through to the end of the bar and up the stairs to the bedroom. Sam and I sat on my bed and Evans sat down on Kevin's facing us. Lyons remained standing examining the contents of the bedroom.

"Do you mind if we turn off the music for a while?" asked Lyons.

The Pink Floyd album had been left playing when we left the room and was now just an annoying ticking sound as the stylus hopped around the innermost track.

"Of course not," said Sam lifting the stylus off.

"You live in Highgate Miss Cooper is that right?" asked Evans.

"Yes, with my brother as we told the sergeant."

"Could you tell me when you were last there?" asked Lyons.

"Yes, I was there this morning before I left for work."

"And what time would that be?" asked Lyons.

"Around eight why?"

"And where do you work?" he asked, ignoring her question.

"I did work at British Petroleum in Moorgate, but today was my last day."

"Oh, so you have a new job?' asked Evans.

"No, James and I are going to do some back packing."

"Oh really? Where?" asked Lyons.

"It's a world trip but we will be starting in Australia."

"Very nice. So, could you describe your movements since you left work?" he asked.

"Well it was my last day at the office, I left there at three, I caught the tube to Waterloo and then the train down to Sway, where James lives. James and his parents picked me up at the station and his father drove us to James' prize-giving. James' brother John picked us up just after nine and drove us here. We arrived about half ten."

"*About* half ten?" asked Evans.

"It was ten thirty," I said defensively. "I checked my watch when we arrived, I told the Inspector."

At what time did you arrive at the station?" asked Evans.

"Six thirty," she answered.

"And you left the prize-giving at...?" he prompted.

"At a quarter to eight," she answered.

"Have you been in London all week?" asked Lyons.

"Yes, it was my last week."

"Thank you. James could you tell me your movements this week?" he asked.

"Well I was at home early in the week. I did some work with my brother on Monday I think. Saw him again on Tuesday and got the train up to stay with Sam on Tuesday evening. I spent the rest of the week at her flat. I went this morning to see my parents and get ready for my prize-giving."

"Thank you. And the uniform you are wearing, that's not a Royal Navy uniform is it?" he asked.

"No, I work for B.P. too. At least I did. I had an accident in the Middle East last month and I have decided to take some time out to consider my future. Captain Le Fevre has given us both six months to decide if we want to continue working for B.P."

"Bad accident then was it?" asked Evans.

"Well it could have been. I was lost overboard joining my ship at night and found with spotlights three miles behind the tanker half an hour later."

"Very lucky," said Lyons.

"Where was this?" asked Evans.

"Off Ras al Khaimah, in the United Arab Emirates."

"Yes, I know where it is. When was that?" he asked.

"Wednesday the 14th of November, the same day Princess Anne got married, around 8pm."

"You didn't lose your uniform then, when you were in the water?" he asked.

"No, I was wearing my suit. I lost that."

"Lucky you didn't lose your passport then eh?" Lyons interrupted.

"Sorry?"

"Well you're off travelling, again aren't you?" asked Evans.

"Yes."

"When do you plan to leave?" he asked.

"Sunday," I answered looking at Sam.

How could I have been so stupid? Knowing we were never going anywhere except Erato I had never considered the need for a passport. I had lost all my identification documents, nobody had considered that, but then I hadn't told anyone; Haji must have told his bosses at Grey MacKenzie because my trip to the Consulate had been arranged. I hadn't given it a thought since then.

"So, you've got your tickets and your visas?" asked Evans

"Is this yours?" he asked, reaching down to pick up my small case.

"Yes," I said.

"Do you mind?" he asked, shaking it in his hand to assess the weight.

He didn't wait for an answer; he emptied the contents onto the bed. My bomber jacket, a pair of jeans, a couple of shirts, socks, shoes and underpants were all the clothes I had brought. He rummaged through the smaller items and photos and picked out the shiny black moon rock.

"What's this?" he asked, examining the black rock.

"Just a stone I found on the beach. Coal probably, it may even be a bit of hardened tar. Who knows?"

He tossed the moon rock to Lyons and picked out my Tarot cards and was about to open the box.

"Do you mind? They are very precious," I said.

He ignored my protest and tipped the box upside own, letting the cards fall into a heap on Kevin's bed

"Not much for a world tour!" said Lyons.

"The rest of his gear is at my place. We'll pick it up tomorrow night when we go back to London," said Sam interrupting.

"Yes of course, silly of me," he said.

"Why the rush to get away?" asked Evans.

"We're both tired of boring Christmases here in England. It's not as exciting as it was when we were children," answered Sam, before I could speak.

I was very conscious that we were digging a big hole for ourselves and reluctant to give away any more damning information.

Lyons continued nosing around the bedroom and picked up the microphone giving it a small tap. There was no sound, so he placed it back beside the stereo system and looked down at the record to examine the label.

"Sing along to this stuff do you?" he asked.

"It's my brother's not mine," answered Sam.

I realised with dread that his eyes now moved down to the tape deck. Kevin had not removed the cassette containing everything Sam had explained, it was still inside the cassette recorder.

Lyons pressed the play button and hearing Sam's monologue, sat down beside Evans and listened to Sam explain our first meeting then go on to detail my accident and my first meeting with Victor. She went on to touch on our bedroom encounter and Lyons stopped the tape.

"Well I don't think we need to listen to that right now. Have your parents heard this?" he said,

"No just my brother," said Sam.

I felt a glimmer of hope expecting him to say he would be back in the morning.

"I'd like you both to come with us so that we can discuss this in more detail. There seems to be a few details you left out about your movements that I would like to know about," said Evans.

"Where do you intend to take us?" I asked.

"Back to our office," said Lyons.

"How long will we be?" asked Sam.

"Well that depends on how cooperative you are," answered Evans.

"We have things to do and a plane to catch on Sunday," said Sam.

"Oh, so you do have your tickets then," asked Lyons.

"Yes, they're at home in Highgate," said Sam

"And what time are you flying?" asked Evans.

"Two o'clock," answered Sam.

"Who with?" asked Lyons.

"James!"

"I meant who are you flying with?"

"BOAC," I answered.

"Well we can check that out very soon; and while my ugly colleague here does just that, perhaps I could see your passports?" said Evans.

He was right, Lyons was not a good-looking man, but there was a meanness in Evans, his contempt for my cards was cruel and unnecessary.

"I did lose mine, in the Gulf. I completely forgot, I have never flown until I went to Dubai. I will have to get an emergency replacement," I said.

"That would be on Monday then, the day after you fly?" asked Lyons.

"We'll just have to postpone the flights," said Sam. "Who are you and who do you work for?"

"We work for the Ministry of Intelligence, and I'm afraid you won't be going anywhere until we sort this thing out. Now I would like you to come with us to talk about how you really got here; you can come willingly in which case I will give you time to say goodbye to your parents, or I can ask Inspector Connolly to arrest you. Which would you prefer?"

"We'll come with you," I said trying to avoid as much stress as possible for Sam's parents. I realised it would only take them minutes to pull our accounts to pieces and besides they now had the tape.

"Bring the brother up. We'll take him too since he knows what's on the tape," said Evans.

Lyons left the room without a word, to fetch Kevin.

'What was I thinking letting Kevin record that damn tape,' thought Sam.

'How could you have known that they would find it? I answered silently. We need to let Victor know what is happening. I will try to contact him,' I said silently.

'Victor, if you can hear me we are being taken by men from the Ministry of Intelligence. We don't know where they are taking us yet or how long they will hold us.'

"Is there anything you want to take with you?" asked Lyons.

"I will need some things from my bedroom," said Sam.

"Off you go then, come straight back here. You have two minutes."

I started to repack my belongings into the rucksack.

"Can I have my stone back?" I asked.

Evans shook his head.

"I think we will hang on to it for the time being," he said.

'Do nothing until you hear from me. Tell them as little as possible about Victor and the other visitors. Say nothing about our knowledge of the bases on Mars and the moon. I will not leave you behind.'

Victor's thoughts reached us both clearly.

Kevin came in with Lyons close behind, and Evans waved the cassette in front of him.

"We'd like to take you along with your sister and Cummings here, for a little chat. They've agreed to come voluntarily rather than upset your mother by arresting you all. Are you going to come along willingly, or do I get Connolly to put the cuffs on you?"

"How long is this going to take?" he asked.

"Let's just see what we come up with eh?"

"Well where are you taking us? I have to be back at college on Monday."

"Shall I have Connolly come up here now?'

"Okay! Okay! I'll come! Do I need to bring anything?"

"Whatever! It's up to you!"

Kevin put a few pieces of clothing into his bag which still contained most of what he'd brought up for the weekend.

"Ok let's go," said Lyons.

"What about Sam?" I asked.

"We'll wait for her downstairs," said Evans.

Sam was already giving her mother a hug when we reached the bar. She was trying desperately to conceal the tears on her face. Neither of us knew if we would see them again before we left.

"Where the hell are you taking my kids?" shouted Fran, with Sam still in her arms.

"We'd just like a chance to talk through some information that may help us understand what happened here tonight. They have volunteered to come and help us," said Evans.

"That's right Ma, it's no sweat really. We'll be back in the morning, well sometime tomorrow," said Kevin.

Inspector Connolly handed Pete a card with his contact details on it.

"You can call me if you need to contact them," he said.

Sam gave her mum a kiss and then gave her dad a big hug and a kiss.

"Love you both," she said.

"I'm sorry about this," I said.

"If my baby is in trouble because of you..."

"It's not James Ma," interrupted Sam.

"Well it seems pretty bloody strange to me!" said Fran.

"They'll be fine," said Pete trying to reassure her.

"You're no bloody use to anyone, letting them take our kids away!" she snapped.

"Ma they just want to ask us some questions, no one has done anything wrong," said Kevin.

Kevin gave his mother a kiss and nodded to his father and we followed the Inspector out of the door.

# THE MILITARY

The empty car park was dominated by the presence of a dull green painted helicopter, which appeared to be owned by the United States Military. Apart from the Stars and Stripes and the letters USAF on the side, there were no other markings on the aircraft.

"Hey a Bell UH-1 Huey!" said Kevin.

"You know your aircraft," said Lyons.

"Just get in and fasten your safety belts," said Evans abruptly.

We climbed into the seats behind the pilot through the open side of the helicopter, Kevin got in the front seat, and I followed Sam into the row behind. Lyons and Evans wandered over to the cordoned area, just beyond where we had landed earlier that evening. They seemed to be discussing the findings of the investigation group, who had now lit the area with spotlights from outside the cordon.

Inside the Huey, the pilot and co-pilot wore unmarked olive-green fatigues and helmets that matched the colour of the helicopter.

"I never thought I'd get to fly in one of these," said Kevin, obviously excited by the prospect.

'Kevin, say nothing now,' said Sam silently. 'When they question you just tell them you know nothing except what was on the tape.'

'No wait a minute,' I said continuing the silent conversation. 'Perhaps we could use the tape as an elaborate hoax, a precaution, in case anything happened to us while we were away backpacking.'

'Good idea. If we all tell the same story they won't be able to dismiss it,' answered Sam.

Kevin shook his head, I sensed him trying desperately to convey his thoughts, but neither Sam nor I could understand what he was trying to tell us.

'What if they use a lie detector or a truth drug?' I thought, and Kevin nodded in agreement.

'Well if they do there's nothing we can do except to try to believe what we are telling them is true. Kevin, you can't be certain what we told you was true, can you?' she thought. 'So, you can tell them you don't know anything. At least it may give Victor time to get us out of this.'

'Sam, is there anything wrong with your alarm clock? I set my watch to it on Wednesday morning and my watch is fifteen minutes fast.'

'The clock is fine, I set it fifteen minutes fast to make sure I get to work on time.'

'That means we landed at ten thirty, the same time we said we arrived, which was actually ten fifteen.'

'That's ok, we still arrived before the ship landed.'

'Yes but also fifteen minutes after Kevin and an hour and a quarter after leaving home.'

Lyons and Evans returned to the Huey and climbed in beside us, shutting the side door as they did so.

The pilot started up the engines and the rotor began to spin slowly.

"Where are we going?" asked Kevin.

"Not far," said Evans.

Lyons leaned forward towards the pilot, presumably confirming the destination. As the rotors began turning faster and faster, the swirling sound they made became something akin to rapid machinegun fire. Eventually the helicopter lifted at the back and then slowly rose into the air, rotating slowly on its axis as it climbed.

No one spoke, it would have been easy to fall asleep but for the noise and vibration. It was definitely the most unstable form of transport I had ever experienced; the noise was incredible and the vibration from the engine and the rotor shook the whole aircraft. There was no comparison with the speed, silence or stability of Victor's ship.

Sam put her head on my shoulder and did her best to sleep, while Kevin tried desperately to see the ground below us and work out where we were headed.

'Do you know what direction we are headed in Kevin?' I asked silently.

He wobbled his head discretely in the Indian fashion, which I took to mean something between yes and no.

'North?'

He nodded.

'How fast do they fly? Two hundred knots?'

He shook his head, keeping his movements as subtle as possible.

'More?'

He shook his head again.

'A hundred and fifty?'

He wobbled his head again.

'One hundred?'

Another wobble.

'A hundred and twenty-five?'

He nodded.

'Victor, if you can hear me, I think we are headed north from Chawton doing around a hundred and twenty-five knots.'

'I'm working on it' he replied.

# CROUGHTON

Itimed the journey at just over thirty minutes, but I could not be certain how fast we were going or which direction we had taken.

'Victor we have landed,' I said silently.

'You are at RAF Croughton,' he replied.

'The helicopter is American.' I responded.

'That will be USAF Croughton then,' he affirmed.

The Huey landed softly on a tarmac landing square, well-lit with flood lights at each corner. The noise and the vibration eased off as the pilot killed the engine. The rotor began to slow above us, and Lyons got up and opened the doorway.

"This is a high security military base, stay by my side at all times and stop immediately if asked to do so. They shoot people who shouldn't be in here," warned Evans.

He jumped out of the helicopter and beckoned us to follow.

"Out you get and keep your head down," he said now standing on the tarmac with his head and shoulders hunched.

Kevin jumped down first, I followed, turning to help Sam out, then Evans followed Sam. We scurried off towards a large building beside which flew the two flags; the Stars and Stripes, and a second confirming that we were at USAF Croughton. We followed Lyons around the building past a number of wooden huts and eventually entered an underground bunker through a large steel doorway.

Inside the bunker there was a small guardroom manned with four uniformed guards. Lyons approached them while Evans kept us out of earshot.

"Are you guys American?" said Kevin.

"I'm Canadian, Lyons is a Brit, we work here with our American allies," said Evans.

"This is an American base then," said Kevin.

"It's a shared base between the RAF and the US Air Force," answered Evans.

Lyons stepped back with a collection of badges. He handed one to Evans and then held out the others for us to take.

"Wear these at all times, without it you're just a target," said Lyons.

Our badges were bright yellow and simply read 'CIVILIAN DETAINEE' written in blue letters; theirs were pale green and read "SECURITY LEVEL 4' in black letters, with photographs, in both front and profile views. Our badges were printed on both sides and attached to long neck chains.

Lyons took us through a set of security doors by sliding his ID tag through a card reader and then entering an access code on a push button panel. He led down the long corridor to an elevator at the far end.

Once again, he repeated the security process, and the lift door opened. Inside there were seven lower levels, each had a slot beside it for the security tags. Lyons pushed his card into the second slot and pressed the corresponding button. The lift appeared to descend quickly but it took time to reach the second level, which suggested that the floors were likely to have high ceilings or separated by layers of earth or some other building material.

The lift opened, and we followed Lyons through several doors until we met two more uniformed guards. One checked the badges of Lyons and Evans.

"Empty your pockets. We'll need your bags, jewellery, watches, belts, handbags, wallets, caps, ties, belts and shoe laces," said Lyons.

We handed over our belongings one at a time and the guard put them all into large plastic crates, which he then took into the guard room. We were then allowed to pass accompanied by the second guard. Once passed the guarded door we stopped outside another open door.

"You, in there," said Evans to Kevin.

Kevin stepped into the cell and the guard closed and bolted the door.

We moved on down the corridor past two more cells and stopped at the third door. Lyons looked at me and shook his head towards the door urging me in. The door closed and was bolted from outside and I heard the group carry on down the corridor and finally Sam's door was bolted.

'Are you ok?' I asked Sam silently.

'Yes, I'm fine. At least I can get some sleep now.'

The sound of footsteps grew louder as they passed my door.

'Kevin if you're ok, ask them for some food.'

"Hey, any chance of something to eat?" shouted Kevin.

There was no acknowledgment from the men, the steps faded away and the door closed leaving us in silence.

There was a bed on one side of the cell, with a pillow and a blanket folded at one end; in the far corner a toilet and washbasin, and above them a camera. I looked around and realised there was a second camera in the opposite corner. I could hear the air blowing through the vent in the ceiling above.

'I am going to try and get some sleep ok?' said Sam silently.

'Me too,' I said. 'Kevin, try to get some sleep, I'm sure they will be back to continue with our interrogation before long.'

I took off my jacket and laid it at the bottom of the bed. Tired and hungry, I kicked off my laceless shoes and collapsed onto the bed, threw the blanket over my body, and put my head on the pillow. I heard a noise in the corner of the room and noticed the cameras move around to focus on the bed. I closed my eyes and said goodnight to Sam.

'Good night Bear,' thought Sam, 'I love you.'

'Good night Sprout,' I answered using Kevin's epithet for her, 'I love you too.'

'Think of another one, I hate sprouts, I've always hated sprouts, that's why he calls me Sprout.'

'I know silly. Love you Princess.'

'Better.'

# INTERROGATION

I was woken by the cell door being unbolted. Lyons opened it and stepped in before I could raise myself. I had no idea how long I'd been asleep.

"Follow me," he said.

I tried to communicate with Sam but there was no response. Either she was asleep, or they had already taken her while I slept.

We walked back through the guarded door to the elevator. This time Lyons inserted his card into the third slot and we descended to the floor below.

He led me through a warren of corridors to a heavy metal door. When he opened it, I could see four similar doors, two on each side of the corridor. We entered the first door on the right, it was an interview room, darkly painted and containing a large desk. Above the desk, hung two lamps with dark shades that prevented any upward light. A microphone hung conspicuously between them. I chuckled inwardly noting the predictably large mirror on the wall behind the desk.

He stood between the two chairs on the mirrored side of the room offering me the single chair on the other side of the desk. Having done so, he left the room and closed the door behind him.

I stared at the mirror in front of me wondering how many faces observed me from the other side. In defiance, I decided to give them something to watch. I pushed my forefinger into my right nostril and cleared my nose, examined the contents, then rolled it into a ball and flicked it at the mirror.

It seemed to have the desired effect, because the door opened seconds later. This time it was Evans that entered the room, followed by another man carrying a mug of strong smelling coffee.

He sat down in one of the two chairs facing me, while Evans stood close to the door behind me.

"Good morning James, I trust you slept well," he said in an American accent. "Would you like some coffee? I'm afraid we don't have any tea in here."

He turned to the mirror and held up his mug then took a seat in front of me.

"I'd like you to tell me in your own words everything that happened to you since your accident in the Gulf," he said.

"Why do you want to know about my accident?" I asked.

"I want you to tell me all about Victor."

"Victor?"

"Yes, the Victor that Samantha refers to in her tape."

I laughed.

"That was a joke."

"A joke?"

"Well not really a joke, a story."

He sat in silence, staring blankly at me, waiting for me to speak again.

"Sam wanted to leave something for her parents in case anything happened to us on our travels. Just something to give them hope that we were ok."

"Very forward thinking of you," he said.

There was a knock at the door.

"Come," shouted the American man facing me.

A uniformed man carried in a tray, which he placed in front of me. On it was a mug of coffee, breakfast and a packet of paper hankies. He was waved away by the American, Evans closed the door behind him and took a seat beside his colleague. He opened the tissues and threw them back to me.

"Much more hygienic!" he said. "Eat!"

The breakfast consisted of scrambled eggs, several rashers of very crispy bacon and three small pancakes with syrup and cream poured over them.

I had no idea what time it was, it felt like the middle of the night. I sipped the black coffee, it tasted bitter unlike the Jamaican coffee that Sam made, so I opened the small plastic container and poured in the cream and added two sachets of sugar.

The eggs were over-cooked, and the bacon incinerated in comparison to the breakfasts I was accustomed to, but I ate them any way leaving the pancakes until I had finished the savoury part of the meal.

"Now, if I was to tell you we tracked unidentified flying objects in Highgate on Wednesday morning, in Sway last night at twenty-two hundred hours and thirty minutes later in Chawton, what would you say?" he asked.

"How many of these things do you detect?"

"And if I also told you that we tracked another object at the scene of your accident last month at the same time as you were in the water and on several days following in the vicinity of Ras Al Khaimah?"

I said nothing while I ate the pancakes giving me time to consider what I would say. When I had finished I sipped the coffee, which seemed more bitter than ever after the sweetness of the honey.

"Your statements last night are all wrong. The timing doesn't make sense. You said you arrived at 22.30, you checked your watch, but your watch was fifteen minutes fast, which means you arrived here at 22.15. You must have left your prize-giving no later than 20.45 real time to drive fifty miles across country roads in ninety minutes, fast drive and short prize-giving eh? And then you just happen to arrive at precisely the same time and place a u-fo is seen landing?"

"Ok! If you want to know where all this stuff came from, I thought I saw an alien while I was fighting for my life in the water. I also thought I saw a UFO in the sky above me, but I was scared, terrified and half out of my mind with panic. When the boat picked me up, I was delirious and ranting, but I calmed down after a while and forgot all about it. I told Sam about it when I got back, it was Sam who thought of using it as a story in case we got into trouble when we were away. The world is a dangerous place these days!"

He sat there in silence sipping his own coffee, so I took my mug and pushed the tray to one side. He took out a packet of cigarettes, lit one for himself, then threw the open packet on the table in front of me.

"No thanks, I don't," I said.

Evans sat silently watching me.

"You have a very vivid imagination James," said the American.

"Is that your real name?" I asked.

His badge said he was Ethan Gervais and the large number seven suggested that his security clearance was much higher than either Lyons or Evans.

"You can call me Gus," he said.

"Well Gus, that's all it was, imagination."

"Come now James! You are on an American Air Force base and you have concocted a story about bases on the moon and on Mars. We have only just ended the Apollo missions, so we can only conclude that these bases are Soviet."

"The bases don't exist! I made them up!"

"You made them up! I thought you said Sam made up the story."

"We both did! It was just her idea!"

There was another knock at the door.

"Come!" shouted Gus.

A uniformed man entered the room and handed Gus a folded note. He read it then showed it to Evans and then passed it back and waved the man away. The door closed, and Gus finished his coffee.

"We are picking up an electromagnetic disturbance emanating from this room. We believe it's coming from you," said Evans.

"How could that be?" I asked. "It must be something from outside."

"These rooms are designed with a dual Faraday shield, nothing gets in and nothing gets out."

I considered the device that Victor has inserted into the back of my neck and I knew that it aided my thought transmission. I also knew that Sam had one too.

"What is this disturbance?" I asked.

"I was hoping you could tell me that," said Evans.

Once again there was a knock at the door.

"Come!" shouted Gus.

Lyons stepped into the room.

"Well?" asked Gus.

"She's talking! The girl!" said Lyons. "She says she is of alien origin."

"We're coming," said Gus.

Lyons left the room closing the door behind him.

"Well it seems your girlfriend is being more cooperative than you are," said Gus.

They rose from their chairs and Evans opened the door.

"You know they are dangerous. They abduct innocent people and perform experiments on them," said Evans.

"That's rubbish!" I said impulsively.

"You think so?" asked Gus. "Are you so sure that Samantha is really one of them or could it just be a way to gain your cooperation?"

They left the room closing the door behind me and I realised I had given them what they wanted. In defending Victor, I had inadvertently implied that I knew more than they did. At the same time, they had implied knowledge of an alien presence on Earth.

I tried again to contact Sam, but I got no response. Perhaps the Faraday shield they talked of was indeed blocking my transmission outwards and hers or even Victor's inward. If Victor couldn't reach us, how would he find us?

I wondered how long I would wait there for a moment and my question was soon answered, Lyons came back and escorted me back to the cell. I tried to contact Sam and hearing nothing tried to contact Victor, but again there was no answer.

I could think of no way to count the passing of time, so I lay down, closed my eyes again and tried to sleep. I had just dosed off when the movement of the bolt woke me again and a uniformed man bought me in the biggest cheeseburger I had ever seen, surrounded by a plateful of thinly cut chips. There were sachets of ketchup, mustard, mayonnaise, salt, pepper and a plastic beaker filled with coke. 'Was it really lunch time already?' I had no idea but ate the food. This time I had no complaints about the cooking.

Hours went by and I was unable to communicate with anyone, even Kevin did not respond with a shout. I paced up and down the cell watching the cameras follow me backwards and forwards.

The bolt slid back on the door and another tray of food was about to be delivered but Evans called out and the uniformed man withdrew.

"James," he said standing in the doorway. It bothered me that he should call me by my first name having continually been so abrupt before. "I'd like you to sit down."

"Why?" I asked apprehensively. "Where's Sam, have you hurt her?"

"I'm afraid Sam is dead."

An uncontrollable anger welled up inside me and I rushed at him screaming.

"Noooooooooooooo!"

Both hands hit him squarely in the chest and knocked him flying backwards into the hall. His head smashed against the far wall and he collapsed onto the floor leaving a trail of bright red blood running down the wall.

The guard dropped the tray and pulled out his side arm.

"Freeze Mother," he shouted.

He smashed his left hand into the panic strip on the wall and a moment later his colleague burst through the door with his pistol stretched out in front of him.

The first guard overpowered me and knocked me to the floor. Before I knew what was happening my hands were secured behind me with a plastic band that cut into my wrists.

His colleague checked for a pulse on Lyons' neck.

"He's alive," he said.

"Don't move him!" shouted the first guard.

The guard's door burst open again and more uniformed men filled the corridor. I was lifted to my feet and pushed back into my cell. The door was slammed and bolted so I could see nothing of what was happening.

I lay face down on my bed and considered what they had said, I realised that Sam could not be dead. Sam had not yet entered the time warp and I knew that we had both returned to the day we first made love. 'If she was dead how could that be?' Victor had told me there was only one future, that our destinies were already written, but Paul had told me that as a Malakh I could change the timeline creating an alternate.

Moments later the door opened, and Gus walked in with Evans behind him.

"I'm sorry James that must have been a shock for you, I should have come myself," said Gus pausing for a moment. "Lyons is ok, he's conscious and the medic says he'll be fine, just a small cut on the head and a slight concussion."

He paused again.

"Boy you sure knocked the wind out a' him!"

"Where is Sam?"

"Come with me," he answered.

Outside the door, Lyons' blood still stained the wall and the floor, but Lyons and the other uniformed men had all gone.

We passed the guard door and the two guards were at their station.

"Get that mess cleared up," said Gus.

"Sir! Already in hand Sir," said one.

We entered the elevator and went back to the third-floor. This time we went in a different direction.

"We would like to take some pictures of you," said Gus, leading the way into a well-lit room with what looked like x-ray equipment, and a doctor or radiographer wearing a white coat with a heavy plastic looking apron. I had seen x-ray machines before, mainly for chest problems. Having contracted pneumonia and developed an abscess of the lung when I was two years old, my chest was often x-rayed when I had subsequent chest problems.

"What have you done with Sam?" I protested.

"I will take you to Sam as soon as we have checked you out," he said.

I allowed them to take their pictures deciding that my cooperation would lead to my being reunited with Sam more quickly. They stood behind the shielding as the machine clicked its way through the exposures.

It was just my head they checked, and I guessed that they were trying to locate the device that Victor had inserted into the back of my neck. I had to wait while they processed the film in a dark room.

"It's there," announced the doctor, "same position, in the pons varolii region."

The doctor pulled down the x-rays and handed them to Gus.

"Thank you Doctor."

"Now Gus," I said. "You said you would take me to Sam."

"Let's go and talk next door," said Gus.

We moved into the next room. It seemed to be a rest room for the medical staff. Gus and I sat at an empty table while Evans stood in front of the doorway.

You seem to have the same metallic device in your head as Samantha. We believe the aliens have inserted this into your brain as some sort of tracking device. Don't worry, you're safe down here," he said, trying to reassure me.

"We've seen this sort of thing before, but usually in a different location," said Evans.

"You're not telling me about Sam!" I protested.

Gus reached into his jacket pocket, pulled out a small cellophane bag, and threw it on the table in front of me. I scrutinised the tiny object and looked back at him in disbelief. It could easily have been a piece of scrap metal; I passed it back dreading that is had come from Sam.

"Follow me," he said picking up the small bag.

He led me to another room with glass windows at the back and what was clearly some kind of operating theatre lay beyond. On the table was the silhouette of a human body covered with green cloth.

I stood motionless at the door; Evans urged me forwards towards the table, then moved forward and drew the cloth back to reveal her angelic face.

I was paralysed with grief. Tears appeared instantly in my eyes and rolled down my face. I stood there unable to speak or move. My whole life had been destroyed in a moment. The future that I had been promised had been cruelly snatched away from me and the pain was unbearable.

I staggered forwards wanting to hold her in my arms. Her head was bandaged, and from the contours of the bandages it was clear her beautiful blonde hair had been cropped short.

I pulled the cloth down and she was clothed in a white gown. I touched her soft cheek, her flesh felt cold. Sliding my arm under her shoulders, I lifted her head and kissed her soft lips.

They stood in silence as I held her lifeless body in my arms. Tears rolled off my cheeks and down her neck dampening her gown.

Gus put his hand on my shoulder, but I continued to hold her.

"Why?" I asked sobbing profusely and dribbling like a baby. "Why have you done this?"

"She wanted it that way," said Gus, his hand still on my shoulder.

"No! That can't be true! He would have known! He would have saved her! Your lying, you killed her!"

"We're not murderers," he said. "We were trying to protect you. She insisted that she went first, she wouldn't let us touch you," said Gus.

"How? How did she die?"

"We don't know why she died. It was a simple procedure, we have done it many times. She simply stopped living."

I recalled how Victor's son has simply chose to end his life, but I could not believe she had deserted me.

I laid her down softly, turned away and walked out of the room. I saw Evans cover her then he and Gus followed me out to the corridor.

"I'm ready," I said, and they looked at me with puzzled expressions. "I am ready for you to operate on me now. Kevin has nothing inside him. He knows nothing except what we told him."

"We are not going to remove it under the circumstances. Not yet anyway," said Gus.

"As long as you're in here they can't reach you," said Evans.

"We need to inform Kevin," said Gus.

"No! I will tell Kevin," I insisted.

"Very well, if you wish. We will take you to him now," said Gus. "We will talk again afterwards."

He led me through the third-floor corridors to another interrogation room. Evans opened the door and Kevin was sitting at the table in an otherwise empty room.

I stepped in and the door closed behind me. Kevin saw the tears still running down my face and leapt from the chair.

"What's happened? Where is Sam?"

I tried to speak, but with every effort, the more my tears increased, and I stood there unable to move.

"Oh my God what have they done?" said Kevin.

I opened my mouth to speak but faltered, my lips moved but my first word went unheard. "... dead, Sam's dead!"

"What are you talking about? How can she be dead?"

"Sh'... she died on the operating table?"

"What operating table?"

"Sh' she wouldn't let them touch me. They wanted the device inside our heads; she wouldn't let them touch me."

"Are you crazy?" he shouted in disbelief.

I sat down in one of the chairs with my back to the mirror and dropped my face into my hands.

Kevin started banging on the door and it was opened in response.

Gus walked off down the corridor and Kevin followed.

Evans closed the door leaving me in the room.

# MESSENGER

I felt her presence.

'James.'

I looked up disbelieving myself, her voice was unmistakeable.

"Sam!" I said aloud.

Her image appeared before me, naked and transparent.

'Don't speak, use your mind,' she said silently. 'They are watching you, but they can't see me. Only you can see me, you are a Messenger.'

'You were dead!'

'Only my body is dead,' she answered.

I started to move but she stopped me holding up her hand towards me.

'Be still.'

'Why did you do it? Why did you let them do this to you?'

'I love you,' she said. 'How could I let them take you from me?'

Another rush of tears flowed down my cheeks, but I made no effort to wipe them away.

'James, I am not alone, my mother noticed, but didn't understand what she saw.'

'You are pregnant.'

'I *was* pregnant.'

'I chose to end my life and join with you not knowing I carried another.'

'But surely...'

'I was taking the pill, I don't know why but I stopped on Monday the sixteenth of November, the day I heard about your accident. Reg and I went our separate ways on the twelfth, the day I saw you off. We met later that day and I told him about my feelings for you.'

'It might be his.'

'No, I had my period, it began four days later, it can't be his, it is yours, ours.'

'But he died with you, he can't be alive.'

'Souls rarely enter the body of a foetus until eighteen weeks or more after conception, but your son had a spirit, it found me here in this dark place and entered our child's body. When I chose to die I had no idea.'

'Where is he?'

'He waits to speak with you. I must prepare you first. He is neither male nor female.'

'I know that spirits may be reborn as male or female.'

'No that is not what I mean. The image you see before you is a reflection of who I was. Before I introduce you to your son, you need to understand what it is you see. It is not the unborn foetus you will see, he bears the image of what he was in his last life.'

'Show me.'

'Come Little Bear. He has no name in his previous existence, just a serial number.'

'How can this be? He is not human, he is not from Earth.'

'He is from Earth; he is from the distant future, perhaps a million years from now, he is not sure.'

'Can he hear us?'

'Yes, I can hear you.'

'He has seen the future, our future.'

'Explain.'

'Those who brought me here are known here as the Tall-Whites, those like me are known here as the Greys. We were sent back through time to begin the creation of our sub-species. We are sexless workers, created not born, but our physical existence and our spirit is as Terran as you.'

'Our masters have created bases on the moon and on Mars for the development and production of a hundred thousand like me.'

'Why?'

'Because we cannot breed. The Earth is over populated, millions must die for our masters to survive. All this can wait. In death I have looked through the doorway to my future. I have seen myself with you, and with Sam as my parents, living on Erato. That is our destiny.'

'How?'

'You are Malakhi, we will join with you now and our thoughts will be hidden from all except you. You must leave here and take Sam's body so that we may be restored, they are of the Earth. You have the ability to travel through space and time, you can also move between timelines.'

'So I have been told but I do not know how.'

'The cards will tell you, they are the doorway. You will see that the cards show you your goal; if you need more, to know how to reach it, more cards will show you the steps. You taught me this in life, 'Identify your goal, work out how to achieve it, moving towards it, step by step.' You must get your cards back.'

'Time is short James, we must join with you now. Take us to Erato with you.'

She moved towards my body and I felt her life force merge with mine, the Grey followed her.

J@ We are one.

S@ You will take our spirits with you and restore my body so that we can become what we were.

G@ You, we, have the power to influence their thoughts.

# ALTERNATE

---

Gus opened the door; this time he was alone.

"What am I going to do with you?" he said.

"You will let us go!" I answered.

"And why should I do that?" he laughed.

"You know what will happen if you do not release us," I said. "You will return the tape to me and release us. Kevin will return to his parents and resume his life. I will take Sam's body and return with her to her world. Kevin will believe we have left together and he will prove the fact to his parents with the tape when the time is right."

"I can't do that," he said. "There would be too many questions if Samantha's death was leaked."

"Look into your mind and you will see for yourself what will happen if you do not release us."

I sensed the remorse in his mind being replaced by sorrow, grief and then anger. I focused on his worst fear and returned it to him, filling his mind with the future that lay before him. My conscience was clear, it was not a threat. I did nothing but allow him to live his own deepest fear, the future.

He left the room in panic and did not return. It was Evans that found me where Gus had left me, having been informed that Gus had left the base.

He took me back to my room and I was left there to sleep through what I assumed must be the night.

Sam was a part of me, and the Grey, our son to be.

J@ That was you Sam.

S@ Yes it was me. You could not feel his pain because of your anger. His son is dying.

512

J@ Yes, I see that now.

G@ You can save his son, have Gus bring him to you.

J@ How?

G@ By creating a different time-line.

J@ In the alternate time-line his son will survive, we will escape, and I will become your son.

S@ What happens in the current time line?

J@ In the current time line his son will die, you will both exist in me. I cannot die, so ultimately, I will escape with you, you have the chance to be born again here, or stay with me and return to Erato.

S@ If we are reborn here in the current timeline, I will have no memory of you, I will not remember this life; you would have to find me again, I would be different, perhaps male. Our son would die with me.'

G@ I too would not remember my previous lives, I would be born again into any naturally born species, or as a Grey; in either case I would have no recollection of my life as a Grey. I am aware now in death, that I once lived in many forms on this world. I must remember that when I am reborn.

J@ We won't know unless I try.

G@ Sleep now, I will remain while you dream.

* * *

I closed my eyes and drifted away, leaving my body. I looked back, and saw Sam's naked form follow me. We were free souls, just as I had been in the time warp. We raced back through time to our first coupling.

I was sitting on her sofa, she lit the small gas fire and then her candles, then two joss sticks in the hearth. She turned off the lights, sat down beside me and produced a hand rolled cigarette from her purse.

I watched as her spirit merged with her body and I merged with mine. She shook visibly, smiled at me and dropped the cigarette.

We kissed, my hand found its way on to her soft thigh and moved up under her skirt. We both stood in silence as I undid her belt. I slipped my hands inside her skirt slowly easing it over her hips, letting it fall to the ground. She reached up and slowly undid my shirt buttons, slipped her hands inside over my chest and pushed the shirt back over my shoulders.

Sam undid the buttons on her blouse, slowly moving from top to bottom; while I stood back savouring every movement. She wore a very pretty white cotton brassiere, which cupped her firm and beautifully shaped young breasts. I eased the straps down over her shoulders, then she slid her hands around her breasts and caressed her erect nipples. I moved towards her and slid my hands around her hips.

She kissed me again softly, then moved away from me and sat on the sofa, her eyes fixed on mine. She touched herself provocatively through her tights and knickers, and I felt her arousal. We knew what the other wanted, we savoured every moment, taking time to explore each other through sight, smell, touch, taste and thought. We were now on our knees and as I kissed her soft breast. She eased her tongue deep into my ear knowing it would stimulate me. So erotic was our simple foreplay, she bought me to climax before I removed my trousers. She undid my belt, eased off my jeans and underpants, and teased me with her mouth and tongue. She stood up and removed her black tights and white knickers together, then laid down on the floor in front of me. My eyes focused on her exposed womanhood, and as I moved towards her I was drawn, by her thoughts, then her scent, and finally the sweet taste of her essence, it was a pleasure I had not known.

We made love there, just as we had before, on the rug in front of the fire. The candle light flickered around us as we both climaxed together, as one.

Our minds exploded, but we were locked together so fiercely that it just went on and on, until we both collapsed exhausted, having shared both the physical and the emotional ecstasy.

We lay naked on the rug together, physically incapable, but our minds raced away together like two wild horses, running out of control together.

Eventually we regained our physical strength and began again as if without a break. By now the candles had burned out, the only light came from the yellow fluorescent light across the street.

The dim yellow light was replaced by the early morning sunshine. We had made love time and time again throughout the night, and finally we collapsed more completely than at any other time, both submitting to a strange sleep.

Together, we rose above our bodies. I looked down at the two of us lying on the rug, my body spooned hers as she lay with her back against my stomach, my arms were wrapped around her and her face turned back towards me at an almost uncomfortable angle, her eyes closed in a blissful smile, and my face in her long blonde hair. It was the most beautiful thing we ever experienced.

* * *

I woke in the cell feeling thirsty. I drank water from the tap and washed the tearstains from my face. If I had slept through the night, it would be Sunday morning and my time was running out. The Erateans planned to leave Earth on Sunday.

J@ Would Victor remain here searching for me if I had no contact with him?

S@ He will not leave without us.

Sam and the Grey were with me, but they were dormant and had no concept of time.

Within minutes breakfast was brought in, presumably prompted by my awakening being observed on camera. The arrival of breakfast reinforced the illusion that it was morning, though there was nothing to verify it.

The smell of bacon and fresh coffee was lifting, I ate greedily as though for the other two spirits sharing my physical existence.

I recalled the remorse in Gus's thoughts and considered what we had done. It seemed that he and his colleagues genuinely believed that the Erateans were a threat to our existence.

I had seen into Gus's mind and understood his fears.

The door was unbolted, and Lyons stood in the doorway. Somehow, I still associated him with Sam's death and my initial thought was to attack him again.

I realised that he was no more to blame for what happened than any of us. 'Did he have the remorse that I saw in Gus?' It was not for me to judge.

"I'm sorry about your head," I said.

"No, it was my fault. I should have realised how much pain it would cause you. I just didn't know how to tell you. This has never happened before, we are not murderers," he said. "Gus wants to see you again downstairs."

I followed him back to the elevator and down to the interrogation rooms on the third-floor. He showed me into one of them and closed the door. Minutes later Gus arrived and took a seat opposite me.

"I'm sorry about yesterday," I said, and his expression changed to reflect his puzzlement. "I didn't mean to frighten you!"

"How do you know I was frightened?"

"Look at me," I said silently. "Open your mind and feel my pain."

"How..." he started.

"Close your eyes," I said no longer using speech.

He hesitated but then closed his eyes and I saw his face contort. Tears emerged from his closed eyes, but they remained shut. He sat motionless, willing to share the pain of my loss and he continued to cry. His eyes opened, and he pulled a handkerchief from his pocket to dry his face.

"I want to help you, but I don't know how?"

I looked into his mind and knew that he spoke the truth. He had shared my pain in his own very personal way and in feeling my grief, he had looked ahead again, to the time when he would lose his son. He knew his son was terminally ill with leukaemia and had perhaps only weeks to live.

"Bring him to me. Go home now and return with your son," I said in silence.

"I can't bring him here!"

"Do you want your son to grow old?"

I knew I could heal his son. There was nothing to substantiate my belief, but I knew what it meant to me for my father to be cured, and I understood what it would do for Gus.

He rose from his chair to leave.

'I will need the cards, they are in the guard room, you will know them when you see them.'

He left, closing the door behind him. Lyons came in minutes later.

"Gus asked me to give you these," he said, handing me the cards. "He said he would be back in forty minutes. Would you like some coffee?"

"Any chance of some tea?" The coffee seemed to make me thirstier than ever.

"Ok, I'll get some brought over. I assume you will want milk?"

I nodded, and he left the room again closing the door.

There was a significant change in his attitude, his cold aggression had been replaced with kindness and consideration. The door opened again, and he sat down where Gus had.

"Where is Kevin?" I asked.

"He's in the cells," he answered.

"How is he?"

"He's pretty shaken up. It's taken longer for him to react than you and he is very angry. He won't eat. He threw his breakfast across the room and he won't talk."

I contemplated ways in which I might convince Kevin that Sam was ok.

J@ Perhaps I could erase his recent memory, but at what point?

S@ He would have to see us together to believe we had left as planned.

G@ We must wait until after Sam's body is safely aboard Victor's ship.'

"What do they look like?" asked Lyons.

His tone conveyed the envy within him, a sincere desire to understand. I knew what he wanted to hear but I could not give him he simple answer. I considered for a moment wondering what he would think if he saw an Eratean in his natural form.

"Do you have a dog?"

"A dog? No, why?"

"What makes a dog appear as an affectionate pet and a part of the family to one person and yet a fierce beast to another?"

"The teeth?" he guessed.

I laughed at his response and tried to rephrase my question.

"Do you have any children?"

"No."

"Well let's try anyway. I just gave my two nieces teddy bears for Christmas. Why do we do that knowing bears are powerful and dangerous wild animals?'

"Because they are cuddly," he said, with more certainty.

"What I am trying to say is that our perception of animals and indeed people is subjective. If you own a dog, you are much more likely to like all dogs. You can look into a dog's eyes and see love and affection in the whites of his eyes, you can see a faithful child who would gladly give his life to protect you. We give children teddy bears and when they grow up they retain the memories of their cuddly toys and view the real thing with associated affection, but either of these animals can become a life-threatening monster."

"So, what do they look like?"

"They look like human beings and yet they are different. Where you might see danger in these differences, I see only kindness and an outlook on life that I can only aspire to. I see friends that are willing to share their knowledge and their lives."

"Do you not feel you are betraying your own kind?"

I laughed again.

"I should apologise, I see only hatred and bigotry in your face and I know that I should not judge you, even worse, I have no idea why or what you are really like. Open your heart and your mind, see what is all around you. Do you travel?"

"Pardon?"

"Do you visit other countries on holiday?"

"Yes, I've been to Spain and to Greece and Austria."

"Why did you go there?"

"Well Spain and Greece for the beaches and the sunshine, Austria for the snow and the skiing."

"Did you mix with the local people, eat their food, learn their language, discover anything about their way of life?"

He never spoke again, and I could only sense confusion in his mind. I was trying to explain colour and hue to a man that could only see black and white.

I longed to see Sam again as she had been, and the knowledge that I would sustained me.

I had never lost anyone so close to me. My mother's mother died before I was born, and my father's parents both died when I was very young, before I was old enough to understand the finality. My mother's father died that summer but despite inheriting my middle name from him, I was never old enough to have really had a close relationship with him. I was too young to know him when he lived in Beaulieu, and in recent years he had lived with my aunt some distance away. Bobby, one of my childhood friends had died in a road accident, but even that was two years after our lives had taken us in different directions. Nothing in life had prepared me for the loss of Sam. Without the knowledge that Sam's spirit existed within me, I would have lost the will to live, trapped in eternity without her.

We were both silent when the door opened. Gus stood in the doorway.

"Leave us," he said, and Lyons did as he was asked.

Gus ushered in his young son from behind him and closed the door.

"This is Ethan Junior," he said.

'Hello Ethan, I am James,' I said silently, knowing they would hear my thoughts.

He was a small boy perhaps eight or nine years old but his pale-dry skin and wasted body made it difficult to judge. He wore an American baseball cap in an attempt to disguise his hairless head and held his father's hand tightly. I turned my chair around and sat down beside the table and they moved towards me.

'Your pa says you have not been well for a while,' I said silently, sensing the way he referred to his father.

He looked up at Gus and then back at me without any anxiety about the telepathy.

"I have acute lymphoblastic leukaemia and I am going to die," he said calmly, his chest wheezing as he did so.

I looked at his father who stood silently, making no effort to conceal his tears.

I sensed a hopeless fight for life within the boy that shamed me. My willingness to accept the end of my own life having lost Sam was pathetic in comparison to the strength in the poor dying child in front of me.

I took my cards from their case.

'Do you play cards?' I asked.

"Sure, I play Gin Rummy with my Pa."

'Can you shuffle?'

"Sure can!"

'Shuffle the cards for me,'

"Okay."

He struggled. The Tarot cards were longer than the ordinary playing cards he was used to, making it difficult for him to hold them in his small hands.

'You trust your Pa Ethan?'

"Sure! Pa loves me."

'Shall we let your pa shuffle your cards?'

"Sure, okay."

He handed his father the cards.

'Now, I need you both to think about what you want most. Don't tell me, just think about it, concentrate your minds. Okay?'

"Okay," said the boy.

His father nodded and began to shuffle the cards. When he had finished, I held out my hands and he passed them back to me. I spread the deck in my hands and offered them to his son.

'Now Ethan I want you to pick out one card; that card will show us what the future has in store for you. Don't show me, show your father.'

He selected a card from the centre of the spread and turned it towards himself to see what he had chosen, he showed the card to his father while I put the remaining pack down on the table beside me.

'I see you have chosen the Ace of Wands.'

He nodded.

'You have chosen life. Describe the card to me.'

"I see a hand holding a stick, a walking stick. The stick has small leaves on it.'

'Whose hand is it Ethan?'

"I don't know, it's coming out of a cloud of smoke. The hand has a glow around it."

'Very good Ethan. The cloud of smoke represents the energy of the universe; as you said, the hand glows with energy, the walking stick is drawing on the energy from the universe and it has become a living tree again. Do you understand?'

He nodded.

'Put your hands together around the card, the way you do in church when you are praying.'

He clasped the card between his hands.

'Hold them out to me.'

I took his hands, closing my own around them in the way Paul had taken mine.

I had expected to give something to the boy but instead I felt his strength being passed to me. Fortified with his energy I closed my eyes and felt it grow inside me, down my arms into his hands and body. I heard Gus sobbing in the hope that his son would live and opened my eyes. Ethan Junior's eyes were still open and staring into my own.

'Thank you Ethan,' I said, releasing his hands. 'Show me.'

He opened his spread his hands like an open book and the card was gone.

'Now you,' I said silently, offering Gus the deck spread in my hands.

He picked a card close to my right hand and turned it towards himself.

'Ah, I see."

He studied the card before him in silence.

Ethan turned to his father and Gus picked him up and held him on his left side, still holding the card in his right hand.

"I'm hungry Pa," he said, and Gus's eyes filled again with tears knowing that his son would not die. He pulled the boy's face to his own and kissed his forehead, sobbing while Ethan Junior sat in his arms breathing silently. Gus tried to speak but gave up unable to utter a word. He opened the door and left with his son leaving the door open.

# CORROBORATION

I sat in the absurdly deafening silence waiting for something to happen, staring into the mirror, half believing I could see through it or even melt it with my eyes like Superman, expecting Lyons or even Evans to return but no one did.

Several minutes must have past and the silence was uninterrupted, eventually I gave up my effort to see beyond the mirror. Stepping out into the corridor, I made my way back towards the elevator. It would be useless to try to get in without a cardkey and code, so I walked past it in search of Sam's body.

I found my way through to the operating theatre but there was no sign of her, her body had been moved and the theatre cleaned. I searched the other rooms and found the x-ray room and several unoccupied bedrooms. Beyond the bedrooms I discovered another room filled with a variety of surgical equipment.

An empty trolley that would clearly have been used for moving patients or bodies, stood ominously in the centre of the room. The wall opposite the door contained four large stainless-steel doors. I opened the first door and confirmed my thoughts, they were cold storage compartments for bodies, but it was empty. The cupboard contained four shelves and it appeared each could be pulled out like a drawer to enable access. Instinctively I was tempted to try the door on the far right next, but perhaps wishing to delay finding Sam's lifeless body I opened the next two in order and confirmed that each was also empty. I braced myself for a moment before opening the last door knowing that I was likely to find her body inside.

I was not expecting to find two covered bodies and the shock made me reel and stumble backwards wondering who the second body was.

J@ Have they killed Kevin too?

S@ Why would they? He had no device inside his head.

Her thoughts reassured me.

I pulled the first shelf out of the cabinet and realised the body was shorter than Sam. I tugged lightly at the cover revealing the top of the head.

G@ It is my body. They brought it here after I was shot trying to escape from another American base nearby.

His body, if intact, was less than four feet tall. I pulled the cover back a little further and revealed the face I recognised. Pulling the cover back further revealed his torso and the extensive exit wound of a high velocity bullet. His skin was the blue-grey colour of a dolphin and at first sight the texture and muscular tone seemed similar to the firm muscular body of a porpoise. There was no sign of hair on the head, face or body.

The eyes were the most significant feature, they were open and appeared to have no eyelids; they were shaped like large sunflower seeds. At first sight they looked completely black and slanting upwards away from the small almost non-existent nose, each eye was nearly three inches long and perhaps an inch wide. On closer inspection there was a very dark brown iris like structure and I realised that the pupils were not aligned, the eyes were looking in different directions.

There were no visible ears but there were small marks where the ear canal would have been. On closer inspection there seemed to be small holes covered with a small skin flap.

The chest and neck appeared to be too small to support the head in comparison to the human physique; the entire torso was firm and smooth. The hands were small, and each had three fingers and a thumb, longer by far than the human equivalent.

I replaced the cloth and pushed table back into the cold compartment without examining the lower body, being anxious to check the other body to see if it was Sam's.

This time the body profile seemed to be the right size. I slowly pulled back the cloth realising it was Sam the moment I saw her bandaged head. Her face looked so peaceful I reached out and touched it. It was cold, as cold as the chilling air spilling from the cupboard. I pulled the cover back further until I realised that she was now naked on the table, and the thought of her lying there that way was painful. I felt the urge to dress her and reached out for her hand. Her body was now stiff with rigor mortis and I realised it would not be possible to dress her until the condition passed.

I kissed her cold lips and tears ran down my face and dropped off onto her cheeks. I wiped the tears away with my thumbs, covered her with the cloth and pushed her body back into the compartment.

I wiped my own face with my fingers and then pulled out the alien body to continue examining it.

"What are you doing in here?" Lyons screamed, having discovered me bent over the alien body.

"Gus left me in here with Sam," I said innocently.

He walked over to the covered body and peeled back the cover, revealing the aliens head, flinching as he caught sight of it. He looked at me and back at the body uncovering the torso before pulling the cover right off.

"So, this is what they look like!" he said.

"You mean you've never seen this body?" I asked.

"Why would I ask you what they look like if I'd seen this one? This is way out of my league!" he answered.

"I assumed that you had access to the rooms on this floor."

He pointed back to the open door and I realised it was marked with the figure six above the security lock. It seemed odd to me that they would put a high security room on the floor with a lower security level.

"This is a level six security wing so technically neither of us should be in here."

"Where did he come from?" I asked.

"What makes you think it's male?" he asked. "It has no genitals!"

I looked for myself and he appeared to be right. The alien had much wider hips in proportion to its tiny torso, but its legs were as thin as its arms and there was no sign of any sexual organs. There was, what appeared to be a belly button and two dark grey nipples, which suggested that it had mammalian origins.

I lifted one of the thin arms, it was firm and muscular despite its looks.

"It has only four digits," I said, holding up the right hand.

Unlike Sam's body, there was no indication of rigor mortis. Perhaps the phenomena did not occur in this species. The body was as cold as Sam's so perhaps it had been there long enough for the condition to dissipate.

"I think we should get out of here," he said. "I have no idea what Gus was thinking of, leaving you here with all the security doors open."

He covered the body, pushed the body back into the compartment and closed the door. I followed him back to the elevator and he closed each door behind as we went.

The third-floor guard room was empty.

Everything seemed normal on the second-floor. The guards were at their station and the doors were all secure. He led me back to my cell.

"I need to find out what the hell is going on," he said. "Don't mention our little friend to anyone, I'm not supposed to have seen them and having done so I may have put myself in danger, even if it was only to find you. I'll be back."

The door closed; I washed my hands and face in the small sink before collapsing on the bed.

'Are you there Kevin?' I said silently but there was no response. 'Kevin, make a noise if you can hear me!'

There was a sudden noise from the corridor and I heard Kevin shouting and banging on the door.

'Kevin, relax! I am going to get us out of here. I'm not sure how but you are going home.'

\* \* \*

# BRASS

T he door opened, and Gus stood in the doorway with a uniformed officer.

"This is Major General Van Doubleday, USAF, he has just arrived from Richards-Gebaur Air Force Base with orders to take you all back to Missouri immediately."

"Get this boy cleaned up while we check out the rest of the cargo," ordered the General.

"Yes Sir," Gus replied. "Guard! Get this boy and his associate cleaned up immediately and get some clean fatigues sent down," he shouted.

The guard escorted me down the corridor to Kevin's door. He looked dreadful and he said nothing. The guard then took us both down to a shower room, opened up a locked cabinet and handed us each a towel and a small bag. Inside the bag was everything we needed to clean up.

I eagerly picked out the toothbrush and a very small tube of toothpaste and scrubbed my teeth, then shaved before using the shower. It felt good to be clean again.

By the time I got out of the shower, the guard had returned with two sets of olive green uniforms and two kit bags for our clothes. Apart from the underwear, which was new, the clothes looked well used, but they were clean and meticulously ironed. I had to turn up the trousers, but it was good to feel fresh.

I was putting on my shoes when Kevin stepped out of the shower. He still wouldn't talk, and I couldn't read his thoughts, I sensed his anger and his grief, guilt too, but his thoughts were too confused. I sensed he blamed me, at least in part for his sister's death.

The guard escorted us both back to our cells and locked us up again.

My door opened, and Gus walked in.

"Leave us!" he said to the guard, and the door was closed and bolted. Gus sat down on the bed beside me and looked down at the floor.

"I don't know what to do," he said softly, raising his head to look at me. "I had planned to get you all out of here before the General arrived, but there is nothing I can do now he's here."

"I was wondering myself how I could escape with Sam and Kevin," I confessed. "We must leave today!"

"In the last few weeks I have got down on my knees every day and prayed for my boy to be spared. I would have willingly given my life to save him. I would have sold my soul to the Devil if it meant he would live. If there is any way I can get you out of here I will do it. I made my promises to God and I'm willing to die to help you as you have helped me."

"You won't have to die, and you haven't sold your soul to the Devil, but I would appreciate your help to get Sam back to her world. I made her a promise you see, and I intend to keep it. And by the way, I could not have saved your son if he had not given me the strength."

"Whatever you say. All I know is that I would have lost him without your help. You have seen the other body," he said, changing the subject, "Lyons told me he found you there. I opened all the doors before I left with my son."

"What did you see in the card?"

"Yes, the card," he said, groping inside his pockets.

"This card," I said, holding it up, "the fifteenth card of the Major Arcana. The Devil."

"Yes, I looked at the card and saw myself and what I stand for, standing over you both, you and Sam, chained up like wild animals. I noticed the horns on your heads, something sinister about you both, frightening and different in some way, and I saw that the chains were loose around your necks. So I undid all the doors, I just thought you may be able to beam out of here or something if you found her."

"Not that I know of!" I answered. "The other body, it's not the same race as my friends!"

"What?"

"My friends are quite different, much more human looking than the body you have."

"My God you mean there are others here?"

"They have been coming here for thousands of years."

"Well Doubleday wants to take you all, including the alien body. I think it's actually the alien he came for! As far as I know these aliens have been here for about thirty years."

"What about Kevin, does he have to go too?"

"He knows his sister is dead and he knows everything you guys have told him which makes him dangerous. I'm sure Doubleday will want to take him too."

"Could you get him off the base if we had the chance?" I asked, hoping we might get a last-minute rescue attempt once we got to ground level.

"I could get you all off the base if it weren't for Doubleday. I would shoot him, but he's too well known around here and they would never let me get you off the base if I started shooting Generals."

"No one else must die, not even injured, it's not their way!" I said. "Can I see Kevin?"

"Yes, I can at least make that happen. Guard!" he shouted.

He stood up and banged on the door and it opened moments later. The guard stood away from it with his side arm drawn in readiness for another violent outburst.

"Put the firearm away son," said Gus, leading me down the corridor to Kevin's cell. "Open it!"

The guard opened the door and Gus allowed me to enter the cell. Kevin was lying down on the bed with his knees propped up and made no effort to move. I turned and nodded to Gus and the door closed. We were alone.

"Kevin, they want to take us to America, but I am going to try to get you out of here."

"I don't care what they do to me anymore," he said. "How can I face my parents knowing that Sam has been murdered?"

It was the first time I had heard him refer to them as such, and an indication of his grief. Both he and Sam always called them 'the Olds'.

"Sam wasn't murdered Kevin, it was an accident. We both had a small metallic transmitter inside our brain. Victor inserted them through the back of our necks, apparently, they moved. They thought that the Erateans were tracking us through these devices and they were trying to help us by removing them. Sam made them perform what was a routine operation on her first. I would have done the same thing for her and she knew that. There was no reason for her to die, she simply stopped breathing. She died of a broken heart."

"You should have made them take you!"

"If I had even suspected that they were going to attempt to operate on her, I would have."

He sat up on the bed and put his head in his hands.

"I've seen her," I said softly.

"So have I!" he said.

"No, I mean I've seen her spirit!"

"Oh come on! Why haven't I seen her then? You expect me to believe that after everything else?"

"I expect you to believe it *because* of everything else!" I answered. "I don't know why you have not seen her."

S@ Let me speak with him.

J@ Is that wise? He might think it's just an illusion of some kind.

S@ Let me try.

'Kevin, it's me, Sprout. I could not bear to lose James and be born again with no memories of who I was, who he was, and who you and the Olds were. It would be like waking up half way through my life with no memories of who I was.'

"Is that really you Sam?"

'Yes silly, it's me, your Sprout.'

"Why can't I see you?"

'Because it is my eternal spirit that talks to you. I am one with James, he carries my soul. See me with your heart.'

530

Sam's spirit left me, and he saw the same ghostly image I saw. He tried to touch her, but the image moved away.

He watched as Sam's image merged with my body again.

'Everything I told you is true. Now I must return to my home-world with James.

"Okay, but your body stays here, for Ma and Pa," he pleaded. You've taken her life, you're not taking her body too!"

"Kevin, Sam died here twenty-six years ago and was reborn remember. Her body and soul are linked somehow, and her soul belongs on Erato you know that!"

"I know, but she's dead and she died here!"

'Kevin, my body must go with me, Ma and Pa need only know what is on the tape. I will return one day, I promise.'

There was a bang on the door before it opened, Evans stood outside holding my kit bag over his left shoulder.

"It's time guys!" he said in his soft Canadian accent.

Kevin washed his face one last time and drank some water from the tap before drying his hands. He picked up his bag and we followed Evans back to the guard room where we collected the rest of our belongings. I put Sam's personal jewellery into her handbag, then put her handbag and her folded clothes inside her rucksack with everything else.

We passed through the main security area at ground level and the steel doors opened to reveal the cold dark December night. There was a fine wet sleet in the air being blown around and I shivered in the cold.

'Victor, we need your help now,' I said silently.

'Follow the General,' came the answer I so desperately wanted to hear.

"Any chance of a jacket?" I asked.

"Bring us three of your jackets and hats," Evans shouted to the guards through the doorway.

One of the guards brought out three jackets and three soft green military caps and offered them to Evans.

"You'll get them back later," said Evans, taking them one at a time and passing them to Kevin and me.

"That's better!" I said. "I thought I was going to die of exposure."

There were no markings on the uniforms or the jackets and I wondered if the guards were actually part of the US Air Force or perhaps CIA or NSA agents.

There was a noise inside the bunker as more guards pushed out two trolleys with a large metallic box on each. Lyons led the way out and Gus followed with General Doubleday. The boxes were sealed with security tags and labelled 'TOP SECRET – SECURITY LEVEL 7'. The boxes were very large, longer than the trolleys and about two feet square. Each one had gas cylinders on the top joined by steel pipe work to the box. There were also valves and gauges beside the cylinders. The trolleys were wheeled out and the huge caskets were loaded onto an open backed truck. Evans climbed into the cab beside the driver.

"In the back lads," said Lyons.

Kevin climbed up and took a seat beside Evans and after looking around to see where the General was going, I followed.

The General climbed into the back of a huge black American car. I saw Gus look over to the truck before climbing into the other side.

Lyons banged the side of the truck and climbed in beside me. The truck started up and we drove around the base and out into the exposed airfield. We pulled up behind a huge American transport plane and the truck stopped. Lyons jumped out and beckoned me to follow. The General's car pulled up beside the truck followed by another truck with more uniformed men.

"Get these caskets loaded," ordered the General.

The men from the second truck moved the caskets onto the plane and we stood waiting in the cold sleet.

"Sir! Cargo has been loaded and secured Sir!" shouted one of the loading crew.

"Leave us!" said the General.

"Sir! Yes Sir!" shouted the soldier.

The crew returned to the truck and drove back across the tarmac; the General turned to the young airman standing at the back of the plane.

"Prepare this bird for take-off boy," ordered the General.

"Yes Sir!" he responded, disappearing into the aeroplane.

The General walked over to where we waited.

"Would you join us Gus?" he said.

'We have very little time.' he said silently.

I realised that his appearance was an illusion.

Gus and I stood in silence as the General stood in front of Kevin, Evans and Lyons. The three of them stood trancelike in front of him for several minutes."

'It is done,' he said silently.

He had somehow erased the recent memory of Sam's death from their mind. The three of them wobbled slightly and looked around unaware of their surroundings, then seeing the General and Gus, accepted the situation.

"Goodbye Kevin."

I did not have to turn to recognise the voice of my lover, but I did. She wore the same fatigues as we did, her golden hair hung in a ponytail beneath her olive cap.

She walked past me touching my hand briefly and spun around to accept a small package from the General out of sight of Lyons and Evans. She continued without stopping and threw her arms around her brother.

"We will be rescued by the Erateans," she whispered into his ear, and placed the package into his hand. "This is for the Olds, play it to them when they need to know the truth."

Kevin hugged his sister and wiped a tear away from his face. I walked over and shook his hand before Sam let him go, then she turned to me and we walked towards the ramp.

"C-141 Starlifter," said Kevin. "I'd love to see the cockpit!"

"Gus, get this boy back to his parents ASAP," said the General loud enough for Lyons and Evans to hear.

"Yes Sir, I'll get the men to drive him back immediately. Have a good trip Sir."

"Drive! Like hell you will. Send him back in the UH-1, I think his folks are keen to see him sooner rather than later!" he shouted. "Thank you Gus. Look after that boy of yours," he added, then turned and followed us up the ramp.

The three of us stood and waved goodbye to Kevin and Gus as the tail doors closed much to the amazement of the other two. When they were out of sight, the two apparitions revealed their true form.

"Where is Victor? I asked, aware now that he had played neither role.

"Friendship, come," said Clay silently.

I turned to the figure still holding my hand.

"Friendship," said Kez, with a smile.

"How did you know Sam was dead?"

"Gus told the General," said Clay. "We improvised."

The engines began to spin up outside and the cavernous cargo bay vibrated. We made our way up to the flight deck where there were two uniformed figures in the pilot's and co-pilot's seats.

"This is Slobodan and Piotr, they will retain the appearance of Terran aircrew until we have lifted off.

Kez took the seat of the flight engineer and began checking the instruments.

"Sit," said Clay, gesturing to the small seat behind and between the two front pilot's seats.

"We are ready for take-off," said Slobodan.

Clay sat in the navigator's chair on the left of the cockpit and fastened his seat belt. I did the same with mine and the aeroplane began to move.

Piotr performed the communication with the tower while Slobodan manoeuvred the huge plane.

"How did you get this plane?" I asked.

"That was easy!" said Piotr, "General Double day has the authority to schedule the flight. It was just fortunate that nobody realised General Doubleday was actually spending the weekend in Florida with his wife."

The take-off clearance came from the control tower and Piotr throttled up the engines.

We sat in silence as the aeroplane accelerated down the runway and Slobodan lifted its nose into the air. We climbed to 30,000 feet for our journey across the Atlantic.

# INTUITION

The noise from the engines at full throttle was overwhelming, so I waited until Piotr levelled out at the end of the long climb and throttled back before even attempting to communicate in any way.

"Where is Victor?" I asked again.

"Victor has business elsewhere!" said Clay. "He asked us to act on his behalf to ensure you and Samantha were rescued."

"Sam is dead."

"We know, Juma also. Kez improvised, you saw what her Terran brother Kevin needed to see. Kez has checked the caskets; we have her body. It seems we have also been successful in obtaining an alien body."

"He's not alien, he's Terran, and he's not male, or female."

Although he said nothing about Sam's death, I sensed that all of them shared my pain. There was no need for me to discuss my grief. The sensation seemed strange, part of me felt that I needed to show my pain, the natural human reaction, as involuntary and uncontrollable as expressing pain after injury. I was being consoled before I had expressed my sadness and that was a new experience to me. Unable and unwilling to suppress it, tears formed in my eyes and ran down my cheeks. At the same time, I felt that they wanted to feel my pain, they almost hungered for the emotions and in return, they gave me hope.

"Juma decided he would contract the Immune System Virus to determine the effect on the Eratean body," said Clay.

"And it killed him?" I asked in disbelief, having understood from previous discussions that the virus could take ten years to develop.

"His body produced antibodies in response to the virus much like the Terran immune system only much faster. What is significantly different about the Eratean defence mechanism is that his mind knew that the virus had embedded itself in the immune system core. There was no way to eradicate it, he also knew that his death would destroy the virus within his body. Because we have developed a collective awareness, the infected body will actually destroy the virus by destroying itself in order to protect other Erateans from becoming infected. He gave me his knowledge and left for Africa."

"Africa?"

"Rather than let his death serve no purpose he went to South Africa and Rhodesia where the spread of ISV170 is worst, there he used his life force to cure young children suffering from other life-threatening diseases. With his life force spent, he simply shutdown his organs to prevent contamination of the Eratean people."

"He chose to end his life, the way Sam did," I said.

"He gave his life to prevent harm to his people. The decision would be the same for every Eratean."

"Why did he risk contamination if he knew what would happen?" I asked.

"In order to fully understand the virus, and hoping to identify a cure," said Clay.

"He needed to be sure and he could not ask another," said Kez.

"Sam asked me to take her body back to Erato. She said her soul must return to her world."

"Until her soul rests it will follow her body," said Clay.

"Can I go and see her?"

"The cargo bay is not pressurised," said Kez.

"I suggest you wait till we are on board our ships. Be patient, we need to get out to sea." said Clay.

I sat back and remembered my commitment to Václav; my Tarot Cards were in a large pocket on the side of my thigh. I took out the cards, shuffled them and turned over the first card considering who I was looking for.

The Two of Swords portrayed a young blindfolded woman holding a sword in each hand; the blindfold suggested confusion about perhaps about her life on Earth, behind her rocks suggested obstacles of some kind, the swords behind her perhaps a problem to be resolved, the waxing moon suggested a new beginning. I concluded that the young woman had some inkling that she was out of place, but she did not know how to find her way forwards; she was ready to learn the truth.

I drew a second card wondering where the young woman may be found.

The King of Wands portrayed a finely dressed king sitting on a throne floating in the sea. I dismissed the rest of the card because my immediate thought was an Island.

G@ Perhaps you are thinking too deeply. I saw a young blind Caucasian woman around twenty years old, just as you see an island.

I drew another card, XXI The World, the final card at the end of the Major Arcana.

J@ But what does it mean?

S@ A map?

J@ yes of course, latitude and longitude. Okay Swords North, the compass point; Wands South, the South pole; Cups East, the Spring; Coins West, greedy banks. First card direction, second card first digit, third card second digit, fourth card third digit, that should be enough, the same again for latitude.

I turned over the first; six of swords, three of cups, nine of cups, ace of coins.

J@ Thirty-nine degrees, ten minutes north.

I started again, longitude; eight of cups, two of swords, ten of swords, ten of cups.

J@ The tens must be zeros, there is only one zero, The Fool. Twenty degrees, zero minutes East.

"Kez, can you tell me the location of Thirty-nine degrees, ten minutes north, Twenty degrees, zero minutes East."

"Of course," she answered. "Just of the coast off Paxos in the Ionian Sea."

"Thank you Kez. Is there anything closer?"

"Well Antipaxos is about the same distance away, but it's only one and half square miles. Paxos is small, I'd say 5 miles long and a mile wide.

J@ How many blind twenty-year-old women do you think there are on Paxos.

S@ Not many.

J@ That is where Václav will find his daughter.

# CAPTAIN GIDEON

"Where are you going to land the plane?" I asked.

"We will ditch the plane in the middle of the Atlantic Ocean. Jenlong and Amulya will rendezvous with us when we are clear of the coast. They will check the area below for shipping," explained Slobodan.

They appeared relaxed with the idea of ditching the plane, so I didn't question it.

"What time is it?" I asked, checking my watch.

"20.22 GMT," said Kez looking at the instrument panel in front of her.

My watch showed the correct time and I noticed that none of them wore watches.

"What day is it?"

"Sunday the 9th of December 1973.

"Then the other Erateans are still here?" I said in anticipation.

"We are on schedule to meet at 22.00 as planned. We would not have left without you," Clay assured me. "We have all accepted Victor's request for assistance and will see the mission through to conclusion."

"We have company," said Slobodan pointing forwards to our left side. A USAF F4-D had taken up a position to prevent us from changing course.

"There are four of them." said Kez, "two on our right and another on our left flanking the lead aeroplane."

"C-141 transport Hotel Charlie Zeero Tree Uniform. This is Captain Francis C. Gideon Junior from the 48th Tactical Fighter Wing, RAF Lakenheath, Delta Yankee Six Fower Tree. I have been given orders to escort you back to USAF Croughton. Acknowledge. Over."

"Delta Yankee Six Fower Tree. This is Hotel Charlie Zeero Tree Uniform. Say again. Over!" Piotr responded.

"C-141 transport Hotel Charlie Zeero Tree Uniform. This is Captain Francis C. Gideon Junior from the 48th Tactical Fighter Wing, RAF Lakenheath, Delta Yankee Six Fower Tree. I say again, I have been given orders to escort you back to Croughton. Acknowledge. Over!"

"Delta Yankee Six Fower Tree. Captain Gideon this is Major General Van C. Doubleday, Deputy Chief of Staff, Operations Headquarters United States Air Force Communications Service. Negative. I say again. Negative. We are returning to Richards-Gebaur Air Force Base on important mission. What exactly is the problem? Over."

"Hotel Charlie Zeero Tree Uniform, this is Captain Gideon Delta Yankee Six Fower Tree, Sir. General Sir. I have orders not to allow you to continue your flight plan. Acknowledge. Over."

"Delta Yankee Six Fower Tree. This is General Doubleday. Well Captain you'd better be damned sure who's giving you those orders. In fact, when you find out who has given these orders, I want to speak to him personally. Over!" bellowed Clay in the General's voice.

'We need time to get out to the Atlantic before we ditch this thing,' he continued silently, 'I want deep water.'

'The real Doubleday must have surfaced, or they would never have discovered us. They will shoot us down if we don't turn back but that could be our opportunity, as long as they don't destroy the aircraft,' said Piotr in the same manner.

Forty minutes passed before there was any further communication from the fighters. They flew alongside us in escort until Captain Gideon broke the silence.

"C-141 transport Hotel Charlie Zeero Tree Uniform. This is Captain Francis C. Gideon Junior from the 48th Tactical Fighter Wing, RAF Lakenheath, Delta Yankee Six Fower Tree, I have orders not to allow you to continue your flight plan, and to use our air to air missiles if you refuse to comply before reaching our mission range. I must insist that you alter course now. Over."

"Delta Yankee Six Fower Tree. Captain Gideon this is Mayor General Van C Doubleday, Deputy Chief of Staff, Operations Headquarters United States Air Force Communications Service, your message is outrageous. I have urgent business at Richards-Gebaur Air Force Base. We are unable to comply with your request and will continue our flight plan. Acknowledge. Over!" said Clay.

Silence prevailed for what seemed like minutes.

"C-141 transport Hotel Charlie Zeero Tree Uniform. This is Captain Francis C. Gideon Junior from the 48th Tactical Fighter Wing, RAF Lakenheath, Delta Yankee Six Fower Tree. I say again. I have been given orders to deploy my weapons if you fail to alter course immediately and follow me back to RAF Croughton. I say again, I have been given orders to deploy my weapons if you fail to alter course immediately and follow me back to RAF Croughton. I must insist that you alter course now. I am commencing my turn across you now. Acknowledge? Over!"

"Delta Yankee Six Fower Tree. Captain Gideon, Negative. I say again. Negative. I suggest you reconfirm your orders. We will continue our current flight plan. Acknowledge. Over!" said Clay.

"C-141 transport Hotel Charlie Zeero Tree Uniform. This is Captain Francis C. Gideon Junior from the 48th Tactical Fighter Wing Delta Yankee Six Fower Tree. General Doubleday is currently at Luke Air Force Base in Florida. I am commencing my turn across you now. Your General Doubleday is an imposter. I say again. Your General Doubleday is an imposter. Over!"

The Phantom moved away and began the slow turn right across us, but we held our course in silence.

"He's re-joining his wing man," said Kez monitoring the radar screen in front of her. "They are manoeuvring into a firing position."

She had hardly finished the words when the crack of 20mm cannon fire raked across our left wing.

"We are losing hydraulic pressure on our port wing," said Kez.

"What is our position?" asked Clay.

"Fifty-seven degrees north, twelve degrees west," said Kez.

"And what is the depth of the sea here?" asked Clay.

"We are on the edge of the continental shelf right now, the depth drops away from two hundred metres to over two thousand metres Sir General Sir," she replied with a smile.

"That's good enough. They will need to refuel or turn back soon."

"C-141 transport Hotel Charlie Zeero Tree Uniform, this is Captain Francis C. Gideon Junior Delta Yankee Six Fower Tree. I am coming across your port bow now, please turn and follow me immediately or we will release our weapons. Over!"

"Push the nose down a little. Let's show them what they need to see before they do any more damage."

Slobodan dropped the nose and let the plane go into a slow descent, while Piotr gradually pulled back the throttle levers for the port engines, bleeding off some speed and giving the plane a yaw to the left.

"Perhaps a little smoke!" said Clay.

I knew what he intended. The F4 pilots were now confronted with the illusion of a growing stream of thick black smoke from the port engines.

"Mayday Mayday Mayday. Delta Yankee Six Fower Tree. This is C-141 transport, Hotel Charlie Zeero Tree Uniform. We have lost power in both port engines. I have a fire alarm. Shutting down both port engines. Activating fire extinguishers. Losing height at Too hundred, Too Zeero Zeero feet per minute. Position Fiver Seven degrees North, Wun Too degrees West. We have five souls onboard. Over," alerted Piotr.

Slobodan shut down the port engines and engaged the extinguishers as Piotr had transmitted.

"C-141 transport Hotel Charlie Zeero Tree Uniform, this is Captain Gideon Delta Yankee Six Fower Tree. I acknowledge your Mayday. I repeat. Acknowledge mayday. Insist you now make U-turn back to British coast immediately. I say again. Make U-turn back towards British coast immediately. We will alert US Navy to deploy rescue aircraft. We standby to escort you back. Acknowledge. Over!"

"Delta Yankee Six Fower Tree. This is Captain Carskadon pilot of C-141 transport, Hotel Charlie Zeero Tree Uniform. Negative. I say again. Negative. Captain Gideon. Have multiple hydraulic failures. Unable to make the turn or correct port yaw. Getting erratic response from rudder. Will not risk losing height by attempting a U-turn with flaps only. Will not, I say again, not attempt landing over land. Acknowledge. Over."

"C-141 transport Hotel Charlie Zeero Tree Uniform, this is Captain Francis C. Gideon Junior Delta Yankee Six Fower Tree. We have reported your situation to base and they will alert the nearest rescue services. I will escort you down to two thousand, Too Zeero Zeero Zeero feet, at which point I suggest you and your crew use your parachutes. The rest of my wing will turn back for Croughton when we reach maximum range, I have been ordered to follow you and ditch when I have seen you and your crew down."

"This is Captain Carskadon pilot of C-141 transport, Hotel Charlie Zeero Tree Uniform, calling Captain Gideon United States Air Force. Negative, I say again negative. We are carrying top-secret cargo and I intend to ditch in the sea in an attempt to salvage or destroy. Cargo must under no circumstances fall into enemy hands. Please alert rescue services and follow us down."

"Captain Carskadon, you are taking unnecessary risks with the lives of your crew. I suggest that all non-essential personnel leave the aircraft at Tree hundred feet. Over."

"Listen son! This is Major General Van C. Doubleday. You'd better be damn sure about the imposter State-side! You will do as the Captain says and alert the rescue services that we are going down together," said Clay in a patronising voice. "We are carrying top secret cargo which must be salvaged if at all possible. If we can keep this baby from breaking up there is just a chance we can do that. I want this operation kept strictly to a U.S. effort. Do not, I repeat, do not engage other NATO forces and that includes the British."

A few minutes of silence followed before Captain spoke once more.

"C-141 transport Hotel Charlie Zeero Tree Uniform, this is Captain Gideon Delta Yankee Six Fower Tree. Request you attempt to alter course Tree Zeero Too, increase your rate of descent to Fower Zeero Zeero feet per minute and maintain speed at Tree hundred knots. The USS Hammerberg is currently Fife hundred miles to our northwest steaming towards us."

"This is Captain Carskadon pilot of C-141 transport, Hotel Charlie Zeero Tree Uniform, calling Captain Gideon. I'll do my best, but I'm gonna have to compensate for this port yaw so if you could show me the way home, I'd be mighty grateful!"

"C-141 transport Hotel Charlie Zeero Tree Uniform, this is Captain Gideon. Follow me guys. Over."

He took up a lead position just ahead of us on our port as Slobodan rolled the plane around using the ailerons and pulling back on the stick, avoiding any use of the rudder, flying in a semi crab-like position, giving the impression we were headed straight for him, but actually flying alongside his fighter holding the same parallel course.

"This is Captain Carskadon pilot of C-141 transport, Hotel Charlie Zeero Tree Uniform. I am increasing my descent to Fower Zeero Zeero feet per minute. Maintain speed at Tree Zeero Zeero knots. Current altitude is twenty-six thousand three hundred feet, Too Six Tree Zeero Zeero. Acknowledge said Slobodan when the turn was completed.

"What now?" I asked.

"Now we wait till we get to ten thousand feet. When we get to ten thousand feet we will depressurise the cockpit, open up the cargo bay and bring Sam and the alien up here," said Kez.

"How are we going to get off this thing before we crash into the sea?" I asked.

"We won't!" said Clay. "We should convince the military that the aeroplane has gone down, and us with it. The best way to do that is to make sure it does sink."

"I'm missing something here!" I said, with a growing anticipation of what was going to happen when we hit the water.

"Don't worry, we will be safely inside an antigravity zone just like we have on our starships."

Clay smiled and pointed to a small spherical object on the floor behind the pilot's seats.

"What does that do?" I asked.

"*That*, is a graviton reactor powerful enough to take this and the USS Hammerberg into space if we needed to," explained Clay.

It took us forty minutes to descend to ten thousand feet, by which time we had flown another two hundred miles northeast into the Atlantic. Three of the Phantoms turned back for base, leaving only Captain Gideon's F4 maintaining position just ahead of us on our port side.

The cockpit pressure was lowered and balanced with the cargo bay and Clay opened the door.

"Follow me," he said.

I followed him back through the plane to the steel caskets that held both Sam and the alien.

"If you can carry Sam, I will carry our unfortunate friend."

I opened the casket and tried to lift Sam, but she was rigid with rigor mortis. I was unable to lift her in a manner that my respect for her demanded.

"Allow me," said Clay. He placed his hands under her and lifted her as easily as I could have lifted a bundle of daffodils. It was the first time I became aware of his immense physical strength.

I turned to the alien body now lying on top of the casket and managed to lift it over my shoulder without too much difficulty.

We made our way back to the cockpit and the two bodies were laid down across the Navigator's desk in front of Kez.

"Now we are ready," said Clay.

"C-141 transport Hotel Charlie Zeero Tree Uniform, this is Captain Gideon. The USS Hammerberg is now Wun Ait Zeero miles northwest. Please change your course to Tree Wun Niner degrees and maintain maximum height. Over."

Slobodan made the course adjustments and eased our descent back to two hundred feet per minute.

"This is Captain Carskadon pilot of C-141 transport, Hotel Charlie Zeero Tree Uniform. Maintaining descent at Too Zeero Zeero feet per minute. Airspeed now Too Zeero Zeero knots."

"C-141 transport Hotel Charlie Zeero Tree Uniform, this is Captain Gideon. I will guide you all the way to the USS Hammerberg. We will commence final descent for approach at Too Zeero miles from target. Over."

Twenty-five minutes later we began our approach towards the Hammerberg. We changed course again and increased our descent to ditch as close as possible to the ship.

Clay placed a square metallic looking key into the gravity reactor, then expanded the anti-gravity zone to the edges of the cockpit using thought control. Suddenly the constant shaking that I had become used to ceased. The fuselage still shook visibly but all sensation of movement ended.

"Let's open up what we can so that this thing goes down as quickly as possible," said Clay.

Clay opened the cargo bay doors at the tail of the aeroplane from the Flight Engineer's desk, while Kez secured the cockpit door to the cargo bay.

The lights on the USS Hammerberg were now clearly visible in front of us, and I recalled the recent memories of the S.S. British Grenadier disappearing into the distance the night it all began.

"Lift the nose up as much as you can and make a sharp turn to port," instructed Clay. "I will neutralise the mass of the front fuselage and with hope the aeroplane will hit down hard on the tail and port wing."

I braced myself for the impact expecting to be thrown across the cockpit when we hit the water. Piotr slowed the airspeed to a hundred and fifty knots.

"C-141 transport, this is Gideon. Try to bring your nose up. Over."

At the last moment, Slobodan did as Clay had requested and the plane reared up and twisted back on the port wing, unbalanced by Clay's manipulation of its centre of gravity.

Piotr killed the engines and the plane stalled as the wing collapsed. The tail must also have been severely damaged by the impact, but our sensation of movement was unaffected. We all sat comfortably in our positions as if nothing had happened.

The fuselage rolled over to the right as the weight of the starboard wing overbalanced the wingless port side. Clay released the antigravity control over the front of the plane and the nose crashed down into the water. The fuselage continued its roll as the port wing sank beneath the water. The last light that I saw was the search light of the USS Hammerberg's helicopter, expecting to pick up survivors and perhaps even some of the undisclosed top-secret cargo.

Clay used the gravity reactor to increase the mass of the broken fuselage so that in seconds we were below the water surface and sinking fast into the depths of the North Atlantic Ocean. Darkness engulfed the cockpit, yet somehow, I was not just aware of everyone's presence, I could see them and the space around me even in the total blackness.

Above us, a search and rescue diver scanned the surface of the unusually calm sea above us, stunned by the speed at which we had rolled over and sunk.

Captain Gideon and his Navigator ejected from his F4-B at three hundred feet, into the dark sky above the Hammerberg leaving the unmanned fighter to crash into the sea beyond.

The helicopter pilot and observer clearly saw the rockets of the ejector seats lift the two men out of the F4, one after the other. They scanned the sky for the expected flares both airmen would have but saw nothing. The pilot waited for two minutes to be sure that a parachuting airman would definitely have hit the water and moved in to search.

Despite the buoyancy devices they wore both pilot and navigator had been sucked beneath the calm surface before they could be found.

Our smashed C-141 now lay on the seabed some two thousand metres below the surface, out beyond the Rockall and Hatton Banks. Once again there was no sense of motion as the wrecked plane finally hit the sea bed.

The blackness of the cockpit gradually became illuminated. The ocean depths in front of us became brighter and brighter until the ocean floor was brighter than a floodlit football pitch. Finally, the shimmering blue shape of an Eratean starship took up position directly in front of us.

The blue hull became translucent and I could clearly see three Eratean figures inside the ship.

"Friendship," said Amulya.

"Friendship," said Jenlong.

"Friendship, I am known here as Captain Francis C. Gideon Junior and this is my navigator Václav," said Victor. "The real Captain Gideon and his navigator are safe and sleeping peacefully in their quarters!"

"Victor! So glad to see you," I said. "Sam..."

'I heard,' he answered silently. There was no need for words.

'Václav, I think you should look for your daughter's soul on the Island of Paxos, in the Ionian Sea. She lives within a Terran woman around twenty years old and I am sorry to say she is blind. It is a very small Island, so I have no doubt that this will help you find her.'

'I thank you for your kindness James.'

Kez opened the cargo bay door behind us. The rear fuselage and tail had broken away just behind the wings; however, the what was left of cargo bay had been evacuated of water.

A second starship filled the space, hovering inches above the cargo bay floor. Through its transparent front, Olga stood waiting.

Victor carried Sam's body onto Olga's ship and Clay followed carrying the Grey. I followed Clay, Slobodan, Piotr; Kez boarded Amulya's ship.

We watched the ocean collapse into the empty fuselage from the safety of Olga's ship, and I imagined the waters of the Red Sea collapsing on the army of Rameses, realising that such things were indeed possible.

Once clear of the wreckage we accelerated away at incredible speed in pursuit of Amulya and Jenlong. With distance between us and the Hammerberg, we ascended from the depths, straight out into space to the waiting starships high above the Earth.

Victor carried Sam's body onto his starship, he laid her on one of four silver-blue seats already in its flat configuration ready for suspension. Clay followed with the Grey laying it on the seat beside Sam's, prepared in the same way.

I moved Sam's rucksack, my small suitcase and kit bag onto his ship, then searched Sam's handbag. I placed the gold Saint Christopher that the Captain had presented to her around her neck and fastened it. I took the simple gold wedding band from my suitcase and placed it on her ring finger. It was intended to be my Christmas gift to her. I straightened the hair on each side of her face and then kissed her cold lips.

'Shall I seal the bodies for flight?' asked Victor silently.

'No wait,' I answered.

I left Sam and the Grey and my spirit entered Sam's cold rigid lifeless body.

J@ Join with me Sam, I want to live with the future we saw together.

Sam's spirit left my body and joined with me in hers.

J@ I will leave you now so that Little Bear can take his place inside your belly.

I returned to my body having restored Sam's spirit to hers.

S@ Join me Little Bear, the foetus inside my womb awaits you.

G@ I will join with you, but not yet. There are things I wish to say while I exist in this form.

Only the three of us could hear our voices, time had stopped. I bent over again and kissed her soft lips and she opened her eyes. I lifted her head and shoulders for all around us to see and all were silent. None of them had ever seen life restored.

# HARMONY

The auditorium grew with each arriving ship, I could see that there were almost as many Terrans as Erateans. Where before Sital, Suzanne and I were the only Terran people, more than half the Eratean members now had guests of their own.

'People of Erato, friendship. I am known as James. She who was known as Samantha and was dead, lives again.'

Victor produced an Eratean himation and gave it to Sam, she rose from the bed and dropped the gown over her head and looked at the people around her, seeing thousands of her own kind for the first time.

'People of Erato, friendship, I am known here as Bernd. It is clear that we have all witnessed something our ancestors witnessed long ago, something transcendent. James, we must conclude that you are Malakhi.'

'I am, but I am at the beginning of my journey to become Trinity, a journey with twenty-two stepping stones. The first was as The Fool, Le Mat; I was New-born of the Earth, at the time of my birth I had no memories of a previous life as a mortal, I was a blank canvas.

'I died on November 14th, but I chose to return to the life that I had, rather than die and be reborn a mortal. On that day I met Victor for the first time. Victor, The Magician, the Magus of Power, my friend and my guide. Victor was my second step. It is my hope, that at the end of his life, Victor will become the Ego to my Id, mediator between the Id and reality, my conscious awareness.

'My choice to return to the life I had, was entirely due to my love for Samantha, a love not realised, a love from the future I have chosen. Sam, Sam is the third step in my journey, The High Priestess, La Papess. It is my hope, that at the end of her life, Sam will become the feminine side of my personality when I become Trinity, my wisdom, my intuition and morality. She would be the Superego to my Id.

'Today, I discovered that Sam carried my child, as unborn son who we will name Little Bear. His life ended too, before it began, when Sam chose to end her life. I carried the spirit of Samantha and the Grey you see here beside me. I have restored Sam's spirit to her once dead body, you see her now before you, but I still carry the spirt of another, one who will be my son. He wishes to speak to you before he returns to the foetus in Samantha's womb. Sam has become my fourth and fifth step, she is The Empress, L'Imperatrice, the mother of my child; I The Emperor, L'Empereur, her mate for life, father to our child, a child who lives as a mortal since he lived before as the Grey, and before that in many life times that I do not yet know of.

'The one who calls himself Paul is my friend and ally, my spiritual counsel and guide, a father and a brother, a mother and a sister, he is both male and female. He exists as a Trinity, he is New-born, Saul of Tarsus; the mortal who lived his last life as Luke the Evangelist, disciple of Paul; the mortal who lived her last life as Mary wife of Clopas, mother of James the Less and Keeper of Knowledge. Paul is my fifth step, The Pope, Le Pape, The Hierophant, he who understands sacred mysteries or esoteric principles.

'Paul has advised me to live as one of you, learn a way of life very different from that on Earth, so that I can one day return and follow my destiny. I ask you all if I can live with Sam and our son until the end of Sam's life. When that time comes, she will choose whether to return to heaven and be reborn as an Eratean mortal, or to join with me for eternity.'

I did not tell them that the Eratean Malakhi still lived among them, it was their world not mine.

'Bernd. James, we welcome the opportunity to learn from you as you learn our ways, there will be a place for you all until the end of Sam's life.'

It was Bernd who stood and replied, but he spoke with the agreement of all.

'I thank you all for your hospitality, please continue with the affairs of council.'

'We meet now as agreed to discuss the investigations agreed at our last meeting. It would appear that many of you have brought with you Terrans who wish to return with us to Erato, we welcome you all to this meeting and in due course, to our world.

It is clear that you all wish to know more about the Malakhi. It is my hope that there will be many opportunities for us to talk with James. Treat him as an Eratean in accordance with our ways, that is what he desires. I now stand down to allow the debate to begin.'

# COUNCIL

Victor stood up and looked around the auditorium, turning his head from side to side before beginning his address, just as he had done before.

"People of Erato and our Terran guests. Friendship. I am known here as Victor. I thank you all for welcoming my friend, the Malakh known as James to our world. It is with great sadness that I must inform you all, that he who was known here as Juma is no longer with us, his body has been recovered by she who is known as Kez, and will return to Erato with her. I will relate our update on the simian virus later.

"People of Erato and our Terran guests. Friendship. I am known here as Samer. I was assigned to select and lead a team to investigate the death of Admiral Souers and report back at this debate. I regret to inform you that our findings are inconclusive. We have been unable to locate the Admiral's body and can find no documents detailing the circumstances of his death. Contact with family members suggests that they also know no more than we do. We have been unable to make contact with any government or military personal that might know the truth about this case.

'Our conclusions are either that the Admiral's death was controversial and being so, the circumstances have not been openly recorded, or that perhaps he is not actually dead. It is possible that he was assigned to a secret project and working in a secret location. Since he was a member of the MJ12 group it is possible that he may have been selected to work with the Tall-Whites; however, Admiral Souers was eighty years old at the alleged time of death in January this year, a relatively old man by Terran standards. Since the circumstances of his death have not been published it is also possible that he died as a result of injuries, contamination or disease that has some connection with the Tall-Whites."

"Thank you Samer," said Bernd.

"People of Erato and our Terran guests. Friendship, I am known here as Joerg. Samer invited me to investigate the death of General Montague on his behalf. I can find no reference to the cause of General Montague's death except that it was recorded in St Louis during February 1958. My conclusions are similar to Samer's. If the bases on Luna and Mars are a joint project between the Terrans and the Tall-Whites, he and indeed Admiral Souers could have been assigned to either. The General would have been fifty-eight years old at the time of his alleged death and would have possessed the experience to head such a project having commanded the White Sands Base. Furthermore, judging by the observations of development on the Luna and Martian bases, it would appear that a presence on these bases may well have been established as long ago as 1957, the year of the General's death.

"Thank you Joerg," said Bernd.

G@ I can confirm that Lieutenant General Robert Miller Montague was the senior military Commander resident on Mars base MU4 between January 1957 and 1963.

J@ I will announce you.

G@ Please introduce me as Little Bear since I had no name in my previous existence, 'the Grey,' sounds as unpleasant as the life that I led.

J@ I am so sorry my son, henceforth you will be known as Little Bear.

'People of Erato and our Terran guests. I would like to relay relevant information from the spirit of the Grey here, who wishes to be known henceforth as my son Little Bear.'

'People of Erato and fellow Terrans. Friendship. I am known here as Little Bear. I can confirm that Lieutenant General Robert Miller Montague was the senior military Commander resident on Mars base MU4 between January 1957 and 1963. MU4 was the fourth and provided accommodation for five hundred Terrans. General Montague was responsible for the construction and development of the twelve Martian bases that existed during his command.' I relayed.

'Thank you for enlightening us Little Bear," said Bernd.

'Please continue, I will give you a full account of what I know after you have finished. If I can confirm any of your findings, I will tell you as you progress,' I relayed.

'People of Erato, and our Terran guests. Friendship. I am known here as Mohammed. I was assigned to select and lead a team to communicate with Mr Kennan and report back at this debate. We have made direct contact with Mr Kennan and made ourselves known to him. I can confirm without doubt that Mr Kennan is no longer a member of any government group or secret society.

'He was willing to listen to our interest in his world and he is definitely aware of the existence of Tall-Whites and his people, but he will not discuss the subject. Mr Kennan informed us that he may be critical of government policy and he has his own opinions about the relationship with Tall-Whites; however, he will not discuss them with any one.

'We were unable to extract any information by analysing Mr Kennan's thoughts however, Mr Kennan was unable to suppress his sustained subconscious thoughts of Nelson Aldrich Rockefeller. Unfortunately, we do not know what if any significance this has. Mr Kennan has spent the last ten years studying and writing at the Institute for Advanced Study in Princeton, New Jersey.

'She who is known here as Michelle, remained concealed in the presence of Mr Kennan for some time after we left him and can confirm that he made no contact with anyone after we had left.'

'Thank you, Mohammed, Michelle,' said Bernd, in acknowledgement of her silent confirmation.

Victor rose from his seat beside me to make his address.

"People of Erato and our Terran guests. I was assigned to select and lead a team to investigate the simian virus. Firstly, he who was known here as Juma gave his life in an attempt to establish its effect on the Eratean body. The virus..."

Victor went on to discuss everything he and his group had discovered about the Simian Virus.

\* \* \*

Nothing more was mentioned of Juma or his sacrifice. They had not dismissed it, I sensed that they all grieved his death but not as I expected.

Knowing that his soul lived on and would return to Erato, his life seemed less significant, it was not the end of his existence.

The debate around me continued. They were discussing the virus, its source and its spread across the globe.

L@ Father, no more.

J@ Tell me what you know.

L@ There are many secret societies on Earth, Freemasons, The Skull and Bones, Bilderbergers, The Elders of Zion, The Knights Templar, the Trilateral Commission, the Vatican and many more. The most foremost is the Illuminati, they have leaders in all the other significant groups. Membership is exclusive to World leaders, heads of state, military chiefs, religious leaders, bankers, highly successful business men in the oil, chemical, and pharmaceutical industries, the rich and powerful. They do not believe that an egalitarian World is possible given the overpopulation of Earth. Society exists in a delicate balance between order and chaos.

L@ The Tall-Whites are Sapiens not aliens, they are the descendants of the Illuminati and a select few scientists, engineers, doctors for example. In my time Earth's population has been reduced to around two hundred million masters and four hundred million menials. They no longer require the masses who will breed and infest their World.

L@ Their motive at this time, is to restore balance to the Earth before over population kills everyone. The simian virus was deployed using contaminated vaccinations across the African continent by health agencies, who were there to save lives; they had no idea what they were doing. The Illuminati use disinformation to set the masses against each other, war has always been a good way to reduce the population. A great deal of work has gone into the search for a virus that would result in infertility; preventing birth is much more effective in controlling population than killing people.

L@ The bases on the moon and on Mars are exclusively for the hybridisation of menials, the Greys. As you know the Greys cannot reproduce, they are sexless creations, clones of a Sapien and Delphinidae chimera, specifically the Cephalorhynchus hectori maui, Maui's dolphin. The developing clones appear as the living species to awaiting spirits.

557

With so few Sapiens, entering the developing foetus is a huge attraction to those that have lived as dolphins or whales.

L@ What the Illuminati do not realise is that all Cetacea can communicate using telepathy. The Illuminati being Sapiens evolved having abandoned it.

L@ Father, in finding my mother, I realise that I be born into a world where my thoughts will be heard. I know that you are Terran and that my mother Sam was also born of the Earth, but her spirit is Eratean and I will be born on Erato. As my physical form grows it will be a Sapien and Eratean hybrid, the first.

L@ When I am old enough, I will return to the Earth as a new lifeform and do what I can to end the misery that exists in my time. You are Malakhi, you will have the powers to help me.

J@ Say nothing of this here. Let me speak for you, I will consider what you have told me.

Pietro informed us that their investigations into the MJ12 group, led them to a group known as the Bilderbergers, and from there to another group known as the Trilateral Commission, and from there to an organisation known as the Illuminati, the enlightened ones. They agreed that these organisations were established by very rich and powerful men. The names were irrelevant, Little Bear had told me that they existed. It seemed to the Eratean council that the common objective of all these groups was the formation of one World Government.

It was agreed that such groups were never democratically elected, but then neither were kings, emperors, dictators nor even popes who have ruled before. The greatest criticism was that such groups were esoteric, understood only by themselves, sustaining power by controlling the exchange of information, and that this factor severely influenced the social and technical development necessary for evolution. The origin of these groups was believed to lie in the Order of Free Masons and the Knights Templar, sworn enemies of the Catholic Church.

A compelling comparison was made to the Roman Catholic Church and its attitude to the use of condoms considering the over population of the world, their use would significantly affect the spread of the ISV170 virus. Perhaps when the Terran people identified the virus, their position would change. All these issues were simply observations, it was clear that there would be no intervention by the Erateans, that was strictly against their philosophy and judgement was not theirs to make. 'Judge no one,' Paul had said to me.

It was clear to all that lives on Earth had been governed more by the large employers than by royalty or government, since the beginning of the industrial revolution. Our lives revolved around money and those that controlled the source of income controlled the world.

They discussed the secret bases on Mars and the moon, and the movement of water from Earth to each. Finally, they performed an autopsy on the alien body. The cause of death seemed to be asphyxiation with no visible means of struggle. That meant they could not determine whether the death was the result of an accident or an intentional act. They determined that the gene structure was similar to that of Sapiens, the body was carbon-based mammalian, and contained the normal basic organs and calcium-based skeleton. The most significant and obscure feature about the body was the structure of the hands. Each hand contained three fingers and a thumb.

The Erateans had not expected the grey alien to share the same basic DNA structure as we did.


\* \* \*


The discussion ended, neither I nor Little Bear added anything to the discussion. Plans were made for the next meeting and one by one the Eratean ships broke away, most to return to Earth but almost fifty began to form another somewhat circular ship, much smaller than the auditorium. Clay took the remains of the Grey to his ship, leaving just Victor, Sam and myself on his. As we broke away from the Council Little Bear's soul passed unseen by Victor into Sam's womb.

The members of Victor's group were well known, Clay, Slobodan, Kez, Amulya and Václav all decided they would join us on the journey home, together with over a hundred others, Eratean and the children reborn as Terrans having been killed on Earth and reborn as Sam had. A few Terrans were ordinary mortals with a superior intellect that had been invited to live on Erato.

Victor manoeuvred his ship into the smaller circular starship for the journey to Erato. Eratean volunteers would each take their turn to remain conscious for short periods during the long voyage home; it was not necessary, the ships course would be controlled by transcriptors, and there was not room for supplies of food and water to last the entire trip even for one person. The short breaks were scheduled.

When we were ready to warp out of the solar system the ship began to move away from the Earth. Sam and I embraced each other and had our last kisses before the Journey home.

Sam held up her left hand to look at the gold ring on her finger.

"I wanted to buy you something special, something no one else would buy you. I considered a necklace, and I was glad I didn't when you brought home the one you're wearing."

"Well let's hope it's a safe trip," she smiled. "So what are we going to call our daughter," asked Sam.

"We don't have a daughter," I answered.

"Not yet, but we will. Little Bear told me. He has seen his sister."

"So, doesn't he know what her name is?"

'White Mist,' she answered silently.

'That's a pretty name,' said Victor.

'It's a beautiful name,' I answered.

'I love you Bear.'

I love you too Princess...Sprout.'

# TIMELESS

## THE EMPTINESS

The travel to Erato was fully automated, the cocoon like shells formed synchronously around our bodies, leaving just Amulya and Pietro remaining conscious to monitor the ships progress. They would wait until the warp field had formed before going into suspension. Others would be woken at monthly intervals during the seven-year journey home, as measured by Earth time.

We knew that soon our souls would be released from our bodies with our physical existence sustained by the transcriptors. Any one of the forty-eight ships had the power and independent transcriptors to ensure our safe arrival.

Little Bear was free to choose to relive lives from his distant past, most of which had been as a cetacean. He found what he craved, spending the entire trip reliving his life as a spinner dolphin. I was mildly envious when I later found out; I knew dolphins love to play, but I had never seen one; the thought of leaping out of the sea and rolling over before slipping back into the water, appeared to be a tempting experience.

Sam and I travelled together, backward in time, stopping briefly at points in our lives, causing moments of déjà vu in our earthbound consciousness.

As we skipped between Sam's life and my own, I saw for the first time the spirits that surround people every day of our lives, unseen yet on occasions sensed by mortals. Some waiting for loved ones to join them, some waiting for the imminent birth of a new child and the rebirth of their soul, as my great grandmother Esther had been, waiting for the birth of my nephew.

My first significant stop was at a careers evening in my final year at Arnewood Comprehensive School. I found myself looking at the Ordnance Survey display and considering a career as a surveyor. Knowing that my destiny would take me to B.P. and the Merchant Navy, I felt that some intervention was required, so I spoke silently to myself, 'Do I really want to spend my life making maps, or would I rather live them?' It was enough, I watched my younger self move across the room to see what the Esso display had to offer. Esso had a huge oil refinery at Fawley across the forest on the west coast of Southampton Water. There were three other boys at the desk asking about Deck Cadet training. I listened to their questions and realised it was what I wanted. There was no B.P. stand but I knew that the seed had been planted. All four of us would end up as Deck Cadets but with different companies.

We arrived at my second year at Ashley County Secondary School, it was the autumn of 1970, the year Ashley and Gore Road schools combined to form Arnewood Comprehensive. Some of my friends had held a séance the night before at Martin's house. Martin was in my year but not in my form. It was Barry that told us about the prediction that Arsenal were going to win the FA Cup that season while the rest of the class laughed and scoffed. I was determined to find out the truth about the incident and so we stepped backwards to the night of the séance and joined the party at Martin's home.

It was a tight-knit group of friends who shared an early lust for alcohol, cannabis and sex. The séance was unplanned, it was Jennifer's idea having discovered the Ouija board amongst the bookshelves and the rest of the group agreed it would be fun.

They sat down at the table and unpacked the board.

"Ok, let's all hold hands," said Jennifer, while the rest of the group laughed and giggled under the combined effect of cannabis and alcohol.

"Don't you think we should all put a finger on the pointer?" suggested Michael.

"Yes, we should, and the proper name is a planchette," said Martin.

"Well how do we know if someone is pushing the pointer thing?" demanded Jennifer.

"We all place just our fingertip very lightly on the top," said Martin. "First we have to invite the spirits into the house."

"Is there anybody there?" said Barry, in a noticeably camp voice.

"Let's do this properly with no more giggling," said Jennifer. "Is there anybody there? We invite you into our house."

Within moments of being asked into the house, the spirit of the previous owner joined us. He looked happy to be back in familiar surroundings and acknowledged our presence by introducing himself.

"My last name was Alexander Kemp, I lived here in this house until 1965 with my wife Elizabeth. I was expecting to find her here having been called. I haven't seen her here for some time now. She's been in the hospital you see."

"My name is James and I am a traveller," I said.

"You are not alone James."

"No, this is my partner Sam."

"I am waiting for my wife Elizabeth to join me; I thought that it was her time. She knows I am waiting for her, but her soul still struggles to let go of the grandchildren. She watches over them day after day while her body lies lifeless, wired up to those contraptions in the hospital."

"Another spirit arrived, then a third and fourth. Before long the room was filled with spirits waiting or watching over someone.

Alexander moved over to the table and rocked the planchette with his fingers, shocking the group around the table, even Martin had never used the board before, it belonged to his father.

"Is there someone there? What is your name?" asked Janette.

Alexander moved the planchette slowly towards the letter A.

"Whose doing that?" screamed Jennifer. There was a general shaking of heads as the planchette moved on to the L the E and the X.

"Alex!" said Charles.

It continued to move onto the A and the N.

"Alexander," said Jenifer.

The planchette on its way to the letter D, swerved up to the 'YES' box above.

"How old are you?" asked Janette.

"No, that's no good! When were you born?" asked Charles.

The planchette moved across the numbers to form the date 1892.

"How old are you?" repeated Janette.

"When did you die?" interrupted Charles, taking charge, of the dialog.

Alexander looked around at us confused by the question unable to grasp the meaning of the words.

"1965," I suggested, and he spelt out the date with the numbers.

"Do you have a message for someone here?" asked Janette.

The planchette moved back to the 'YES' box and then spelled out the name Elizabeth.

"There's no Elizabeth here," said Jennifer. "Is there someone in your family called Elizabeth?" she asked Martin.

The planchette went on to spell out the surname Kemp.

"Does anyone know an Elizabeth Kemp?" asked Jennifer again.

Everyone shook their heads and one by one removed their fingers from the planchette.

"Someone is pushing it around," said Sue, angrily.

"Ok let's put it away and put some music on," suggested Martin.

If we were to witness the prediction that Arsenal would win the FA cup that season, it seemed that I would have to act before they discarded the board. I moved the planchette using telekinesis. Jennifer screamed, and the room was silent as they witnessed the pointer move around the board autonomously.

"A, R, S, E, N, A, L." said Charles.

"Arsenal," said Janette.

"What about Arsenal? Who is this?" asked Charles, accepting that they were witnessing something unexplainable.

I moved the planchette around in small circles indicating that I did not want to tell them.

"Is there something you want to know about Arsenal?" asked Janette.

I moved the planchette to the 'YES' box and then spelled out 'FACUP'.

"Oh my God!" shouted Janette.

"Arsenal will win the FA Cup," scoffed Peter oblivious to the unexplainable movement. "No chance!"

"No, you idiot. Who is moving the damn thing?" added Sue.

I rocked the cup back and forth on top of the 'YES' box.

"I don't care. That's good enough for me! I will get my brother to put a bet on it for me," said Charles.

I moved the planchette around in circles aggressively and then to the "NO" box. Then backwards and forwards between the G and the O.

"Go! It wants us to go," said Janette.

I pushed the planchette across the table and onto the floor and Jennifer screamed in horror at what she had seen.

"I think we should do as it says," Janette urged.

"Oh come on! Let's put some music on and party," said Charles still hoping to seduce her that night.

"I'm going home!" said Jennifer. "I want to call my dad. Janette if you want a lift you had better be ready when he comes."

I do not know why I spoiled their fun or even if it was my own consciousness, perhaps Sam had ended the séance so abruptly. The party spirit died away quickly, and people began to drift away. We left them and continued to move backwards into our past.

It was Easter Sunday, April 6th, 1969, three weeks before my twelfth birthday. I was singing in the church choir for what would be the last time at a major festival. It fascinated me to see myself in my robes. I wore a black cassock and crisp white surplice and ruff which had been washed and starched for the Easter weekend. I smiled sensing the pride I had felt wearing RSCM Chorister Medal. It was the first time I wore it, the broad red ribbon signified that I had passed the third and final tests. I was the first chorister to be awarded the red ribbon at St Luke's, alas just few weeks later my voice would break, and my treble voice gone forever. I realised that Harry Gale had coached rather than pushed, I just loved to sing.

We stopped again, on New Year's Eve, 1968. Sam was fourteen years old and partying with friends for the first time. She was sitting beneath a dining table with her newfound friend Christine. Two pretty girls content with their own company avoiding the boys, drinking cider together and getting drunk for the first time. They had known of each for some time, but it was the first time they had actually met and talked. Instinctively realising how much they had in common, they were destined to become best friends. Sam realised that she had not said goodbye to her. She moved into her body and did the best she could to say goodbye to the friend she had just met.

"One day I will go on a long journey and I won't have the chance to say goodbye, so I will say it now. Good bye, I'm going to miss you," she said, wrapping her arms around her and hugging her tightly.

"What the hell are you talking about girl? Have you gone bloody mad or are you just pissed?" replied Christine, laughing at her outburst.

"You will understand when I have gone."

Tears of sadness filled Sam's eyes, realising she could not make her understand.

"Oh you daft thing, you stay there, and I'll find us another bottle of cider girl!"

Back we went through our past through the years of my childhood to the summer of '68. I lay basking in the high tender branches of a thirty-foot western hemlock; my younger friend Adrian lay in the tree close beside. The thin branches at the top of the trees barely held our weight; bending downwards, they opened a window to the world, allowing the sun to shine through, and us to watch the fields around us. It was the last summer before secondary school for me, and the end of an era. There was nothing spectacular about the scene except that it was one of pure happiness, and perhaps the last time I played as a child, significant enough to make me relive it one more time.

On a cold afternoon that February, Sam took us back to her discovery of Bob Dylan. Woody Guthrie had died in the previous October and Guthrie had been Dylan's idol. He was a great influence on his life and his music. In January Dylan made his first public appearance since his motor cycle accident at a pair of Guthrie memorial concerts and was once again in the news. We watched and listened as Sam sat with a group of friends, listening to Dylan's early albums for the first time. She was deeply moved by his lyrics and she loved his distinctive claw hammer style playing the guitar.

Sensing Sam's emotions reliving her memories of Dylan, Victor found us in the emptiness. He asked us to follow him while he relived some of his experiences. Together he took us on a detour away to some of the events he had experienced during his trip to Earth. Sam's emotions soared again as we witnessed the twenty-one-year-old Dylan record his Freewheelin' album at Columbia Studios with his producer Tom Wilson. At the time, Victor had entered the building, concealing himself from everyone, wishing to hear the youngster record his powerful songs on several occasions between July '62 and April '63.

In May 1961, I was only four years old, Sam was not yet seven, and Victor had arrived on Earth just over two months before. We relived his meeting with John F Kennedy and Nikita Khrushchev, in a small gathering of starships similar to the one Victor's group had formed after my first Council meeting. It was a brief encounter but an auspicious one. Negotiations between the two men were at their most encouraging, plans were being made to begin to end the nuclear arms race. It seemed tragic to know that two years later John Kennedy would be shot and killed by Paul. I comforted myself knowing more about what Kennedy had achieved and wondered how the Russian people would feel about Khrushchev if they knew he too wanted peace between the two super powers.

Victor's presence on Earth was over and it seemed only Sam and I had a past here.

Shortly after my second birthday in '59, I had been hospitalised with pneumonia, which in turn caused an abscess on my left lung. The local doctor's diagnosis was that I had a chest infection, but my father was not satisfied and took me to Southampton Chest Hospital. It had been established just a few years before in 1952, by the chest specialist Ernest Chin, fortunately for me, it was one of the best in the country.

The earliest memory of my childhood had been a year or two later, sitting on my mother's knee in the front seat of the car crying with pain, while my father drove through the darkness from dentist to dentist, searching for someone to remove another rotted tooth. I had no idea that the cause for these all too regular trips was consuming bottle after bottle of penicillin syrup that rotted my first teeth. I had been in hospital for over a year when I was finally discharged, but I still needed the antibiotic medicine for several more months.

We watched the surgeon, known to his wife and friends as Paul Chin, perform the operation that would save my life, the bottom lobe of my left lung was infected and had to be removed.

A frail old woman stood at the side of the operating table. She had been watching Mr Chin work, but she realised we were there and looked up at me.

"It's you isn't it," she said.

"Who are you?" I asked politely.

"My name is Eliza Jane, I am your grandmother. I was waiting for you."

"Waiting for me?"

"I did not expect you to survive the operation."

"Oh," I said not realising how close to death I had been.

"You are not alone."

"No, I travel with Sam, my partner."

"Then my presence is not needed here," she said quietly.

"Yes, it is needed," Sam answered. "Please watch over him for me, watch over him always."

She had died on June the 25th that year, shortly before I was admitted to hospital, having been crippled with arthritis, and confined to either bed or chair during the last years of her life.

Sadly, my saviour, the surgeon Mr Ernest Favenc Chin MRCS FRCS, died that evening, 5 December 1959, crashing his sports car on the journey home to his wife Margaret in Nether Wallop.

We saw my grandmother again at my baptism in Beaulieu Abbey. She was already too weak to stand, so she sat quietly beside her husband Francis.

She had only held me once, shortly after I was born. My grandfather was concerned that she might drop me, but she insisted; my mother stood by in case it was too much for her.

Finally, I witnessed my own birth at my home in Sway, at two o'clock on May 2nd, 1957; then there was nothing, I had no existence on Earth before that time, only Sam's past existed.

# PELONA PEAK

W e moved back through Sam's birth to her previous existence on Earth as Victor's son. Having never chosen a Terran name, I use the name Samuel for disambiguation.

Samuel was just a young boy in his previous life, as Victor had said, just twelve Eratean years old when the ship crashed near Pelona Peak, sixty-five miles south of Datil, New Mexico on the afternoon of Friday June 13th, 1947.

A very hot and humid afternoon was followed by a violent electrical storm that filled the night skies over New Mexico. A lightning strike caused two different starships to collide and veer off course. The Eratean ship was moving considerably faster than the other, and they ultimately crashed some two hundred miles apart.

Samuel survived the crash, one of his friends, the son of Amulya, was fatally injured and died three days afterwards, the other two of his Eratean friends died instantly, the daughters of Pietro and Václav. Samuel's Terran captors, would later know him as Ebe, an acronym for Extra-terrestrial Biological Entity.

Samuel was able to move his two dead shipmates and the graviton reactor away from the wreckage, on three separate trips, five miles south-east of the crash site to the lake, Line Gap Tank, in the Gila National Forest. He took the graviton reactor on the first trip and hid it, carrying it as far as he could into the lake. He returned to tend to his dying shipmate and then repeated the exercise with the two dead Erateans, weighting their bodies with rocks tied up inside their himations. He remained at the crash site for the next three days nursing his shipmate, hoping to be rescued by the rest of the group. His shipmate, the son of Amulya, chose to end his life knowing he would not survive, by which time Samuel was too weak to carry his body to the lake and hide it.

On July 15th, 1947, Samuel was found by another specialist unit starving and extremely dehydrated. He gratefully accepted the water offered to him but declined the Terran food offered to him. In the hours that followed, he too was transferred to Sandia Base.

Samuel's body underwent an autopsy examination at the Sandia Base in New Mexico, on the south-eastern edge of Albuquerque. The scene was more distressing for me than it was for Samuel; to him, his body was just a vehicle for his mind and soul, but to me it represented Sam's previous existence. The autopsy took place under the supervision of Rear Admiral Hillenkoetter, General Twining, Rear Admiral Souers, General Montague and performed by Doctor Detlev Wulf Bronk. After the examination, the body was frozen and later moved to Wright Field, Ohio.

\* \* \*

The second ship crashed on the edge of a ranch near Corona New Mexico, two hundred miles to the west, close to the spot where the ships collided. The wreckage was scattered over a two-hundred-yard area. It was discovered by chance the day after the crash by rancher Mac Brazel, while out checking for damage after the previous night's storm, at the J.B. Foster sheep ranch, eighty-five miles northwest of Roswell. Not realising the significance of what he had discovered, he ignored it and continued his work.

Ten days later, pilot Kenneth Arnold reported that he had spotted what he described as nine disk-like objects flying in formation near Mount Rainier Washington. He approximated the speed of the ships to be around twelve hundred miles per hour. The nine Eratean ships had left an undersea base off the coast of British Columbia, and were flying south-east on route to New Mexico, to assist in the search for the missing ship and its crew; each circular ship formed from sixteen triangular ships, flying in their circular configuration.

The sighting gave rise to numerous reports over the next few days and by the July 4th, 1947, the press were printing reports of hundreds of 'flying saucers' in the skies across the nation.

With no radio in his little shack, Brazel was oblivious to the reports until he drove into Corona on July 5th and heard about the saucers and a reward for anyone who recovered one. Realising that the wreckage may be worth something Brazel returned to the wreckage with his wife and two children, they gathered what debris they could carry and took it back to their home.

Two days later Brazel entered the office in Roswell suggesting that he might have found a 'flying saucer'. Sheriff Wilcox did not hesitate, he phoned nearby Roswell Army Air Field, home of the 509th Bomb Group, and spoke to Major Jesse Marcel, the group intelligence officer.

Marcel drove into Roswell with Counterintelligence Corps Officer Sheridan Cavitt, picked up Brazel and headed out to the ranch. There he examined what Brazel had collected and loaded it into the boot of his car. Shortly afterward returning to Roswell Base, Colonel William Blanchard, the base Commander, gave the order to cordon off the area and begin an investigation.

On July 8th, 1947, four small grey bodies were discovered by a special unit of the US Air Force.

Colonel Blanchard issued a statement to the press the same day. In it, Lieutenant Walter Haut confirmed the Air Force had a 'flying disc' in its possession.

Major Jesse Marcel was ordered to fly to Fort Worth to show what had been found to Brigadier General Roger Ramey, head of the Eighth Air Force, and Blanchard's superior officer. Before Marcel and the wreckage arrived, Lieutenant Haut's statement was hastily retracted; General Ramey publicly retracted Blanchard's 'flying disc' press release, telling the media that what had been found was a weather balloon with its radar target. The smashed remnants of a genuine weather balloon were then forwarded on to Wright Field, Ohio while the grey bodies and the real wreckage were sent to Sandia.

* * *

Due to the remote location, the second site at Pelona Peak was not discovered until August 1949. Two ranchers reported the find to the sheriff of Catron County, New Mexico. The sheriff took photographs, then notified Sandia Army Base. A recovery team was dispatched to take control and collect all evidence of the crash.

* * *

Samuel would remain a prisoner at the top-secret base for four years before finally choosing to end his life, dying of sadness in 1951.

# EPITAPH

## SAILING

---

The little boat was sailing well in the summer breeze. Paul opened another can of beer and passed it to me as I held back the light weather helm on the tiller. He was content just to sit back against the leeward side, feeling the occasional light sea spray on his face as the boat rode the waves.

"Cheers," I said.

"You didn't change the timeline."

"Really?"

"No, Gus just saw what would happen if he hadn't brought Ethan to see you. He was always supposed to do what he did. So, continue. Tell me all about life on Erato," said Paul.

Success is not measured by what one brings,
but rather by what one leaves.'

Unknown.

28457360R00343

Printed in Poland
by Amazon Fulfillment
Poland Sp. z o.o., Wrocław